PRAISE FOR JOHN LOVE'S
FAITH

"Sophisticated, inventive, and beautifully written, *Faith* is a cut above the rest. John Love has made an excellent debut."

—Allen Steele, author of *Oceanspace* and The Coyote Chronicles

"Gripping and original."

—David Moles, Theodore Sturgeon Memorial Award-winning author

"The beautiful, brutal bastard of Iain M. Banks and Peter Watts— absolutely brilliant."

—Sean Williams, author of *The Resurrected Man*
and *The Grand Conjunction*

A NOVEL
BY

JOHN LOVE

NIGHT SHADE BOOKS
SAN FRANCISCO

First Edition

ISBN: 978-1-59780-390-8

Night Shade Books
http://www.nightshadebooks.com

To Sandra, Helen and Ian

PART ONE

His pregnancy convulsions dragged him out of unconsciousness. They were stronger and more urgent. Through his delirium he perceived a drip-drip-drip of blood from something which was not even a corpse any more in the impact harness above him. He held his right hand in front of his face, unsheathed and retracted his claws, and made himself count from one thumb across four fingers to the other thumb. The convulsions went away and he slumped back.

When he woke again his head felt clearer but he couldn't detect anything except his head; he was eyes and ears and nose and mouth, deep in an impact harness, watching and hearing and smelling and tasting the wreckage of the lifeboat around him. Hours must have passed since the crash and still the crash had not finished. The forces, counterforces, creakings and reverberations of the impact were still going on as the hull settled.

His convulsions came again, and he used the pain to make himself reinhabit his body. Consciousness returned, warily, to his arms and chest and stomach and legs, and he probed for damage. There was a dull throbbing pain in his side, quite distinct from the sharper pain of the convulsions: in view of what he had to do, both the dull pain and the fact of his pregnancy could be hindrances. The thought that his death in the lifeboat would have been a bigger hindrance gave him some ironic amusement, but not for long. Not even the foetus inside him was as important as the need to get out of the wreckage and *tell* someone. Thinking this, he sank back and fell asleep.

When he woke it was midday. The hulk of the lifeboat still creaked and groaned, recounting the minutiae of its crash like an old person repeating the details of a surgical operation. He got up, stretched, and wasted valuable time on a task he could not leave without performing, though he knew its result. Not only were the others dead, all seven of the people he managed to get into the lifeboat before the ship was destroyed, but they were *over*dead. Between them, they had enough death for seventy.

He continued checking the hulk. There was no communications equipment functioning or repairable. He considered searching the wreckage for weapons, but decided that would be a waste of time; he knew about the desert predators on Bast 3 but he was, after all, a Sakhran and should need no weapons. A voice inside him, perhaps the foetus, said *You're a pregnant Sakhran, and you aren't made for deserts.* He ignored it. Time was beginning to worry him.

He didn't have much of a plan, but then he wasn't in much of a situation. The lifeboat had crashed in a desert which extended for at least ninety miles in each direction; he had limited food and water, and pregnancy would impair his hunting skills; and there were no Commonwealth settlements or bases in the desert.

He would simply walk.

If he kept in a straight line, avoided the rock outcrops and stayed in the open, he might be seen by one of the patrols overflying the desert. It wasn't much of a plan, but to survive the crash and then not give himself any chance was unthinkable. He gouged a large arrow in the sand in his chosen direction, and did a final check for supplies. Then he moved off. A few minutes later, four shadows detached themselves from the darkness of some neighbouring rocks to follow.

After he left the wreck, the sand underneath it started teeming. As in most ecologies on most planets, nothing on Bast 3 would be left to waste.

●

His name was Sarabt. He was a Sakhran, lately a resident of Hrissihr in the Irsirrha Hills of Sakhra, and more recently (until a few hours ago) Weapons Officer on the *Pallas*, a Class 091 cruiser and the guardship of Bast System. He was one of only two Sakhrans who had attained officer status on Commonwealth ships, the other being Thahl, also of Hrissihr although Sarabt only knew him slightly.

Bast was the seventh Commonwealth solar system to receive a visit from the unidentified ship which some Sakhrans called Faith. More significantly, though, it was the first of the four previously Sakhran solar systems which the Commonwealth had absorbed; the others were Horus (the system with Sakhra), Anubis and Isis. Horus was the Commonwealth's richest and biggest solar system. It was heavily guarded already, but rumours were rife—they had even reached Bast—about steps being taken to defend it if Faith went there. It was said that an Outsider Class cruiser, the Commonwealth's ultimate warship, was already on its way to Blentport on Sakhra.

There were nine Outsiders. One of them was the *Charles Manson*, commanded by Aaron Foord, with Thahl as First Officer.

Sarabt looked back. He had covered a good distance, and the wrecked lifeboat was already being heavily scavenged. The arrow he had drawn on the ground was gone, obscured by the shifting of the sand and the movement of what lived in it. Soon nothing would be visible from the air, even if a patrol did fly overhead. He had to stay in the open, but that meant he would be visible not only to patrols but predators. He had been briefed about the predators of Bast 3. Normally they would not have concerned him.

Bast was by far the smallest and poorest of the ex-Sakhran systems. The planet Bast 3 was almost uninhabited, except for a few flyblown Commonwealth military bases and some almost unviable mineral extraction plants. Bast 4 was a larger and more temperate planet, and contained most of the system's population, but the Bast system as a whole would hardly be ranked as a major asset. The *Pallas* was the only warship of any size stationed in system. Everybody assumed that Faith would go first to Horus, or maybe one of the other two. Instead it had been Bast, and the *Pallas* didn't have a chance.

The engagement was very short. He had heard someone in the lifeboat say that most orgasms were longer, though their outcomes were less certain. They had only got one brief sighting of the unidentified ship, but for Sarabt that was enough.

Three hundred years ago the same unidentified ship had visited Sakhra, and left it devastated. One Sakhran recognised what the ship was, and wrote the Book of Srahr, and when they read it they turned away from each other. The Sakhran Empire went into a slow but irreversible decline, and was later absorbed by the Commonwealth. Sakhrans were mostly agnostic, and they called the ship Faith out of self-mockery. Faith was something they didn't understand and didn't want; it had come to them suddenly and without invitation; it would not be denied; and when it left them, which it did as suddenly as it came, they were ruined. They would never recover.

On balance, Faith seemed a good name.

The Commonwealth first used the term Unidentified Ship; it now used Faith as well, but for quite different reasons. The ship was often shrouded, but when it became visible, those who survived said there was something about its appearance to which recordings didn't do justice. Only a female name seemed right, with its accompanying female derivatives. So the terms Unidentified Ship and It became Faith, and She, and Her.

Sakhrans knew what She was; the Commonwealth didn't. The Commonwealth knew She visited civilisations and left them ruined and declining, but not why; and Why was the product of *what She was*. Sarabt knew this even better than most Sakhrans, for two reasons: he had read the Book himself, and now he had actually seen Her. He needed to survive, to help stop Her doing to the Commonwealth what She did to Sakhra three hundred years ago.

It was a limited ambition. He didn't expect he alone could stop Her or save the Commonwealth. He didn't even (he told himself) have any particular feelings for the Commonwealth. It had features he didn't like, but it wasn't a ravening Evil Empire; it worked tolerably well, gave him a good career, and only occasionally showed him unpleasantness or bigotry. So we should *stop Her* this time, he thought; stop Her doing to the Commonwealth what She did to us. It was an unusual thought for a Sakhran, at least for one born after Srahr. There was no telling where it might lead.

And that gave him another reason to survive. He wanted to contact Thahl. He wanted to know if Thahl had ever had thoughts like this.

There were four of them, each one about his own size and weight. They were reptilian: low-slung, six-legged and very muscular. Their mottled skin, like the desert, was the colour of unwashed underwear. They trotted alongside him desultorily. Their faces were expressionless. So was his.

Every time he felt a pregnancy convulsion, and they were now coming more frequently, he masked it with a sudden unsheathing of his claws which caused the four predators to break formation, but every time he did this they took fractions of a second longer to break and regrouped fractions of an inch closer. As the sun rose higher in the pewter sky, and the day grew as hot as the night had been cold, he became more and more conscious that they belonged in this place, and were adapted to it; and that he didn't, and wasn't.

He had been travelling for part of yesterday, all of last night, and part of today. The pain in his left side, the dull pain which was quite separate from the convulsions, would not go away; it dogged him like the predators. He diagnosed it, as far as diagnosis was possible while half-running and half-walking, as a puncture in his minor heart. That meant that without surgery he would be dead in another twenty-four hours, but he was able to assign it a lower priority because he knew he would die of premature childbirth within twelve, or perhaps be killed by the predators within six. If he hadn't been pregnant he could probably have outrun them, but if he hadn't been pregnant he would not have needed to.

He might not even have been here: in accordance with regulations, he had reported his pregnancy to Captain Matoub of the *Pallas*. Matoub should have required him to stand down, but, aware of his abilities, had asked him to embark on what became the ship's last journey.

He shrugged. Sakhrans did not waste time wishing for the non-existence of facts. Actually, as he continued with the predators loping alongside him, he became aware of one fact which might operate in his favour. Back on Sakhra he had always lived in the Irsirrha Hills; he had never lived in Blentport or any of the other Commonwealth lowland cities, so the poison glands in his hands and feet had not been removed. This would be significant. The ability to augment his claws with poison might give him another full hour.

His claws. Again he unsheathed them, and again the predators hissed and moved away. He hissed back. The inside of their mouths was bright pink; the inside of his was dark red. They returned to their normal forma-tion, alongside him. They seemed to have less trouble in keeping the pace than he did in setting it. Two hours passed.

The sun rose higher, sweating reflections out of quartz veins in the boulders and rock outcrops which were occurring more frequently, and still they stayed loping unhurriedly alongside him. In this fashion another two hours passed. The scene was totally devoid of any element of drama, and it was this, rather than his own deteriorating condition, which made him sense that his calculations were slightly off and their attack was imminent.

He slowed down, sauntered carefully over to the largest boulder within reach, turned with his back against it and waited for them. Amazingly they squatted before him in a semicircle, watching him earnestly. For at least half a minute the tableau remained stable, and he found himself fighting an impulse to start addressing them as though they were a gathering; then the one on his left attacked. He almost felt sympathy for it as his foot whipped out and raked parallel poison trails across its muzzle, for he realised as he watched it shrink back vomiting that these predators had the same inner contradiction as Sakhrans: their social organisation was weak. There wasn't enough keeping them together.

Just like us, he thought idly, as he jabbed a hand into the eyes of the one which he'd pretended not to notice climbing the boulder behind him and crouching to spring, *when they come together they're always less than the sum total of the individual parts.* He reached back, grabbed the poisoned and blinded predator, and tossed it screaming on top of what was now the corpse of the first. It was a foolish act, a gesture which took no account of his physical condition, and it brought on a new and deeper series of pregnancy convulsions which bent him almost double. The two remaining predators, who had started to back away, now looked at him with renewed interest as he staggered and fell forward on his knees, hands clutching his abdomen; and now, of all times, he started to feel the first mixed sense of wonder and outrage at something *separate from himself* causing movement inside his own body.

All his calculations were wrong, he thought irritably, all of them; the attack was earlier than he expected and the advanced convulsions were worse than he had imagined and *if you don't get up and get back to the boulder and find time to rest you'll lose this child, it'll die, you'll carry a dead thing in your belly.*

His vision blurred, but he saw the remaining two moving towards him.

Their mouths were very pink, opening and closing in unison: absolutely perfect unison. He shook his head and the double vision cleared, leaving one in front and one, he realised just before he felt the first tearing and clawing at his back, behind. He fell face down, almost welcoming the shift in the focus of pain away from his abdomen. The second one joined the first. His face was pressed into the dust with their weight and he felt their tearing at him shift, subtly, from random to rhythmic; he was no longer being attacked but being eaten.

He had often watched something similar, back on Sakhra: one of the huge herbivores, run to exhaustion by a hunting party, giving up and allowing itself to be eaten, still standing. He made a decision. There were two alternatives, both involving his death, but only one involving his death now. He would not die in that way; it was obscene.

He bunched his arms and legs underneath him, then screamed and rolled onto his back. The two predators either jumped away from him or were sent flying, he was not sure which. He stood up, feeling dust and gravel where he bled, and with his forearms covered in vomit which he knew somehow was his own; its colour was like the dust, and as he spread his clawed fingers it formed a shaking web between them. When had he vomited? How did he recognise it as his? He put the questions aside for now, though the second one particularly interested him.

The two predators crouched where they landed, staring up at him wide-eyed. He sheathed and unsheathed his claws. His tongue licked across his teeth. He shut down the poison glands in his hands and feet. He would not need them now.

Only when he finished did he stop to analyse his motives. It was not that without poison the act of killing them was slower, or more vengeful; it was simply fitting, because it introduced a proper element of balance. Without poison it was more risky for him, though only marginally so. But anything less would have been a discourtesy to the child he had let die inside him.

He lay down on his back, spread his legs, looked up at the pewter sky and pushed. It was not an act of birth but an act of defecation. He buried it in a shallow grave and turned quickly away before the soil started crawling.

Ten hours later he stood unsteadily on a low ridge overlooking a shallow dust bowl—stood, because he could walk no further, but knew that if he were to lay down, or fall down, he would never get up again—and considered what he saw with a mixture of astonishment and amusement.

He had been taught that life, while it happened, had no real meaning. Meaning could be assigned later by others, but life, while it happened, was only the total of a series of random accidents, each one operating *on-off* like a binary gateway, either *this* or *that*, to give it its particular direction; but not its meaning. And now *this*.

He revised his ambitions. They were limited already, and he made them more so. Never mind living long enough to see Her again and help others stop Her. He wanted only to know if Thahl had similar ambitions. If he could live long enough to get spotted by an aerial patrol drone, perhaps he'd have time to communicate with Thahl.

The wounds on his back and the septic trickle from the birth rupture in his lower abdomen attracted clouds of flies which he was no longer strong enough to keep brushing away; he endured them with a herbivore's patience, his secondary eyelids flicking horizontally every now and then. Something small and multi-legged erupted from underneath a rock by his feet and made for the cover of another rock, froze as his claws whipped out in reflex, and sank into the sand like a brick into mud. The rocks around him seemed to sing with the refraction of sunlight. The air quivered. A few minutes passed. He counted them, and with them the ironies of pure, binary accident which were the only life-shaping force he understood or recognised. Sakhrans called them Binary Gates, and liked reciting them. It appealed to their sense of irony.

One, that She had moved on Bast rather than Horus or the other former Sakhran systems. Two, that the only ship in Bast able to engage Her was the *Pallas*, on which he was an officer—one of only two Sakhran officers in the Commonwealth. Three, that when his ship died around him—that was not an accident, but a certainty—his particular abilities meant he was the only one among several qualified pilots to get a lifeboat away with some survivors. Four, that the lifeboat crashlanded and the others aboard all died. But five, that it landed and he survived. Yet, six, that he had no communications equipment and could only try to walk out of the desert and find a command post or be spotted by a patrol before the predators, premature childbirth, or a ruptured minor heart killed him. But, seven, he had lived through the first two of those. But, eight, the third one—his heart—was still counting away, unevenly but inexorably, the time he had left.

He lost count. No, he concluded, there could be no overall meaning. There usually wasn't, when you reduced events to their building-blocks. Accidents occurred, chances fell; gates opened here and closed there; but there was no hidden force insisting on an overall direction. Nothing *made* him survive the crashlanding or predators. No sinuous enigmatic force had willed it, any more than if he dropped dead now it would have been willed. If he dropped dead now, it would mean only that his abilities weren't enough.

And yet, he stood swaying on the ridge, a slight dark figure, and wondered if all his teaching was wrong. For below him in the dust bowl lay the ninth and final irony. He had no idea it would be there when he laboured up the shallow incline; he had thought to skirt the slope but his innate tidymindedness, or maybe it was obsessiveness, made him keep to his straight path, even if straight meant up.

And now, below him in the shallow dust bowl and almost but not quite within hailing distance, sat a small Commonwealth command post. He continued to stand on the ridge, unable to walk forwards. A few more minutes passed.

●

"Fucker," said Sergeant Madsen, mechanically and without malice. The way he said it, without emphasis on either syllable, gave it an everyday cadence. If he had spoken it as part of a longer sentence, it would have been hidden in the other words.

He was talking to a dismantled drone lying on the bench in front of him. He'd been working on it for four hours, and couldn't get its optical circuits to function. Unknown to Sarabt, this was the tenth and possibly final irony. If it had been working properly four hours ago, it would have been quartering the area of desert where the lifeboat crashlanded, and would almost certainly have seen him.

Madsen was just about to give up on it. The optical circuitry wasn't responding to any of his efforts. He leaned back and listened to the door of one of the outbuildings banging in the wind.

Only a Sakhran would be polite enough to describe it as a Command Post. It was a collection of three sheds (two plus an outside toilet) to which Madsen and two others had travelled by tracked groundcar. It was the only collection of buildings anywhere near the area where they had calculated, from the lifeboat's last known trajectory, that the crashlanding might have occurred. Their orders were to set up at the command post and quarter the desert with the remotely-piloted drone to spot any survivors. It hadn't worked. The drone was a low-budget, short-range model, and its optical circuits were trashed. Ironically (would Sarabt have seen this as the eleventh irony?) it had been assembled by Sakhrans, as part of a failing Commonwealth re-employment project.

In fact, the whole thing was rather half-assed. Yes, they'd told him, it would be easier just to quarter the desert with a flier, but all piloted fliers (Bast 3 didn't have that many) were commandeered. In case, they told him, She came back.

Hynd looked round the door.

"Luck, Sergeant?"

Madsen shook his head. "S'not gonna work. Give up, is best. Where's Stockton?"

"Toilet," Hynd said, and added, "Wanking himself silly."

Madsen snorted, not in disgust but because he always snorted rather than blow his nose, and returned to the drone. It was spread out on the workbench like a dissected bat. He folded up the pinions and fabric of its wings, folded back its jointed body, went to return it to its carrycase, and found it wouldn't fit.

"Get him to come fit this back in its box. We'll have to go back for another one."

"Should've brought two," Hynd muttered as the door closed behind him, but Madsen heard.

"Three," he shouted at the door. " 'Member who made them."

He snorted again, for the same reason as before. His personal hygiene was not of the first quality. While he waited for Stockton, Madsen remembered that his scalp itched. He scratched it—an event he had been saving, as a treat, for just such a moment. White flakes flew around his head and settled on the workbench, where they were camouflaged by dust.

Stockton came in, still buttoning his fly, and, at a nod from Madsen in the direction of the workbench, commenced unpacking and re-packing the drone. Like Hynd, he was of average build with regular and not unpleasant features, but there was something not right about him. He had tastes he couldn't share with real people, so he kept them to himself; and made frequent visits to the toilet. His colleagues often said he might have been Outsider material. He had all the required deviances and loner tendencies, and lacked only the talent.

Second time round, the drone still didn't fit. Part of its nose with the malfunctioning optic—if it had *really* been a bat, it would be part of its head with the left eye hanging out—refused to go in the carrycase. Stockton was about to start again, but Madsen couldn't face the tedium.

"Oh, leave it. Tell Hynd, take the groundcar and bring another one… No, tell him bring another three."

"Another *three*, Sergeant?"

"He'll understand."

Stockton went out. A moment later he was back.

"Sergeant, you'd better come and see this."

He got up, at first wearily; then, seeing Stockton's face, he straightened, hurried to the open doorway, and stood, with Hynd and Stockton, gaping at the figure which stumbled down the incline towards them. A slight, dark figure.

"He needs help," Stockton pronounced.

"Oh, you think?" Madsen roared, and ran towards the figure, the others following. The figure bumped into the groundcar which stood directly in its way—still trying to keep a straight line—and continued, and when they reached it, it did not fall into their arms, or fall down, but stood before them swaying.

Sarabt was still wearing his Commonwealth officer's uniform, but only the top half. Below his waist he was naked. Madsen smelt, then saw, the bloody ruins hanging from his lower abdomen and between his legs.

"Oh, you poor bastard," he said, "you were pregnant, weren't you?" He took Sarabt by the shoulders and gently lowered him to the ground. The secondary eyelids were flicking horizontally, and the mouth worked soundlessly, but his thin face held no expression.

"Mmmmmmmmm," Sarabt said, and "Ssssssssssssss."

"Later," Madsen said. "Rest. Rest is best." He turned to Stockton, who was already rushing back to the shed, and shouted "Tell Command to get a medical team here, *now! Sakhran* survivor of *Pallas*, premature child-birth, can't be moved."

The smell from between Sarabt's legs was shocking, even to Madsen, but Madsen stayed with him. *He lost it,* he said to himself, *it died. Probably buried it out there, they do when they lose them, they bury them immediately. Along with their name and their past and their future.*

Now that Sarabt had stopped moving, flies were circling thickly around the area between his legs. Madsen went to cover him with his jacket, then thought better of it; better not touch or cover any injuries before help arrived. Instead he began waving his hands a few inches above the injured area, just to disperse the flies. He thought how strange it would look to Stockton if he returned; to Stockton, of all people.

Stockton returned just then, but was too preoccupied to notice.

"Mmmmmmmmmm," Sarabt said again, and "Sssssssssss." It was no use. The words stayed inside him. His lips wouldn't shape them.

"They're on the way," Stockton said. Madsen nodded.

Stockton brought a cup of water. Madsen propped Sarabt in his arms so he could take it. He accepted it gratefully, though he spilt most of it; the cup was too big for his narrow carnivore's mouth.

He seemed to be more comfortable propped up in Madsen's arms, so Madsen stayed holding him, with the other two sitting close by in the dust. Arranged thus, they waited for help to arrive. His smell had got worse—Sakhran blood had a smell which humans found unendurable—but they stayed with him.

The medical team arrived in two fliers which landed vertically nearby, but there were also at least eight others which continued overhead and into the desert, in the direction from which Sarabt came. Madsen remembered the drone and exchanged a weary glance with Hynd.

An hour later he started talking, though he was incomprehensible to any but the Sakhran doctors with the medical team. One of them turned to Madsen.

"Sergeant, he keeps saying he wants you to put in a call to Thahl."

"Get the location. Stockton'll do it, won't you?"

"He means," the Sakhran said, "the First Officer on the *Charles Manson*."

"Oh, shit."

Not even ordinary warships would take non-military calls when they were on a mission: custom, as well as regulations, forbade it absolutely. Outsider Class ships, like the *Charles Manson*, were the most unreachable of all. Officially, they were almost nonexistent.

"I'll fix it, Sergeant" Stockton said quietly. "I'll get the *Charles Manson* for him."

And somehow he did.

●

"Commander," Thahl said, "I've been told I have an urgent personal call. May I take it?"

Foord raised an eyebrow—a gesture missed by most of those on the Bridge because of the soft lighting, though Thahl noted it—and said "Yes, of course. Do you wish to take it privately?"

"No thank you, Commander, I'll take it here."

He spoke softly into his comm, nodded, and waited. No call came through. A couple of minutes passed. The soft lighting seemed to darken, as if the Bridge had its own artificial summer evening. It turned almost to twilight. Movements flickered discreetly round its edges, and low nuanced voices murmured.

No call came. Sarabt had died before they could connect him.

PART TWO

"I t won't happen again" the convoy leader repeated. "Probably."

"What caused it?" asked Copeland.

"A malfunction in the remote guidance system."

"I didn't ask what it was. I asked what caused it."

"These malfunctions are quite common in freighters, Captain."

"I'll try again. What. Caused. It."

Pause. "We don't know."

"You can't be certain it wasn't Her."

The convoy leader stayed silent.

Come on, Copeland thought, *it's only a double negative*. But he didn't bother to press for an answer.

It was Her.

In a convoy of thirty-one unmanned freighters, number Twenty-Nine had suddenly broken formation and embarked on a peregrination of its own for nearly three minutes, after which it had re-inserted itself in the line-ahead formation of the convoy. It was not uncommon for remotely-piloted freighters to do such things, and since returning it had responded perfectly to signals. There was absolutely no evidence that anything external was involved. And, at Copeland's repeated insistence, they had checked and rechecked that, most thoroughly.

He knew it was Her.

"You can't be certain it wasn't Her! Probably Won't Happen Again is no good to me!"

The convoy leader's image, on Copeland's small chair-side comm screen, showed none of the anxiety this outburst had caused among Copeland's crew on the Bridge, only a dogged will not to be bullied; he was a civilian.

Copeland knew about civilian pilots, and knew about people who wouldn't be bullied. He remained silent, and let his silence grow loud and long, never for a moment taking his eyes off the comm screen. Finally, the convoy leader started to fidget under his rancid gaze.

"Captain, I...."

"Until," Copeland resumed, his voice now soft, "you can tell me exactly what caused the malfunction, I'm assuming it was Her. That means my ship remains on alert, and if any ship in your convoy breaks formation again I may order it destroyed. That includes the manned lead freighter. *Your* manned lead freighter."

"Captain, I...."

"Stay on, I haven't finished with you yet."

Copeland was large and overweight, an unreasonable and fractious burden for his Captain's chair, even though it was reinforced. He had the complexion of a piece of uncooked pork, and eyes like the heads of embedded maggots. His gaze switched abruptly from the chair-side comm screen to the main screen at the front of the Bridge, where the convoy of freighters, thirty-one idiot unmanned ships led by one idiot manned ship, stretched for miles, identical nose to identical tail. It continued to lumber on undisturbed, and Copeland continued to lumber in his chair, disturbed. He was not reassured. His instincts were usually pessimistic, and usually accurate.

He refocused his glare on the Bridge officers in front of him, silhouetted against the forward main screen, and barked "Status reports."

"Scanners: there are no sightings. Maintaining alert."

Copeland referred to his Bridge officers, and had them refer to themselves, by their function and not their name—an archaic military custom of which he was one of the few remaining practitioners.

"Weapons: everything powered up and on immediate readiness."

"Engineering: immediate readiness on all drives."

"Signals: maintaining open channels with Anubis 3 and 4. They detect no other ships." Pause. "Convoy leader is waiting to report, Captain."

Copeland swivelled to face the comm screen. His chair creaked as he did so.

"Convoy leader," he intoned, "I'm pleased to tell you that I'm now able to accept your status report."

The face on the screen started to frown, then thought better of it. Most ship's captains took status reports at much longer intervals than this. Copeland took them every thirty or forty minutes; he treated them as recitations, to help him focus.

The convoy leader checked his own instruments. "We're two hours twelve minutes from arrival at Anubis 4. Guidance systems are functioning. No further incidents. But..."

"Acknowledged."

"But I respectfully request, once again, that you move your ship closer. We want a *proper* escort."

"Respectfully denied."

"Commander, Anubis 4 needs this convoy urgently."

"Be precise. The convoy is going to the moon of Anubis 4. And it needs this convoy no more or less urgently than it needed any of the previous convoys."

"Previous convoys were delivered before *She* started appearing. Do I have to remind you that you volunteered to handle the escort of this convoy yourself?"

"I volunteered because it was politically impossible to order any smaller ship to handle it." And, he added to himself, no other ship in Anubis would have a chance, not if She appeared here. I won't send others to certain death when I can send myself to, well, to perhaps not-quite-certain death.

"Captain, unless you give us closer escort I can only assume that you're using us as bait! You're inviting an attack."

"I can hardly defend you without one."

He slammed the channel shut before the convoy leader could see past the apparently clever rejoinder and realise that he meant Yes, I am. As the small comm screen went dark he scanned the unmoving silhouettes of his Bridge officers for any reaction. He found none. They knew exactly what he meant, but they felt his gaze on their backs and took care to remain like cardboard cutouts.

"Pilot, he said two hours twelve minutes until Anubis 4. Is that accurate?"

"Yes, Captain."

"It's too long."

"It's as fast as the convoy will go, Captain."

Copeland's disgusted snort was violent enough to jerk his body, which in turn brought a creak from the contour chair on which he was beached untidily and asymmetrically. Over the last hours the creak of the chair had assumed the character of a second voice, prefacing and echoing his shifts of mood (and of posture, which was the same thing) like an extra person, a familiar. The Bridge officers tensed when they heard it, then cancelled their tensing, then grew tenser in case he had spotted their tension before they cancelled it. It was a process which came close to perpetual motion.

Some members of his crew asserted that Copeland's mind was as small as his body was large, others that it was as agile as his body was ponderous. He knew of the existence of both opinions and took care to ignore them equally.

●

Anubis and Isis were both ex-Sakhran systems: much larger than the almost negligible Bast, but much smaller than Horus, the Sakhrans' home system.

Bast, where the *Pallas* had been destroyed, was light-years away. The Commonwealth spanned twenty-nine solar systems; but the MT Drive, discovered almost by accident three centuries ago, compressed the spaces between solar systems to nothing, and removed distances from awareness. So, when the other twenty-eight systems got news of what had happened in Bast, it was like hearing muffled sounds in another room of the same darkened house.

The news had reached the *Wulf*, Copeland's ship, just after it passed the mid-point of its journey from Anubis 3, the system's major planet, to the moon of Anubis 4. Copeland had promptly gone to full alert, dropped back from the convoy, and waited for the equivalent of footsteps in the hall and the turning of a door-handle.

He knew it was Her.

He knew She was in the system. Even before he heard about the events in Bast, he knew She would be coming, not just to this system but for *this convoy*. That was why he overrode the normal protocols and transferred escort duty from the small Class 072, which would normally have done it, to his own ship. The *Wulf* was a Class 095 cruiser, by far the highest designation in the small Anubis Fleet which, until now, had been more than sufficient for the security of the system. It was a silver needle nearly fifteen hundred feet long, as small and predatory in the wake of the freighters as a Sakhran stalking a herd of herbivores. It had three-percent sentience.

The *Wulf* maintained speed and distance from the freighters, enough of each to be ambiguous: it might be guarding them, stalking them, or playing them out as bait. Copeland wanted Her. It might be a match. Fifteen hundred feet was about the same size as She was; without Her extraordinary abilities, of course, but with *his* unusual instincts.

Copeland had commanded the *Wulf* for years. Now, for what it was worth, he could claim to be the greatest living authority on its construction and performance. It was his ship; he and it, like a long-married couple, had moulded their lives to each other. If it was physically possible, they would have started to look alike.

His brother, fifteen years his junior, had recently accepted command of a Class 097 in the huge Horus Fleet; he was the first of his family to leave Anubis for a century, but Copeland was not envious. Horus Fleet had problems of its own. An alien ship. *Two* alien ships, the first an Outsider sent by Earth to engage the second, sent by nobody knew who. But She hadn't gone to Horus, not yet; She would come *here* first, or so his instincts told him.

How would She make Herself known? Her firepower and performance were at least equal to an Outsider. And, since nobody knew where She came from or what She was, there were other abilities which were almost unguessable: shrouding, communications, unprecedented tactical shifts. How would She make Herself known, in *this* system, when She moved against *this* convoy?

Anubis 4, the system's outer planet, was a gas giant. Unusually, it had only one moon: airless and featureless, but with huge deposits of bauxite and associated minerals. This convoy, like the three previous ones, was intended to land on the moon where its cargo, and the freighters themselves, would be used to construct a large extraction plant and mining complex. Construction was already well under way; when it was finished it would probably get a proper city name, but until then it was simply called Khan's, after the geophysicist who had founded it.

The freighters, like those before them, would be cannibalised for the mining complex; they would never leave the moon.

From time to time, communications had been disrupted by bursts of static. Copeland, suspicious enough already, had become even more so when freighter Twenty-Nine experienced its guidance malfunction. That too, they had told him, like the static bursts, was probably caused by electrical discharges from Anubis 4—normal on gas giants, and likely to increase the closer they got. He had not been reassured; nothing ever fully reassured him. After a particularly strong burst of static, they had even proved to him that there was a correlation with some sudden turbulence in Anubis 4's atmosphere at exactly the same time. He accepted what they said, but then started watching Anubis 4's cloud cover in case *She* was manipulating it.

He knew She was there. He knew She would come for them. He didn't know what She would do, but he suspected it would be almost anything. She was like the bastard child of Moby Dick and Kafka: invincible and strange.

"Further orders, Captain?"

"She's there somewhere. Worry about Her."

For the next hour his orders were scrupulously observed. His eyes, from their two open graves in his face, watched the forward screen almost without pause. Occasionally other crew members would enter the Bridge on routine business, but they gave or took their messages in whispers and with glances back at him—an indication of his contagious mood. Even during a formal alert, the Bridge of any warship, except an Outsider, remained accessible for legitimate errands, and was usually bustling. The Bridge of the *Wulf*, without any explicit orders from Copeland, had become like the Bridge of an Outsider: quiet, withdrawn, a place where communication was sparse and nuanced.

The hour started to stretch out. His instincts had produced the mood which infected the rest of them, and made time pass so uncomfortably, but nevertheless most of them trusted his instincts—a trust justified when, just as the hour passed, he activated the alarms and yelled for battle stations, moments *before* the screen showed the convoy breaking up.

●

"Freighters Twenty, Twenty-Four and Twenty-Nine no longer respond to signals," the convoy leader yelled. "This isn't like the last time. They aren't coming back. Their remote guidance systems have been completely burned out."

"It *is* like the last time," Copeland said, "because you don't know what caused it or where it came from. Do you?"

"No, Captain, but I've ordered members of my crew to board them and take them in manually."

"Cancel those orders."

"But....."

"I'm taking personal command of those three. Re-form your convoy without them and get under way."

Copeland cut the connection and watched on the forward screen as the line of freighters moved slowly ahead; automatic filters on the screen compensated for the brief sequential blaze, one by one, of their crude chemical motors. The three which had broken formation stayed where they were, a tight huddled knot of spheres and girders behind the main line of the convoy, like the dot at the bottom of an exclamation mark.

It was as though someone had made a deliberate gesture, and Copeland knew who: not where, why, or how, but definitely who.

"Signals, I want that answer."

"I've just got it, Captain. Anubis 4 have rechecked their satellites around the moon and the planet. They say there's nothing out there, anywhere in the outer system. Except us and the convoy."

"Scanners."

"Nothing in the inner system either, Captain. Not even anything of ours. All traffic ceased when we lifted off, as you ordered."

"And the convoy?"

"Nothing new to report, Captain. Our monitoring shows nothing to suggest that the breakup was caused by any external signal."

"Alright. Maintain battle stations. Pilot, reset previous course and speed, and go back to our previous distance behind the convoy."

He settled back lopsidedly into his chair. As it creaked, he added "And Weapons, destroy those three freighters."

●

Coming to the end, Copeland thought. Or nearly the end. Always most vulnerable when it seems we might have made it.

"Well?"

"It seems we might have made it, Captain. Scanners still show no other vessels."

"Alright. Get me Khan's."

"Convoy leader to *Wulf*," piped the chair-side screen.

"Yes?"

"The convoy is ready to go into landing formation, Captain."

The forward screen showed the manned leader and twenty-eight surviving freighters strung out in a loose, miles-long line ahead. Beyond them, a similar shade of grey, was the naked single moon of Anubis 4 on which Khan's gleamed like a dropped coin. Beyond that, and dwarfing everything else, was the planet itself, with a roiling opalescent cloud-cover of plum and ochre. Like most gas giants, its atmosphere made it look out of focus.

"Captain, the convoy is ready to go into landing formation."

Copeland's chair creaked; it, too, had felt the strain of the last few hours. "Thanks. I'll say when."

"I have Khan's, Captain. It's Ms. Khan herself."

"*Doctor* Khan."

"Apologies, Captain. Putting her through now."

"Doctor Khan, this is Copeland."

"Captain Copeland, you're very welcome...."

There was a burst of static. Copeland was immediately wary, but said nothing.

"I said you're very welcome. I hear your journey was not completely uneventful."

"Yes, we lost three and it may not be over yet....Doctor, excuse any discourtesy, but I'd like to get the rest of the convoy landed and then we can talk. Agreed?"

"Of course. I'll instruct my staff to make arrangements direct with the convoy leader. We'll meet later, I hope."

"Yes, I'll look forward to it."

Copeland shut the channel, and looked round at the unmoving silhouettes of his Bridge officers.

"I don't have to remind you," he reminded them, "that we're not finished yet. Something caused those malfunctions. I believe it was Her. We're still at battle stations. If She moves, it'll be now."

There was another wave of static.

"Signals, what *is* that?"

"Just more electrical discharges from the planet, Captain."

"As strong as that?"

"....Yes, Captain."

"Convoy leader to *Wulf.* Convoy leader to *Wulf.*"

Copeland realised the chair arm screen had come to life without his having noticed; he had been preoccupied.

"Yes, what is it?"

"I now have landing clearance from Doctor Khan's staff. I need your permission to group the convoy and start landing procedures."

"Go ahead. We'll remain on standby until the last one is down."

"I have your permission to go ahead?"

"I just told you."

Another wave of static.

"So I have your permission to go ahead."

Muttering, Copeland closed the comm link. Reminding himself not to relax for an instant, he relaxed for an instant and watched the forward screen. Slowly and solemnly, as solemnly as only mindless things could manage, the twenty-eight assemblies of spheres and girders were jerking and shuffling into a tight line ahead, the manned lead freighter marshalling and fussing them. A few minutes passed, punctuated by occasional bursts of static and an icily polite argument between the convoy leader and the Landing staff at Khan's over the length of intervals between the freighters' individual landings. This was something Copeland expected; it had happened with each of the previous convoys. The freighters were so large that ground around each one needed to be cleared before the next could be allowed down, since once they landed they would never fly again. Copeland, lulled by the detail of the argument, almost hotsoaking in it, started thinking things like *Khan sounds OK, I've never met her, I'll enjoy meeting her,* so that the slowly gathering emergency did not immediately register.

It did not register when the convoy leader took seven minutes to get the freighters into landing formation, an operation which should have taken less than five. It did not register when the communications interference mounted gradually from being an exception to becoming the rule. It registered only when, for the third time, the freighters' remote guidance systems malfunctioned.

And this time, it was all of them. The entire formation broke, and freighters cartwheeled solemnly across the screen as if from the centre of an unseen explosion.

"Captain," Signals said, "we have a …."

"Convoy leader to *Wulf!* Convoy leader to *Wulf!*"

"…a strong override signal. Those freighters are being jammed. It's coming from…"

"Khan to Copeland. Captain, we have an emergency."

"Coming from where? The planet?"

"No, Captain, from the *moon.* Planetside."

Copeland swore and hit the alarms.

"Convoy leader to *Wulf.* Convoy leader to *Wulf.*"

"Somebody, shut him up… Weapons, stand by. Scanners, pinpoint that signal. Pilot and Engineering, ready for immediate move."

"Khan to Copeland. Captain, we have an emergency."

"Doctor, it's *Her.* You bet it's an emergency. This is the biggest emergency you've ever had."

"But how? Where?"

"Just over your horizon. How, I don't know. That comes later. Your people missed Her, and so did we until now."

"Captain, handle this any way you like, but I need those freighters."

"Been there all this time… Her shroud is perfect when She's not moving…No drive emissions," Copeland muttered, half to himself. "Scanners, I want that signal pinpointed! Weapons, Pilot, Engineering, I want immediate…"

"Captain," someone on the Bridge shouted, "*look at the screen.*"

"Convoy leader to *Wulf.* Convoy leader to *Wulf.*"

The end of the emergency had registered as slowly as its beginning, but now it was over. The twenty-eight freighters were regrouping into classic landing formation; if anything, more smoothly and tidily than before.

Copeland subsided. His chair creaked.

"Convoy leader to *Wulf*."

"Copeland speaking. Why didn't you call?"

"Captain..."

"Never mind. Just tell me, what *was* that? And if you say a malfunction in the...."

"*Cap*tain," the convoy leader snapped, "whoever is preparing this convoy to land, *it isn't me*."

On the screen they were continuing to regroup, briskly and very precisely.

Copeland's control came close to leaving him. *You asked how She was going to do it,* he told himself, *and now She's shown you.* He was already seeing three moves ahead. Expressions of horror at what was about to happen were passing across his face like cloud-shadows across Anubis 4.

"Scanners, Captain. The override signal is unstoppable. Source is 02-05-03."

"So. She's closer than I thought."

"Just below the horizon. Do we engage Her now?"

"Of course not! Don't you understand yet? Copeland to Khan. Copeland to Khan."

"Yes, Captain?"

"Doctor Khan, did you hear that last call from the convoy leader?"

"I did. It seems we're getting our freighters after all."

I'd really enjoy meeting her, Copeland thought. I wish there was more time.

The screen showed a very precise line ahead landing formation emerging; Copeland caught himself admiring its tidiness.

"Doctor, I need to know, very quickly, what defences you can deploy down there."

"Captain, what you need to know is that we have nothing Down Here capable of stopping twenty-eight freighters from crashlanding on us."

"Then you must...."

"No, Captain, there's no time to evacuate, and nowhere to go."

Freighter One was peeling off to commence descent. Freighter Two was moving forward to follow it. The rest held their formation tidily. One at a time, thought Copeland incredulously, She's even going to observe that last detail and crashland them one at a time.

"It seems we've run out of choices, Doctor."

"It seems we never had any, Captain. Go ahead. Do what She wants."

"Copeland to convoy leader. Abandon the convoy. Take your ship out of the area. You have ten seconds." Ten seconds during which Copeland reflected on his own slowness, the inadequacy of his scanners, and how he'd had the instinct to know She would come here, but not the imagination, or the strangeness, to guess *how* She would make Herself known.

"Convoy leader, confirm you're now clear."

"Confirmed, but...."

Copeland cut the channel. He took a deep breath.

"Weapons, destroy the freighters. One at a time, as each one peels off for landing."

Freighter One had already commenced landing descent when the *Wulf's* particle beam found it and reduced it to less than dust. The screen filtered out the momentary flare. Focus shifted. Freighter Two was peeling off downwards and again the particle beam stabbed out, again the screen filtered and refocused, and showed nothing; no wreckage, not even the afterimage of wreckage. Three moved forward and peeled off, and the beam stabbed out; flare, filter, refocus, nothing. Four moved forward and peeled off, and the beam stabbed out; flare, filter, refocus, nothing. It became a rhythm, the dispassionate rhythm of a culling.

Copeland had no language for what was happening. From the empty space on the screen where Three and Four had gone, and where Five and Six were going... his gaze wandered to a spot he couldn't see, just below the horizon of Anubis 4's single moon. He tried to imagine Her there, and tried in particular to imagine Her commander—for surely, whatever She was and wherever She came from, there would be something inside Her like a commander—who had done *this*.

She could easily have attacked the convoy direct. She could easily have destroyed the *Wulf*—though he would never, never have said this in anyone's hearing—and then destroyed the convoy. But *this* had such flavour, such symmetry: to get them to do it for Her, while She scrupulously observed the one-at-a-time landing protocols which they themselves had negotiated. He had no language for it. *Foord*, he thought, *if it's true that they're sending you to face Her at Horus, I hope you're strange enough. I'm not.*

Again the particle beam stabbed out. Again. Again. Seven, Eight, Nine. The freighters were unmanned, non-military and therefore defenseless, which somehow made it worse. The filtered wreckage-less frame on the screen, the dark area where the beam waited for them and where they entered passively, was like the curtain across an abattoir door.

Ten. Eleven. And then a roaring swamped the Bridge and something rose over the horizon of the moon.

It was a patch of empty space. Just like the empty space around it, but something was wrong. This was like a patch of empty space from another day, or seen from another angle. It was different; and it moved.

Copeland screamed as the forward screen erupted with light and a deep violet afterimage settled across his eyes like a piece of hot iron. When his sight returned, the screen was still shuffling filters and the *Wulf* was left bobbing in the wake of whatever had passed. The screen cleared, voices returned to the comm channels, and normality crept back, injured, to the Bridge. The disruption had been total but lasted no longer than a heartbeat. The Weapons Officer was first to recover and, without speaking, resumed firing on the freighters. Twelve. Thirteen. The screen filtered the glare of the explosions almost gratefully. After what had just passed, that was easy.

"Khan to Copeland."

"Engineering! I want damage reports. Scanners! I want..."

"Khan to Copeland."

"A moment, please, Doctor. Scanners! I want..."

"Yes, Captain, I have it. Unidentified ship, dimensions equivalent to a large cruiser; shrouded, but we can track Her drive emissions. Emerging from planetside of the moon and travelling on ion drive, about seventy percent."

Fourteen. Fifteen.

"Travelling *into* the system."

"Yes, Captain."

"Towards Anubis 3."

"Yes, Captain. And She's still putting out that override signal."

Copeland's head cleared like the screen, totally but perhaps too late. Suddenly the decision was easy.

"Captain, we have damage reports."

"No time. Pilot, Engineering, I want immediate pursuit on ion drive at eighty percent." He hit the alarms. "Signals, tell Anubis 3 what's happened, and tell them what's coming. Weapons, stop destruction of the freighters *now*. Copeland to Khan."

"Captain, those freighters will crashland!"

"I said *now*. Copeland to Khan. Doctor, did you hear that?"

"Captain, Anubis 3 has defences. I don't. There are two thousand people down here."

"Doctor, I wish we were down there with you, it's the safest place to be. If –" Copeland gasped as his impact harness whipped round him. All the seats sprouted impact harnesses; it looked like the ship was attacking its own crew. The alarms increased a semitone, and red Final Warnings flashed from screens and displays. On the forward screen, Sixteen was halfway through landing descent, Seventeen was following and Eighteen had shuffled into position behind it. "If you don't see what She's done, I can't explain. No time."

"Two thousand people, Captain."

"I'm sorry. No time."

The manoeuvre drives flared. The *Wulf* was wrenched round a hundred and eighty degrees in little more than its own length, but even before the ion drive cut in it was already moving too quickly for its own gravity compensators. Under the force of the turn Copeland was flattened in his chair, blood from his nostrils and the corners of his mouth running *up* his face, the turning screws of pressure in his eardrums drowning the roar of the drives which in turn drowned the blaring of the alarms, his eyes swivelling left-right-left as a swarm of assorted movable objects, under the force of the turn, slammed against opposite walls with the unison of a shoal of fish changing direction.

The turn was completed, the ion drive cut in, and the *Wulf* left for Anubis 3. The alarms ceased. The floor of the Bridge was strewn with rubble. Someone had activated the rear screen, but Copeland didn't look back when, exactly as he'd expected, Sixteen veered away from Khan's seconds before impact and careered off into deep space. Seventeen did the same. And Eighteen.

"And that," Copeland told them, "is what will happen to the rest of the convoy. She never attacks undefended civilian targets, remember?"

The *Wulf's* ion drive reached and held eighty percent. It was fast enough for the star field on the forward screen to start becoming a tunnel shot with rainbow colours; then the filters cut in and readjusted the spectral bands. *She only gave us a fraction of Herself,* he thought sourly, *like a chess grandmaster playing hundreds of games. We only got a fraction of Her.*

"Someone get this mess cleared up. Then I'll take damage reports. Do we have a visual on Her yet?"

"No, Captain. She's still shrouded. But Her speed's dropping slightly."

"Hold our speed at eighty percent. We stay at battle stations."

"Signals, Captain. Anubis 3 has acknowledged. And we have a message from Doctor Khan. It says, 'Thank you, I understand now'."

Copeland laughed softly. A pity there was no time.

"Pilot, hold our speed at eighty percent. We'll keep chasing Her."

"For how long, Captain?"

"Until She catches us."

A minute passed. There was no time.

"Well?" Copeland said.

"Like you thought, Captain. She's stopping."

"Is She still shrouded?"

"Yes, Captain."

"Right, listen. She's going to turn and face us. When She does, She'll drop the shroud. If you get a visual of Her, send it to Anubis 3 and keep sending it for as long as you can; it might help them later. Tell Anubis 3 to keep defensive positions only. After engaging us there's a chance She'll simply pass out of the system; that's what She's done before, and in any case, after us they don't really have anything."

No time. I should say more. I wish I'd met Khan.

"Captain, She's stopped."

"Cut speed to thirty percent. Hold battle stations. We have the rest of this time to ourselves."

He settled back in his chair, which creaked loudly, and waited for Her image to form on the forward screen. As it started to form, he thought Face of God

PART THREE

Thahl spoke softly into his comm, and nodded. Foord raised an eyebrow and asked "News?"

"I'm afraid so, Commander."

"Afraid?"

"Ansah, Commander. Her trial is over. "

Foord said nothing, and was careful to give no outward indication of what he felt.

"I'm sorry, Commander," Thahl added. He didn't entirely understand the dynamics of human relationships, but in his time aboard the *Charles Manson* he had acquired a feeling for things unsaid. He knew Ansah once meant something to Foord, but wasn't sure what.

The soft lighting seemed to darken, as if the Bridge had its own artificial summer evening. It turned almost to twilight. Movements flickered discreetly round its edges, and low nuanced voices murmured.

"There's something else, Commander," Thahl added. "We've been ordered to Horus. To engage Faith when She comes there. Your sealed orders and mission briefing have been transmitted."

Foord rose, and turned to Thahl. "You have the ship. I'll view the orders and briefing in my study."

He never called it a cabin; he used it as a study. It was large and sparse, like the apartment he kept on Earth, and, along with the Bridge, the only uncramped space on the ship. Everywhere else was crowded with functionality.

Without being asked, the screen in his study showed him a digest of his orders and briefing, and he scanned both without surprise. He found, as expected, that they hadn't repeated the mistake they made at Isis. At Horus—the solar system of Sakhra, Thahl's home planet—it would be different. He would meet Her alone, as he had always insisted.

He knew what had happened to the *Pallas* at Bast, to Copeland's *Wulf* at Anubis, and—most recently, and most dramatically—at Isis, where they had sent Ansah. She would be their scapegoat; he knew the outcome of her trial, from Thahl's voice and from his own instincts. *When I form any kind of attachment with people they usually leave, in one way or another.* In the privacy of his study his heart nearly broke, a process to which he allotted five minutes; then he spoke into his comm.

"Thahl, do you have the transcript of Ansah's trial yet?"

"Yes, Commander."

"Put it on my screen in here, please…Thank you."

As the words began to form on his screen, he tried to put pictures in the spaces around and behind them; to imagine what it must have been like for her. Isis trials were inquisitorial, not adversarial, so she would have been facing them alone, without counsel. She would be looking at them with her head slightly cocked to one side, the way she used to look whenever she felt threatened.

●

She looked at them for a moment, with her head slightly cocked to one side. Then she poured herself a cup of scented tea from the immaculate service of white fluted porcelain set before her—not easy considering the manacles, though even these, in deference to the occasion, were slender bracelets of chased silver. She made the operation last long enough for the Chairman to decide to repeat his question.

"Commander Ansah, I'm giving you, on record, a second chance to exercise your rights. Think carefully. You're charged with desertion and cowardice. As a result of these offences…."

"Alleged," intoned a lawyer member of the Board.

"….alleged offences, this city has been subjected to an unprecedented and humiliating attack. Ships have been lost. Crews have been lost. You've been told the penalty you face if found guilty. You have the right to refuse

to stand trial here on grounds of possible bias and to elect for trial on
Earth. You don't seem to regard that as very important, but I do; more
important, for instance, than the dignity of this Board, so I'll ask you
again. Will you elect for trial on Earth?"

"I'm not interested in where I stand trial."

"Unless you formally *elect* for Earth, it will be here."

Ansah shrugged. The Chairman nodded and leaned back.

●

The next day, Ansah was back in the same room. It was large and formal,
almost ballroom size, with a geometric parquet floor, furnishings of red
mahogany and buttoned velvet, and watered-silk wallcoverings. As before,
she sat in a comfortable keyhole-back armchair, with a circular drum table
to one side, set out with a tea service of white fluted porcelain and silver.
She faced the same large curving bay window, through which sunlight
streamed, silhouetting the figures who sat before her at the long table
whose curve matched that of the window. When she had last faced them
there were six and they called themselves a Pre-Trial Directions Board.
The same six were there, but now there were six more, and they called
themselves a Supreme Court. *The* Supreme Court.

The trial would be in camera, in view of possible public reaction; it
was not even widely known that Ansah was on the planet. Her ship had
returned to Earth, with—the story went—her aboard in custody. There
was no public gallery, no media presence, and just a handful of security
guards. Ansah had only one guard assigned to her, and he was unarmed;
but he was a Sakhran.

These procedural matters, which were considered unusual but necessary,
had been settled at the Pre-Trial Directions Hearing. Other matters, however, would proceed exactly in accordance with the Isis Legal Code: the
conduct of the trial would be inquisitorial and not adversarial, the verdict
would be decided by a minimum three-quarters majority of the twelve,
and once the verdict was given, the complete record of the proceedings
would be put in the public domain. There would be no right of appeal.

The Chairman recited some of these matters, in order to put them, and
Ansah's acknowledgement of them, on the record. He went on to tell her
his name and those of the eleven others. As on the previous day, she chose

not to remember them, and decided instead to identify them to herself as First Voice, Second Voice, and so on.

She went to pour herself some tea. The Sakhran guard behind her, without apparently asking anyone's permission, reached in front of her and gently unlocked the manacles. (*Those wonderful hands!* she thought.) She smiled her appreciation and he smiled back. His teeth were very pointed. The inside of his mouth was dark red.

Someone started reciting charges. The sun Isis rose higher on the left-hand side of the huge bay window, making the figures at the table grow more indistinct, blurring the edges of their silhouettes. She was not unduly concerned at being unable to see their faces clearly. Voices, with their nuances and inflexions, could tell her as much as faces; on her ship, she had acquired some skill in analysing voices.

Third Voice was speaking.

"Commander Ansah, will you please tell us your occupation?"

"Commander of the Commonwealth ship *Sirhan*."

"And what kind of ship is the *Sirhan*?"

"An Outsider Class cruiser."

"That's not just any kind of ship, is it?"

"No. It's considered the Commonwealth's ultimate warship."

"How many Outsider Class ships are there?"

"Nine."

"These nine ships, they're outside the normal military command structure, aren't they?"

"Yes. They report to the Department of Administrative Affairs on Earth, not to the military authorities. But that's not why they're called Outsiders."

"I'm aware of that, Commander, we'll come back to that....Tell me about your title. You're Commander, not Captain. Can you explain that?"

She smiled faintly. "It's a kind of symbolism."

"Symbolism?"

"The Department likes to reinforce the idea that *it* is the Captain of each of the nine. Those who command from day to day are Deputy Captains; Commanders."

"So this, symbolism, actually provides a double emphasis. The Commanders are doubly reminded that these extraordinary vessels are.... Instruments of the Department?"

"Yes. The Department even uses that word. Instruments."

"An unusual word. Does it mean that each of the nine is absolutely bound to honour the letter and spirit of the Department's orders, in every detail?"

Again she smiled faintly. "I see where you're leading."

"Just answer the question, please."

"I'm sorry. The answer is Yes."

"Commander." This was another voice. She had heard three so far today, including the Chairman. Yesterday she had heard six, including today's three, so she called this one Seventh Voice, and committed it to memory.

"Commander Ansah, what brought a ship like the *Sirhan* to Isis?"

"Faith."

"Please answer in more detail, Commander. For the record."

"A single unidentified ship with extraordinary capabilities, making apparently random, motiveless and highly successful raids on several Commonwealth systems...Is that enough?"

"Yes, thank you, Commander, that's excellent....So again, what brought your ship to Isis?"

"Faith had made eight attacks on the Commonwealth. The last two were on ex-Sakhran systems, Bast and Anubis, so it was thought that Isis and Horus might be next. The Department deployed an Outsider to each of them. I got Isis."

"Or we got you....Thank you, Commander."

There were glances and shufflings of paper among the figures at the table. The sun Isis streamed through the curved bay window. It was now almost directly overhead, and its white-gold light drew dust motes circling up to the ceiling. The window showed the city outside; it was breathtakingly beautiful. Only very occasional hints of its smell penetrated the large room's climate control.

"Commander Ansah." This was Second Voice, from yesterday. "Department Of Administrative Affairs...Is that a euphemism?"

"It's a less than completely accurate description of the Department." She spoke the words with exaggerated carefulness, in a gentle mimicry of the way a politician or lawyer would speak them. It drew some smiles, as faint as her own, from a couple of those at the table; though not from Second Voice.

"Your orders from the Department. Did they give you absolute freedom of judgement and action in the event of an engagement?"

"You know they didn't, or none of this would have happened. In particular, the city outside wouldn't be smelling like it does." She took care to keep any inflexion out of her voice.

"Just answer the question, please."

"No, my orders didn't give me absolute freedom of judgement and action in the event of an engagement. Or any freedom of judgement and action."

"And we've heard that you're absolutely..."

"...absolutely bound to honour the letter and spirit of the Department's orders, in every detail. Yes; you've heard that."

"Was your ship assigned to a task force of five Isis ships?"

"Yes."

"What were the ships?"

"There were four heavy cruisers, and..."

"Yes, go on, Commander. Say it. And?"

"And the battleship *Thomas Cromwell*."

"Yes, that's the pile of radioactive rubble that's still in orbit above us and fouling up our communications, isn't it?"

"Over two hundred people died on that ship. I think," Ansah said carefully, "that you didn't mean to sound so dismissive."

"I had friends and colleagues among those two hundred, Commander."

"I think," the Chairman said, "this would be a good time to adjourn for lunch. It's been a long morning. I suggest we reconvene in ninety minutes."

Chairs scraped, heels clacked on the parquet, and voices resumed then receded.

The Chairman continued sitting for a moment after everyone left. He was thinking about the wording of Ansah's orders, and her apparent indifference about where she stood trial. The wording of her orders was unusually explicit and constraining; someone would have to be primed to ask her why. As to her indifference about where she stood trial, he'd initially thought she was being theatrical; now, he wasn't sure.

Desertion and Cowardice. It seemed a simple case when he first read the pleadings, and that should have warned him. Most things, he had learned, were not simple when you saw them up close.

They took her in an unmarked flier to the De Vere Highlands, a few miles north of the city. Highlands was something of an exaggeration: they were more like gently rolling hills, but they did give a good view of De Vere and its surrounding countryside. They landed in Marling Park, a small formal garden, far enough into the Highlands to make it unlikely that there would be many lunchtime visitors from the city. Ansah walked at leisure, taking in the view, and the Sakhran maintained a discreet distance.

De Vere was an elegant, formal city of white marble and stucco, with palladian architecture, piazzas, colonnades and garden squares. It was the legislative and financial centre of Isis 2, and of the whole Isis system. It was not the biggest city, but was arguably the most beautiful and well-kept; though almost everywhere on Isis 2, city or parkland or country, was beautiful and well-kept. The De Vere Highlands were just far enough, and high enough, to afford a pleasing view of the city's more expensive districts, without seeing the stains on its buildings or smelling its air.

The Sakhran took out his lunch: dried shredded meat in a leather pouch. He caught up with her and offered her a piece. It tasted vile, as she expected, but she smiled her thanks. Again she thought, Those Wonderful Hands.

Thirty seconds later, she was still chewing. She considered discreetly spitting it out when the Sakhran wasn't watching her, but realised there was never a moment when he wasn't watching her; so she steeled herself, swallowed it, and signalled her relish to him. Deadpan, he acknowledged with a brief nod. She walked on.

A little further, she encountered two families—four adults and five children—picnicking under some wireweave trees. The Sakhran momentarily grew wary, but nobody even looked at Ansah, much less recognised her. This was not surprising. Outsider officers kept low public profiles, and in any case Ansah was supposed to be already heading back to Earth for her trial.

She genuinely didn't care where her trial was held. Its outcome was inevitable, as inevitable as that stupid engagement where five stupid ships had stupidly believed that they could go up against *Her*. Those five ships had been more than just a task force, they were actually the bulk of Isis

Fleet: quite a large Fleet, considering the size of Isis, but that reflected the wealth and political connections of the system's leading citizens. Isis attracted such people.

The Commonweath's most characteristic state was one of orderly turbulence, in which Fleets played a central part. Its twenty-nine solar systems had all kinds of conflicts: political, religious, cultural, historical, economic. The last one tended to be the root of the other four, so that trade wars between the systems often blew up into real wars. Hence the Fleets, which were funded partly by the systems themselves and partly by Earth. Earth used its funding to dispense favours, create obligations, and play the systems against each other.

Most of Isis 2's wealth came from its finance houses and banks. Of the four ex-Sakhran systems in the Commonwealth, Isis had by far the highest per capita income and standard of living, if you excluded Sakhrans from the calculation. And it showed, not least in the view of De Vere which Ansah was admiring.

The exclusion of Sakhrans from the calculation also showed in the view; unlike the other ex-Sakhran systems, Isis almost ghettoised Sakhrans in residential areas outside the cities. The irony was that Sakhrans themselves preferred living separately. The authorities had preferences of their own: they preferred that Sakhrans' relative poverty, and their blocky functional buildings, be kept at a distance. Accusations of racism, which came regularly from other Commonwealth systems, were mainly but not entirely justified.

Mainly But Not Entirely. Most things, Ansah reflected, were not as simple close up. Her time on the Sirhan had taught her that. When you look close up, simple issues pass out of focus, dissolving into Ifs and Buts. She even sensed that the Chairman might be realising this; there were things she had noted, detailed nuances of his voice and body language...

No, enough of that. The outcome of this trial is inevitable.

She suspected that the Department had already forgotten Isis and was concentrating on how to defend Horus, where She'd probably appear next. There were rumours that they were sending Foord there. It made sense; Foord was the second best of the nine. The best was Anwar Caal, who commanded the *Albert Camus*, leadship of the Outsider class, but they'd keep him in reserve; if Foord failed at Horus, Earth would be next.

Ansah once had a relationship with Foord. Given their two natures it worked well, with only occasional violence on either side. Foord, despite all his obsessions and compulsions, had given her something she still valued: a quiet friendship of equals. Ansah had heard that he didn't do relationships anymore; apparently his affections were now directed elsewhere. A shame: she could have done with some of his quiet friendship now.

The pilot leaned out of the flier and gestured to her to return. She nodded. None of them—pilot, Sakhran, or Ansah—had said a word to each other.

Second Voice resumed.

"Commander, you were telling us your ship was assigned to a task force of four heavy cruisers and the battleship *Thomas Cromwell*. The *Thomas Cromwell* was destroyed, as we've heard. What happened to the others?"

"They made it back, but they were all damaged and suffered casualties."

"Would you say heavy casualties, Commander?"

"Compared to what?" The moment she said it, she realised where she'd been led.

"Why, compared to *your* ship, Commander! But then, your ship was hardly an active participant in the events, was it?"

Ansah did not reply, and Second Voice went on.

"Let's go back to those orders from the Department, Commander. They placed your ship specifically under the command of Isis Fleet, didn't they?"

"Yes. They were quite specific."

"And they said that if the unidentified ship was detected entering Isis system, the task force was to move out and engage it, directed and led by the *Thomas Cromwell*. Is that correct?"

"Yes."

"So what happened when the unidentified ship *was* detected entering Isis system?"

"The task force moved out and engaged it, directed and led by the *Thomas Cromwell*. Four hours later Faith had completed Her attack, and five Isis ships were destroyed or damaged."

"And what of your ship? The *Sirhan*?"

"It returned undamaged, and with no casualties, after taking survivors off the *Thomas Cromwell*."

"It returned *after* it took survivors off, because *after* it took survivors off you ordered it to leave the scene of battle. You deserted, Commander! You ran away! That's correct, isn't it?"

"Everything except Deserted and Ran Away."

"And how would you characterise what you did?"

"I can only answer that by going back to my orders. I'd like to say something about my orders."

"In good time, Commander. Let's not leave what you actually *did*, not just yet. I want to be clear about this. If you never Deserted, and you never Ran Away, how would you characterise what you did?"

"A moment, please" said the Chairman, to Second Voice. "We can come back to that. Let's hear her first. Commander, you wanted to say something about your orders?"

She paused before answering.

"The Department made a stupid decision. Those orders cost you most of your Fleet. All Outsiders fight best alone." She noted the stirrings and mutterings among the silhouetted figures, and added for good measure, "We're like Sakhrans. We don't work in teams."

"Commander, if it was so stupid…"

"Which it was. I bet it won't be repeated at Horus."

"…If it was so stupid, why was the Department so insistent that you should be under Isis Fleet's command?"

"I don't know. Maybe your leading citizens used their political connections."

Second Voice resumed.

"You're the one who's on trial here, Commander. For your life. Let's return to the issue. If you never Deserted, and you never Ran Away, how would you characterise what you did?"

"I was protecting my ship. And giving the next Outsider, when it faces Her, a better chance than I had."

"Commander—"

"No, let her go on," the Chairman said. "I want this, for the record."

"During the engagement I realised that She can never be stopped by conventional people in conventional ships. She can only be stopped when an Outsider engages Her alone, without any constraints like those on me. I don't know who She is, where She comes from, or why She's doing this, but I know that nothing except an Outsider, alone, will be good enough to stop Her."

She paused, almost embarrassed: it was one of her longer speeches to the Court, and it sounded like it was turning into a defense, which she hadn't intended.

In front of her, Isis was starting to set. Shadows of dusky pink and dark red were settling over De Vere; evening light slanted through the great curving bay window, enriching the dark reds of the furniture. That, and the lengthening silence of those in front of her, broken only by a couple of murmurs, reminded her of the Bridge of the *Sirhan*.

"We'll return to these matters in detail tomorrow, Commander," the Chairman said eventually. "We have much we need to ask you about the engagement."

"And," Ansah said, "about what She did *after* the engagement."

The Chairman glanced up at her sharply. "That too," he snapped. "Court is adjourned."

●

The following morning statements were taken from some of the surviving officers and crew of the *Thomas Cromwell* and the four cruisers. They gave detailed accounts of how the engagement had been fought, and how the *Sirhan* left them. They generally tallied, and Ansah placed on record her agreement that in all material respects they were accurate. The Court asked her if she wished to reserve her position in respect of any discrepancies, but she declined.

"And that is it, is it, Commander?" This was Fourth Voice.

"I'm sorry," she replied, genuinely confused by the grammar. "What is what?"

"That's what you want to tell us about the events of the engagement, is it?"

"Oh, I see....Well, I've acknowledged that those statements are substantially correct, and there's what I said at the end of yesterday's session. Did you want me to add something?"

"How about, you know, something along the lines of a defense?"

"Just questions, please," the Chairman reminded Fourth Voice, "and not rhetoric."

"So you've agreed with the survivors' accounts, and you've referred us to what you said yesterday. What you said yesterday boils down to this: your

orders tied you to our ships and stopped you fighting Her properly. Is that
it? You think that's enough from you?"

"Yes."

"Well it isn't, Commander. Frankly it stinks."

"You've recently acquired knowledge of things that stink."

There was a silence.

"Perhaps," the Chairman said, "you should have thought before you
said that, Commander."

"No, Mr. Chairman," Fourth Voice said. "That's all right. Let her have
that one, on us."

After the engagement with the five Isis ships, which She had won so
brilliantly and shockingly, and with the *Sirhan* having left the scene of
battle to pick up survivors, there was nothing to stop Her turning towards
De Vere. She did so.

It was a matter of record that She never attacked undefended civilian
targets. This time, however, She did attack a civilian target, but in a most
unexpected way.

She went first to one of the city's poorer southern suburbs, consisting
mainly of Sakhran ghettoes, where She hovered mysteriously over one
area for a few minutes, then turned and set off towards the city centre.
Later it became apparent that She had scooped up some faecal waste—
both human and Sakhran—from a sewage treatment plant, synthesised it
in large quantities, carried it stored under high pressure back to De Vere,
and released it as a spray above the city. Then She left, and passed out of
the system.

The effect was incalculable. It was, as the Chairman had described it,
unprecedented and humiliating. It was also particularly apt: Isis was fa-
mously obsessive about the beauty and fragrance of its cities, and of its
people. The story spread rapidly over the other twenty-eight systems. Isis,
and De Vere, would forever be known as the place where She had done
this.

And the smell and stains absolutely would not go away. Sakhran faeces smelt many times worse than human faeces, and left stains on De
Vere's palladian facades and colonnades and piazzas which responded only
gradually to even the most high-powered of hoses. The city's renowned
formal gardens also suffered; Sakhran faeces killed rather than fertilised.

It was the first thing She had ever done which might, just possibly, hint at a motive. Or maybe not; nobody knew anything about Her, and She had never made or answered any communication. And yet, it was said throughout the Commonwealth, how exquisitely judged! And how exquisitely executed! Until you remembered the five Isis ships and their crews.

"No, Mr Chairman." Fourth Voice said. "That's all right. Let her have that one, on us. Commander, I'm bound to say that your attitude towards this trial is at best questionable. You've refused to call witnesses in your defense, you've refused to cross-examine any witnesses we might call, you've refused to appoint a legal adviser or to accept our offer of one, you only answer our questions partially, and when you do it's as if you're doing *us* a favour. Either pull out of this trial altogether—and we advised you of your right to do that—or participate in it; but don't insult us. That unidentified ship does enigmatic silences and hidden meanings much better than you do."

"I'm sorry," Ansah said, "if my attitude to the trial has offended you. Frankly, the trial isn't going the way I wanted."

"You're not the first defendant to think that."

"No, I mean the way I *wanted*. It's been concerned too much with my personal guilt or innocence."

"I rather thought that was the idea of a trial, Commander."

"No. If you find me guilty, you're wrong. If you find me innocent, you're wrong."

The hazy outlines behind the long curved table exchanged whispers and glances. Ansah could imagine their expressions, and remembered a phrase Foord sometimes used for such people: clitoris-faced and labial-lipped. She waited a while, calculating when best to speak, then said loudly "Forks." She was gratified to see a couple of them, including Fourth Voice, actually jump.

"What was that, Commander?"

"Forks. A road with two forks. Sakhrans call them Binary Gates. Two alternatives, one for Guilty and one for Innocent. But I made earlier decisions at earlier forks. The fork I'm facing now, at this trial, is so far down the road that wherever I go, it won't alter the main direction."

"So you're not Guilty and you're not Innocent. What are you?"

"When I was sent to Isis I received sealed orders for this mission. When

I decided to open them I knew that sooner or later that decision would kill me. As you know, those orders put my ship under the control of Isis Fleet if there was an engagement with Her. I could have refused to obey them, and died there and then. I could have accepted them, joined your Fleet and fought in a battle which I knew was already lost; and died then. Or I could have withdrawn my ship, knowing that I would have to stand trial; and die now."

"Do you mean to tell this Court that—is something amusing you, Commander?"

Ansah had been smiling faintly. "I'm sorry. I had a bet with myself that if anyone used the phrase Do You Mean To Tell This Court, it would be you."

"I'll use it again," Fourth Voice snapped. "Do you mean to tell this Court that when a Class 101 battleship and four Class 097 heavy cruisers—let's leave *your* ship out of it, shall we, since that's what you did—when those five ships engage a single opponent, far from having even a limited expectation of success they're inevitably going to be defeated?"

"Yes. And they were."

"Commander, listen to me carefully. You're on trial for your life. *Why* did you leave those ships to Her?"

Ansah paused.

"They didn't have a chance, and I told them. That's on record. I asked them to get out of my way and let me engage Her alone, and they refused. That's on record. They couldn't accept that they were facing an invincible opponent. They couldn't accept that giving way to an Outsider—something completely abhorrent to them—was their only chance of survival. So they lost; and that's on record."

There was a few seconds' silence from the figures at the table. Then a new voice spoke; she called it Ninth Voice.

"Commander Ansah, I'd like to ask you about your ship. The *Sirhan*, as we've heard, is an Outsider Class cruiser. I understand that Outsiders are believed to be capable, on present documented evidence, of at least matching the performance and firepower of this unidentified ship. Is that correct?"

"On present documented evidence."

"Then wouldn't such a ship be decisive in the engagement, especially when added to those five others? Why should it be more likely to fail *with* those five than without?"

"You've heard me tell the Court there are nine Outsiders."

"Yes."

"Do you know how much each one is worth?"

"Probably something that sounds good when you recite it: the entire cost of Isis Fleet, or the entire annual gross product of Bast, or something similar."

"That will do well enough. And do you know their political status?"

"I thought you'd already told us, Commander…and I believe that I'm supposed to be asking you questions."

"Then please ask that one. It's important."

Pause.

"Commander, what is the political status of the nine Outsiders?"

"They're Instruments of the Commonwealth, outside the normal command structures. They report directly to the Department of Administrative Affairs. They fight alone, not in a team."

"Yes, we know all that, you already told us. Why is it important?"

"There are people…" Ansah paused, and began again. "There are people who say that if She can only be stopped by an Outsider, then maybe it's better if She isn't stopped at all."

"And are you familiar with that attitude, Commander?"

"I see it wherever I go. It's like we're carrying a disease. Outsiders have a certain reputation. They're accountable to nobody, at least nobody anyone would recognise, and they're run on lines most miltary people wouldn't understand. So people treat them as alien ships, crewed by aliens."

"How do you mean, Crewed By Aliens?"

"People of unusual ability, otherwise they wouldn't be there. But people who don't fit into any conventional authority structure, because they're too ambitious or unambitious, too political or apolitical, too stable or unstable. Most of them are sociopathic, many are psychopathic. Most of them have done terrible things."

"Is that the real reason they're called Outsiders?"

"Yes."

Some of the figures facing her glanced at each other, but said nothing. To fill the silence, Ansah added "And there will never be any more than nine.

They're expensive, but the Commonwealth could easily afford to build fifty."

"Then why only nine?"

"Would any rational system deliberately inject a disease into itself? Nine is all the Commonwealth could possibly take. They were conceived in back alleys, built in secret, launched almost in guilt, and commissioned without ceremonies. They're even named after ancient killers and loners and assassins: *Sirhan, James Earl Ray, Charles Manson.* They're like some shameful medical condition. And yet they're the only Commonwealth ships which might defeat Her."

"And the only time," Ninth Voice said quietly, "the only time an Outsider has ever faced Her was here, in our system. And you turned away."

"Yes."

"Don't you think it's time you told us how you remember that engagement? Not statements or recordings, but how *you* remember it."

"I remember when I first saw Her. It's true what they say, it's not like seeing pictures of Her. When She unshrouds, there's something about Her actual presence which you don't forget.

"She's a bit smaller than an Outsider, but a very similar shape, a thin silver delta. But on Her, the shape looks different. Like She's only the visible part of something larger.

"I remember seeing Her pick off the others one by one. It was obscene; they didn't have a chance.

"I remember requesting the *Cromwell*, again and again, to withdraw that ridiculous task force and let me engage Her alone. All my requests were refused, and all of them are on record.

"I remember thinking that She could have destroyed those cruisers, but She only disabled them. There were casualties, but there were also survivors.

"I remember how She kept probes on the *Sirhan* all through the engagement. She made no move against us, and we made none against Her, but Her probes were on us all the time, and they were much stronger than ours on Her. Ours gave us nothing.

"And I remember the *Thomas Cromwell*, because that's where the end came. The *Cromwell* tried to keep Her at long range and use its beam weapons, but She turned suddenly, in Her own length, and charged down its throat in less than a nanosecond, too quickly for the *Cromwell*'s electronics to refocus. That's the first time I've seen a ship do something in battle which was both pure reason and pure impulse. It was done so suddenly that it even outpaced computers. It looked instinctive; yet logically it was perfect, and She executed it perfectly.

"I remember one other thing. She could have used Her own beams and vaporised the *Cromwell*, but instead She used conventional closeup weapons. Again, She left survivors. I don't know if that was intentional. I don't know Her motives. Nobody does. She never communicates."

"So, Commander, we've come to the point where you turned away."

"Yes, I turned away. I took survivors off the *Cromwell* rather than chase Her, because I knew…"

"A moment, Commander. You say She was heading here, and you didn't chase Her?"

"Yes. I knew She'd never attacked civilian targets. And I knew there were people on the *Cromwell* I could save. Even knowing what She did to your city, I'd still do the same."

Ansah remembered how, on the Bridge of the *Sirhan*, She was first registered by the scanners: blips and echoes and simulations denoting a single ship of similar dimensions to the *Sirhan*. And then She unshrouded.

Ansah had watched in disbelief as She moved among them like a living thing, the way Ansah always imagined the *Sirhan* appeared in comparison to ordinary ships. Faith made even the *Sirhan* look like an ordinary ship. She looked like She belonged in empty space; like She was actually a *part* of empty space, a small part made solid and visible. And the rest looming around Her, unseen.

There were low chimes from a gold carriage clock on the long table. It was well into evening. During the pause, and in view of the unexpectedly late hour, tea was served. The silence refocused to a muted clatter of porcelain and silver among the indistinct figures at the long curved table. Even in here, the smell of faeces persisted round the edges.

"Thank you, Commander," the Chairman said. "I think none of us realised how late it was. The Court is adjourned until tomorrow morning."

The trial wore on for another few days, but that was its last substantive chapter. There came an afternoon, seven days later, when all depositions and statements had been read and considered, all recordings of the engagement played and studied, all theories of Faith's nature and origin weighed, and all matters of Ansah's record and conduct assessed; and the Chairman found himself ready to bring the trial to a close.

"Commander Ansah."

She stood and faced him. The Chairman studied her through the gathering twilight as Isis set over De Vere, turning the air velvet. She was a beautiful woman, tall and elegant. She was Commander of an Outsider, and he knew she had done terrible things; he'd seen them in her record. Yet she wasn't unlikeable; even here, at her trial, she had shown glimpses of a self-mocking sense of humour. How had she found time in her life, which wouldn't last much longer, for such a career? And how could she have done those things?

"Commander Ansah, these proceedings are concluded. The Court will adjourn to consider its verdict on the two charges against you: Cowardice and Desertion."

He realised, only after he said it, that the final words he would speak to her in these proceedings, the final words on the transcript until the announcement of the verdict, would be Cowardice and Desertion.

The Chairman felt a mounting unease. He knew that an injustice was going to be done, but he genuinely didn't see how to make it right; and even the injustice would have some trace elements of justice. Nothing was simple.

The outcome was inevitable, like the fate of those five Isis ships; she knew that. But there was something he still might do for her.

"Ebele Ansah, please stand. The Court has now reached its verdict," the Chairman told her, three days later. "On the charge of Cowardice we find you Not Guilty. Unanimously. On the charge of Desertion we find you Guilty. Eleven votes to one."

Ansah gazed back at him, without any visible emotion.

This was what the Chairman had done for her. For three days he had argued against the Cowardice charge, insisting they find her Not Guilty. Their opposition was furious, but he would not be moved. Sensing his mood, some of them had even tried to compromise with a verdict of Not Proven, but still he would not be moved. So, Not Guilty of Cowardice was what he had done for her, but Guilty of Desertion was inevitable.

Even she knew that.

"Commander, you know the sentence."

"Yes," Ansah said. "I request the Court to allow me to carry it out on myself, in accordance with military custom."

"That's granted, of course. You have until midnight. The Court Secretary will bring you the necessary substances."

"Thank you."

"Commander," the Chairman said, "would you like us to provide you with a companion of some kind?"

"Yes. I'd like my guard, if he agrees." She turned to the Sakhran. "Will you?"

"Of course," he said. It was the first time they had spoken to each other.

●

The pictures faded from where Foord had imagined them, in some quasi-space behind the words of the transcript; then the words themselves faded from the screen. He turned away. His grief for Ansah had come, occupied its allotted time, and gone; much like his relationship with her. What it left was a sense of unfamiliarity, the knowledge that she was no longer a part of the universe. It would make the shape of his life different. The rest of his life, for as far as he chose to see it, would be devoted to Faith. *We were made for each other. We belong together.*

He recounted his mission briefing from the Department. It was an irritating document, overwritten and portentous (the Department always knew more than it let on, or thought it did) and ultimately of no use to him. *Everyone wants to know what She is and where She comes from. Me, I'm interested only in what She's done. I've studied what She's done, and I know how to defeat Her.*

"Thahl."

"Commander?"

"Lay in a course for Blentport on Sakhra, please."

PART FOUR

1

I t was a late autumn afternoon, and the sun Horus bled through a bandage of clouds. He arrived alone, cramped and tired after the journey. Foord was disappointed, but not surprised, when they didn't come out to meet him.

Almost before he stepped out, the Sakhran landchariot which brought him clattered back towards the lowlands, its driver hissing and flaying the team. He looked up at Hrissihr and saw the great black disc daubed over one of its buttresses. A srahr: he remembered reading about it in his mission briefing from the Department.

The srahr (unlike the name of the historical figure, it is not written with a capital S) is recurrent in Sakhran culture. It is the silent letter in their alphabet, and the symbol of zero and infinity in their mathematics. In their past legends it is the mark of apocalypse, and in their present legends the mark of the unidentified ship, which for reasons of their own they call Faith. This ship came once before, over three hundred years ago, and they know it will soon return. You are not the only visitor they are expecting.

He gave the black disc a cursory glance, aware that they would be watching for his reaction. Then he turned his attention elsewhere around the massive hillcastle, noting details with the habitual precision of a warship commander. The wind swore down at him and he tasted two distinct liquids, one from his watering eyes and the other from his running nose.

Hrissihr rose before him like the fist of a subterranean arm. He counted off one minute, concluded the Sakhrans would not be coming out, and walked into the main courtyard. Several doors led off it, each one—he knew from his briefings—the entrance to a separate Sakhran apartment. Hrissihr looked like the castle of some single absolute ruler, but it wasn't; it was the home of many Sakhran families, although, being Sakhrans, they stayed behind their own doors and rarely met socially. Tonight was to be an exception, with a dinner in the little-used Main Hall to mark his arrival.

The walls of the courtyard were hung with iron braziers, some containing fires which spat as he passed them, others empty beneath old soot-smears, recording the departure of Sakhran families to the Commonwealth lowlands, or to other hillcastles higher and further away. In the wind from the Irsirrha Hills, dead leaves rushed across the flagstones and clamoured against the shut doors. He picked up one; it was dark grey-green, its veins dry and spatulate. He tossed it away and the wind snatched it.

Sulhu chose that moment to appear.

"Commander Foord! You're very welcome."

Together they walked across the courtyard, Foord treading the dead leaves noisily and the Sakhran avoiding them gracefully. A few doors opened, and other Sakhrans peered warily from their apartments at Foord; either he was carrying some disease, or was the disease. Sulhu, though, treated him warmly, as if they'd known each other for years and this wasn't the first time they had ever met. He took Foord's arm and looked up at him as they walked, smiling a dark red mouthful of pointed teeth and chattering in perfect if rather sibilant Commonwealth.

"Your journey here wasn't too tiring, I hope? I've been looking forward to this meeting. My son Thahl has told me all about you. I'm delighted that you could come up here and visit us while your ship is on Sakhra. Come in, come in...."

●

"You haven't seemed completely at ease tonight, Commander Foord. I hope the food wasn't to blame."

"The food was fine, thank you. The fact is, I rarely get invited anywhere twice. I don't make a very good guest."

"Yes, my son Thahl says you call it Social Awkwardness. Then there's also the long journey, and Director Swann's opposition to your visit here. My invitation was well-meant, but perhaps not well-judged."

"It was both, and very much appreciated. Also, my visit here is a useful reminder to the Director that I don't take orders from him." Swann was Director of Horus Fleet—regular military—and found having an Outsider at Blentport deeply insulting.

The silence lengthened. Sulhu's eyes were unwavering behind the occasional horizontal flicker of their secondary lids. His ophidian face, usually rather immobile, seemed to crawl under the play of firelight.

"Alright, Commander. You've had an evening of small talk over dinner with my neighbours. Let's not continue it. Can we talk freely? You're off the record here, you know."

Most Sakhrans were natural linguists, but Foord found Sulhu's near-fluency disconcerting; it made him sound like he understood humans as well as he understood their language.

"You mean, Talk Freely about what I'm doing here?"

"Everyone knows what you're doing here, Commander. Me especially. My son Thahl gave me an outline of your orders."

His son Thahl sat deferentially silent and to one side, partly hidden in shadow. The dinner to welcome Foord had finished and the rest of those who attended—only a minority of those living at Hrissihr—had gone back to their apartments across the courtyard, or across other courtyards, and closed their doors behind them. Their empty chairs remained in a crescent round the dwindling fire. There had been much about the dinner—soft low light, murmured conversations, carefully judged understatement—which reminded Foord of the *Charles Manson*.

Foord turned and glared pointedly at Thahl, who showed no obvious embarrassment. The slender Sakhran darkwood chair on which Foord sat, although much stronger than it looked, still creaked under his weight.

"As well as being your son, Thahl is an officer on my ship. Those orders are confidential. Or were."

"I said Outline, Commander, not details. Everyone knows them in outline. And in any case, Commonwealth law recognises no secrets within a

Sakhran family."

Since Sakhrans reproduced asexually once or twice in a lifetime, the father-son bond was strong; it was the only bond which was, since all the others had weakened over the last three hundred years. Hillcastles like Hrissihr provided the minimum for life, housing families of two, or sometimes three, who ate together only rarely. Fathers died, sons grew into almost the same identity, and reproduced; then died, and their sons grew into almost the same identity, and reproduced; then died. Sakhran society was conservative and minimal.

Foord knew all that from his long association with Thahl, but the detailed point about Commonwealth law had been covered in his briefing, and he should have remembered it.

"Of course," he said hastily, and to both of them. "My apologies."

Sulhu nodded, deadpan. "You're not a very good guest. I won't be inviting any more Socially Awkward people here."

The evening wore on, and still Foord stayed talking. Despite his misgivings, and with all the issues looming in the background, he found himself enjoying it: Thahl's father was good company. Thahl himself hardly said a word, having clearly decided to leave them to each other.

"I was watching you, of course, when you saw the srahr," Sulhu said. "Later I watched you examine a dead leaf. Both are getting numerous. We're well provisioned here for our winter, but are your people provisioned for theirs?"

"What makes you ask that?"

"I listen to Commonwealth broadcasts, Commander. I read Commonwealth journals. They all refer to Faith as a distant thunder. They hint that whole systems, including this one, may be battened down if She comes. I'm old and diseased and will soon die, so few things worry me; but that does."

Tall narrow windows were scored down one wall of the Hall, like claw-marks. Foord stood up, stretched, and strode over to gaze out of one of them, his heels clacking on the flagstones. He was tall and powerfully built, dark-haired and bearded, a fourth-generation native of one of the Commonwealth's heavy-gravity planets. He exuded a musky odour, like a lion. People meeting him for the first time found his quietness and reticence so at odds with his appearance as to be unnatural, almost threatening.

"Why does it worry you?"

The Sakhran laughed drily. "Because they've sent *you* here. The prospect of being anywhere nearby when you find Her is not appealing."

"But you're old and diseased and will soon die."

Sulhu inclined his head, in the way of acknowledging a hit. Foord thought, *It must be all this time around Thahl. I'm beginning to learn irony.*

"Well," Sulhu said, "there's also the fact that my son will be on your ship."

"No. There's something else that worries you. Something you haven't told me." It amounted to calling his host a liar, so Foord spoke carefully. "But I think you will, when you've worked out how to say it."

He continued to gaze through the leaded glass where the cold blaze of Blentport and its surrounding cities was spread out far below, prominences flaring now and then as ships landed for refit or lifted off to join the cordon around Sakhra. Under the huge Sakhran night, the spaceport seemed both mighty and vulnerable; like a beached whale, its size made it weak.

"An impressive spaceport," Sulhu observed. "Much more impressive than anything we had. And yet, do you know how it got its name? When Sakhra became absorbed by, or rather was Invited To Join, the Commonwealth two hundred years ago"—Sulhu's vocal irony, like all other forms of Sakhran irony, was light and subtle—"we pointed out Srahr's tomb and asked that no human should ever go there uninvited to read his Book. For no better reason than that, a man named Rikkard Blent did. We caught him before he entered and later returned his still living body to the lowlands. The Commonwealth never actually retaliated, except—rather injudiciously if you ask me—to name Blentport after him."

Sulhu paused for a moment. When he resumed, the irony had drained from his voice.

"To name its biggest spaceport after a silly man who thought he could come up here and just read the Book of Srahr. Srahr was the greatest of us, Commander. Poet, philosopher, soldier, scientist; and, unfortunately, author. We never recovered from his literary career... Must you go back tomorrow morning, Commander?"

"I think so. The refit has to be completed."

"If you could stay until the afternoon, I had in mind a hunting trip."

Foord smiled. "Cyr would have liked that."

"He's your Weapons Officer, isn't he?"

"She."

"Ah. Tell me about the people on your ship."

Foord told him.

"But if they've done those things, why aren't they dead? Or in prison?"

"Because they're too valuable. And I've Done Those Things, too."

"You see, Commander," Sulhu went on, "There's something wrong about this mission of yours." His hands raised themselves from his lap, just enough to silence Foord, and returned to rest. "Let me think about how best to put it to you."

Not for the first time that evening there was a loud roar as some military transports dipped low over the Irsirrha on their way down to Blentport. Suddenly aware that he was shivering, Foord walked back to stand by the fire.

"Yes," Sulhu said as the noise from the ships died away, "that's a good cue. It's common knowledge—I didn't get this from my son, it's in all the broadcasts—that Horus Fleet has been ordered to maintain a defensive cordon around Sakhra, and that if She appears in the system, you're to go out and engage Her singly, and they're to stay put."

"Yes, the Department made a terrible mistake at Isis. They insisted the *Sirhan* should join the regular forces, and not fight Her alone. They don't want to repeat that mistake here. If anything, they've gone to the other extreme."

"But Horus Fleet is the biggest in the Commonwealth, outside of Earth. Do the people who give you your orders really think the whole Fleet isn't equal to Her?"

"Maybe they think She isn't equal to me."

"I was in Blentport a few days ago and I watched your ship land." A carnivore's lightning-bright smile. "I can't imagine much that would equal it. But here's my point: what will happen after you destroy Her?"

Foord had some difficulty hiding his surprise. "I can't say. My orders aren't specific."

"No, not what you will do afterwards; what will *happen*. This is a matter which has interested me for a long time." Thahl, who had been almost silent all evening, shifted uneasily, but Sulhu went on. "Why is the Commonwealth expanding?"

Again, Foord had some difficulty hiding his surprise. "Is that all you were thinking how to say?"

"All?"

"Well. There are obvious reasons: economic, political, military, probably in that order."

"I hardly think so. Economically the Commonwealth already has an abundance of unused resources, politically its systems are if anything more divided than they were before it acquired them, and militarily it has never encountered an enemy strong enough to justify making itself bigger; though that may change now."

Foord was beginning to feel tired, and remembered the journey which would be waiting for him the following day.

"Then maybe none of those. Maybe cultural: just sheer curiosity."

"Better, but it still only explains the process in terms of itself. New systems are acquired because they're there." Sulhu's tone was almost bantering.

"Then," Foord's was almost irritated, "since you've obviously thought about it, what's your answer?"

"It's very strange, Commander. I've studied cultures like the Commonwealth. They seem to expand for no good reason, at least none they're conscious of. Almost as if something external was making them."

"What made the Sakhran Empire *stop* expanding three hundred years ago?"

"Two things, Commander: Faith, and Srahr's Book. And it didn't just stop expanding, it declined. When you see this," he gestured around him, "you must find it difficult to imagine that we once built ships....though nothing like yours, of course, or like Her...."

Sulhu turned and gazed deliberately past Foord towards the windows. His hands tightened slightly round the obsidian goblet he was holding.

Foord read the gesture accurately. The subject was important, but they'd only touched on it; it needed a whole new conversation, and it was too late. He stood.

"It's been a pleasure. Thank you for your hospitality."

Sulhu smiled and inclined his head. His eyes were dark, simultaneously deep and depthless. "For me, too. I expect to invite you back one day, Commander."

Outside, the wind from the Irsirrha howled through the empty wings of Hrissihr. The last fires in the wall-braziers crackled in the courtyard, and their distant cousin in the hearth hissed and stirred in response.

2

The interior of the Sakhran landchariot was dark and dirty, cramped even for Sakhrans. The seat barely extended halfway up Foord's back, and was inadequate for even one of his buttocks. Because he was reluctant to put his feet on the opposite seat (though he could not have made it much dirtier) he spent most of the journey back from Hrissihr peering between his knees at Thahl, who peered back impassively.

Thahl's face was thin and ophidian, flesh stretched taut over muscle. In fact his whole body was flesh stretched taut over muscle. His skin was purplish grey and made up of tiny diamond-shaped scales, which undulated from the movement of the strange musculature beneath them. The undulation pushed the scales into minutely different angles so they reflected light at different moments and intensities, like the play of light on water. There was nothing much, either in appearance or demeanour, to distinguish a younger Sakhran like Thahl from an older one like Sulhu.

Foord was already uncomfortable and cold, and the journey had barely started; and yet, when he recalled Swann's annoyance, not just at Foord's going to Hrissihr but going there in a landchariot, he thought it was worth it.

"How long will the journey back take, Thahl?"

"About as long as your journey here, Commander, since that was also by landchariot and covered exactly the same route."

"Ah."

"Of course, most of the return journey will be downhill, so it's likely to be quicker. While on the other hand," Thahl continued, relentlessly deadpan, "traffic towards Blentport will be much heavier than traffic towards Hrissihr...."

Foord sighed. They could be irritating, sometimes.

There was nothing much to see, yet. The road from Hrissihr was cut into rock, so one side showed only a sheer face hurtling past, and what might have been an impressive view on the other side was obscured by grey, clinging mist (they had made a very early start) and grimy windows.

Foord turned his attention to a web in the bottom corner of one of the windows. In it hung the dry hollow carcase of something like a fly, jerking with the movement of the landchariot. Foord scraped the window-pane so particles of paint and wood fell on to the web, to tempt its maker to emerge, and watched bemused as the web itself folded over at the points where the particles landed, a silver glistening of digestive juices dribbling down its strands.

The road wound backwards and forwards across the face of the Irsirrha. The landchariot clattered on, leather creaking and wood and metal rattling, the driver occasionally swearing at the chimaera, they occasionally swearing back. Foord yawned; he had not had a good night. They'd given him an apartment in one of the empty wings of Hrissihr, but their beds, like all their furniture, did not accommodate his bulk easily. He started to doze.

A spider perched on his shoulder. He jerked awake and tried to brush it off. It was Thahl's hand, gently tugging.

"My apologies, Commander, but it's time for you to check in."

"Yes, of course. Thank you." He snapped open his wristcom.

"Yes, what do you want?" Smithson's voice answered.

"This is Foord."

"This is me, on the Bridge. What do you want?"

"Checking in. We're on our way back from Hrissihr."

"Yes, we know that. Your wristcom tracker says where you are."

Foord sighed. "We should be with you in," he glanced at Thahl, thought better of it, sighed again and went on, "in about three hours."

"No. There are delays. All the roads into Blentport and the cities are clogged. It seems everyone's coming to the lowlands. Is it some local thing we don't know?"

Foord shot an inquiring glance at Thahl, who shrugged; not the Sakhran gesture but the human one, with his shoulders. "What about the refit, Smithson? Is it proceeding well?"

"It is now. Swann agreed that *we* come before everything, and he's told his people they have to work round the clock."

"How did that happen? When I saw Swann, he said he'd never let our refit take priority over the defensive cordon. Outsiders can take their turn, he said. He practically prodded me in the chest."

"Yes, well, he did all that with me too. But I encouraged him to see it differently." Smithson deliberately paused; he was leaving a space for Foord to congratulate him, so he could receive the congratulation ungraciously and imply it was patronising, and that listening to it kept him from valuable sharp-end work. It was part of his ritual. Foord saw it coming and simply went on.

"What's been completed?"

"All drives and weapons have been overhauled and tested. Scanners and minor systems have been overhauled and are due for testing presently. And right now I'm watching them load on board those two missiles you told them to build."

"Did you make sure they were built exactly to my specification?"

"Yes."

"Exactly?"

"*Yes*....Commander, what were you thinking of? Why take on a couple of primitive things like that?"

"Just a hunch. I have an idea they might be important."

"I have an idea they might be a waste of space."

Foord let that pass. "How are relations at Blentport?"

"How are relations at any port we put into?"

"I asked you about Blentport."

"They started out badly, and got worse because of the refit. Swann's people have been told to give me priority, and they are, but they really don't like me." Occasionally, as now, Smithson would lapse into theatrical self-pity. Foord had never known anyone for whom self-pity was less appropriate. "What about *my* feelings? What happened to common courtesy? I mean....."

●

Like a piece of gently mocking Sakhran conversation, the road wound backwards and forwards across the face of the Irsirrha. It was a track of loose stones and mud, devoid of signs or distance markers.

One side of the landchariot still showed only a rock face rushing past, but on the other side, now the mist had cleared, there was a sheer drop filled with heavy forest: huge trees with green-grey foliage as dense as fur, casting green-black shadows. Because Foord was looking down on them, and because they grew so close together, it was difficult to see properly just how tall they were, or how far into the distance they reached, but both figures were big: about six hundred feet and hundreds of miles respectively.

Occasionally there would be a break in the forest and Foord would catch glimpses of dark torrential rivers and granite palisades; and other hillcastles, all smaller than Hrissihr and showing only one or two sullen plumes of smoke. Hrissihr was the only large hillcastle so close to Blentport and the lowlands; the others were much further away, high in the distant mountain ranges which dwarfed even the Irsirrha. Humans hardly ever went up there. There was a rumour in the lowland cities that somewhere, high in the heavily-forested mountains, was a thousand-foot tree.

There was no other traffic yet; there wouldn't be until they got closer to the lowlands and started hitting Commonwealth towns. The driver—Foord knew him only as a surly expanse of diamond-scaled back and shoulders visible through the grimy front window—hissed and swore and whipped the team.

"Thahl," Foord said, "you omitted to calculate that this landchariot has six chimaera pulling it, not four like the one which brought me."

"You mean, Commander, that that will affect any estimate of our travel time? But this is not a fresh team, unlike the one which brought you. The driver will have to rest and water them in an hour or two."

"Oh." Foord subsided.

Rituals. At least Thahl only did it privately, this gentle pisstaking; never in front of others, or when it genuinely mattered. Smithson did it publicly, privately, whenever and wherever he liked.

Foord commanded one of the nine deadliest warships in the Commonwealth, crewed by uniquely talented and dangerous individuals, yet they all had these rituals they enacted with him. Often they would change the rules at random, on the possibly anarchic basis that random rule changes were part of the rules. And Foord usually went along with it; anything to get the most from them. In any case, as well as being their Commander he was also one of them. He had done things as terrible as any of them. Except, of course, for Thahl. As far as Foord knew, Thahl had done nothing more terrible than any other Sakhran; he was not, by Sakhran standards, psychotic or maladjusted. He had simply completed all the necessary officer courses, usually with grades well into the top five percent, and had specifically asked to serve on an Outsider. He'd never wanted anything else.

The Department appreciates that you have a Sakhran First Officer; you know a lot about him, but maybe less about them. Your ship's Codex, as usual, has more detail, but you may prefer this modest summary.

Sakhrans contain elements of mammal and reptile; and other elements, still unclassifiable. They reproduce asexually, but our cultural preconceptions still lead us to refer to them as males.

They have a slight build, but extraordinary physical abilities; the deadliest intelligent humanoids known to us. They evolved to compete with their planet's other spectacular carnivores: Angels, Coils, Diamondfaces, and even the dreadful Walking Air. Sakhrans can outkill them all.

Their neural synapses and metabolism, their musculature and reflexes, are quite unique. Their bones and claws and teeth are like titanium. Thahl is smaller than you, but much faster and stronger. You have often been heard to say that you wouldn't last ten seconds against him. Ten seconds is optimistic.

But they work best as individuals, not in teams. This could be connected with the next point.

You have had a long working relationship with one Sakhran, which may have obscured an important fact about Sakhrans generally. They were not always like they are now. Their society, their institutions, their Empire, even their everyday technology, declined rapidly—it was not a collapse, but a rapid decline—three hundred years ago, after the first visit of the unidentified ship and the writing of the Book of Srahr. We know no other culture which has declined in quite the same way. This may not impinge on your professional relationship with Thahl, which appears to have worked well; but with other Sakhrans, it may be significant.

The landchariot lurched on.

"Thahl," Foord began, "I was sorry not to see your father before we set off this morning. Was he unwell?"

"Not unusually so, Commander. He's old and diseased and will soon die, of course, but that wasn't why he didn't appear. I think he was concerned that if he saw you again he might delay you by restarting last night's conversation."

"I enjoyed last night's conversation. He asks very good questions."

"He's very ignorant."

A few miles later, as if there had not been a gap of distance and silence in their conversation, Thahl added: "My father asked me to give you a message, Commander. First, to thank you for coming up to visit him. Second, that whatever happens, he expects to invite you a second time."

They were still in the Irsirrha, but they had left the higher slopes and the road didn't double back on itself so much; it was straighter, plunging down between walls of dripping forest on either side. The view was smaller-scale, but didn't seem so. Higher up, what would have been a much more impressive view had been obscured, by the mist and the sheer density of the trees. Here, the forest had thinned out enough to see how massive the trees really were; although the trees of the higher Irsirrha were even taller, these ones still towered four hundred feet over the road, often standing in groups of three or four as if talking privately together. Somehow, they made the air around them seem like the air in a cathedral.

They were set far enough apart to see the green-black shadows they cast on the ground, and the armoured secondary foliage bursting in frozen waves around their lower trunks, and the dark mouths of openings in the coils of their massive roots. Sakhra had many species of trees, but Sakhrans had a particular name for tall trees generally; they called them Shadanth, or Vertical Rivers.

The gradient softened. The road widened but was still mainly loose stones and mud, and still showed no signs or markers. The trees on either side were no less tall than before, but were set back further from the road, leaving a verge of mud and grass, dotted with tall clumps of silver-green bladeweed. As they turned a bend they encountered the first traffic they had seen all morning, another landchariot coming directly towards them at a speed almost matching theirs. They swerved to a halt and the two drivers had a brief and spiteful conversation—at least, to Foord it sounded spiteful—before the other driver lashed his team and clattered away towards the highlands.

They remained stationary.

The driver, without turning round, said something. Thahl leaned out of the window and a long, sibilant conversation ensued. When it finished they both sat silently, long enough for Foord to start hearing the noises of the forest; then the driver's whip exploded over the six huge backs of his team, and they shot forward.

"What was that about?"

"It may be nothing, Commander. The driver has heard something… Can I suggest you check in again?"

"Thahl, what is this? Does it have any bearing on the ship?"

"Nothing like that, Commander. A rumour of a local evacuation. But it may affect our journey time and it would be prudent to check in more frequently from now on."

Foord snapped open his wristcom.

"Yes?" Smithson said. "What do you want?"

"An update on the refit, please."

"Scanners are done and tested. Minor systems await testing."

"We may be delayed getting back."

"You will be, Commander. Traffic's got worse, it's so tight you can't…"

"No," Foord said, not eager to hear Smithson complete the phrase, "it's up here. There may be further delays in the highlands."

"Why don't we send one of the ship's fliers for you? Or even better, get Swann to send a Blentport flier?"

"No. We've been through this before. I told you I wanted to make this journey by landchariot."

The answering noise from Foord's wristcom was moist and disgusting. In a gesture characteristic of his species Smithson had plunged his hand, and by symbolic extension Foord's, into one of his lower abdominal orifices.

"Well, Commander, whenever and however you get here, we'll have completed the refit, done the testing, got their people off and ours on, in four hours."

"*Four* hours?" Foord and Thahl exchanged glances. Even Thahl looked surprised.

"Yes? Why not four hours? What's wrong?"

"I expected eight at least."

"Well. It's four."

Again, the ritual; Smithson left a gap into which Foord was supposed to put praise which Smithson could accept ungraciously. All the same, Foord couldn't let it go unacknowledged.

"Last night at Hrissihr, I was thinking you'd need most of today to complete. I didn't expect we might leave so soon. Thank you."

"With the trouble we've had here, they might not *let* us leave."

"Trouble?" Foord asked, carefully. "What trouble?"

"An incident in a bar with two of our crew. Cyr's dealing with it. It's always an incident in a bar, isn't it?"

"Where is Cyr now?"

"She's at Swann's offices."

"Tell me what you know, *now*."

"Two of our crew got called names in a bar. There was a fight, the others got hurt, Cyr took our two aboard and isn't releasing them. It does happen every time, doesn't it, Commander?"

"Get Cyr to call the moment she returns from Swann. If I haven't heard in thirty minutes I'll check in again."

A clattering and hissing and squealing as two more landchariots passed them going the other way. A sickening jolt as they crashed through a pothole. The driver swore, the whip flew and crackled electrically, and they hurtled on.

●

"Why have we stopped?"

It was an hour later. The road was wider, the gradient shallower, and Sakhran landchariots heading up into the Irsirrha were more frequent. The forest still towered over the road on both sides, however, and they had seen nobody except Sakhrans.

"Why have we…"

"The team have to be rested and watered, Commander."

"Fine, then let's get out."

"We'll only be here a few minutes."

"Half an hour, you said earlier."

"No, we'll be going sooner than that."

"Nevertheless, I'm getting out."

"I wouldn't advise it, Commander."

"Why?"

"There may be trouble here."

"Tell me about it outside."

They stepped out into a large forest clearing where the road from the Irsirrha crossed two others. It was full of landchariots, of Sakhrans hissing and chimaera squealing; of wheels foundering in mud, smoke from damp wood fires, the sodden flapping of canvas and hammering of tent-pegs.

With a sudden vicious blow at the leader's chest their driver smashed the harness from his team, whereupon they lumbered over to a pothole full of muddy water, drank, and settled; this, apparently, amounted to resting and watering. The driver had already turned his back, pointedly, and stalked off to sit alone on a dead tree-trunk some distance away. He unsheathed his claws at another Sakhran who was doing no more than amble past.

"What is this place, anyway?" Foord demanded.

"It's the last gathering-place before the lowlands, Commander."

"Gathering-place? Sakhrans, gathering?" Foord was surprised to hear himself speak so sourly. He put it down to discomfort from the journey: cramp, and a throbbing headache.

"These are hunting-parties, Commander, from Hrissihr and from some of those smaller places you saw on the way down. They come here to exchange news and trade carcases."

"They appear to be doing little of either. They look like they hate each other. Their chimaera look like they hate each other."

"Then perhaps they've just come together to reaffirm it, Commander."

They walked across the sullen clearing, between groups of Sakhrans whose expressions were unreadable, past tents and fires, and around landchariots festooned with carcases, mostly of giant wild relatives of chimaera. Other carcases hung from poles, heads lolling, or sat in heaps in the mud ready for flensing. Many had throats cut. Some were partly eaten.

"Anything here remind you of the *Charles Manson*, Thahl?"

"I'm not sure I understand, Commander."

"Oh, you know, this comradeship"—again, Foord was surprised at his own sourness—"this golden glow of social intercourse."

Thahl glanced at him but did not reply.

They sat down on a tree-trunk, the wood of which was damp and rotten and teeming with white grubs. Foord's throbbing headache was getting worse.

"So what's about to happen here, Thahl? And why didn't you warn me earlier?"

"I only suspected it as we drew in, Commander."

The throbbing had become louder and more pronounced, almost loud enough to be an external noise.

Thahl stood up. So did most of the other Sakhrans. They looked like they were smelling the air, but Foord recognised it as their posture for listening.

He suddenly realised there *was* an external noise.

"Thahl, what's going on? What's that..."

Thahl had relaxed slightly; he turned an expressionless gaze on Foord.

"I know what it is now, Commander. But it's too late to leave, and it could still be dangerous. Please stay close by me."

Three military groundcars entered the clearing. They settled with a low whine and disgorged twenty soldiers who set about moving Sakhrans away from the centre of the glade. They carried only light sidearms and behaved with impeccable courtesy. Their demeanour was carefully low key, and although well drilled, they seemed to have been chosen for their non-threatening appearance; they were of average build with regular features, definitely not Special Forces like those Foord had seen in Blentport.

At the edge of the clearing, coming up the road from the lowlands, loomed the source of the throbbing background noise: three tracked military lowloaders carrying enough equipment to erect a large scanner emplacement and several particle beam and missile units. The throbbing was due to the heavy muffling of their engines, which were now idling as they waited—Foord gasped when he realised this—to move into the centre of the clearing.

"Thahl! I thought you said the military *never* came into the highlands. There's going to be murder here."

"I don't think so, Commander. But please stay close."

Slowly, carefully, the soldiers made a space for themselves in the centre of the clearing. Their patience and diplomacy were remarkable; they persuaded the Sakhrans back, easing their way with smiles and thanks, requesting space with gestures carefully drained of sudden movement, speaking softly and politely, treading as if on broken glass. There were only twenty of them; any one Sakhran, armed or unarmed, could easily have killed five or six, and there were nearly seventy Sakhrans. But Sakhrans together were less than Sakhrans individually. Foord had often read about it, but this was the first time he had ever seen it demonstrated, and he was astonished. He glanced at Thahl and thought, *Is this is what you lost? Did a book make you like this?*

It was over in a few minutes. Twenty men, chosen by someone very cleverly, had persuaded seventy Sakhrans to move aside and allow the Commonwealth to make its first military entry into the Sakhran highlands in two hundred years.

The Sakhrans stood singly, or in twos and threes, and watched the lowloaders lurch into the clearing. Foord let out a breath and walked back to the landchariot with Thahl, who gestured to the driver. By the time they were inside, the main scanner emplacement had been mostly erected and the particle beam and missile units were being unloaded. Smithson could not have done it much better.

"They were very good," Foord said.

"Yes, Commander. I was afraid you might be endangered, but they handled it well."

Foord looked askance at Thahl, a gesture he had learnt from Thahl himself.

"You're more Worrier than Warrior."

"It keeps you alive, Commander...and I think we'll see more of this as we get closer to the lowlands. I think I know what these rumours of evacuations are about."

"Well?"

"We'll see more military incursions into the highlands. Later, we'll see some of the outlying civilian populations being moved into the lowlands."

"I don't understand."

Thahl waited politely until he did.

"You mean they're gambling that if She defeats us, and comes for Sakhra, She won't attack the cities if they've been turned into civilian targets?"

"Yes, Commander."

Foord swore to himself.

"I think," Thahl added, unnecessarily, "this may not be a pleasant journey."

The driver's whip exploded and the landchariot clattered out of the clearing and down towards the lowlands.

3

The landchariot hurtled on, now a dark wheeled box full of so many varieties of brooding that even the chimaera fell silent and ran faster as if merely to get away from it.

They passed their first roadsign. It was crooked and untended and read, in blue letters on a rustpocked white background, BOWL BLENTPORT (Pindar, Framsden, Cromer, Meddon). As it flashed past the landchariot, Foord leaned out of the window to look back at it. The reverse side was blank.

The road was wider now and verged with grey-green tussocky grass, the terrain more level and less heavily wooded; they were in the vaguely-defined border between the end of the lower Irsirrha and the start of the foothills, which would eventually slope down and level out at the rim of the Great Lowland Bowl. They were making good time; but all around them, the details which it was Foord's lifelong habit to note and store were mounting.

It began when they left the clearing. As the road sloped gently downhill and they got closer to the foothills, the forest gradually thinned out, becoming the exception rather than the rule. Fields predominated, with trees—usually smaller varieties, like cloudclaw and armourfern—making borders between them. The fields, of course, were not Sakhran; Sakhrans didn't farm, though a few did work on the human-owned farms which characterised the foothills and the edges of the Bowl. But Foord had noticed these fields on the way up to Hrissihr, along with occasional farmhouses; there were people and vehicles around them, smoke from chimneys, the sound of engines running. Now they were deserted; the farmhouses showed streams of furniture and possessions vomited out of open windows and doors, and churned tracks in the mud.

There were other figures, however. Every quarter-mile or so there would be a military vehicle, usually a small groundcar, with a couple of soldiers. This seemed to be the message: evacuate to the lowlands *now*, leave your possessions, go *now*, this is an emergency, and if you go *now*, we'll post guards against looting; an easy task, since no humans would be left to do any looting, and the remaining Sakhrans would be in the highlands.

Sakhra's diameter is about 1.5 times that of Earth, large for an Earth-type planet. Its atmosphere and gravity, and the length of its day, are all close to Earth normal. Its topography is unusual. The largest continent, Shaloom, covers most of one hemisphere; its main feature, taking up sixty percent of its land area, is the Great Lowland Bowl.

The Bowl was thought to be an ancient impact crater, but that theory is discounted now; anything making a crater that size would have destroyed the planet.

The Bowl's cross-section is irregular, sometimes deep and sometimes shallow. Most of the Commonwealth settlers on Sakhra live there. Some Sakhrans also work and live there, but most remain in the traditional hillcastles in the mountains and highlands.

Sakhra's other hemisphere consists of oceans and archipelagos, and has huge natural resources: mineral deposits offshore, and precious metals and precious stones in the mountains of the larger islands. (There may be similar finds in the mountains of Shaloom, but for obvious political reasons these are not prospected.) The Commonwealth's main economic activity is the extraction and processing of these commodities, and their transport to, and distribution from, Blentport.

Landchariots hurtled past them every few minutes, in the direction of the highlands. And, also heading for the highlands and also every few minutes, they encountered more military traffic: low-slung groundcars with opaque windows, light armoured vehicles, and, so far, five more convoys of tracked lowloaders taking scanner and missile and beam installations up into the Irsirrha.

Then, when they started to pass the farms, they saw the other half of the evacuation: the civilian traffic from outlying farms and villages, mostly pickups and trucks and offroaders, laden with people and packing cases. The traffic had not yet reached crisis proportions because the human population in the foothill areas was quite sparse, but further down, when it met the normal lowland traffic, it would be unimaginable. And then there was the roadblock. Or rather, there wasn't.

"Are you a local resident, sir?"

"No. Do you want to see my papers?"

"Are you going to the lowlands, sir?"

"Yes. My papers?"

"Not necessary, sir, if you're going to the lowlands."

The soldier paused as a couple of freighters roared overhead, on their way down to Blentport. The sky—a grey inverted bowl shot with high trailing clouds, like the roof of a giant mouth streaked with mucus—had again started to be full of them, like it was last night.

"Are you sure you don't need to see my papers?"

"Yes, sir, as long as you're going to the lowlands." He was already losing what little interest he had in Foord. "Safe journey."

Across the road, on the side leading up into the highlands, where they had seen a stream of landchariots and military vehicles, but no civilian traffic, there was not merely one soldier but nine or ten, all heavily armed, and a large armoured sixwheel. Both its gun turrets were pointing down the road in the direction of traffic *from* the lowlands, but that may have been coincidence.

Foord's wristcom buzzed. He snapped it open.

"This is me," Smithson said. "Is that you?"

"Smithson, where is Cyr? Why hasn't she called?"

"She's still with Swann. And it's forty minutes since *you* said *you'd* call in thirty minutes."

"I know, we were delayed... The traffic is getting heavier, but we're still aiming to be back in about two hours."

On Foord's wristcom, either a toilet flushed or Smithson laughed. "I don't think so, Commander. It'll get worse as you get closer. You wouldn't believe what it's like now, down here."

"Is the refit still on target?"

"Yes, be done in three hours. I've got total priority. At least nine ships, including three Class 097s, are stuck down here and can't join the cordon, because of me," he said proudly. "It's going well. But whether we leave in three hours, or wait twelve for a post-mortem on that alehouse brawl, is Cyr's problem. And yours."

"*Post-mortem?*"

"Nobody's dead, Commander, it was just an expression."

An expression, thought Foord, which he had used deliberately. "Smithson, if we're ready to leave in three hours we'll leave! Do you understand?"

Smithson hated being asked Do You Understand; he took it as a personal insult, a fact of which Foord was aware. "Call Cyr, please," he went on quickly, "and tell her I want the details of that incident. And she's *not* to hand our people over to Swann. And even if Horus doesn't set tonight, two things are certain: we leave when the refit is done, and we leave with *all* our crew."

Foord felt like adding another Do You Understand, but decided it would be ill-judged. He snapped the wristcom shut.

●

At Pindar the evacuation really started to show itself. Foord looked out of the landchariot as it turned a bend into the main street, and swore.

Coming here from the highlands was like jumping from air into treacle. Pindar was the last Commonwealth settlement he had passed on his way up to Hrissihr yesterday, and the first on their way down today: a small market town with a longish narrow main street lined with houses and shops and civic buildings, all slightly uncared-for and all built on the same modest scale. It would have taken a direct bombing better than it was taking the evacuation.

They were embedded in traffic. Most of it was town vehicles, with a few trucks and offroaders from neighbouring farms, some of which had passed them on the way down, sounding their horns. They were not sounding their horns now. Pindar was gridlocked but eerily quiet.

Military groundcars were positioned at intervals along the main street, turning it into a one-way through road to the lowlands. The traffic was like a stream of food passing down a long mouth, with the groundcars as inward-pointing teeth.

It looked like much of Pindar was already evacuated. The main street resembled a table-top onto which the contents of buildings had been emptied like the contents of pockets. For collection later, Foord thought, as though the urgency dwindled once *people* were put on the road, and pointed in the unvarying direction of the lowlands.

Thahl was right. And this, thought Foord, must be happening all the way around the rim of the Bowl. Here, though the crowding was heavy, it was still rather small-scale, just one modest town in the foothills; the entire population of the foothills wasn't that large, but if *this* was happening here, it was the tip of something far larger. And something quite desperate.

They can never do it, Foord kept thinking. *There isn't time. They can't turn the lowlands into an undefended civilian area!*

They could, and they were; not completely, but perhaps just enough.

Foord opened his wristcom, told it to seek the local broadcasts, and listened.

The broadcasts talked of hotels and commercial buildings in the Bowl being requisitioned. Of camps erected on unused land between lowland cities. Of the mobilisation of hospitals and social services and charities to take the sudden—but, as they described it, temporary—influx of people. Of special comm links to enable those who had relatives in the lowlands to contact them and arrange accommodation (the preferred option). Of detailed arrangements for farms to leave one or two people behind to tend crops and animals.

The broadcasts used as much of the truth as humanly possible, but no more than necessary. They said—it was common knowledge anyway—that *She* may be coming to Horus, and that people in outlying areas were being moved temporarily to the lowland cities where they could be better protected. It was, they repeated, only temporary, until the *Charles Manson* lifted off from Blentport to engage Her.

They didn't simply have one official broadcast repeating this message. They got existing presenters to insert it in existing programmes, not merely reading a prepared text but speaking around a summary they'd been given, so they could preserve some spontaneity. Even so, Foord heard similar phrases being repeated by different voices. The most common was We Have To GET You, To Where We Can PROTECT You. Once or twice, though, he actually heard the phrase Drawing The Wagons Into A Circle. He suspected the authorities hadn't fed them that; their plan might be desperate, but they weren't stupid.

They mentioned that large military detachments were being deployed to the highlands to prevent looting of evacuated properties. They did not mention that they were also moving defence emplacements to the highlands, or creating the impression (hasty and partial, but maybe just enough) that the lowland cities were undefended. Such an impression could not be other than hasty and partial. They could never move *all* the military out of the lowlands, even if they wanted to. What they wanted was to move the most visible garrisons. The fixed defence emplacements around the Bowl and especially around Blentport would remain, but would be visibly undermanned.

Foord left the wristcom on speaker. It scrolled up and down all the lowland frequencies, repeating substantially the same material. Foord and Thahl listened in the landchariot as it moved, at walking pace, through Pindar. The web in the window continued to salivate.

"This is their endgame, Thahl. We haven't even left to engage Her. She hasn't even *appeared* in Horus yet. And they're gambling that if She defeats us and comes to Sakhra, this—*this*, will keep Her from attacking the lowlands!"

The broadcasts continued to murmur out of Foord's wristcom. We Have To GET You, To Where We Can PROTECT You.

"It may not work, Commander, but it's all they've got. Their ships can't fight Her because they've been told to stay in the defensive cordon, while *we* fight Her. If She comes here, it means She's destroyed us and destroyed their cordon. They have to have an endgame, even one like this."

Foord did not answer for a while. Then, "You of all people. I thought you'd be outraged at the military going into the highlands."

"Commander, the way *they* see it, they're decoying Her away from the cities. If She comes, those in the highlands know they won't have a chance against Her."

We Have To GET You, To Where We Can PROTECT You. Nothing is simple, Foord thought but did not say. He snapped his wristcom shut. Immediately it started buzzing.

"Foord."

"Cyr, Commander. I've just left Director Swann's offices."

"And is he still demanding we hand over our people?"

"No, Commander." She laughed, rather unpleasantly. "He almost disappointed me. Before I could invoke our priority he invoked it for me. Keep them, he said, and just go. He's desperate to get us off Sakhra."

"Good. Should I know who did what to who or will it keep?"

"You can guess most of it, Commander. It does happen every time, doesn't it?"

It was a voice-only channel, but Foord nodded; he knew that Cyr would read the quality of his silence. Outsiders were always treated, especially by regular military forces, like the carriers of a disease. Everyone knew the Department recruited most Outsider crew members from prisons, and psychiatric hospitals, and orphanages; sociopaths and psychopaths who could never work with regular forces. And when one or two of them walked into a bar, or were seen anywhere in public, the results were almost inevitable. Most were not openly aggressive, which made them even more of a provocation; they were loners or depressives who tended to sit in corners, in ones or twos or small groups. On this occasion, two were set upon by four from a Horus Fleet cruiser, also on Blentport for refit.

"Was anybody killed?"

"No, Commander. Our two went immediately back to the ship. I refused to hand them over to Swann, and now he's given up. The other four were all injured, one of them seriously, but he won't be permanently scarred or disabled: I checked with the hospital."

"Alright, Cyr, thank you…No, wait, something's happening here."

The traffic jamming the main street of Pindar had been strangely quiet. Now, Foord could hear klaxons and sirens, and soldiers shouting at vehicles to move to one side of the road, further and further to one side until they mounted the pavement. Something huge was coming.

Foord should have realised what it was from the low throb of its engine, or the shape of the shadow it cast, but he didn't until it was upon them: a tracked lowloader, like those in the clearing earlier, but much larger. There were others behind it. They carried more beam and scanner units, and missiles so tall they towered precariously over Pindar's buildings, and they moved through the main street in the opposite direction to everything else: in the direction, of course, of the highlands. The lowloader was so long that as it passed the landchariot, and continued and continued to pass, it seemed that its bulk was standing still and they were moving past it. Then it passed by and the illusion ended, but as those behind it followed, each of them equally tall, there was another illusion: that of a city moving through a town.

"What's that noise, Commander? Are you all right?"

"It's OK, Cyr, a military convoy is passing through. Stay on, I want to speak again when it's quieter."

The lowloaders continued: there were seven of them, followed by groundcars, sixwheels and other vehicles. When they had gone, and their engine-noise had receded, the traffic was ushered back into the centre of the road and continued at walking pace. The sirens stopped. The abnormal quiet returned.

"Cyr."

"Commander?"

"That convoy gave me an idea. Cyr, I intend to return to the lowlands, and to the ship, in this landchariot. Contact Swann, please. Tell him where we are, and tell him to get a military escort to clear the way for us. Invoke our priority, it seems to work."

Cyr did not reply immediately.

"Cyr? Do you think that's pushing him too far?"

"No, Commander." Foord realised, from the inflexion of her voice, that she had been laughing quietly. "I think he'll do anything....I'll call him now. We are heaping insults on him, aren't we?"

Foord snapped his wristcom shut, and thought, *This is like the running joke in ancient movies, where one person gets repeatedly clobbered.* He thought also, *She never asked why I have to go by landchariot, though she probably thinks it's self-indulgent.* The fact was, he didn't really know himself. Instinctively, it just felt fitting. He could have rationalised it by saying it was done out of respect for Thahl, but that wasn't true. Thahl had already told him, firmly but in private, that he thought the idea was unnecessarily risky as well as a provocation to Swann.

Between Foord's knees, and across the landchariot's dim interior, Thahl stayed expressionless and silent, though Foord had known him long enough to know he was amused at the indignities being piled on Swann. Sakhrans' quiet humour was strangely at odds with their capacity for violence.

Foord looked above Thahl's head at their driver. He had never seen anyone's mere neck and shoulders radiate so much repressed anger. The driver had said nothing to Thahl since leaving the clearing, and nothing at all to Foord; his turned back carried far more expression than Thahl's face.

●

When they finally got out of Pindar the road widened; traffic was heavy but faster. In both directions—toward the lowlands and highlands, the latter now entirely military vehicles—it was an unbroken stream. Cyr called back to report that Swann, although outraged that Foord should enter Blentport by landchariot, had agreed almost gratefully to the suggestion that a military escort would hasten his return and, hence, departure. They would be met, Cyr said, by a specially picked detachment who would escort them at high speed the rest of the way down.

The foothill country opened up and the landchariot clattered on, between fields of dark gold corn stubble where suddenly-empty houses stood alone as if daubed there in anger; fields of waving barley where cloud shadows raced each other across the ground; between fields of naked brown ploughed earth where flocks of white birds, or things like birds, wheeled screaming. And everywhere in the fields were swarms of giant Sakhran butterflies, iridescent violet and purple, looking for the farm animals on whose excrement they fed; they preferred it warm, so they would cluster around anal orifices. The farmers called them Buggerflies.

The sky was still full of freighters going to and from Blentport. As two passed overhead, much too low and much too fast—they were huge ships, and their passing seemed to go on and on, like that of the lowloaders—they encountered their escort. Swann had wasted no time.

Two sleek, low-slung military groundcars, with sirens blaring and lights flashing, came up behind them from the direction of the highlands, overtook them and waved them down. The landchariot juddered to a halt, the chimaeras' hooves scuttering and kicking up stones and mud. Three soldiers got out of each car. They were from heavy-gravity planets, each one of them bigger than Foord, and they wore dark blue Special Forces uniforms.

"Commander Foord and Officer Thahl?"

"Yes."

"I'm Kudrow. Major Miles Kudrow." He was not unlike Foord, even down to the thick dark hair and beard; but younger and larger. The five standing behind him were equally large, and looked impressive even to Foord. "I've been ordered by Director Swann to escort you back to your ship."

"Thank you, Major. We didn't expect you quite so soon."

Kudrow nodded, politely. "Commander, my orders were to escort you in this landchariot."

"That's correct."

"Can I suggest you transfer to the cars? We'd make better time."

"Thank you, Major, but I particularly want to complete the journey by landchariot."

"Of course, Commander. We'll get you there as quickly as we can. One car in front, one behind, sirens and lights. We've already called ahead so a lane will be cleared when we hit the main highway."

"Thank you, Major."

Kudrow opened his wristcom and spoke into it. His wristcom, and Foord's, buzzed in unison. "Our numbers are stored, Commander. Please call me if we're going too fast, or too slow. See you in Blentport."

They moved out into the road, one car in front and one behind, the sirens and flashing lights clearing the way. Generally the traffic moved aside in good time, leaving them free to rush past in the left-hand lane; vehicles which didn't move quickly enough were made to, diplomatically but efficiently. Kudrow seemed to have got the landchariot's speed exactly right, and kept it thoughtfully constant. They were making good time, having neither to slow down or to rush beyond the chimaeras' capacity.

The road was wide, still partly stones and mud, but starting to show patches of proper surfacing. The area was still predominantly agricultural, although crops and livestock had given way to commercial-scale market gardening: huge fields growing the prized Sakhran black tulips and blue roses. It was a more prosperous area: they passed through a couple of market towns and saw several farmhouses, all notably larger and better-kept than Pindar. The towns had fatter names, too: Framsden, Cromer, Meddon.

After twenty minutes, Foord's wristcom buzzed.

"Kudrow, Commander. We'll be taking a left turn in half a mile."

"Trouble?"

"No, Commander. I've called ahead and there's a detour we can take to reach the main highway: a farm road which cuts off a few miles. My people are keeping it open for us."

It came up in a couple of minutes, a small turnoff guarded by a sixwheel. Kudrow's car, in front of them, signalled and turned smoothly, flashing its lights at the sixwheel as it did so. The landchariot, and the second car behind, followed.

But it wasn't a road, or even a track. It was just a clearing. Kudrow's car skidded round, throwing up stones and mud and turning in almost its own length to face them; and with impressive speed and precision, and before the car stopped moving, Kudrow and his two passengers jumped out and were at Foord's side of the landchariot, guns levelled. Foord could even read the name-tags of the other two: Lyle and Astin. The guns were pointed unwaveringly in his face—directly at him, with such geometric precision that their muzzles appeared to him as perfect black circles. Not even ovals, but circles.

"Get out, please. Both of you."

For most of the morning Foord had seen Thahl gazing impassively from the seat opposite, but now the seat was empty, the landchariot's other door hanging open—*when did that happen?* Foord had neither seen nor heard him move—and as Foord stepped out he saw the second car, which had stopped behind them, and waved desperately to the three inside it, who wouldn't meet his gaze.

Time fractured. Foord glimpsed the results of what Thahl did before he saw him do it. Events should have been sequential, but Thahl's speed broke them into pieces and when Foord tried to put them back together, they no longer followed each other properly. He seemed to remember them before they happened.

The guns were pointed unwaveringly in his face. Kudrow was explaining that they could *not* allow an Outsider to compromise Sakhra's defences, and would *not* rely on an Outsider to defend them against Her, that was unthinkable, and the only way to stop it was *this*.

Foord looked at the three in the second car, and concluded they'd washed their hands of it. He couldn't remember if he concluded that before or after Kudrow spoke.

The guns pointed unwaveringly in his face were now on the ground, because Thahl had broken the forearms of Lyle and Astin. Thahl had not used his poison, because they were still alive where they fell, and were screaming. Their screams drowned the sound of Kudrow's voice, explaining why they had to kill Foord. No, that came earlier. The voice drowned by the screams was Thahl's. He was saying to Kudrow, *Please don't, You know you don't have a chance, Don't make me do this, Just walk away. Just leave the gun.*

Kudrow reached for his sidearm. *No,* Thahl said, *Please don't,* his pleading tone ridiculously at odds with what he had done. Thahl snatched Kudrow's pistol, infinitely quicker than its owner, and tossed it away. Foord noticed that Kudrow's severed hand was still clutching the grip, and Kudrow was screaming, so maybe it was his screaming *now* which was drowning out his voice *then.*

It should all have been sequential—blurringly fast, but still sequential —except that Thahl's speed splintered it. Foord had seen Thahl in combat before, but not like this. This was a single glimpse, *on-off,* of things that were impossible; as if Thahl had opened his private jewel-box of impossibilities, flourished it in front of Foord's face, and snapped it shut.

Time slowed, and the pieces rearranged themselves. Thahl had kicked the guns away from the three on the ground. Kudrow was still screaming. The others were unconscious. Then Kudrow fell silent. Foord tasted brine along the sides of his tongue, the taste that comes before vomiting: a reaction not to the violence, but to its strangeness.

And one last detail: their driver had said and done nothing while it happened. He was sitting where he had been all along, flicking the chimaera with his reins and waiting for the journey to resume.

Finally, when he had recovered, Foord strode over to the second car. Thahl followed him at a distance. The three inside hadn't had time, from when it started to when it finished, even to open the door.

Somehow, Foord correctly picked out the senior one.

"Did Director Swann know anything of this?"

"No, Commander."

"And you, you all washed your hands of it."

"Yes. We told Major Kudrow we wanted no part of it. He said, Look the other way."

"Your name?"

"Lieutenant Traore, Commander."

Foord turned to Thahl, and their eyes met. Foord shook his head slightly, then turned back to face those in the car. He could see them all let out a breath; they saw what passed between him and Thahl, and were praying they'd read it correctly.

"Alright. Lieutenant, please call Director Swann, now, and tell him what happened here. And tell him we're going into Blentport in this landchariot, and he's to give authority for the roads to be cleared for us. We want to see his fliers and VSTOLs and groundcars ahead of us all the way to Blentport, clearing a path. Do you understand?"

"Yes, Commander."

"As soon as you've arranged that, we'll leave here. You and your colleagues are to stay put. And please arrange medical help."

He stood for a while listening to them make the call, then turned to Thahl.

"How did you know they…"

"More Worrier than Warrior."

Foord nodded, wryly. Thahl's quiet friendship and gentle mockery had been like a soothing antiseptic balm after the orphanage; yet still he could do things like this.

4

The journey was turning feverish. The road was now a six-lane carriageway, the middle and outer lanes jammed with a thrombosis of traffic and the inner lane cleared for them, cars and trucks shunted to one side by the military. The oncoming three lanes were an unbroken procession of military vehicles: more lowloaders and groundcars, tankers and multiwheels and personnel carriers, each one with its own battery of sirens and lights. Ahead there were VSTOLs hovering low over the road, low enough to force traffic into the outer lanes. Their road was being made for them as they travelled it.

They were in the flat country leading to the rim of the Bowl: immense and drab, partly fields and partly industrial wasteland, littered with lowgrade and failing development: warehouses, factories, workshops, silos, apartment blocks. Some of them were soiled with brown stains from their partly-exposed steel skeletons.

Foord's wristcom buzzed.

"Commander, it's Cyr. We've got a situation."

"Situation?"

"It's the crews of the Horus Fleet ships. They're stuck here until our re-fit's completed and they're gathering round our Grid—not doing anything yet, just watching. And when I refused to hand over our people to Swann, civilians and military started gathering too. They don't seem to know what they want yet, but Swann won't order them away because he says their mood is unreadable and he can't predict the consequences. And now the news of what Thahl did …How long until you arrive, Commander?"

"About ninety minutes."

"It may get worse. And when you do arrive, it'll take something excep-tional to get you through this crowd and on board. You won't reconsider the landchariot?"

"Not now."

"A moment please, Commander…Smithson says he has an idea about what to do when you arrive. I'll call back."

"Thank you, Cyr."

The landchariot sped on. The landscape stretched either side of the highway, reflecting the sky's greyness as if it was a stretch of ocean.

Now that they were approaching the edge of the Great Lowland Bowl, there was a strangeness about what they saw. The country was too unre-lievedly flat to see the actual rim yet—it wouldn't be visible until they were almost on top of it—but the strangeness had to do with how its presence was felt and almost seen. Freighters and warships, going to or from Blentport, appeared to fly into and out of the ground at a distant point on the horizon where the rim was located but not yet visible; at the same location and for miles beyond, the air was coloured with rainbows from the rivers which fell in torrents over the edge; and occasionally, there was the sense that beyond every rise in the horizon there was not simply more land, but emptiness—a difference in the quality of the landscape, like the difference felt near a coast before the sea was visible. And it did things to the air. Above the rim, so high above it they couldn't be seen properly, were flocks of white things floating on the roiling air-currents. They weren't birds, but they had wings over thirty feet across. Angels.

Blentport is situated in the Great Lowland Bowl. It is the headquarters of Horus Fleet, and the Commonwealth's biggest port outside of Earth. It has landing and takeoff capacity for warships, freighters and liners: nine large and ten minor Grids, each able to repair, rebuild or refit a ship.

Commonwealth cities grew rapidly in the Bowl. Blentport grew rapidly too, because Horus Fleet was needed to protect the natural riches of Horus system; but the cities grew faster, making one huge conurbation surrounding the port.

You will have consulted your ship's Codex about Blentport. Remember, however, the following:

First, how it got its name.

Second, its unique "City Centre" location. Population pressure in the Bowl conurbation is high, and Blentport is inevitably affected by (or even the cause of) the political and social pressures around it.

Third, its capacity. It can only refit, at any one time, less than half of Horus Fleet—adequate for most situations, but not for what you will find when you arrive there. The enforced deployment of the entire Fleet to a defensive cordon around Sakhra will precipitate a serious emergency, with more ships than it can handle putting in for refit.

Your ship has total priority, but the situation is volatile. The effect of anything ill-considered on your part is something you may be able to imagine better than the authors of this briefing.

They hung poised over the rim, and Foord froze. The traffic lurched forward and their road, along with all the others, commenced its long spiral descent round the sides of the Bowl. As it did so the Bowl effectively vanished; its curvature was so vast and shallow that it was no more discernible, from its own surface, than the curvature of a planet.

They were in a huge but ordinary landscape, occasionally hilly and occasionally flat. Their road was cantilevered out from the Bowl's sides where the gradient was steep, almost flat where it was shallow. There were junctions with other major roads which forked off into the interior of the Bowl, and these roads too followed the ordinary demands of the landscape: sometimes raised on columns and sometimes at ground level, sometimes on embankments and sometimes in cuttings.

Overlaying the landscape was the Bowl's metropolis. There was no single name for it: people tended to cling to the names of the original cities and districts, perhaps because the Bowl conurbation was too big for any single name. The cities and suburbs did not fill the Bowl levelly or evenly, like water, but crept up its sides, like brandy. As soon as the landchariot entered the multilane road spiralling down, outlying buildings rose and crowded alongside it. Some were quite mundane, like the suburbs of any city: schools, apartment blocks, shopping malls, leisure centres, vehicle workshops (including, as they passed through one of the seedier districts, workshops for landchariots).

The traffic was as heavy and slow as it had been on the rim, except for their lane, which the military still cleared ahead of them. But now they had entered the Bowl, there were more junctions and more delays. They came to a major junction and slowed, waiting to take the turnoff to the interior.

Foord said "Thahl, about the driver…"

"What of him, Commander?"

"Why is he so angry? I can feel it coming off him in waves."

Thahl paused. "Commander, when you decided to return to Blentport by landchariot, was it something you considered important?"

"Yes. Also to make a point to Swann, but it was important to me. Why do you ask?"

"The driver believed it was important to you. That's why he agreed to take you."

"I don't understand."

Thahl waited politely until he did.

"You mean, because of the evacuation he won't be allowed to leave… and if he has to stay he'll have his poison glands removed?"

"Yes, Commander, that's possible."

"Does he know?"

"Yes, Commander. I discussed it with him back at the clearing. He said he agreed to take you in and he'll take you."

"Thahl, we must stop this. I had no idea. I'll call Swann and get a flier…"

"I wouldn't recommend it, Commander. Don't try to stop him. He'd sooner kill you than be persuaded not to take you in."

●

Foord snapped open his wristcom.

"Yes, Commander?"

"Cyr, we've entered the Bowl. We should be at the ship in an hour. How is the situation there?"

"The refit is almost finished, but we're now fully surrounded. Our Grid is full of crews from the other ships, stranded here because of us. And Port personnel. And troops from the Port, who are supposed to keep the others away from us but aren't. They've been coming since we last spoke."

"Anything else?"

"Yes. Swann came to the ship. Asked to come aboard."

"What the fuck"—Foord rarely swore audibly; this was his quota for the day—"What the *fuck* made him think he could come aboard my ship?"

"That was almost exactly, word for word, what Smithson said to him."

"What did he want?"

"He said the mood of the people around us was difficult to read, and said he wasn't going to force them off our Grid without first trying a better way."

"Better Way? I thought you said Smithson had an idea."

"That's what he meant. Smithson had asked Swann to get the commander of the garrison at Blentport, Colonel Boussaid, to help. Smithson met Boussaid at one of Swann's receptions when we first landed—"

"One of those I didn't go to?"

"Yes, Commander. Smithson was impressed by him."

"Smithson was *impressed*?"

"Yes, he said Boussaid's one of the few real people at Blentport. Anyway, Swann only wanted to say that he'd get Boussaid to help you when you reach Blentport. That was all."

"So Smithson asks Swann for Boussaid's help, Swann turns up personally to say yes, and Smithson..."

"Yes, Commander. Tells him to fuck off." She laughed. Her voice was dark and beautiful, but she could also make it ugly. "We're still piling indignities on him, aren't we?"

Foord knew that Thahl was smiling; not by any upward turn of the corners of his mouth or change of expression in his eyes, but Foord *knew*. He snapped his wristcom shut.

The landchariot hurtled on.

"Thahl, it's too late now, isn't it?"

"Late, Commander?"

"For the driver. Now we've entered the Bowl."

"Yes, Commander."

After a while, Foord said "Are you sure? I could put pressure on Swann, maybe invoke our priority, and...."

"And what? Refuse to lift off?" Privately, Thahl regarded *Are You Sure* much as Smithson regarded *Do You Understand*.

"Alright, but this law about removal of poison glands.....you of all people...."

"Commander, that law will almost certainly be repealed soon. Most humans here think it's wrong. "

They hurtled on. Cyr did not call back. The driver said nothing. Thahl said almost nothing, and Foord did not reply to it. In the window the web still quivered and salivated over the particles of wood and dry paint Foord had dropped into it—perhaps the most apocalyptic event of its recent life.

The journey was beginning to tighten around them.

They kept to the fast multilane roads, which meant they drove through the suburbs between cities more than the cities themselves. Often their road would rear itself up on columns and rise over sunken or congested areas, covering them like a smear of cosmetic. It passed through districts which were once open grassland separating the original cities but now, with economic ebb and flow, were variously rich and poor.

They drove through wasteland scabbed with empty buildings where businesses had grown and died. Through a vast and deafening open market where carcasses hung dripping from hooks with signs like Wild Chimaera's Handkilled By Sakhran's, or Angel's Freshly AirSnared (someone had added And Freshly Fallen). Through political and financial districts, where people occurred rather than worked, lounged in pavement bars, or dined luxuriously in unnamed restaurants where menus carried Angel and chimaera dishes, but had the good taste not to show prices. They drove through civic districts with huge public buildings, flowing and organic, some of them honeycombed so that they softened sunlight into granular latticeworks, and some of them designed to appear not designed but on the brink of metamorphosis into some higher form. They drove through, or around, or over, districts so different they didn't seem to belong on the same planet, yet were linked to each other as inextricably as nerve-ends; a universe apart but a postcode away.

And sometimes, after feverish speed, there was feverish slowness; where gridlocked junctions were like archipelagos, and even their military escort couldn't clear a path immediately. At these times the atmosphere grew as thick and heavy as standing water, as though the vehicles cramming the road were shadows cast on an ocean floor by objects floating above in still salty froth.

Even when they were travelling at speed, it seemed that the landchariot stood still while the cities and suburbs moved and unfolded around it, trying on different sets of clothes, changing and rechanging obsessively and restlessly, unable to decide what they were. The road and its traffic wound on, and around, and in, and out, like a stream of antibodies seeking a source of infection.

5

They were directed by the military, who obeyed Swann's orders to the letter, through the gridlocked junctions and on to a major six-lane highway leading directly to Blentport. After thirty minutes, they found themselves rushing alongside a thirty-foot high chainlink fence, with vast grasslands rippling beyond it: the outer perimeter fence of Blentport. The road to their right was choked with traffic, and the air above them was full of VSTOLs. They hurtled on.

Later, his wristcom buzzed.

"Commander Foord?"

"Who is this?"

"Khalil Boussaid. *Colonel* Khalil Boussaid, commander of what remains of the garrison at Blentport. Most of it has headed for the hills. Literally."

"Thank you for calling, Colonel. Smithson says you're the only real person he's met at Blentport."

"I think," Boussaid laughed, "he meant only that most of the others have gone... Commander, we have a very troubling situation here, and I want to get you back on board your ship without anyone getting hurt. I'm waiting for you at Gate 14. You need to continue round the perimeter fence for twelve miles..."

"*Twelve miles?*"

"Blentport is a very large place, Commander. And please hurry. Things are worsening here."

"Thank you, Colonel."

The fence rushed past on their left. It loomed thirty feet high, jewelled with electronic monitors, bristling with swivelguns, and crackling with high voltage, and this was only the outer fence; the two inner fences got progressively stronger. To the lowland cities, Blentport was an old and central presence, a slow heart surrounded by rapidly growing organs; it limited their growth and fuelled it, linking them as they strained to grow away from it. Maybe that was how the Commonwealth viewed Earth.

From the few glimpses Foord had got of Blentport from his ship as it landed, he remembered it as a vast yellow plain as big as the cities around it, with its three concentric fences looking like cell walls to prevent it and the cities from infecting each other. From ground level it looked like the only large area of living land they had encountered in the Bowl, a wind-swept expanse of yellow-green grass. From above, the great gates were spaced at regular intervals in the fences to allow the approach roads to spiral symmetrically inwards, but from ground level the sheer scale reasserted itself and the distance between gates, which had looked negligible, became interminable.

The landchariot sped on. They started to encounter roadblocks, but each time they were waved through by soldiers who knew very well who they were. The traffic was thinner and moved faster, as more of it was bled off at the roadblocks. The vehicles still sharing the road with them were mainly articulated trucks on their regular runs, with their cabled flanks and multiple wheels towering above the roof of the landchariot and more than filling the window on Foord's right, where the web ignored them and continued to have wet dreams of small cataclysms.

In the distance, sirens wailed, both the high unbroken harmonic of military groundcars and the two-tone of VSTOLs, the latter both military and ambulances, but they were less frequent now; either the evacuation of the military had reached and passed its peak or the landchariot had left it behind. *The evacuation*, thought Foord sourly. Sakhra had the Commonwealth's second-largest fleet, and almost all of it was deployed in a defensive cordon against just one ship. Her. The evacuation was their way of saying that they expected Her to defeat Foord's ship *and* penetrate the cordon.

Foord was watching a truck thunder past on the right in apparent silence, and realised its noise was drowned in the roar from the left as a

Horus Fleet ship, probably an 078, lifted off from the distant centre of Blentport. It looked overladen and undermaintained, and rose as heavily as a methane bubble through mud, barely clearing the tops of the distant control buildings as it made its belated, and bloated, way to join the cordon. Apparently, the *Charles Manson*'s refit was nearing completion and Blentport was returning to other work.

There was a gap in the perimeter fence up ahead, an approach road leading to a gate.

"Take it!" Boussaid yelled in Foord's wristcom. "Take it, it's Gate 14!"

They took it. So, immediately, did some of the smaller and slower groundcars which were bunched behind them on the inside lane. Sirens blared and four military sixwheels, which in the noise and chaos Foord had not noticed waiting in the verges, lurched forward to block the approach road. The landchariot slewed to a halt within a few feet of their slabsided flanks. The groundcars immediately behind halted, and vehicles behind them, on the inner lane of the main road, but unable to see what was causing the holdup, skidded and sounded their horns.

The military sirens died out. The horns from behind did not. Voices were raised behind them as soldiers set about moving back the vehicles which had followed them into the approach road. The arguments reached a crescendo and died abruptly when someone, Foord hoped a soldier, fired a shot, Foord hoped into the air. A moment of silence was followed by a gunning of engines and churning of wheels as the vehicles behind backed off. Then the landchariot was alone, faced by sixwheels and ringed by soldiers whose positions, faces and weapons were unwavering. The wind rolled hugely over the Blentport grassland. The traffic roar from the main road seemed a long way away.

The soldiers lowered their guns, and one of them spoke into his wristcom. Immediately Foord's buzzed.

"Boussaid, Commander. They know who you are. Follow them to the middle gate, they're expecting you."

The Sakhran driver, who had given no sign of being able to speak Commonwealth, but was fluent in the language of levelled and lowered guns, did not wait for instructions. He lashed the team forward just as the sixwheel directly in front gunned its engine—it squealed, like a metallic chimaera—moved aside, let them pass through the outer gate, and followed close behind.

A half-mile in silence, with the swivelguns on the outer fence tracking them all the way, and with the tall waving grasses of Blentport looking as though any minute they would crash down in torrents to engulf the road which so tentatively parted them, and then came the middle fence, as high as the first; then a gatehouse, bigger than the first; and another assembly of military vehicles and soldiers, also bigger than the first. They were passed through quickly and politely, and escorted another half mile to the third fence and gate. The third fence was thirty feet high, partly chainlink and partly stone. From the amount of visible and conventional defences covering it (swivelguns, heat and motion sensors, lasers, arclights) Foord could imagine what else was hidden inside it, or, because it was camouflaged or microminiaturised, simply invisible on its surface.

Everything about the third fence area was bigger: the gate and gatehouse (both large, solid, real stone constructions, unlike their more makeshift equivalents on the two inner fences), the military vehicles, and even the soldiers themselves.

Boussaid, however, was not big; he was about Thahl's height, balding, and plumpish. He was standing alone in front of the gate in the third fence.

"Commander Foord! You're very welcome."

All around him were lights and sirens, troops running to and fro, military vehicles gunning their engines, crews barking out orders; yet somehow, without shouting, Boussaid's voice carried to the landchariot.

Foord got out, followed by Thahl, and went over to Boussaid, who shook hands. His face seemed open and amiable and generous, which normally would have made Foord instantly suspicious.

"The only real person on Blentport. Did Smithson really say that?"

"I'm told he did. He also said you can get us back to my ship. Can you?"

"Of course, Commander."

"And the landchariot?"

"You can ride it right up to your ship, if you wish…But first," he motioned casually towards the gatehouse, "let's go in and talk. I need to brief you on this situation. I keep a small room or two in some of these gatehouses, and I have one just here. Come in, come in…"

The gatehouse was a two-storey stone building, blocky and squat, not unlike some Sakhran buildings. Foord noticed as they approached it that its outlines were softened by creepers trained along its walls and even—he did a doubletake at this—some hanging flowerbaskets and windowboxes. Three plates and three water-dishes were placed in an orderly line outside the main door, where a large tortoiseshell cat, orbited by two silently fighting kittens, surveyed them impassively. They walked through a couple of anterooms and into a small inner office.

"The kittens are Dollop and Globule. I haven't thought of a name for their mother yet."

"Fundamental Particle?" suggested Thahl.

"A nice idea, but not a name for a cat. I could give you a whole dissertation on the naming of cats…perhaps when you get back."

"Perhaps," agreed Thahl.

"Do all your gatehouses have hanging baskets and cats and windowboxes?"

"Most have cats, Commander. Members of the garrison make pets of them, or vice-versa. Flowerbaskets and windowboxes, no—only the gatehouses where I keep a small room, as here."

There was a desk but no other obvious office furniture, only a couple of armchairs and a sofa. Standing in front of the desk, Foord saw several documents arranged neatly—nobody would ever completely eliminate paper—which were annotated in red, green and blue, in a hand which, even upside-down, Foord could see was regular and careful. Boussaid's writing implements were set out on the desk; they were old-fashioned, functional, devoid of personal insignia, but well maintained. Foord's own personal possessions were similar. He began to like Boussaid.

Apart from the documents and several comms, the only other object on the desk was a still photograph, in a plain wooden frame, of a woman and two children, all three slightly plump, amiable and open-faced. Boussaid let Foord look at it for a while before he spoke.

"Ever see people after a really bad brawl, Commander?"

"Oh no, Colonel, never. When we put into a port, nobody is ever less than totally welcoming."

"Usually," Boussaid continued imperturbably, "the aftermath of a brawl here on the Port is messy. Cracked heads and broken bones; blood; missing teeth; people battered from head to foot, usually in an area equidistant from each."

Foord's smile began just as Boussaid's vanished.

"But not this time, Commander. I've just visited some Horus crew members who were involved in this incident with your people. They're all badly injured, one of them very badly. Probably you know this. I certainly expected it. What I didn't expect was the *way* they'd been injured. It was neat and clean and deliberate, and very vicious; and totally disproportionate." He shifted his gaze, from Foord to Thahl. "It's as if *you* attacked them, apart from the bit about Vicious and Disproportionate."

Unusually, Thahl was taken unawares. He became suddenly and diplomatically absorbed in the indicator board on the wall: nineteen lights, one per grid.

"Or *as if*," Boussaid went on, "Faith was already here, disguised as two of your crew. That's how clean."

Sixteen of the lights, Thahl noted, flashed red, indicating a ship present. This included the light for Grid Nine, which housed the *Charles Manson*.

"I'm sorry it happened, Colonel. But it does happen every time."

Thahl saw Foord and Boussaid lock eyes and remain so for some time without either speaking. Finally Boussaid broke contact. He flipped open his wristcom, said "Confirmed. Start now," snapped it shut and said to Foord "I've just activated certain plans, Commander."

Before Foord could reply, he noticed a red light go out on the indicator board; a small ship lifting off from one of the minor grids. Through a window he watched it ascend, noiselessly and vertically.

His wristcom buzzed.

"You'd better answer it, Commander. It's connected with my call."

Foord did so. "Commander, it's Cyr. I've just received a call from the garrison commander's staff, with orders which they say have your authority."

"What are the orders?"

"To be ready for your arrival here in about thirty minutes, and to be ready, at any time from now until you arrive, to go to Armed Shutdown. Are those orders confirmed?"

Even Thahl could no longer maintain the polite pretence of interest in the screens. Armed Shutdown was the last resort of a grounded ship under heavy attack; it made it impregnable and immovable. To Foord's knowledge it had never been used before by a Commonwealth ship in a Commonwealth port; not even by an Outsider.

Foord glanced briefly at Boussaid.

"Yes," he said. "Confirmed."

"I hope Boussaid knows what he's doing, Commander."

"I'm with him now," Foord said drily, "and I believe he does."

He closed his wristcom, slowly and thoughtfully. From a distance, another ship lifted off and another of the red monitor lights went out. This one was a very large ship, a Class 097. For the first few hundred feet of its ascent it rode on its noiseless magnetic drive; then its atmosphere boosters cut in, their multiple trails looking—and sounding—like a set of giant fingernails screeking across the grey slate of the sky. Foord waited until the noise receded.

"Armed Shutdown, Colonel?"

"It may come to that. Or it may not, it's hard to read…Excuse me." He opened one of the comms on the table and spoke into it without activating the screen. "He's here now, start sending, I want him to see for himself…. Thank you." He activated the comm screen, and spun it round to face Foord, whose expression did not change.

"This is presumably from one of your VSTOLs?"

"Yes. I have four hovering over Grid Nine at the moment."

Thahl's expression didn't change either, but only because his face was made that way. Inside, there was a surge of feelings he couldn't precisely identify when he saw his ship—a slender silver delta, sixteen hundred feet long—on Grid 9. At times he'd felt he might not see it again. The sound of Foord's voice jerked him back.

"And the people crowding the Grid, who are they?"

"A large part of Blentport's civilian population. Plus the crews of Horus Fleet ships waiting to join the cordon, plus a large detachment of my troops."

As if on cue, the comm screen went blank. Boussaid had not deactivated it.

"And that's it. Nothing has happened yet but anything might. And I may be one of the last people on the Port prepared to do anything about it."

"You said you could get me back to my ship. How?"

"A couple of hours ago, Commander, I sent a large detachment from what's left of my garrison to clear Grid Nine."

"And?"

"As I said, they're still there, among that crowd. They reported initially that the mood was too tense to attempt any dispersal. Then they said that unless I actually ordered them back they'd stay, to maintain a discreet presence and contain any disorder. I understood." He paused, then laughed softly. "They've become like the people they were sent to disperse. With most of my garrison in the highlands, and the problem of how to get *you* through *that*, particularly when you insist on doing it in a landchariot, the last thing I want to do is even hint at mutiny." Again he laughed. "You may already have protected us from Faith, Commander, because every minute your ship remains here, Blentport becomes less and less worthy of Her attention as a target."

Out of Foord's sight, Thahl smiled privately and thought *I like him, how he looks askance at the world. Smithson was right. He usually is.*

Another ship roared overhead. Another light went out.

"I've tried to defuse the situation by hurrying the liftoff of the Horus Fleet ships grounded here, some of them before their refits have been completed, but too many of them are still grounded. The call I made just now activated plans to take you—yes, and your landchariot—under heavy escort to your ship on Grid Nine, and to get you and Thahl safely aboard. I'll be going along in the lead escort vehicle, with what remains of my garrison."

"How do you intend to get us aboard?"

"You'd think it ridiculous if I told you, and there isn't time to argue. Call it a last throw of the dice. Just go along with whatever happens."

Foord thought about what Smithson had said, added his own impression so far of Boussaid, and said "All right, Colonel. And thank you."

"One more thing before we move off, Commander. When we reach Grid Nine, and when you see what happens there, you may start to question my judgement, so remember this. I believe it's inevitable that someone, almost certainly a member or members of my garrison, is going to die before we get you back on your ship today."

6

Nobody hated Foord except Other People. Nobody would ever refuse him cooperation (indeed, left to themselves they would heap it upon him) except that there were Other People. Other People had to be considered. Other People still clung to preconceptions, still harboured gangrenous prejudices—in short, hated him—and clicked their tongues at the vast majority who would otherwise have flocked to welcome the Commander of an Outsider. These Other People even hated the *shape* of an Outsider, because it was unlike ordinary ships: elemental and simple, a slender delta without corrugations or excrescences or power-bulges.

Always it was Other People. And Other People when asked would cite others, who when asked would cite others, so that wherever the *Charles Manson* made planetfall and Foord had to leave his ship to have dealings with what Other People would call the real world, he would find himself shunted through a series of shadowy anterooms where conversations died as he entered and restarted as he left and where always those Other People, the ones who really did hate him, had gone just moments before, leaving a chair still warm or a drink half-drunk or something daubed on a wall. He understood this and recognised that many of them genuinely believed it. In his absence, he knew they would turn to each other and remark on how much some *Other* People hated him.

When he and Thahl left the gatehouse and walked back to the landchariot they found it surrounded by heavy armour, with guns peering down at it from all angles. The six medium-calibre rapidfire guns trained on the landchariot's rear belonged to the two triple-turreted sixwheels which had followed them through the outer and middle gates; the slender swivelguns ahead, along the top of the inner fence, would coldly track anything which moved; and the heavy-calibre guns massed further ahead were mounted on ten huge armoured twelvetracks waiting to escort Foord safely across the last few miles to Grid Nine, where, it seemed, most of Blentport waited to watch him rejoin the *Charles Manson*. Or watch him try to rejoin it.

Outside, a loudspeaker emitted a single harmonic and some three or four hundred troops apparently sprang from the ground and started milling silently around the ten huge twelvetracks. A second harmonic and they disappeared inside them, as if soaked up. A third, lower harmonic and the inner gate began to open: it was a large section of the fence, a chain-link and girder latticework over thirty feet wide, and it took its time. The ENTER NOW sign flashed, the driver's whip uncoiled and spat in the heavy air, and the chimaera, heaving their great grey buttocks from side to side and forced forwards only after some abortive plunges to the left and right, reluctantly took the landchariot through the gate. The ten twelvetracks immediately clotted around it, two in front, three on either side and two behind, as though parcelling the infection entering a wound; and then the whole cavalcade—in scale, a mongrel dog escorted by ten elephants—started down the long wide road leading to the Grids at the heart of Blentport. The same slow mechanisms which had prised the gate open now closed it deafeningly behind them, causing a great voiceless flock of white birds to rise from the grass and resettle, like shaken powder.

The swivelguns on the long curve of the inner fence, either side of the gate for hundreds of feet, tracked them through in finely graduated arcs and continued to track them into the distance; and then, ten minutes later when Boussaid signalled the gatehouse from the lead vehicle that they were ENTERING GRID AREA NOW, swung away and forgot them.

●

"Grid 19," Boussaid announced over Foord's wristcom, unnecessarily, as they passed a junction in the road where a large sign said GRID 19. "One of the outlying minor grids. About fifteen minutes to your ship, unless we encounter anything on the way."

"Looks like we already have," Foord replied, referring to a VSTOL which was now following them, hovering silently a hundred feet directly above with full grappling tackle hanging underneath it like entrails.

When Boussaid did not answer, Foord shouted, over the noise of the escort vehicles, "Is that VSTOL responding to your orders?"

"Yes, Commander. To about the same extent as this escort."

Grid 19 spread out below them to the left. It was a sunken concrete and metal latticework about a thousand feet long by four hundred wide, criss-crossed with walkways and surrounded by antigrav generators set into the lawned slopes curving down to its surface, and by derricks and cranes bent over it like a mixture of tall and short surgeons over an operating table. It was ringed by a wide tree-lined road along which were more low buildings, mostly engineering facilities. The rest of the Grid's capacity was underground. It was a minor Grid, so it would be capable of refitting anything up to light cruiser size, perhaps Class 079 or 080, but nothing larger.

It was almost deserted. Not only did it not house a ship, but there were hardly any people—just a few at some windows, Foord noted, speaking into wristcoms as the landchariot and its escort passed by.

Grid 14 contained a Class 047 light cruiser. As Foord looked down from the raised road and saw the Grid swept clear of everything except the ship, whose flat tapered hull shone like the blade of a throwing knife, he knew immediately what was going to happen next, even before the liftoff alarms started blaring and Boussaid started yelling through the wristcom to take cover.

"You mean we should crawl under the landchariot, Colonel?"

"I mean that ship is lifting off *now* and I have no idea what it's going to do next!"

"Aren't you supposed to have an idea?"

Boussaid cut the connection.

Outside, the liftoff alarm had risen a semitone and the escort vehicles were closing in a protective circle around the landchariot, which was lurching with the panicked movements of the chimaera. The two VSTOLs overhead increased their height and moved away to either side of the road.

"Commander," Thahl began, "perhaps we should…."

"No time. That ship's only an 047 but if he's really going to attack, we're finished. A hundred of those escort vehicles couldn't stop him."

But to Foord it was already clear what the ship was going to do. He settled back and watched as it lifted off, with the silence and precision of the magnetic drive used for atmospheric manoeuvres, and moved towards the raised road. The escort vehicles—much less silently but with equal precision—tightened their outward-facing protective circle around the landchariot. Despite their size, they looked like models arranged on the road by a giant invisible hand, a hand which had now returned holding a silver knifeblade towards them. The ship came closer.

It paused only once. Then, as the dust and exhaust fumes churned by the vehicles began to settle, and in a silence which was broken only by one noise which had been mounting all the time, the noise of the chimaera screaming, it passed slowly and deliberately no more than thirty feet above them. It was only an 047, but its long flat hull seemed to go on forever. The chimaera screamed not in fear, but in outrage at the wrongness of its noiseless passage above them. The ship disturbed the air no more than if it had been a long silver trapdoor sliding endlessly open, and it went on and on.

Later, Foord learned that the four injured men were crew members of that ship.

Foord remembered the 047 more vividly even than the final events which were to precede the *Charles Manson*'s liftoff from Grid Nine, not because it proved him right about its intentions—it was only making a gesture at Foord; an actual attack was impossible—but because it proved something else, something Foord had always understood intellectually but had never seen demonstrated physically.

The ship was only an 047, but Foord had not exaggerated when he said that a hundred escort vehicles could not have stopped it; yet a thousand such ships could not have stopped the *Charles Manson*. There were different orders of magnitude. He sat in the lurching landchariot, darkened by the never-ending shadow of the 047's passage, and reflected on them.

The ship finally passed overhead, continued a few hundred feet and then rose into the grey sky; it could have done that directly from Grid 14, but a gesture was a gesture. Foord opened his wristcom and made one of his own; for him, a rare one.

"Colonel Boussaid?"

"Yes, yes, I know, you were right, it didn't attack."

"I owe you an apology. We both knew it wouldn't attack, but you were commanding an escort and I wasn't. Only one of us could afford to be clever and rely on assumptions. I'm sorry."

"Thank you, Commander, that's gracious. But we haven't made it yet. The last bit is the biggest gamble."

Orders of magnitude, thought Foord. The 047's power dwarfed that of the escort vehicles like a boulder would dwarf a handful of pebbles. Yet there was another scale of power looming beyond that: the power of the *Charles Manson*, which would dwarf an 047 like a mountain would dwarf a boulder.

And then there was Faith. And Faith—he remembered what the priests at the orphanage had beaten into him—can move mountains.

7

Grid 9 spread out below them and Foord saw his ship again for the first time in two days. And because its shape was the symbol he most recognised, because it stood at every junction in his personal roadmap, because it joined lines which for other people were joined by symbols of home or family or friends, for a moment he saw only his ship and did not see what had happened around it.

Grid 9 was full to bursting. There were dozens of maintenance and service vehicles and cargo vehicles, large and small, called in to Grid 9 from all over Blentport to speed the refit, and simply abandoned where they stood when their work was done. There were thousands—maybe five or six thousand—variously sitting, standing or walking around the Grid and the grassy slopes leading down to it. They had gathered there, slowly at first as the other refits were abandoned to give the *Charles Manson* priority, then more quickly as news spread of the two incidents of last night and this morning. They were mainly Blentport workers from this Grid and others, and officers and crew from Horus Fleet ships; but there was also a scattering of the slate-grey uniforms of Blentport garrison, at least three hundred. Foord assumed they were the detachment Boussaid sent earlier, who hadn't quite mutinied, but didn't return when ordered.

Officers, crew, Blentport workers, garrison members: they each had their own shifting motives, which might turn against each other, or focus on the *Charles Manson*. Their ambiguity hung murmuring over the whole Grid. It seemed, simultaneously, to stop short of open hostility and to go beyond it.

And in the middle of it was the *Charles Manson*. It was beautiful, a clean silver shape sixteen hundred feet long, tapering from a width of three hundred feet at its stern, where the main drives bulged, to a pointed snout so sharp a man could actually prick his finger on it. It was as concrete and emphatic as a noun written on a page, with the scattering of people and vehicles around it like prepositions.

"Soon be over now," Boussaid said in the wristcom. Foord heard tension, or maybe it was tiredness, in his voice.

The convoy reached the turnoff leading down to Grid 9, then halted. One by one the escort vehicles cut their motors to idle. As their engine roar diminished, the murmuring of those crowding the Grid crept up the approach road to replace it. It was an indistinct sound, as indistinct as the motives which produced it.

The two VSTOLs which had shadowed them since they entered the inner gate moved off to join five others—not four, Foord noted, but five now—hovering directly over the *Charles Manson*, for what purpose and on whose orders Foord could not begin to imagine.

"Neither can I," Boussaid replied when Foord called him, "so forget them. They can't matter now."

Most of the people on the Grid and on the grassy slopes around it were now standing and looking up at the convoy, then back at the ship. The murmur of their voices increased, maybe a semitone. Their mood was as unreadable as the ship. The *Charles Manson* remained still and silent, with every port and orifice closed and opaqued.

The engines of the escort vehicles thundered anew, and they and the landchariot moved down the approach road.

The *Charles Manson* carried many missiles, of all shapes and sizes and designs. The last fifty, including the two strange ones made to Foord's specification, had only been loaded that morning. The special lowloader which had transported them now stood abandoned at the point where the approach road joined the Grid. So, instead of sweeping dramatically out into the choked arena, the convoy halted. The escort vehicles disgorged troops who set about lining the approach road to hold the crowd back, a job which they did amid much heel-clattering, saluting and mutual barking of orders. A corporal strode briskly towards the lowloader, presumably to drive it out of the way. He climbed the access ladder up its mountainous flank and disappeared into the cab. For a while nothing happened.

"What's keeping you?" yelled one of Boussaid's sergeants.

"It won't tell me its start code."

From the modest crowd clustered around the entrance to the Grid came a modest ripple of laughter. It increased when another sergeant grabbed a loudhailer and demanded that The Driver Of This Vehicle should Make Himself Known. It subsided slightly when, after a hurried conference, a man was found who knew how to circumvent the start codes of cargo lowloaders. He too climbed the access ladder up its side and disappeared into the cab. A moment later its multiple engines coughed mightily into life, and the lowloader lurched forward. The laughter redoubled, and began to spread to those crowding the main arena of the Grid, when the lowloader ploughed into the side of a small robot welding vehicle which, after being bulldozed for several feet, sprang into brief reflex life, extended a telescopic arm and caressed the lowloader's flanks in a search for hull-plates. Clever, thought Foord, and genuinely unexpected. But it's very high risk, and it won't last.

For now, though, the fiasco continued. Eight of the ten escort vehicles roared forward and formed a large semicircle where the approach road joined the Grid, a semicircle into which nothing was allowed except the landchariot and the two remaining escort vehicles flanking it. Thus the landchariot finally clattered out onto Grid 9; and the moment it did so the semicircle became a circle, the escort vehicles joining behind it to package it in the same manoeuvre they had executed at the inner gate.

There was only a modest crowd gathered at the approach road; most people had stayed in the main arena of the Grid. Those nearby, having seen the landchariot's entrance onto the Grid and perhaps having caught a glimpse of Foord or Thahl inside, now moved away. As they did so, soldiers poured out of the escort vehicles to move them further away; more soldiers than there were people. The convoy, still maintaining a circle around the landchariot, moved towards the *Charles Manson* at the centre of the Grid. The troops had to march after the convoy. By stages their march became a trot, then a run, then a ragged dash. *Don't overdo it,* Foord prayed silently to Boussaid. *Genuine cock-up, not slapstick. Be careful.*

The ragged dash was, in any case, unnecessary. The convoy only moved fifty metres or so before it encountered another knot of abandoned vehicles, among and around which a few groups of sightseers stood or sat, waiting to be moved away. The convoy halted. Usefully, this allowed the troops to catch up with it, and since their original orders had been to move people away, they moved *these* people away. Less usefully, they did not ask whether any of those moved were in charge of any of the abandoned vehicles. After a hurried conference, it was decided to bulldoze them clear.

Almost inevitably, the main obstruction was a cargo lowloader. This one, however, was smaller than the previous one. Its brakes were not powerful enough to withstand the two escort vehicles bulldozing it; they gave way suddenly and it was pushed clear, skidding into the side of a second, smaller, vehicle. The smaller vehicle tottered, then crashed onto its side and burst into flames. It was a fire truck.

Foord watched as alarms sounded and a column of black oily smoke climbed skywards, as slowly and deliberately as if it was made of bricks being laid one on top of the other. He started to think that Boussaid had overdone it. But the escort vehicles carried full firefighting equipment and were around the fire truck in seconds. The fire was smothered in foam. The column of black smoke, its source cut off abruptly, hovered vertically like an exclamation mark without a dot, then slowly dissipated. There were some ironic cheers from those crowding the Grid, but not from all of them; some noticed the speed and precision with which the convoy had dealt with the fire, so at odds with how it had entered the Grid.

The convoy moved on, trailing a line of straggling troops like a freshly-whipped court jester dragging a pig's-bladder, lurching from fiasco to fiasco, leaving in its wake a swathe of damaged, dented, charred and overturned vehicles. It picked its way through the congestion and around the crowds in a mazy series of diagonals and curlicues, and with an elephantine solemnity which deepened as the mocking laughter around it increased; but always coming a little closer to the *Charles Manson*. Foord went many times to call Boussaid and congratulate him, but didn't; the effectiveness of the plan would soon wear off, and Boussaid must be desperately trying to assess how much further it would take them. And what to do when it failed.

●

When they saw the convoy edging closer to the *Charles Manson*, people started moving away from the outer edges of the Grid and towards the centre, where the ship stood. By the time the convoy had got within fifty metres of the ship, several hundred of them were waiting. Their mood was not yet openly hostile; a few of them were still laughing.

The convoy halted. During the brief pause, the six VSTOLs hovering directly above dropped lower until their grapples and undercarriages hung only a few metres above the ship's dorsal ridge. The impression was not one of people converging on the ship, but of the ship having pulled them in, on invisible lines, almost like fishing for them. This impression remained even when the fragile mood Boussaid had created started to waver, and the first brittle noises of violence began.

As Boussaid's last troops poured out of the escort vehicles for the last time to clear the crowds for the last fifty metres, Foord hardly gave his ship a glance. He was aware, as he watched heavily-armed figures striding past the landchariot's windows, that this time the mood was different because the tension was mutual. The first angry clashes with the crowds were isolated, but they spread and got to within seconds of a full-scale riot. With fifty metres to go, Boussaid's plan was exhausted.

A few shots were fired in the air and the crowds fell back. Immediately, the escort vehicles broke their circle and moved forwards toward the midpoint of the *Charles Manson*'s hull, noticeably not threatening any collisions with people or things as they had done before. They moved for the exact point on the hull, about midway, where Foord had told them the main airlock was located, though there was no interruption of the hull's surface and no external marking to indicate this.

The ship, which dwarfed everything else on the Grid, was the least noticeable thing there; it made no movement or noise.

The soldiers funnelled back to plug the gaps between the escort vehicles, apparently without any order being given. The clatter of their weapons and shuffling of their boots as they made final positional adjustments died out only seconds after the brief roar of the escort vehicles' engines, and the first warning shots, also died.

They weren't funny anymore. In less than half a minute, and without overturning anything or setting anything on fire, they consolidated their final position—a gauntlet between the landchariot and the *Charles Manson*, a fifty-metre avenue lined so deeply on either side with vehicles and armed men that the crowd beyond it was largely obscured. And whether by accident, or as a final gesture in the last wavering moments of their protection, almost as many guns seemed to be pointing inwards as outwards.

Conventionally, the inactivity of the *Charles Manson* should have seemed menacing, but the ship's silence and immobility was so profound it seemed to come from inside, as though its interior had been swept by an instantly fatal disease. It had done nothing while a near-riot boiled around it. It had done nothing while the gauntlet was formed and the escort vehicles had charged directly at it, the two vehicles leading each of the gauntlet's parallel lines slewing to a halt only moments before collision. It had done nothing while Boussaid, who was the first out of one of the two lead vehicles, ordered a few of his men to assemble where the main airlock was located and to guard it. Foord noticed there were as many guns pointing at the airlock as there were pointing at the crowd. He snapped open his wristcom.

"You never told me the bit about covering our airlock. I assume that's for appearance."

"Look at them, Commander. Appearance is double-edged."

Foord closed his wristcom, frowning at whatever it was Boussaid had meant, and glimpsed through the forward window a flicker of muscles in the driver's neck and shoulders—this time he did not use the whip, merely jerked the reins—and they moved forward. Right to the end, Foord thought, the driver timed the landchariot's moves with absolute precision.

The landchariot eased forward between the lines of the gauntlet, creaking and rattling in the sudden silence and dropping bits of dirt behind it. Fitful movements rippled along the lines in its wake as people craned and dodged to see inside it. The chimaera breathed heavily and rhythmically as they walked, like masturbating dinosaurs; for them, it was the last stage of a long journey.

Still the *Charles Manson*'s airlock did not open.

The overhang of the *Charles Manson*'s hull was a sheer silver cliff-face. It dwarfed everything else on the Grid, but its silence and stillness was profound; there were times when Foord almost doubted it was there. The landchariot reached it and halted. Foord took a final look at the web in the corner of the side window—he had no way of telling whether it looked back at him—and glanced across at Thahl, who nodded.

Thahl was careful to step out first. He helped Foord down and followed an unwavering three paces behind, a quiet slight figure, as Foord walked round to the front of the landchariot.

Boussaid had already detached himself from the group at the airlock and had taken a couple of steps forward, but paused at a gesture from Foord, who turned and looked up at the Sakhran driver.

"Don't, Commander, it *isn't necessary*," Thahl hissed, but Foord ignored him.

"I understand you don't speak Commonwealth," he said to the driver.

The driver gazed down at him, closely but without expression, and apparently confirmed this by not replying.

Thahl stayed where he was, watching Boussaid (who had stepped back to rejoin the group covering the airlock) and Foord; he had become absorbed in the calculation of relative angles and distances between himself, Foord, Boussaid, the airlock and the two lines of the gauntlet. He knew that Foord was still talking to the driver, but had stopped listening; the words didn't interest him.

"I speak enough Sakhran," Foord was saying, "to say Thank You, but somehow that would seem patronising. So…"

The driver did not open his mouth, even to spit, but his gaze, dark and expressionless, never left Foord. His secondary eyelids flickered horizontally. The Grid was silent for the moment and the chimaera started to shuffle restlessly, as if in embarrassment. One of them farted.

Three paces behind Foord, Thahl completed his calculations.

"So…"

Foord floundered; the words wouldn't come. He was still floundering as the driver died. A sliver of barbed stainless steel from somebody's needle-gun—it was impossible to say whose because needleguns discharged silently, but they were standard issue for Horus Fleet crew, and for Blent-port garrison—nuzzled greedily into his throat, sweeping him from the landchariot to fall in a crabbed heap at the feet of Thahl, who leaped the corpse without looking at it and made straight for Boussaid.

The difference between Thahl and everybody else was less than a second. While the first long second after the shot was still beginning, and while the reactions of everybody else were still beginning with it, Thahl whipped between their not-yet-moving bodies like a cat between dustbins and reached Boussaid. Normal time returned. In the middle of the group covering the airlock were Boussaid and Thahl. Boussaid had fallen to his knees and Thahl stood behind him, his left hand pulling Boussaid's head back by the hair while the unsheathed claws of his right hand were touching, but not yet piercing, his throat. Had the two soldiers who were closest to Boussaid and quickest to spring to his aid been able to stop themselves when the poison claws were unsheathed, they would have done so; but they were built on the same scale as Foord, and their momentum was irreversible. They came at Thahl from behind. He dropped them both, one with the heel of his right foot and the other with the elbow of his left arm, without turning to face them and without breaking his grip on Boussaid, to whom he returned his full attention before either of them hit the ground. He had understood that they would have pulled back if possible, and had taken care not to kill them.

Thahl knew, because he had calculated, that he probably had no more than twenty seconds to live. The guns of Boussaid's troops were trained on him from all sides—those around him and Boussaid swung away from the airlock and towards him, and those along the twin lines of the gauntlet followed soon after. He settled down to wait for the shock of what he had done, and the mixed motives of those with the guns, to corrode their hesitation.

It was impossible, and had never been his intention, to shelter behind Boussaid. He was an open target. Nobody had yet fired because his claws remained at Boussaid's throat, as precise as micromanipulators; but not all of them regarded the safe return of Foord, or the survival of Boussaid, as a priority. Once they had thought that through, somebody—perhaps whoever had shot the driver—would turn his gun on Thahl, or on Foord, standing alone and all but forgotten near the landchariot, or even on Boussaid himself. It would take, Thahl estimated, about twenty seconds. (Foord made it ten to fifteen, because from where he was standing he could see something Thahl could not see: a look almost of acceptance on Boussaid's face, as though he had known all along that he would have to die to get them across the last few metres to the ship. Foord remembered the photograph in his office, and his heart almost burst.)

Then, at last, the *Charles Manson* came to life.

There was something alien about the ship's instant shift from extreme silence to extreme action. It was unrelated in scale to any external event; it was not caused or provoked; it did not build up in any stages of lesser action, which might at least have been understood as a response or warning. It was abrupt and jagged, like the darting of a tarantula.

The *Charles Manson*'s hull was no longer featureless or quiet. Blaring with lights and alarms, throbbing as if with disease, it sprouted blisters which swelled and split open to reveal the mouths and lips and orifices of its closeup weapons array. Nobody had even bothered to preset them on particular targets. Some of them tracked backwards and forwards or up and down, others were aimed directly into the Grid, others vaguely into thin air. It did not matter. There were proximity lasers, coilguns, tanglers, friendship guns, disruptors, breathtakers, harmonic guns, motive beams, and others whose use in a confined area on a planetary surface would have been excessive even if the *Charles Manson* were under direct attack from the whole of Horus Fleet; and they sprouted from a ship crewed by people who had lost, or never had, the motives of people. Thahl had designed his move on Boussaid to win a specific period of time, a period he had calculated to within seconds; now, it seemed, there was all the time in the world.

The main airlock irised open. A ramp tongued out of it to the ground. Many of the *Charles Manson*'s crew of sixty-three had, like Foord, received Special Forces training, and now ten of them moved quickly, but carefully, down the ramp to surround and cover the group around the airlock, the group in whose midst were Thahl and Boussaid. Behind them at the top of the ramp stood Cyr, darkly beautiful, carrying a single handgun with which she motioned Foord to come aboard, and behind her was the *Charles Manson*, massive and motiveless, threatening everything and explaining nothing.

One by one, the men surrounding Thahl laid down their weapons. Some of those along the lines of the gauntlet did the same, but others kept their guns trained on Thahl, or swung them round to cover Foord as he started walking. Thahl read their postures carefully, remembering that postures were not, as with Sakhrans, an auxiliary language, and tried to anticipate which of them would fire first and at who. His grip on Boussaid neither tightened nor relaxed.

As he walked towards his ship—now such a short distance, the last few metres of a long and unpleasant journey—Foord was trying to anticipate the same event as Thahl. If anyone did shoot, he thought it would be one of those in the lines of the gauntlet. It might be a shot in the back—in which case he could do nothing, short of walking to his ship backwards, which he did not intend to do—but that would be relatively deliberate, and on balance less likely. No, if it happened it would be someone's judgement snapping, the act of someone who had endured all this but could not endure seeing him walk past unharmed; perhaps a shot from ahead, but more likely from either side, where he felt faces and gun-barrels swivel as he passed, as if each one was connected to him by gossamer wires, anchored in his flesh with little pins.

His calculations were less exact than Thahl's, but nevertheless he got it right. When it happened it came as he expected from the side, from someone in the line on his right, someone he was just about to walk past. Everything went smoothly: he sensed a figure in the line tensing, saw the gun-barrel start to move towards him, and long before he was in any danger Foord turned and drew his own handgun and was looking down its barrel at the face of a young soldier, so young he had acne, looking suddenly terrified at the thought of what he had tried to do. Foord's finger relaxed on the trigger. So far so good: his reflexes had been up to it, he wouldn't need to shoot, and he knew Thahl would have reached the same conclusion. Then, to his extreme surprise, he found himself looking down the barrel of his gun at only half a face, trying to decide whether half a face could still wear a frightened expression when the other half was gone.

The shot had come from the *Charles Manson*. From Cyr, standing at the top of the ramp in the open airlock.

Foord was so surprised that for a moment he was unable to move. Unaware that he was still looking down the barrel of his gun, he watched the young soldier's body rise in the air and commence a long back-somersault, limbs flailing with momentum but not with life; and as it landed, as the men kneeling around it saw its face and started to turn their gaze on him, he decided he had nothing to say to them. He turned away and started walking back to his ship—such a short distance, now—unsure if he would ever reach it, but certain there was nothing else he could do. *Unnecessary*, he kept repeating to himself under his breath, the second syllable keeping unconscious time with his long strides, *Unnecessary*. It was an arid word, as arid as his anger.

He tried to project the manner of someone neither frightened nor guilty, but merely bent on an important errand elsewhere. He walked briskly (but did not break into a run; that would have been fatal) while around him everything, every single thing, which Boussaid had kept at bay for so long now started to happen. There were shouts from the crowd for revenge, only half as bitter as his own impulse to give up and let them take it. The VSTOLs settled lower over the *Charles Manson* and turned their guns towards the open airlock. Soldiers who had laid down their guns were snatching them up and starting to level them. Foord continued to walk.

When the first sounds of gunfire came from behind him he did not tense or turn around; when it continued for some time he assumed, correctly, that they were killing the six chimaera and probably raking the landchariot and the driver's body. With some difficulty he put it out of his mind, even the web in the window, and continued to walk. He neither slackened nor increased his pace. The two lines of the gauntlet moved in his wake as he passed between them, as though they were trying to fill a vacuum generated by his passage. He was now only a few paces from his ship but he knew that the lines would break before he reached it, and that then he would die in a way quite unlike any he had ever imagined.

Ahead of him he saw his crew retreating. Slowly and carefully, and with guns still levelled, they were backing up the ramp to the main airlock. For the first time he looked at their faces, pleased he could recognise each of them. He also noted, with a satisfaction which was ridiculous in the circumstances, that they hadn't made the obvious mistake; they hadn't tried to come forward and cover him back to the ship, which would have merely hastened the inevitable. Thahl had not joined the retreat and remained standing over Boussaid, and Cyr was still standing in the open airlock. Foord avoided looking at either of them. It must have become quiet again, because Foord was suddenly aware of a small but inappropriate sound, the buzzing of his wristcom. He ignored it—though a part of him tried to imagine how it would look if he answered it—and continued walking. Such a short distance now.

Having calculated that the lines would break when he was still a few paces away from his ship, he half-hoped that they would not. It was part of the nature of irony, whose ability to turn back on itself he was beginning to understand like a Sakhran, that the lines of the gauntlet would take longer to break; long enough for him to begin to think he might have a chance of reaching his ship after all. So he was only half-surprised to find himself no more than two or three paces from the foot of the ramp, and almost level with Thahl, when the lines finally broke and the roar he had been expecting went up behind him. Only then did he take a last look at Thahl. And the irony turned back on itself again.

Thahl leaned forward and said to Boussaid, "I'm sorry, Colonel." As Foord walked past him and started to ascend the ramp, Thahl moved the talons of his right hand until they pierced Boussaid's throat, once, then lifted the body and threw it writhing into the path of the soldiers who were rushing after Foord. The deliberate obscenity of the gesture made them stop just long enough for Thahl to follow Foord up the ramp and through the airlock, which immediately irised shut behind them. Just before it closed, Foord took a last look back. Medical staff from the escort vehicles had already surrounded Boussaid, and there was the approaching siren of a VSTOL ambulance, which Foord knew would be too late; the antidote to Sakhran venom needed to be administered within seconds.

"It was unnecessary," Foord said quietly to Cyr as he strode along the cramped main corridor of his ship towards the Bridge. "I know how accurate you can be with a handgun, or any weapon. You could have wounded him. There was no need."

"But Thahl..." began Cyr.

"What Thahl did," Foord said, still speaking quietly and without turning around, "was unavoidable. What you did was gratuitous."

A few moments later, though this was not yet known on the *Charles Manson,* the irony turned back on itself a third time.

Thahl had had no intention of killing Boussaid; he had not used poison but had just given the appearance of having done so, to cause enough distraction for them to reach the ship. It had been his last throw of the dice; his claws pierced flesh without injecting venom. But Thahl was not aware that Boussaid had a heart condition. The shock and speed of Thahl's attack triggered a massive heart seizure, from which he died.

The *Charles Manson* rested for a few more minutes on Grid 9, alien and impregnable; a single, self-contained denial of everything around it. Then, quietly and without requesting clearance from Blentport, it engaged magnetic drive and lifted off unopposed. At the requisite altitude it switched from magnetic to ion drive, left Sakhra's atmosphere, and passed without ceremony or recognition through the silver ranks of Horus Fleet. At about the time that Boussaid's doctors realised they were dealing not with Sakhran venom but with a heart attack, Horus Fleet was closing the ranks of its cordon behind the *Charles Manson*; like a woman folding back her disarranged clothes as a customer passes out of her apartment.

PART FIVE

1

Foord gazed around the Bridge. One by one, they fell silent.

"After this," he waved a hand at the food set out in front of them, "it's just pills and hyperconcentrates. This is our last proper meal, until the mission is over."

"And before the mission is over," Smithson said, tasteless as always, "one of us will betray you."

Smithson was a mixture of reptile and mollusc, and other unclassifiable things, in a humanoid shape. For a nonbelieving nonhuman who had only travelled infrequently in the Commonwealth, he had a disconcertingly thorough grasp of human cultures and religions. *And he just uses it for pisstaking,* thought Foord, gazing at him speculatively. Smithson gazed back as if he knew exactly what Foord was thinking, which might well have been the case. Smithson was tall and grey and moist, and his eyes seemed to see everything; they were large intelligent eyes, as warm and golden as urine.

After a few moments, Smithson shrugged. For him, shrugging meant the brief extrusion and retraction of a secondary limb from his lower torso. Foord chose to regard the gesture as conciliatory.

Their last meal together started without ceremony, and proceeded quietly. There was some conversation, but it was muted and commonplace, scarcely louder than the sound of cutlery on plates. Thahl was still eating when the others had finished, but they had seen him eat before and registered no reaction; it was not really living meat, just a preparation from the ship's culture vats served at body temperature and grown with a nervous system incorporating motor responses. Thahl was always careful to eat it more tidily and slowly than he would have eaten real prey.

Smithson, who had finished eating before any of them, was an extreme herbivore. He ate concentrated vegetable slime: it went everywhere. He absorbed it subatomically, as efficiently as carnivores extracted sustenance from meat. He even ate like a carnivore, quickly and violently, always looking around him as he chewed.

Foord had insisted that their infrequent meals on the Bridge should be taken together, and defied any of the humans to object. Rather to his annoyance none of them had, although his liberal gesture did irritate Thahl and Smithson: they both found humans' eating conventions unsettling, though for different reasons, and would have preferred to eat alone.

The Bridge was a circular compartment set deep in the ship's midsection. Bridge officers sat at consoles arranged in a circle which followed the shape of the curved walls. All of the walls were screen, a screen so thin it had almost been painted there. It showed a linked projection of what the external viewers saw from their thousands of positions over the ship's hull; normally it showed what was humanly visible, but it could be locally magnified or filtered or altered in wavelength to make visible displays along any electromagnetic band. Merely integrating the thousands of viewers to provide a continuous and infinitely-variable 360-degree projection inside the Bridge was an exceptionally complex task, requiring a computer almost the size of Foord's thumb.

The Bridge screen was where the *Charles Manson*'s nine-percent sentience most frequently communicated with the crew. Often—like a very good butler—it would anticipate their requirements before they were spoken, and patch in a local magnification or headup. Or, with its own equivalent of a polite cough, it might display something unasked which it considered important. Usually it anticipated correctly. Very occasionally Foord would overrule it.

The meal finished as quietly as it had begun. Gradually their conversation returned to matters connected with the mission. Relays clicked and mumbled and voices whispered from comms, an unnoticed background noise. The Bridge was twilit and muted, its occupants murmuring over consoles like surgeons at an operation. Foord himself, after the events preceding liftoff from Sakhra, felt immediately more comfortable here. The ship was his world, far more than any of the places where he made planetfall. On real planets, among real people, he could be surprisingly vulnerable, and often had to be saved from his ill-judged liberal impulses by others like Thahl or Cyr or Smithson. But on his ship he was supreme. It was his *home*, far more than the arid apartment he kept on Earth, and far more even than his home planet, where he was no longer welcome.

They were fifty minutes out of Sakhra, headed for Horus 5, the outer planet of the system, where She was expected to make an emergence.

●

Foord gazed around the Bridge. One by one, they fell silent.

"Status reports, please," he murmured.

"Sakhra says they've detected no emergence, Commander," Thahl said, on Foord's immediate left.

"And your view?"

"They're probably right. If She had entered the system undetected, our instruments should by now have picked up some residual ripples, and all they're showing is normal background interference."

"And Director Swann, has he called again?" Foord asked, implying a continuation of the subject of background interference.

"Not so far, Commander."

Foord passed to Joser, on Thahl's left. Joser was of average build, with suspiciously pleasant and open features. He reminded Foord of the priests at the orphanage.

"Could there have been an emergence?"

"She has emerged undetected in other systems, Commander, but our scanners are more sensitive. On balance, I think not."

"Thank you."

"Also, the amount of energy released by a ship emerging from MT Drive at the periphery of a solar system is so large that..."

"Yes, thank you." Foord's gaze continued round the circle of consoles to the next one, opposite him.

"The weapons array," Cyr said, "will work satisfactorily. If," she shot a glance at Joser, "we can locate Her. We may already have failed to do that."

"The signature of a ship emerging from MT Drive into the solar system would be so large that…"

"That you would have detected Her. But you aren't sure," Cyr said, quite unreasonably.

Foord raised an eyebrow.

"Status reports," he quietly informed the air just above their heads, "should be confined to facts unless I ask for opinions, and should be addressed to me."

Tension subsided abruptly. The ship's environment was cramped and potentially explosive and Foord kept everything, especially personal interaction, low-key. Conversation was by undercurrents, nuances and inflexions, by things left unsaid. A raised eyebrow on the *Charles Manson* was equivalent to a raised fist anywhere else.

Cyr tossed her dark hair and smiled, formally. "You're right, Commander. For my part I apologise." She thrust up three manicured fingers, waited just long enough to make it a gesture, and counted off. "One, long-range weapons array. Two, medium-range. Three, closeup weapons, including the two missiles built to your specification. I listed them all together because the report is the same: they all tested perfect after the refit."

Foord thanked her elegant fist, still raised, and added "Take special care of those two missiles."

●

"It was unnecessary," Foord had said quietly to Cyr, fifty minutes earlier as he strode along the cramped main corridor of his ship towards the Bridge. "I know how accurate you can be with a handgun, or any weapon. You could have wounded him. *There was no need.*"

Ten minutes later, she reported to his study.

"You wanted to see me, Commander."

"Come in. Close the door, please." She did so, and remained standing.

Outsider crew members were allowed individual leeway over uniform.

Cyr's was a dark blue tunic with a box-pleated skirt, over a white long-sleeved shirt. She had several others like it, all personally and expensively tailored for her. She wore it because she knew it aroused Foord. It made him remember the uniforms of the girls at the orphanage, one of whom he had raped.

"You know why you're here." Foord did not make it a question, and she did not give it an answer. She merely stared back at him.

Foord often wondered how much of her was human. Certainly the outside—that was almost more than human—but inside she could seem full of poison. She was disturbingly beautiful. Her face, like that of a classical statue depicting something like Justice or Liberty, was too perfect to be alive. Her hair tumbled over her shoulders; it was black, with hints of violet iridescence like birds' plumage or (which Foord thought more appropriate) beetles' wing-cases. Her lipstick and manicured nails were also, today, dark blue; other days they might be maroon or dark grey or purple or black, to match her other tailored tunics.

Despite her intelligence and beauty, Foord found her cold and predatory and often disgusting.

"Why did you kill him?"

"He was about to kill you."

"You could have wounded him."

"I couldn't be sure he'd drop his gun."

"Why did you kill him?"

"*Because I wanted to.*"

Foord locked eyes with her, then looked down at his desk, where he had placed a heavy hardwood ruler, nearly three feet long. It was a souvenir; the priests at the orphanage had used it on him, often, and he was minded to use it on Cyr. She saw him eyeing it and knew what he intended. It would be totally against regulations, even the deliberately ambiguous Department regulations written for Outsiders, but Foord's authority was such that Cyr would have accepted it.

He wanted to do it, more than anything except destroy Faith, and he infuriated himself by finally deciding not to. He knew she would have accepted it, but not to atone for the life she had taken so unnecessarily. She did not perform acts of atonement.

"Why did you kill him?" he repeated.

"*Because I wanted to*," she repeated; and added, as a thought she did not speak, *To make sure you lived.*

"I thought this would be pointless. Just go."

She held his gaze for a moment; then turned to leave, the pleats of her skirt fanning out.

●

Foord thanked Cyr's elegant fist, still raised, added "Take special care of those two missiles," and passed to the console on her left.

"The MT Drive has been shut down since we used it to make the Jump to Horus system," announced Smithson. "All the others are…"

"Is it operational if needed?"

"Of course it is. But if you're thinking of using the MT Drive inside a solar system…"

"Just give me an itemised report on the Drives, please. Do you understand?"

Smithson bristled, not an easy accomplishment for someone so moist, and snapped "*Yes*, Commander, I understand. Itemised." He shifted in his strengthened chair, extruded a limb from his stomach and held it aloft in a ghastly and deliberate imitation of Cyr, and began counting. "One, Photon Drive. Two, Ion Drive. Three, Magnetic Drive. Four, Manoeuvre Drive. Five, Six, Seven, Fusion Drive, Fusion Power Core, Backup Power Core." His auxiliary limb extended and retracted a digit as each item was counted, and in a further imitation of Cyr he added "I listed them all together because the report is the same: they all tested perfect after the refit."

"Thank you," Foord said, with genuine enjoyment. On the *Charles Manson*, conversations were often coldly venomous; even on a good day, they could be as distant as conversations between Sakhrans. But, unlike Sakhrans, those on his ship were somehow *more* than the sum of their individual selves, and that was what gave him enjoyment.

Like an invisible clockhand the initiative moved on round the Bridge; and juddered to a premature halt, on Foord's right.

"Kaang?"

She was absorbed in some task or other, and did not hear him. He watched her for a moment, thinking how ordinary she seemed: slightly pudgy, with a pasty complexion and medium-length fair hair cut in an uninteresting bob. She did not look remotely like someone who, at her one particular task, was so gifted that Genius was an inadequate term; although, it was fair to say, in every other respect she was almost worthless to him.

"Kaang, I'd like your status report, please."

"I'm sorry, Commander. We're fifty-nine minutes out of Sakhra. I'm holding us on photon drive at thirty percent, as instructed. We're crossing the Gulf and heading for the outer planet, Horus 5. Detailed positions are on the screen."

"Thank you." Foord reclined his chair. "No further orders."

Thirty percent of maximum speed on photon drive was still enough to produce relativistic effects. Stars burned fitfully at the edge of darkness, like Sakhrans' autumn fires. Without the automatic compensating filters and rectilinear adjustments of the Bridge screen, infrared radiation would start to become visible, red light would shift to green, green to violet, and violet to invisible ultraviolet. And the cold stars ahead and behind would crowd into an ever-narrowing sector, becoming finally a corridor to and from infinity. But none of that happened, because the ship compensated for it, and compensated for its compensations, until the screen gave them a workable visual analogue: a necessary lie. It did this quietly and unnoticed and without needing instructions. The *Charles Manson* was nine percent sentient; no other Commonwealth ship was more than five percent.

The ship was a graceful silver delta, slender and elongated. It was just over one thousand six hundred feet long, and three hundred feet wide at its widest point, at the stern where its array of main drives was concentrated.

Radiating from the Bridge were the other inhabited sections where the crew of fifty-seven, excluding the six on the Bridge, were embedded. There was no room for any place where the entire crew, or even part of it, could gather; no crew member was likely to see more than six or seven others during a mission. It was a quiet and nonsocial environment, compartmentalised to the extent that if an inhabited section became irreparably damaged (unlikely, but not impossible) it could be shut off and forgotten and its functionality transferred elsewhere, leaving the ship free to go on without it as if a diseased part had been amputated.

●

"Cyr?"

"Nothing since my last report."

"Smithson?"

"Nothing since her last report."

"Commander," Thahl whispered, "I have Director Swann again. He asks why you haven't yet ordered maximum speed to Horus 5."

"Tell him..."

"He insists you speak to him, Commander."

"Insists."

"His word."

"Later. My word."

And the Outsider Class cruiser *Charles Manson*, Instrument of the Commonwealth, plunged on at its own chosen speed. It was a silver jewel-box full of functionality: drives and weapons and sentience cores, bionics and electronics and power sources, scanners and signals and life support, all packed to almost dwarf-star density. Externally beautiful, but internally dark and cramped, like a silver evening gown hiding ragged underwear.

The Outsiders took existing technology as far as it could possibly go; as far as it would ever go. They were not the largest of the Commonwealth's various warships, but they were the closest to perfection, and would not be improved upon until the currently stale physical sciences were shaken by the next major breakthrough. At an unvarying thirty percent photon speed the *Charles Manson* went on to its appointment, silent and catastrophic.

2

HORUS SOLAR SYSTEM. *Your ship's Codex has all the detail. This summary may, however, suggest some of the system's more unusual, and usable, features.*

Horus is a main sequence star, 1.6 times the size of Earth's Sun, and at a similar stage in its life. It has three inner planets, then the Gulf, then two outer planets separated by an asteroid belt.

Horus 1 and 2 are respectively 59 million and 90 million miles mean distance from Horus. Both are uninhabited; Horus 1 is molten slag and Horus

2, bare rock. Horus 3 is Sakhra: the third of the inner planets, 118 million miles mean distance from Horus.

After Sakhra comes the system's first unusual feature: the Gulf between inner and outer planets. From Sakhra to Horus 4, the Gulf extends for 980 million miles, the largest empty space in any known solar system. It ends at the orbit of the system's second unusual feature, the planet Horus 4.

Horus 4 has a mean distance of 1100 million miles from Horus. It is the most massive planetary body in the known galaxy. Its mass and density and gravity are extraordinary: it has some of the properties of a small neutron star, as well as those of a large planet.

The Asteroid Belt extends 400 million miles, between Horus 4 and Horus 5. It too is unusual, both in its extent and in the number and size of its asteroids; many are the size of small planets. Almost certainly, the Belt is Horus 4's doing: the remains of two or even three very large planets inside the orbit of Horus 5, torn to pieces by Horus 4's gravity.

Horus 5 has a mean distance of 1540 million miles from Horus, and is the system's outermost planet: a gas giant with a thick hydrocarbon atmosphere and a swarm of moons.

If She makes an emergence in Horus system, you will face Her alone and unconstrained, as the Department promised. If that happens, you may find the unusual features of this system helpful, though of course the authors of this briefing would not presume to advise you on how to engage Her.

Foord had no intention of considering any advice on how to engage Her, whether it came from the Department or the Sakhran authorities or even his own crew, unless it suited him. He had been reflecting for some days on the strategy and tactics he would employ if She emerged at Horus, and had found something which seemed genuinely to have escaped everybody's notice.

For the next few days, just as for the last few days, all the planets of Horus system would be roughly in alignment: like an antique clockwork orrery, with its brass balls quivering on the ends of their brass rods.

Maybe, Foord had thought, when She emerges at Horus 5, at the outer edge of the system, She'll wait for us to reach Her. Why? Because, he imagined, She'll want to meet us there, almost formally, so She can fight us all the way through the system, planet by planet, back to Sakhra. And why should She do that? Because, Foord further imagined, She would think it fitting; because She would have found out that in *this* system alone, She could enter into a single combat with the only other ship in known space able to match Her.

It was a recurrent daydream, or conceit, of Foord to think about Her so. But it also suited his purposes. He had analysed Her known capabilities and previous documented encounters, and the features of Horus system (using the *real* data on his ship's Codex, not the Department's rather patronising and flippant briefing) and had concluded where it would be best to engage Her: in the Gulf, and in the outer parts of the system. So he *wanted* to fight Her all the way back to Sakhra.

For the same sound operational reason, She would probably have done a similar analysis and reached a similar conclusion—that is, if whatever lived inside Her worked and thought in that way.

●

Things were as quiet and well-ordered as usual on the Bridge. So, after the meal had finished and he had taken status reports, Foord decided to go for a walk; there was something he needed to see.

"Back in twenty minutes," he told them, as the Bridge door irised shut behind him. "Thahl, you have the ship." The others glanced up, but said nothing.

He walked through the cramped main corridor. It was more like a burrow, with conduits and cables and wires and circuitry pressing down from above, prodding sideways from the walls, and pushing up from the floor: a burrow through the ship's densely-packed working parts, which occupied almost every inch of its sixteen hundred feet. The main corridor forked into secondary burrows even more cramped, and he followed them, occasionally having to stoop.

The secondary burrows looked unmade, like a building site. Their walls were unfinished plaster and cement. They were lit by naked light fittings, which worked efficiently (everything worked efficiently, whatever it looked like) but were fixed at random angles and irregular intervals. This was what the *Charles Manson* really *was*, inside itself. Its crew, human and nonhuman, moved like germs through its elegant but densely-packed body.

He continued walking until he reached one of the ship's many weapons holds. In this one were stored the two missiles built to his specification at Blentport.

This was the first time, after carrying their picture in his head, that he had actually seen them. He remembered the skepticism in the Blentport machine shops when he'd explained what he wanted. Of course we can build them, they'd said, but why *should* we? He knew Smithson would have made sure they were built exactly to specification, but he still needed to see for himself.

They towered over him. They were low-tech almost to the point of being primitive: ugly and utilitarian, made of blue-black welded cast iron plates, with a drive bulge at the rear which swelled so fatly it looked like a growth. He wished he'd asked Blentport for more, though two should be enough, if they worked, and if the occasion for using them arose. He knew exactly how and when and where they'd be used, but he still wasn't sure how the idea had occurred to him. It was as though it had always been there, but dormant. After looking at them for a couple more minutes he turned and made his way back to the Bridge.

He met only two other crew members on the journey there, and one on the way back. He greeted them by name and rank, and they greeted him with a muttered "Commander." They had to struggle past each other like termites. The ship's burrows were imperfect and unfinished, cobbled together almost as an afterthought to accommodate mere people.

He returned to the Bridge, greeting them, and being greeted, quietly. He sank back into his contour chair. The Bridge was murmurous and discreet, with restful soft light and muted sounds in different registers and keys. Like any good butler, the ship had unobtrusively but thoroughly attuned itself to Foord's preferences. It made the alarms, when they sounded, discreet and murmuring; understated, like him. It had done the same for the electronic noises at the Bridge consoles, and for the Bridge lighting, without his having to instruct it. *Like Jeeves*, he thought, and that reminded him of his father's old books, now neatly shelved in his study: Shakespeare, Dickens, Austen and all the usual classics, plus some P.G. Wodehouse.

Time passed. They continued through the Gulf towards Horus 5, at an unvarying thirty percent.

"Commander," Thahl said, "I have another call from Director Swann."

"Is it on the same matter as before?"

"Yes, Commander. He says She could make an emergence at any time. He demands to know why we aren't making more speed towards Horus 5."

"Is Demands an advance on Insists?"

"I don't know, Commander."

"The answer is the same, Thahl. Tell him, Later."

"Yes, Commander."

Cyr looked across her console at Foord and half mouthed, half whispered, Piling Indignities On Him. It was as though their conversation in his study had never taken place. She and Thahl had already moved on from what had happened at Blentport, but for different reasons. Cyr considered it trivial. Thahl, being a Sakhran, would not waste time wishing for it to unhappen.

Foord looked around the Bridge.

"We'll do this as I said at our first briefing. We'll cross the Gulf at thirty percent photon speed, switch down to ion drive, and make a wide pass around Horus 4. A *very* wide pass. Then we'll cross the Belt to Horus 5. Questions?"

There were none. Foord went on.

"Director Swann seems to think we should rush to keep our appointment with Her. I think we don't need to. When She makes Her emergence, I believe She'll wait for us." He paused for effect, looking round at them, and added "Why should that be? ...Well, I found out something recently. Something which nobody seems to have noticed."

"You mean that thing about the planets being in alignment?" Smithson asked. "I thought everybody knew that."

Foord's moment hung in the air, dissolving.

The ship plunged on. Round the circumference of the Bridge screen, and at the consoles which followed its circumference, components clicked and hummed and shone, reporting the fiction of the ship's movement—fiction because it moved through a medium whose absolute motion, geared down from universe to galaxy to solar system to planet to ship, was too vast to discern; and fiction also because its own movement, like that of space, was subdivided into the movements of its larger and smaller parts. The slender arrowhead hull moved towards the outer planet of Horus system, and the scanners and weapons tracked endlessly back and forth through a notional sphere of which the star Horus was centre; the synapses in its Codex, the aggregation of its nine sentience cores, moved back and across and back in latticeworks; the subatomic particles in its bionics and electronics moved in orbits around their nuclei. The ship was an illusion moving through an illusion. With nine percent sentience, it only nine percent knew itself. It faded in and out of self-awareness, not unlike people.

Foord yawned and settled deeper into his contour chair. "Status reports, please."

Joser hit the alarms. "Commander, an unidentified ship has just entered the Gulf."

3

"Battle stations, please," Foord murmured.

Darkness grew like fur on the Bridge. The main lights dimmed, leaving only the glow from the consoles and from the stars on the circular Bridge screen. Seats extended to full harness configuration. Alarms sounded politely through the ship's inhabited burrows.

"Thahl, please request the intruder to make identification."

A tall beaker of amber fluid—a sleep and defecation inhibitor—had appeared in Foord's chairarm dispenser. He sipped it thoughtfully.

"Well?"

"No reply, Commander."

"Keep trying, will you? Joser, position of intruder, please."

"12-19-14, Commander. *Behind* us, coming from the direction of Sakhra."

"Thank you. Kaang, please turn us to face that reference. Then hold."

There was a muffled bump, which just failed to ripple the fluid in the beaker which Foord had left balanced on his chairarm, as the photon drive shut down and the gravity compensators cut in. Other compensators swept the screen invisibly, turning the starfield from an analogue to a real image.

"Joser?"

"Preliminary readouts indicate that the intruder is a Class 097 cruiser of

Horus Fleet, Commander. A visual will follow shortly."

The *Charles Manson* turned, manoeuvre jets playing like fountains from the outlets grouped round the nose, midsection and rear of its hull, Kaang first activating jets for the turn and then others to counter it, and others to counter those, and so on; normally an operation left to computers, but Kaang did it manually for greater speed. The starfield stretched around the circular screen as if it was a tight skin inside which the Bridge rotated. The ship came to rest.

"Joser, you're sure that's a Horus Fleet ship?"

"Yes, Commander."

"Sure enough to attack it if you were Her?"

Joser blinked at the strangeness of the question, but said "Yes, Commander. I'm now getting detailed readouts which are quite definite. And the visual is coming up now."

"Thank you. Superimpose it when it's ready, please. Thahl?"

"Still no reply to our requests for identification, Commander."

"Then get Horus Fleet Directorate at Sakhra, please."

"I've already done so, Commander. They absolutely deny ordering any ship to shadow us."

"Then please get me Director Swann personally."

"Here's your visual, Commander."

From a widening point dead ahead, the imaginary skin round the circumference of the Bridge screen was ruptured and a locally-magnified image slapped against it, like a plaster over a wound. The visual was so good that for a moment the details were more prominent than the whole: silvered overlapping hull plates, rings of manoeuvre drive blisters like plague scars, oxidation streaks, and, clearest of all, Horus Fleet insignia and identification markings. The ship was large and heavily built and looked close enough for collision.

"When we stopped and turned," Joser said, "it switched down from photon to ion drive. It's approaching us very slowly, at about five percent. And it's on battle stations."

"Yes," Foord said. He noted the hooded viewports like eyeslits in a perhaps-empty suit of armour, and the weapon ports housing extended nozzles which tracked back and forth.

"Commander," Thahl said, "I have Director Swann."

"Thank you. Put him through, please."

Silence.

"Has something gone wrong, Thahl?"

"I'm sorry, Commander. Director Swann just cut the channel."

"Position of intruder is 12-18-14 and closing slowly," Joser said.

"Cut the channel? I don't understand."

"I told him you needed to speak urgently. He said 'Later', and cut the channel."

Foord smiled faintly.

"Commander," Cyr spoke for the first time, "we're still at battle stations."

"And?"

"And I have no orders. I'd like to ask if you intend to…"

"If I intend to attack that ship?"

"Our orders were quite explicit, Commander."

"Yes, I got a copy of them. I know what may have to be done."

"Commander," Joser began, "for the record I must…"

"No, for the record you mustn't. Please confine yourself to readouts of the intruder's position. Can I have the latest one?"

"12-17-14 and closing slowly."

"Thank you. Thahl?"

"Still no reply, Commander. From the intruder, or Director Swann."

"Get me the Director's chief of staff, please. Tell him I have a message."

"Intruder is now 11-17-14 and…Commander, he's decelerating!"

Foord glanced up at the screen. Manoeuvre jets were blazing in sequence from the front of the ship like a visible scale played up and down organ pipes. Scanners and weapons peered ahead from the dark semicircular recesses of their housings. The Bridge screen, before it was asked, patched in a view from another angle, showing the name and Fleet ident, SABLE 097 CX 141, bulging over the corrugations of its flanks. The ship came to rest.

"Kaang, please take us forward slowly on ion drive, no more than five percent. Thahl?"

"I have Director Swann's chief of staff, Commander."

"Oh, and Cyr: no further orders for now. Thank you, Thahl. Put him through on sound only; visual won't be necessary."

"Commander Foord? I'm not getting your…"

"Forgive me. You're Director Swann's chief of staff?"

"I am. Commander, I'm not getting your visual."

"But you can hear me clearly?"

"Yes, Commander."

"Then please give the Director this message. Tell him that it appears that the *Sable*, a Class 097 cruiser of Horus Fleet, number CX 141, has disobeyed orders and shadowed us into the battle area. Emphasize the word Appears. Tell him I have orders to engage and destroy an unidentified ship whose specification—are you recording all this?"

"Every word. Please go on, Commander."

"An unidentified ship whose specification is largely unknown, but whose documented abilities include evading and confusing scanners." He glanced briefly at Joser as he said this. "Horus Fleet has been recalled to defensive positions around Sakhra, and my orders entitle me to rely on Horus Fleet to ensure that I engage that ship alone."

"Commander, we've already received an enquiry from one of your officers on this matter. I assure you we're treating it with the utmost urgency. If any ship has broken formation it will be ordered back and if necessary brought back by force."

"I think," Foord said, "that you may have misunderstood. Let me complete the message, and then I'll leave it to you to pass it to the Director. This unidentified ship—I'll use the name Faith, most people do now—can evade and confuse scanners. My orders entitle me to rely on Horus Fleet to ensure that I engage Her alone. The ship shadowing us has repeatedly failed to identify itself. Please tell the Director that I must assume this ship is Faith, and that somehow She's contrived to appear on our scanners as a Horus Fleet ship. I'm therefore going to engage and destroy Her."

"Commander," Joser said quietly, "I must tell you on the record that I have detailed readouts on that ship, and it's definitely a Class 097. Drive emissions, dimensions, mass, they can't be faked."

Foord appeared not to have heard, though in the sudden silence on the Bridge that was quite impossible.

"Thahl, you've continued to request identification?"

"Yes, Commander. No reply."

"Continue sending, right up to the moment we open fire."

"Commander," Joser persisted. "It would be..."

"*Don't*!" Cyr snapped, before Foord could answer, "Don't say it would be murder!"

"Thank you, Cyr, that's enough," Foord said.

But for Cyr, it wasn't. "Unsolicited comments," she hissed at Joser, "from unproven Bridge officers, are not helpful."

"Thank you, Cyr, that's *enough*."

"Commander," Thahl said, "I have Director Swann."

4

"Commander Foord."

"Director Swann."

"This conversation is long overdue."

"It's overdue; don't expect it to be long."

"I've been handed a message from you." On the screen, Swann looked like a badly-drawn cartoon of Foord. He too came from a heavy gravity planet, and had the same large frame and the same dark hair and beard; but his frame was less toned, and his hair and beard less well groomed, than Foord's. "Let me make sure I understand you. You're about to destroy a Class 097 cruiser of Horus Fleet. Is that correct?"

"Position of intruder," Joser said, "is 11-17-14 and holding."

Foord glanced at the magnified section of the circular Bridge screen. The large silver ship remained at rest, the only movement coming from the nozzles in its weapons ports and scanner housings which tracked side to side, side to side, much as an underwater current might move the minor appendages of something long since drowned.

"I'm about to engage a ship which I have to believe is Faith," Foord said.

"*Have* to believe?"

"I'm at war with everything in the system not in the immediate vicinity of Sakhra, where my orders tell me I can assume it belongs to you. And I'm at war with anything which follows me into the Gulf and fails to identify itself."

"You attack that ship, Commander, and you're at war with Horus Fleet."

"We both know that isn't true." *But if it was, we'd probably win.*

"Commander, listen to me."

"Holding on ion drive at five percent, Commander. Shall I continue?"

"Thank you, Kaang, yes."

"Commander, listen to me. The *Sable* shadowed you without my knowledge and in defiance of my orders. I now know what made its Captain commit this error. It'll be the last error of his career, but it *is* just an error. The *Sable* has a crew of ninety. It's only an 097. It wouldn't stand a chance against you."

"Not if it's really an 097. But why hasn't it identified itself?"

"*Stop* this, Foord! That's a real ship with real people. I can prove it to you, I have documented evidence that the *Sable* joined the cordon and then broke formation and followed you."

"Not enough. She could have heard all that when She monitored your comms, and decided to appear as the *Sable*." Foord knew this was almost inhumanly unreasonable, but it was how Swann would expect him to behave. Perversely, he was enjoying it.

"Commander, please listen to me. The Captain of the *Sable* has been under strain recently. He broke the cordon because…"

"You're making my point. I don't need to know his motives, but if She became aware of them through monitoring your comms, that's another reason to doubt whether that ship is any ship of yours."

"Commander, if that's Her out there and not the *Sable*, why hasn't She already attacked you?"

"If She always attacked when people like you expected Her to, I wouldn't have been sent here."

It continued. The more desperate Swann's voice got, the more even Foord's stayed. The more dishevelled Swann looked, the more poised Foord appeared. They were both acutely aware of the contrast.

"Still no reply to requests for identification," Thahl said. "Shall I continue sending?"

"Yes, I think so, though it seems pointless…I'm sorry, Director, but it also seems pointless continuing this conversation."

"Then let *us* try ordering the *Sable* to identify itself to you."

"You mean you haven't already?"

"Let *me* try. Personally. I'll order its Captain to call you now."

"Not enough. It could still be Her."

"Then we'll send out two or three ships of our own to bring it back. On tractor beams if necessary."

"Not enough. They could be two or three of Her. Anything in Horus system, not in the cordon, I'm at war with."

Swann played his final card.

"If the *Sable* doesn't identify itself, I could send out two or three ships...."

"You already said that."

"...to destroy it, Commander."

"Not enough. I can do that myself. Director, I want you to treat us how *you* want to treat us, like we're infected. I want you to leave us so alone that we can assume anything else we meet is hostile. If *any* ship of yours leaves the cordon, it's hostile."

"Then you *are* at war with us."

"Orders, Director."

"If I had your orders I would..."

"Have you ever in your life had orders like mine?"

"I've never in my life had to deal with anyone like you, Commander. Whatever I thought about your ship coming here, I still offered you courtesy and hospitality and you ignored it. I arranged receptions to welcome you and your crew. I gave your ship's refit total priority. I gave you assistance to return to your ship. I even made sure that the unspeakable events on your last day here didn't stop your liftoff. So please, tell me what will stop you destroying the *Sable*."

"Nothing, Director. I can't and won't stop."

"Commander!" Joser said. "Scanners have just registered an emergence at Horus 5."

"Do you have detailed readouts?"

"Yes, Commander. It's Her."

5

"Yes, Director," Foord said, "you did hear me correctly. I said we've detected an emergence at Horus 5. I said our first readouts indicate a ship matching the known specification of Faith. And I said I refuse to move."

"You have orders," roared Swann, "and I demand you obey them!"

"I have orders to engage Her alone. I've now got two unidentified ships, one at Horus 5 and one here in the Gulf."

"Then *fuck off*, and engage Her alone, and I'll see to it that the *Sable* doesn't follow you."

"I can see to that myself. What's the difference?"

"Ninety lives, if that *is* the *Sable*, which you now know it is. Come on, Foord. She's *arrived*. She's here waiting for you, like you always wanted. Somewhere down here we've probably picked Her up too, and they're probably checking and rechecking before they tell me. And then there's the cordon to complete, which was held up so *you* could leave Blentport, and the evacuation into the lowlands, and the civil chaos when the news breaks that She's here, which is something you couldn't begin to imagine because you don't spend much time among real people, do you?"

"What's the point you're trying to make?" Foord said, adopting a tone of puzzlement. He was beginning to overdo it, he thought.

"A moment, please." Swann's face turned to one side, where someone off screen was whispering to him.

Foord too turned away from the screen. "Positions, please," he asked Joser.

"The *Sable*, I mean the first intruder, is 11-17-14 and holding. The second intruder is 99-98-96 and holding. Readouts on the second intruder conform to Faith's known profile; heavily shrouded on all wavelengths."

"Foord," Swann resumed, "that was the expected message, and our readouts match yours. So stop talking about unidentified ships. That ship at Horus 5 *is* Faith, and that ship which shadowed you into the Gulf *is* a Horus Fleet ship!"

Foord glanced at Joser, who nodded vigorously.

"Then I'm about to order the destruction of a Horus Fleet ship. I will *not* engage Her until I know for certain that I'm engaging Her alone."

"When this is over, Foord"—Swann's voice had lost its desperation; now it was oddly calm—"when this is over I'll make sure that whatever's left of the Commonwealth knows what you did, and disowns you."

"It's already disowned us."

"Commander. Please. My last try. Give me two minutes to contact the Captain of the *Sable*, and I'll make it go away. Two minutes, Commander."

"You have as long as it takes me to give the order. But I'll speak slowly."

6

The Bridge was silent as they watched the big silver ship on the magnified section of the screen, in an effort to confirm visually what the scanners had already told them. Slowly, gradually, it happened. One by one the weapons nozzles ceased tracking and retracted into their housings; a dull red aura spread from the stern as the ion drive restarted at low intensity; manoeuvre jets flared and fountained in shifting combinations; and then, quite deliberately, and with the same lack of communication which had characterised its first appearance, the *Sable* turned away.

Not once, thought Foord, did it make any contact with us. Not even now.

On the Bridge, banks of subdued red warning lights continued to glow at every console. Alarms continued to murmur at discreet intervals.

"Position of *Sable*..." began Joser, then stopped as Foord glanced up at him sharply. "...of *first intruder*, is still 11-17-14, but the turn will register shortly. And..."

"Excuse me. Thahl?"

"No call yet, Commander."

"Thank you. Please keep us at battle stations. Joser?"

"Position of second intruder is still 99-98-96 and holding. No detectable movement or activity on any waveband."

The ship on the screen continued to turn away. Now it was almost sideways on, repeating the view the screen had patched in earlier. Like before, SABLE 097 CX 141 bulged over the long contours of its flanks. Class 097s were heavy cruisers. The *Sable* was bigger than the *Charles Manson*, but much less powerful; like Foord against Thahl, it wouldn't have lasted ten seconds.

"Commander," Thahl said, "I have a call from Director Swann."

"Thank you. Put him through, please."

"Well, Commander Foord."

"Well, Director Swann."

"As you can see, the *Sable* is leaving the Gulf. When can I expect you to do the same, in the opposite direction?"

"As soon as we've tracked him for a reasonable distance."

"Of course," Swann said, magnanimously. He was visibly more relaxed; his face had the equivalent of a spring in its step. Foord's manner, on the other hand, was precisely the same as before. "But when you've tracked him I want you to go, Commander! Do you hear?"

"What will happen to him, Director?"

"You know perfectly well what will happen to him."

"And his crew?"

"That's another matter. But for Captain Copeland, it's all over."

"Copeland?"

"Yes. It was his brother at Anubis."

●

"If *you* can't stop Her," Swann had said to Foord, as the *Charles Manson* was making ready to re-engage photon drive and head through the Gulf towards Horus 5, "then She'll have to get past Horus Fleet to reach Sakhra. If the Fleet can't stop Her, neither will Sakhra's normal defences, but by then the evacuation will have progressed and if She ever reaches here She'll find military areas full of civilians and most of the movable defences gone to the highlands. If everything else fails I'll gamble on Her not attacking civilian targets."

Foord had not answered.

"And don't give me any of your silences, Foord, not after what your people did here! My family have been evacuated too. They're taking the same risk as everyone else. I was born here, and so were my parents *and* my children, and I'll defend it any way I see fit."

Foord had not meant his silence to imply disapproval. Insofar as the evacuation interested him at all, which was not very much now that he'd left Sakhra, he could see it made some sense; Thahl had persuaded him of that. His silence was merely a suggestion that they both had other things they should be doing.

"We're just about to move off, Director. Was there anything else?"

"We need you to stop Her, Foord; but..."

"But you think the cure is worse than the disease?"

"Your ship isn't a cure. It's another disease."

Foord had blinked a couple of times at the empty patch on the screen, where Swann had cut the connection, and then returned his attention to the Bridge.

"Joser, please keep a continuous check on Her position and confirm every ten minutes. Kaang, please take us out of here, heading 99-98-96, on photon drive at thirty percent rising to ninety percent."

The conversation with Swann had taken place forty minutes earlier. The *Charles Manson* was now about one-quarter of the way through the Gulf, holding at ninety percent photon speed. The Bridge screen had cut in with filters and compensators at twenty percent to adjust for relativistic distortion of the starfield, and at seventy percent had blanked out entirely and substituted a simulation which showed Horus 5 in outline, and beyond it, at 99-98-96 and unmoving, a white dot which represented *Her*. It seemed very faint on the screen, like the last living thing in a wasteland; or the first, of millions.

At regular intervals Joser would murmur "Position of Faith is still 99-98-96 and holding. No detectable movement or activity on any waveband," and Foord would acknowledge politely. That, and the muted voices of the others as they made regular status reports or conducted routine conversations with other parts of the ship, was the only human noise on the Bridge. When the *Charles Manson* went to battle stations, there were changes of degree which were barely perceptible; relationships were a little more carefully delineated, Foord was a little more courteous and attentive to detail, and noise and light were a little more subdued.

Foord was starting to feel distaste at what he'd done, as if he'd been pulling wings off flies; Swann was only trying to protect his people. He took a sip from the tumbler of inhibitor fluid put out by his chairarm dispenser. It was half-full, exactly as he left it since the encounter with the *Sable*, and when he replaced it it slid down into the chairarm, was replenished, and slid up again. It was a tall tumbler, filled almost to the brim, but no vibration disturbed the surface of the liquid. Had it done so Foord would have been quite disoriented. For generations, it had been an established convention that space travel was dull: empty of events, and almost devoid of distance.

It was empty of events because events could be anticipated by the ship, and either avoided, evaded, compensated or filtered, before or while they happened; so that at ninety percent photon speed the ship enabled gravity, light, elapsed time and sensory perception to function inside it exactly as if it was at rest.

It was almost devoid of distance because distances between stars could be sidestepped by the MT Drive, and distances within solar systems could be eaten up by the ship's array of lesser drives. Since the development of Matter Transfer, distances between stars had ceased to have much meaning. Most interstellar cultures, like the Commonwealth and the old Sakhran Empire, had developed MT Drive almost by accident. It was still only partially understood. One of its features was that it could not be used within solar systems; to engage it anywhere near bodies of planetary mass would be catastrophic. Distances within solar systems, however, were no more than a minor irritation for ships with photon and ion drive.

All that, plus the existence of instantaneous communication using principles derived from MT physics, made it possible for a Commonwealth of twenty-nine solar systems to function as if each system was an apartment in the same block, divided only by thin walls and a darkened hall and staircase—darkened, because nobody needed to go out there anymore. The Gulf in Horus system was the nearest anyone would get to the old pre-MT days of space travel, when people travelled physically through the nothingness between stars, instead of sidestepping it as they did now; an MT Jump, and an emergence from it, took the same time whether the distance was one light-year or a hundred.

"Position of Faith," Joser said, "is still 99-98-96 and holding. No detectable movement or activity on any waveband."

"Thank you," Foord replied, giving Joser a sidelong glance. Maybe, he thought, Joser would say that Foord had been unreasonable over the *Sable*; or that Foord had compromised on the Department's orders. Either way, it'd sound good when whispered back to the Department.

"You have the ship," he told Thahl. As he left the Bridge, he turned to Cyr. "I'd like to see you in my study, please. In five minutes."

●

Foord's study was almost adjacent to the Bridge, a very short walk down an adjoining corridor. When four minutes fifty seconds had elapsed, Cyr walked the short distance, knocked on the door, and waited. When Foord called Enter, she did so, and like last time she closed the door behind her and remained standing.

Foord was seated at his desk. He looked up at her.

"I'd like to ask you about Joser."

"I know I spoke hastily on the Bridge, Commander, but I meant it."

"No, it's not that. He makes you uneasy, and I'd like to know why. You have permission to speak freely."

He spoke as if their previous interview hadn't happened. She noticed there was no ruler on the desktop.

She paused, and said "On the Bridge, when he told you It Would Be Murder…"

"Or tried to, until you shouted him down."

"He told me later that he'd only said what any ordinary decent person would have said."

"And your point?"

"Nobody on this ship has any right to be ordinary or decent… I don't trust him, Commander."

"Tell me why."

"Three reasons. One, he's always manoeuvring for position, as if he's expecting what he does and says to be played to an audience later. Two, his work's mediocre; he might be acceptable on an ordinary ship, but not on this one. Three, and following from One, I think he's a Department stooge."

"He wouldn't be the first," Foord said drily.

"Do I still have permission to speak freely, Commander?"

"Of course."

"He's dangerous. Get rid of him, get him off the Bridge, any way you can. Not because he's a stooge, we've had them before, but because he's *fucking mediocre*."

Foord was silent for a couple of minutes, thinking.

"Thank you," he said eventually. "That's helpful. I'll see you back on the Bridge."

She turned and walked out, aware that he was watching the seat of her skirt, and the swaying of its pleats.

●

Foord yawned, settled back in his chair, closed his eyes and listened again to the muted background noise on the Bridge. It always reminded him of long summer afternoons from his childhood when he would lay alone with eyes closed on a crowded beach, and would listen: to the sea, to the sharp voices of other children, to the lower voices of their parents tossing everyday remarks tiredly back and forth like beachballs, and to the doppler effect of someone running towards him and past him, on the way to someone else. His childhood had been complex and solitary, but not unhappy; at least, not until the darkness came.

He had prepared carefully and thoroughly for what was about to happen, as he always did. He knew how he would destroy Her. He had worked with the ship's Codex, the aggregation of its nine sentience cores, to extract from the onboard computers every last detail of the structure of Horus system and the known and suspected abilities of Faith. He had then constructed an intricate mechanism of initiatives, responses, failsafes and fallbacks. And now the entire mechanism, like the *Charles Manson* itself, was under way—as dense as a mountain of lead, as precise as an antique clock movement, and so finely balanced that his will needed only to touch it as lightly as a feather to move it all in a given direction. So he could afford to relax, for now.

"Commander," Thahl said, "we're now within twice the maximum distance at which She's been known to monitor communications. You asked to be notified."

"Thank you. From now until further notice, no external communication will be made or accepted without my prior authority. Please inform Sakhra; and then close their channels."

It seemed everyone wanted to know about Faith: who She was, where She came from, and why She was doing this. Foord, however, was genuinely indifferent. All that concerned him was that She was an opponent—the only one, apart from another Outsider, who might match him. Others were working on Her identity and motives, and if anyone found anything they'd tell him. With a kind of cold irony which was almost Sakhran, he looked forward to destroying Her *before* anyone could find out who She was.

Almost everyone who served or commanded on an Outsider did so because, for various reasons, they would be unacceptable on an ordinary ship. Foord rarely thought about why he would have been unacceptable; but it might have been his reluctance to believe in things. He considered that other people, particularly those who gave him his orders, believed far too much in their own existence and in that of the universe. Human senses, unaided, could perceive the universe across a range of 10^{-4} to 10^{+4}. Optical and mechanical devices increased the range: 10^{-10} to 10^{+10}. Electronics made it 10^{-25} to 10^{+25}, and the knowledge of which the *Charles Manson* was perhaps the last product made it 10^{-50} to 10^{+50}. Upon the perception gained at each stage a body of knowledge was constructed, and upon that construction grew further constructions—philosophical, political, cultural, social. There was the clockwork of Newton, then the relative chaos of Einstein, though Einstein only wanted harmony; then the smaller and deeper chaos of quantum uncertainty, and then back to a post-Newtonian clockwork. Beyond that was a deeper and vaster level of chaos, not yet quite visible; by the time it was, people would no longer be travelling in things like the *Charles Manson*.

Each stage proved its predecessor an illusion, and waited to be proved an illusion by its successor. But they all continued to be part of the same accretion over time; because, Foord thought, they all shared the quality of illusion. In the universe which was currently believed to exist, Foord served current institutions by applying current knowledge and techniques to the orders he was given, but the difference between Foord and those who gave him his orders was that they believed it had a meaning, whereas he knew it did. But only in terms of itself.

●

Eighty minutes later, the *Charles Manson* passed uneventfully out of the Gulf and crossed the orbital path of Horus 4, giving the planet a wide berth as Foord had stipulated. Kaang commenced deceleration for entry into the Belt. As photon drive subsided to seventy percent and below, the simulation disappeared from the Bridge screen and was replaced by a real visual, overlaid by rectilinear filters and compensators to correct for spectral shift; and these overlays themselves dwindled and disappeared as the photon drive subsided to twenty percent and below.

"Switching to ion drive" said Kaang.

"Position of Faith is still 99-98-96 and holding," Joser said, not needing to raise his voice above the faint velvet thud which, together with a brief play of lights from Kaang's console and a grunt of something which might have been approval from Smithson, was the only indication that a switch of drives had occurred.

"And no detectable movement or activity on any waveband," Joser added.

"Ion drive engaged," Kaang said. "Ninety percent and falling."

"Thank you," Foord said. "Joser, from now on I'd like those positional checks every five minutes. Smithson, Cyr, I'll be requesting your status reports when we complete deceleration, so please have them ready. Oh, and Joser, one other thing…"

●

The *Charles Manson* entered the Belt on ion drive at exactly thirty percent, and slid through it unhurriedly and without incident. Status reports were given quietly and received politely, while the ship picked its way between bodies ranging in size from large boulders to small planets. It stolidly maintained its own up and down as asteroids rolled and turned around it; the surfaces of the bigger ones loomed on the encircling Bridge screen, sometimes below them like floors pocked with craters, sometimes to either side like walls veined with crevasses, sometimes above them like ceilings from which mountain ranges hung inverted. Foord stole a glance at Kaang, and thought, *We may have to come back through the Belt a lot faster than this. And with less leisure for observation.*

The asteroids grew smaller and dwindled away to the rear and the last phase of the journey began, the crossing of space between the Belt and Horus 5. Foord called for the adoption of the final stages of battle stations. Bulkheads slid across corridors to seal off the Bridge and the burrows of the ship's nine other inhabited sections—no more than a ritual gesture, since each section was self-sustaining and its functions could be transferred elsewhere if damaged, and in any case Foord tended to run his ship as if the bulkheads were always there. On the Bridge, and in the sub-centres of each inhabited section, seats configured to full harness. Communications were shut off, except through Foord. The Codex told its sentience cores to tell the onboard computers to ignore everything outside the mission parameters. Finally, the ship switched to a navigational sphere of reference of which it was the centre.

Until further notice, the ship designated itself the centre of the universe.

The caretaker went out into the darkened hallway. He had put a lot of time and care into his preparations, as he always did. He had forgotten the tenants of the twenty-nine apartments who summoned him when they heard footsteps in the hall and on the stairs; it was their business to speculate about the cause and origin of the footsteps, his to make sure they were never heard again.

7

Horus 5 clamoured over all wavelengths. It boiled with upheavals—gravitational, magnetic, ionospheric, volcanic, tectonic—and continued to exist because of them, borrowing and re-borrowing its existence from the accountancy which decreed that creation and destruction must balance each other. The red upper levels of its atmosphere were shot with lightning and swirling with vortexes; at its surface there was enough pressure to liquefy rock, and more heat than had ever filtered down from Horus; and in the purple and ochre of its middle atmosphere it bred new hydrocarbon-based lifeforms to replace the old ones it was destroying. They were strange and beautiful things, tinting the thick atmosphere as they slid through it. It was said they were sentient, and lived in family groups.

Horus 5 would still have clamoured if nobody was there to hear it, but now it had the *Charles Manson*, floating almost at rest just inside its orbit; and something else, perhaps not unlike the *Charles Manson*, floating at absolute rest just outside. The *Charles Manson* was approaching very slowly, on a course which kept the planet between them.

"Status reports, please."

"Nothing, Commander," Thahl said. "Sakhra has not attempted to communicate. Neither has Faith."

"All our probes have been blocked, but otherwise She's inert," Joser said. "And shrouded. We've detected no probes from Her. Her position is 99-98-96 and—"

"Use the self-centred sphere of reference from now on, please," Foord said with a trace of impatience.

"I'm sorry, Commander. Her position is 09-07-09 and holding."

"Proceeding on ion drive at one percent," Kaang said. "At a range 1.91 from Horus 5."

"All weapons are at…" Cyr began.

There was a hiss of static from Horus 5. It ceased abruptly, and the Bridge returned to its customary near-silence.

Cyr glanced pointedly at Thahl, and waited.

"I'm sorry, that was an unusually big atmospheric discharge."

"Are you sure," Foord asked Thahl, "that's all it was?"

"Yes, Commander." Since they were not in private, Thahl did not bristle at the question, except privately. "It coincided with an upper atmospheric prominence on the planet. I've adjusted the filters."

"Thank you. Cyr, please continue."

"All weapons are at immediate readiness, Commander."

"All drives," Smithson said, "are at immediate readiness."

"Including MT?" Foord asked quickly. "She might head out of the system, not in."

"Yes, Commander, I know that. I said, All drives."

Foord glanced up at the Bridge screen, the entire front semicircle of which was taken up by Horus 5. The planet's upper atmosphere was purple and ochre and, predominantly, dark red; it was heavily filtered but it still bloodwashed the Bridge, almost but not quite matching the shade of the red Battle telltales which glowed politely from each console. Foord had seen many gas giants before, some more spectacular than this one—they were common in the outer reaches of main-sequence systems like Horus—and he was accustomed to being able to gaze directly into their faces for as long as he wanted. With this one, however, he couldn't quite. He looked away, frowning.

"Joser, can you increase the screen filtering, please? I still find that light a little livid…Thank you."

"Range now 1.88 from Horus 5, Commander," Kaang said. "Do you wish us to come to a halt yet?"

"Not yet, thank you. I'd prefer to be a little closer, say 1.85 or less… Thahl, about that burst of static just now."

"Yes, Commander, I've made the adjustments."

"Thank you. I just want to be sure that That Planet," he lounged in his seat against the backdrop of Horus 5 and talked about it as if he was talking about someone at a neighbouring restaurant table, and intending to be overheard, "doesn't intrude into conversations on the Bridge. That's all."

They didn't balk at his obsessiveness, even now when they were about to engage the strangest opponent they would ever face; in fact, to some extent they shared it.

She was motionless, and inert on all wavelengths. They could easily bend their long-range viewers around the planet, as (presumably) could She; but there was nothing to see, because She was shrouded. She always went shrouded into engagements, only becoming visible later, usually at some point of maximum psychological impact. The shrouding didn't hide Her drive emissions, so if She moved, She could be tracked; but when She didn't move, as now, She was invisible.

The Bridge screen had patched in a small insert showing a simulation of the other side of Horus 5, with a white dot marking Her position, and Foord looked at it and thought, *Whatever happens next I've won the first point; I knew you'd wait. I would, if I was you.*

"Our range from Horus 5 is now 1.85, Commander," Kaang said.

"Thank you. Disengage ion drive and bring us to rest, please."

With an almost insolent lack of haste, and a negligent precision like that of a diner's fork suspended between mouth and plate during conversation, the *Charles Manson* brought itself to rest relative to Horus 5. The move was accomplished by the disengagement of ion drive—as always, Kaang made it barely perceptible—and a brief fountaining of manoeuvre drives round the front and midsection of the hull.

Soon, thought Foord, it will start. The two of us are already closer to each other than we've ever been.

He looked round at Cyr and Smithson. "Commence launch procedures, please." It was a strangely low-key start to an engagement which, he knew, would either end his life or change it.

From a series of small bays near the ship's nose, a swarm of slender objects slid out horizontally. From a larger ventral bay a single object, of a much different shape and size, dropped vertically towards the planet.

●

A few days earlier, when the *Charles Manson* had made planetfall at Sakhra, and before he had gone up to Hrissihr, Foord had attended one of Swann's welcome receptions—as it turned out, the only one he would attend. It was a large-scale event, with figures from lowlands business, media, political and military circles. It was held in a ballroom in one of the exquisite civic buildings which Foord had seen on his way through the Bowl; this one was the Friendship House at Three Bridges, a few miles outside Blentport. Foord was there with his Bridge officers and a few other crew members. Each of them performed as they usually did on such occasions.

Cyr was gliding elegantly among the guests, for the most part ignoring the men (though this was not reciprocated) and making conversation with the women; she could make them feel ugly and untidy just by standing near them, even though she was still wearing her uniform and they were wearing evening gowns. She was well aware of her effect on them, but behaved as if she wasn't.

Kaang was the centre of a group of Horus Fleet pilots, apologising for herself as always. Every time they were invited to events like this, her reputation went before her. Pilots would introduce themselves, would ask her how she did it, and would leave baffled or resentful, or worse, when they found she couldn't tell them. It was a gift she had been born with, and didn't understand. It made her many times better than they would ever be, but with none of their effort. They hated her for that, and also, perversely, for the fact she was not arrogant about it; for the fact that it embarrassed her.

Smithson was pleased to discover that someone had prepared thoroughly enough to have included, just for him, some concentrated vegetable matter; in deference to the elegance of the occasion, it was presented as small solid cakes rather than bowls of slime, but it was palatable. (Cyr told him later that Swann had called her, personally, to check on his dietary needs.)

Smithson was an Ember. His planet, Emberra, was unusually rich and self-sufficient. Emberra had made it clear to the Commonwealth that it would decline any Invitation To Join, and the Commonwealth, wisely, didn't press the point. Instead it negotiated a network of trade agreements and political treaties, making Emberra a partner but not a part of the

Commonwealth. Embers were thus not often seen on Commonwealth planets. Smithson quickly found himself the centre of an openly curious, but not initially hostile, group.

"So what's your real name?" someone asked. "Is 'Smithson' a human nickname or translation or something?"

"Ember names are long multisyllables, sometimes a paragraph long. They identify us by summarising our lives and accomplishments. 'Smithson' is a human approximation of the last two syllables of my name."

"Doesn't it cramp your style a bit?"

"How do you mean?"

"When you're rolling in bed with a female, do you whisper her *full* name?"

"Yes, but we speak quickly. Especially when we're fucking each other senseless."

Eventually, someone else asked "So how do you come to be working for the Commonwealth?"

"Well, I…"

"And how, of all things," a lady interrupted, "do you come to be working for the Commonwealth *on an Outsider?*"

"I had to leave Emberra," he said, straight faced. "I'm not welcome there. I killed my children and ate them."

She laughed uncertainly. As he walked away from the group, which he did without any formal leave-taking, he heard someone say "Even more gross than Foord," and someone else answer "Yes. A seven-foot walking column of snot."

Of the rest, Joser was conversing easily and working the room—in the few months since he joined the *Charles Manson*, he had shown himself to be more socially adept than any of them—and Thahl was conversing less easily, but tolerably well. He was not the only Sakhran present; Swann had taken care to include several on his guest list, including Thahl's father Sulhu, who had politely declined.

After some perfunctory and awkward circulating, Foord spotted Smithson alone and called him over. They skulked together in a corner of the elegant ballroom. That was when Foord had asked him.

"Let me be clear, Commander." Smithson was about to say I Don't Understand, but caught himself just in time. "You want me to devise something to use when we meet Her at Horus 5, but it's not vital whether it succeeds?"

"Not absolutely vital."

"Why do you think She'll wait at Horus 5?"

"Not your concern. She'll wait. As to whether it succeeds...I want one of your Ideas. The first time we encounter Her, I want something unusual. Something singular. If it doesn't succeed, I still get to see how She responds to it, and that's almost as valuable."

"And you tell me this now, a few days before we lift off?"

"I'm not asking you to invent a new branch of physics. I'm not asking you to build something never seen before."

"Stop telling me what you're not asking, Commander."

"Just use our existing weapons, but put them together into something unusual. Something singular. I already told you. Have one of your Ideas."

"When I have an idea," Smithson muttered, "I usually start from the premise that it will work..." But even while speaking, he began to sort and pick through the possibilities.

A string quartet had been setting up on the main stage for the last few minutes. Just as it struck up, Joser came over to join Foord and Smithson.

"Thank you," Smithson told him, "but I don't dance."

"Commander," Joser said, "Director Swann will be making a welcome speech very soon. I thought it might be useful if you were to spend a little more time with him and his party."

"Useful?"

"He's holding this reception for *us*, Commander. I do think we might...."

Foord reluctantly complied, and Smithson was left alone, still pondering. That was how he came to devise the thing which dropped out of the *Charles Manson*'s ventral bay which now sped towards Horus 5.

●

Foord looked round at Cyr and Smithson. "Commence launch procedures, please."

From a series of small bays near the ship's nose, a swarm of slender objects slid out horizontally. From a larger ventral bay a single object, of a much different shape and size, dropped vertically towards the planet. The smaller objects were conventional missiles, released in a swarm on randomly-varying orbits round Horus 5. The large single object was a Breathtaker.

Breathtakers were usually miniature closeup weapons, designed to enter an opponent's hull and burn away atmosphere; they would consume any gas, whatever it was, and leave behind a perfect vacuum. The object Smithson had put together was, in effect, a large and long-range Breathtaker, but it wasn't designed for Her. At least, not directly.

The missiles were launched amid a surge of noise and light at the same time as the Breathtaker dropped silently out of the ventral bay. Nobody seriously believed this would stop Her detecting the Breathtaker's launch—Her superiority in all areas of scanners and signals technology was well known—but they tried it anyway. Similarly, nobody believed any of the missiles would actually get through, but the speed and manner of Her response, how She detected and countered them, would be illuminating.

Foord had originally wanted to launch twenty-nine missiles at Her, one for each Commonwealth solar system. Warming to his theme, he had decided to give each one the name of a Commonwealth system.

"I don't think that's a good idea, Commander," Cyr had said.

"Why not?"

"We know She'll almost certainly destroy them. So how will it sound if I keep announcing Horus Destroyed, Anubis Destroyed, Alpha Centauri Destroyed, Bast Destroyed, Sirius Destroyed..."

That had been exactly Foord's intention; he liked its irony. However, he caught sight of Joser listening attentively. "Yes, all right, I see what you mean."

"...Isis Destroyed, Aquila Destroyed, Vega Destroyed..."

"Yes, *all right*. We'll just number them, Cyr."

"One to twenty-nine, Commander?"

"One to twenty-*eight*. Keep one back." He glanced at Joser. "The Commonwealth always keeps something back."

Not yet under power, the Breathtaker dropped down through miles of Horus 5's thickening atmospheric soup, through reds and purples and ochres. It had onboard motors, but it looked nothing like a missile. Its motors would take it towards Her, but it would never make impact. What it did would not be aimed directly at Her; only the *result* of what it did.

Smithson had devised and built it in a hurry, and could not, of course, test it. As far as anyone knew, nothing like it had been used before. It might fail to work, or it might work and still be destroyed by Her. If She destroyed it, it might, like the missiles, provide some insights into Her abilities. If it failed to work, it might still leave Her wondering: was its failure genuine or double-bluff?

On the Bridge screen the Breathtaker started to glow. Foord watched it fall further and further until the swirling atmosphere of Horus 5 swallowed it.

A few minutes later, Cyr said "Commander, we've received the first confirmation."

"Thank you, Cyr."

The Breathtaker was preset to descend to the middle levels of Horus 5's atmosphere, to send its first confirmation to the *Charles Manson*, and then to fire its motors and commence a low-level orbit of the planet which, in about ten hours, would take it to a point directly below Her.

It was a large matt black sphere, made of heavy overlapping plates and designed to withstand the pressures found in the middle atmospheric levels of a gas giant. It contained hundreds of small Breathtakers, and a crude but large thermonuclear device. When it completed its low-level orbit and was directly underneath Her, it would send its second confirmation; the thermonuclear device would detonate and the Breathtakers, augmented and amplified by the blast, would smash a temporary vacuum in part of Horus 5's atmosphere, a *shaped* vacuum, long and thin, pointing up at Faith. Into it would rush some of the liquid metal hydrogen which existed at Horus 5's lower levels. The vacuum would very quickly be closed as Horus 5's atmosphere rushed in to fill it, but by then, if the theory worked, a large slug of liquid metal hydrogen would be accelerated through the vacuum, directly at Her. The vacuum would act like a giant coil gun, miles long.

Maybe it wouldn't work; maybe it would work but miss; maybe it would work but Her defensive fields—flickerfields—would hold it. Whatever happened, it would be singular: worthy of Her, and of Smithson. If She survived, which Foord fully expected, it would still leave Her wondering. That is, if whatever lived inside Her thought that way.

Joser filtered down the light from the Bridge screen a little more, and time passed quietly; the missiles and Breathtaker would need ten hours to reach Her. One by one each of the Bridge officers wound down his or her routine tasks, and communications with crew members on other parts of the ship gradually tailed off. The ship hung at rest relative to Horus 5; it was closed to communications from outside, and its parts were closed off from each other, as were those who inhabited it.

It waited, serene and invincible. As long as the parts which made up its whole continued to believe they didn't need or care for each other, the whole could never be destroyed.

8

An hour passed uneventfully.

"Kaang," Foord said, "if you want some rest, it would be better if you took it now. We'll need you later, when the missiles start reaching Her."

"Thank you, Commander, but I'd rather stay. She may not wait until later."

"It could be hours," Foord said, with a trace of irritation. "And do you intend to keep the ship on manual?"

"Yes, Commander. You know I prefer manual. I'm faster than the computers."

She spoke as if explaining housekeeping arrangements; on any other subject, if she had an opinion at all, she would have been more hesitant and probably wrong. Foord let it pass. Whatever else *She* has, he thought, She doesn't have a pilot like Kaang. Nobody does, not even the other eight Outsiders.

Across the Bridge, he and Cyr made brief and unexpected eye contact, and realised they were both remembering the same thing: the day Kaang first joined them.

●

Although it could fly in planetary atmospheres, the *Charles Manson*—like all nine Outsiders—had been built and fitted out in Earth orbit, to preserve secrecy. After its first proving flight, it was kept in orbit to receive its pilot for the second, and definitive, proving flight. When Kaang was brought up by orbital shuttle to join them, they knew of her by reputation; but they were disappointed at the pleasant, but unremarkable, young woman who entered the Bridge and reported for duty.

After the usual formalities, she smiled hesitantly at Foord as she took her place and reminded him—inconsequentially, it seemed at the time—that this was to be the *definitive* proving flight. Thahl, who was interim pilot, offered to take her through the controls, but she politely declined; if, she said, it was satisfactory to Foord, she would prefer to begin immediately. He agreed, and what followed was almost beyond his belief. She took the ship out of orbit and flew it, not like a sixteen-hundred-foot heavy cruiser, but like a single-seat interceptor. She made it pitch and somersault, roll and yaw, turn in its own length, and almost turn itself inside out. She switched through the array of drives from ion to magnetic to photon to nuclear to ion, from ninety percent to rest and back to ninety percent in each of them, until it seemed ready to collide with itself. She played it like a virtuoso would play a perfect instrument, to the highest level of its performance; the closest to both its perfection and its destruction. For two hours she kept it exactly balanced between the two, on the edge of fulfilling or losing the new life she had shown it. It was sublime, and terrifying. And when it was over, she resumed the hesitant smiles and awkward commonplaces.

That was seven years ago, when he had first taken command of his ship. Since then, he had learnt only three things about Kaang. First, where computers made millions of low-level calculations every second, she could jump them intuitively to see patterns; so could all good military pilots, but she was always faster, and always right. Second, the Department wanted her as pilot on the *Albert Camus*, the leadship of the Outsider Class, but she had declined politely; she had always, she said, wanted to serve on Foord's ship. (He'd once asked her why. Embarrassed, she said it was because he understood she was only a pilot, and nothing more).

And that was the third thing he knew about her. Apart from her abilities as pilot, she gave him nothing of any use. She was almost worthless to him.

●

Two more hours passed uneventfully. Cyr broke the silence every few minutes with status reports on the missiles: they were all launched accurately and did not, so far, require any additional guidance or in-flight correction. A long way below them, the Breathtaker continued to plough through the heaving middle levels of Horus 5's atmosphere. The lifeforms around it, who tinted the air and who might be sentient, watched it quizzically as it thundered past them. It would kill some of them when it started functioning, a fact which concerned Foord, but not enough to decide against using it.

"Cyr?"

"The Breathtaker is on course and on schedule, Commander; just over seven hours to go. And functioning perfectly." She glanced at Smithson.

Foord looked at the beaker on his chairarm; it was quite steady. Conceitedly, he thought it important not to look too much at the headups on the Bridge screen. If something happened, he didn't want to look like he'd been waiting for it. So when it did, he wasn't; he missed the first warning flicker of headup displays on the screen.

"Commander," Joser said, "missiles Three, Eleven and Eighteen are gone."

"How?"

"They're just not there anymore. If She fired on them, we didn't detect it."

"Any pattern to it?"

"Not that we can see. They're all on random orbits, and they weren't close together. It seems as random as their launch pattern. And whatever She did, we didn't detect it."

"Yes, you said that. It's still data, so no doubt your people will analyse it."

"Yes, Commander."

"Thank you. You can turn the alarms off now…and Joser, this is likely to happen again. Don't sound the alarms each time."

Two hours passed; then "Ten, Fourteen and Fifteen have gone, Commander. No attack on them was detected."

Thirty-five minutes later, one more. Ten minutes, two more. Two hours, and getting closer to impact, two more. Fifteen minutes, and another seven. Fifty-five minutes, three more.

They tried, unsuccessfully, to discern some mathematical progression in the times and numbers of their destruction, or some spatial pattern determining which ones were destroyed, and how they were destroyed.

Nothing. Especially about how they were destroyed.

Foord tried to tell himself that it was still data, that they could still analyse it and draw conclusions. But it wasn't, and they couldn't. She had given them nothing. She had stayed silent and shrouded, and yet twenty-one of their missiles, so far, were gone. *This isn't a simple military engagement. It's already stranger than that, and will get stranger still.*

"And the Breathtaker?"

"Still exactly on schedule and course, Commander. Now ninety-one minutes to go."

Foord frowned slightly.

"Are *all* the readings from the Breathtaker satisfactory, Cyr?"

"Yes, Commander. Atmospheric pressure is well within its tolerance, the turbulence hasn't deflected it, and all its onboard systems are functioning."

"I see."

The Breathtaker was beginning to worry him. He still assumed that She would destroy it, but he hadn't expected it to get so far without apparent detection or response. If it got much further he might start thinking it could succeed, and then the engagement would end early—something he didn't want for a number of reasons, all of them ambiguous. Or, if She did respond, it might be something unreadable and patternless, as with the missiles. As with Her visits to Commonwealth solar systems. As with everything She did.

It was like throwing a stone into water, and watching it sink without ripples.

"Joser—"

"If it's about the Breathtaker, Commander, we've scanned the entire length of its projected path since its launch."

"Like you did with the missiles," Cyr muttered.

"Even She," Joser continued, still speaking to Foord, "might find it difficult to put any beam on the Breathtaker through all that atmosphere."

"Thank you, Joser." Foord noted the Might, but let it pass. "Cyr, any further observations?"

"No, Commander."

Another hour passed. Five more missiles went, and then two; the last two. The Breathtaker continued to plough its way through Horus 5's lower atmosphere with bovine unconcern—an unconcern matched, apparently, only by Her. Suddenly time was running out.

"Breathtaker's due to detonate in six minutes," Cyr said. Foord nodded.

"She's going to move," Kaang announced. She looked around, aghast at the flurry of activity this remark had produced, and added lamely "I'm sorry, I was talking aloud. I mean *thinking* aloud. I mean, I *think* She's going to move. I mean, She *must* know it's there… "

The Bridge of the *Charles Manson* had many kinds of silence, for use on different occasions. The one which now lengthened around Kaang was the shape of pursed lips.

"It's fine," Foord said, eventually. "And I agree, She must have detected it. We never made it to be undetectable."

"Even if She hasn't detected it yet, She can hardly fail to when it starts making holes in the atmosphere and shooting bits of Horus 5 at Her. Can She? And then, all She has to do…" Joser trailed away.

"All She has to do is outrun it, which She probably can, and watch the slug of hydrogen lose momentum and dribble back to where it came from. We never expected it to succeed. We expected it to make Her respond, and make Her wonder."

Of course we did, said the silence on the Bridge. The Breathtaker was a powerful weapon, but crude and unproven, and easily avoided. In fact, if it could only survive another few minutes, and if Smithson's theory and cobbling-together worked, an absolutely devastating weapon. But easily avoided.

Cyr spoke something into one of her command needlemikes, and after a moment nodded.

"The Breathtaker has sent its second confirmation. It's in position, directly underneath Her."

"Arm it, please," Foord said.

Cyr touched a sequence of panels, and looked up at him.

"The arming signal has been sent and received, Commander. Detonation in two minutes."

"Now She'll move," Kaang whispered.

But She didn't. Another minute passed, somehow.

Now perhaps She'll move, thought Foord. He shot a glance at Joser, who was now the focus of a nest of command needlemikes. Joser shook his head; She continued to do nothing, or nothing detectable. Foord frowned—something he was now beginning to do regularly—but made no further comment.

"Forty-five seconds to detonation," said Cyr.

It would have been a good moment for Joser to hit the alarms and announce a sudden change in Her position, or the sudden approach of a swarm of unidentified objects, but none of this happened. They entered the last thirty seconds, then the last ten, and Cyr started counting down. At Five, Joser said "It's gone, Commander! Like the missiles, no detectable attack but there's nothing there."

"Zero." Cyr said. Then, "No detonation. There's nothing there."

Joser turned to Smithson. "I don't know what She did, but your weapon is gone."

"Then," Smithson said, "we should both be disappointed. Me, because my weapon is gone. You, because you don't know what She did."

Joser did not reply. He couldn't; he was hitting the alarms.

"Unidentified object approaching, Commander."

"That's better," Foord said, and genuinely meant it. "What, where, how many and how long to impact?"

"If its speed stays unchanged, just over nine minutes. Apparently a single object. Position 06-04-08 and closing. Travelling on low ion power, from the direction of Her last position. Readings suggest a missile, but a large one, about three times the size of those we launched. More results are coming in, and we should have a visual any moment."

If; Apparently; Suggest; About; Should Have. Cyr was right, thought Foord. Mediocre. The weakest of us, in the area where She's the strongest.

"Thank you. Please superimpose the visual, and give me the rest later. Kaang, ion drive, please, at forty percent in reverse for ten seconds; no more. Just move us further out, and hold."

If the ion drive made any noise, it was not enough to be heard above the soft and, as always, discreet murmur of the alarms. If it produced any emission from the outlets around the ship's snout, it was not enough to be noticed on the forward section of the Bridge screen, which would have filtered it out anyway. And if it produced any sensation of movement—which objectively it did not, because the gravity compensators would have dealt with it—it was only the illusion of the ship standing still for ten seconds while the red screen image of Horus 5 receded.

"It's changed course to match our movement, Commander," Joser said, "but it hasn't changed speed. Eight minutes forty seconds to impact."

"Thank you. Another ten seconds on ion drive at forty percent, please, Kaang. This time to starboard."

Again the object matched them, again without changing speed.

"Here's the visual, Commander," Joser said.

On the screen directly ahead, a hole opened in the face of Horus 5. It was a black rectangular section of space, as though punched through the planet by some industrial machine, and in the middle of it floated a featureless grey sphere.

"Just over eight minutes to impact, Commander, and I have a full set of results. I'll put them up on the screen."

Foord studied the superimposed rectangle carefully. Joser's text scrolled along its lower edge. Unasked, the screen began generating a series of schematics of the object from other angles: ventral plan, dorsal plan, side view, rear view. It wasn't a sphere—that was only an illusion created by its angle of approach, which was head on to the *Charles Manson* and closing—but a cylinder. A long, thick cylinder whose snout was blunt, whose rear bulged in a manner suggesting both photon and ion drives, but whose exterior was blank and featureless. While Foord gazed at it the alarms continued to murmur on the Bridge and throughout the ship, but the normal onboard business of the ship was still conducted as quietly and calmly as if they were silent. If anything, more quietly and calmly.

"Good," Foord said eventually. "Joser, your results suggest that it's three times bigger than one of our standard missiles, but seven times heavier. So what's happening inside it?"

"I'm sorry, Commander, the interior's too heavily shrouded."

"But your people are working to penetrate the shroud."

"Yes, Commander."

"And what else can you tell me?"

"The hull is a conventional mixture of alloys and ceramics. It's on ion drive at the moment, but seems also to possess photon drive. Its guidance system is obviously active and self-programming. And She must have launched it at us only a few minutes after we launched our missiles at Her."

"Thank you, but most of that's on the screen. Do you have anything to say about how She kept this hidden from us until now?"

"I'm sorry, Commander."

"He means No," Cyr whispered.

"Cyr, you have about…seven and a half minutes. Particle beams first, then closeup weapons. Kaang, hold us at this position for now. Joser, please turn *off* those alarms."

The *Charles Manson*'s particle beams were dull blue, the colour of bruises. They stabbed out once, in two parallel and almost-solid lines. They reached the object, but what followed was unexpected. It threw up a flickerfield to meet the beams, a shimmering white aura which enveloped it. It lasted only for the nanoseconds of impact and no more—no vessel, even Faith or the *Charles Manson*, could sustain a defensive forcefield for any longer than the bare minimum, the millionths of a second needed to survive—but instead of the inevitable blinding concussion as the beams hit the field and either stabbed through it or were deflected, the field merely assumed their shade of dark blue and sank back into the object. The silence which followed should not have lasted so long.

"Six minutes forty seconds," Joser said. "Still closing. No variation in course or speed."

It was the first recorded appearance of a flickerfield which was energy absorbent and not energy repellent, and it robbed Foord of nearly half his weaponry.

"Cyr?"

"*Her* flickerfields are like ours, Commander, they only *repel* energy. You've seen recordings of Her other engagements."

"I know. So why has that thing got an energy absorbent field?"

"For whatever it's going to do next. Which won't be just to make impact."

"So don't…"

"I know, Commander. Don't use beam weapons."

"But everything else."

"Six minutes ten seconds to impact," Joser said.

He knows it won't be impact, Foord thought, *but he's too sloppy to think of another word.*

"Use everything else, Cyr. *Everything.*"

"Yes, Commander."

"Imagine it's some frightened kid at Blentport."

She glanced at him, but did not reply. She was already sending orders through a nest of command needlemikes which had grown up around her.

"Five minutes fifty seconds to impact." *How*, thought Foord, *did we suddenly get so short of time?*

Without needing any formal confirmation, the ship—having heard the conversation, and exercising its usual discretion—placed its entire resources at Cyr's disposal. As Foord became increasingly polite and punctilious during a crisis, Cyr became increasingly passionless; Foord's last remark, which he was already regretting, had been easy for her to ignore. Under her direction the *Charles Manson* turned the whole of its conventional weapons array on the approaching object, Cyr's curiously flat voice ordering in rapid succession the use of harmonic guns, friendship guns, tanglers, disruptors, plasma clouds, and finally missiles: missiles with conventional explosive warheads, with micronuclear warheads, with bionics-disruptive and hull-corrosive warheads. And one by one, the object's flickerfield met and repelled them, in a series of jarring concussions which the Bridge screen duly filtered out.

"Nothing's reached it so far, Commander," Cyr said. "I can try again, but…"

"Four minutes ten seconds to impact."

"…but its flickerfield was reinforced by what it absorbed from our beams."

"Thank you, Cyr. Discontinue for now, but have closeup weapons ready. We'll resume this at close quarters."

"They're ready now, Commander."

"Thank you. Kaang, when I give the word, take us towards it; ion drive, fifty percent."

"Standing by, Commander."

"But not yet…I think something's happening to it. Joser?"

There was no reply. Foord glanced up.

"Joser?"

"Commander, the object is slowing down."

"Deliberately? Or is it damaged?"

"I think…Commander, I think we may have hit it. I'm getting readings which suggest it may have sustained internal damage. Its drive emissions are…”

“One moment, please. Cyr?”

“None of our weapons reached it, Commander. I don’t think it’s damaged.”

“Neither do I. I think it’s slowing deliberately. But why?”

“Commander,” Joser continued, “it’s almost at rest now. And its drive emissions are clearly…”

“Get us out of here, Kaang! Photon drive, ninety percent, random evasion!” His voice sounded strange. It wouldn’t carry.

“Have you seen the screen, Commander?” Thahl asked.

“Kaang, I said Get us out of here!”

“Out of *where*, Commander? Where are we?”

“The screen, Commander,” Thahl said loudly. His voice sounded strange too. “*Look at the screen.*”

Apart from the object, which was still dead ahead, the Bridge screen was empty. Horus 5 was gone. The stars were gone. The distance between the stars, and the ability to measure it, was gone.

Some of the Bridge instruments sounded failure or overload alarms. Others stopped registering altogether, and fell silent. Elsewhere around the Bridge, needlemikes and navigation computers and scanners and sensors were jabbering impossibilities at each other; ordered to disprove what had happened, they were pouring out proof in stream-of-consciousness torrents. The stars and planets were gone, not merely as electronic images on the main screen or as phosphor-dot smears on computer displays but as solid objects, as sources of gravity and energy and positional reference. They were *gone*.

The size of the universe was the distance between the *Charles Manson* and the now-stationary object facing it.

From outside, a single concussion shook the ship. It was repeated, repeated again, and became a continuous vibration. It was soft and low-register, as discreet as one of the ship’s own alarms, and pitched well below the threshold of actual discomfort; but to the ship, it was more profoundly wrong than the stars’ apparent absence. Very little of what went on outside the *Charles Manson* should ever have been felt inside. The ship tried to define the new situation—it couldn’t fight what it couldn’t define—by telling its sentience cores to analyse what had happened, and they variously shouted, warbled, beeped and murmured back at it their inability to do so. For a moment the Bridge, unthinkably, became deafening, then the ship told them to stop. It was at least able to do that, but not much more. If it had been more sentient it would have defined what it felt as human panic, while the humans and humanoids who inhabited it remained inhumanly calm.

"Presumably," Foord said, "that object has put something like a force-field around us."

"Around us and itself, Commander," Joser said. "It's about ten times more powerful than our flickerfields, and…"

"*Ten* times?"

"…and it's continuous. It's blocking everything from outside—light, gravity, radio waves, X-rays, infrared, ultraviolet… For all I know, the universe could have ended the other side of it."

On the screen, what had been space was now a confined space, a compartment they shared with Her missile, and with nothing else; depthless black and infinitely close. Joser's voice still sounded strange. So did Foord's. So did everybody's. The reason was—

"That vibration, Joser. What is it?"

"Similar to a tractor beam or motive beam, but not powerful enough to damage the hull, or to activate our flickerfields. Very low register. And very localised."

"I see," Foord said slowly, covering for the fact that he didn't, yet. There was something, but it was still unclear.

"What do you mean, *localised*?" Smithson spoke across Foord, completely ignoring him. "Answer carefully. Localised *where*?"

"At the stern, I think."

"Fuck what you think. Localised *where*?"

"At the stern."

"Smithson?…" Foord began.

But Smithson was already roaring orders down several needlemikes at once. He looked round briefly at Foord, snarled "No time. Work it out yourself."

The vibration ceased. There was another concussion from outside. Then it resumed, louder, and this time there was a second noise accompanying it, a noise from *inside* the ship. A noise like the scraping of fingernails down a blackboard. Unless someone actually *was* scraping their finger-nails down a blackboard, there was only one explanation for such a noise.

It came from the stern.

"Of *course*," Foord said. "The MT Drive. That beam is trying to activate our MT Drive." His stomach was knotting and clenching, but he spoke calmly.

Across the Bridge, Smithson started clapping two temporarily unoccu-pied hands together in a heavily sarcastic, and moist, parody of applause.

Foord was irritated. "It's *your* MT Drive," he told Smithson. "She's got Her hand in *your* clothes. Do something."

The noise from the stern got steadily louder.

"I already am," Smithson muttered. He was now no longer merely op-erating his controls but fighting them.

The MT Drive struggled to obey Her tractor beam and activate itself, and those on the Bridge struggled not to think about what would happen if it succeeded. The noise from the stern was still increasing. It penetrated even the needlemike circuitry, distorting voices to rasping bass and over-laying them with static; communication would soon be impossible. It activated the Prayer Wheels (the stasis generators used to contain the MT Drive, so called because they were wheel-shaped, and made things around them stand still) which were essential to the Drive's activation.

A convulsion rolled the length of the ship, as though the burrows and corridors had become a pinball machine with giant ballbearings. Round the Bridge six glasses of inhibitor fluid fell simultaneously to the floor and smashed, were replaced by the chairarm dispensers with six more which also fell to the floor and smashed, and were replaced with six more. Smithson fought back and gradually regained control. The convulsion died away, but it would be the first of many. And from the stern, the noise of the MT Drive's awakening continued unabated.

"Cyr," Foord shouted, in the last few seconds during which he could be sure of being heard, "whatever happens, keep all weapons powered. I think She may fly past us, into the system."

"Commander?"

"I said, Keep all weapons powered. I think She may—"

The second convulsion began. And the the third, and the fourth, rolling up and down the length of the ship until they met and became continuous.

When ships activated their MT Drives inside solar systems—there were only five known cases, all of them years ago—they disappeared without survivors or wreckage; they were never heard of again, even as rumours. The consensus view, which was necessarily tentative since MT had been invented almost by accident, was that they had contracted instantly to mathematically dimensionless points. Every MT Drive was now loaded with inbuilt failsafes to ensure it could never activate if any one of an array of sensors registered planetary or other large bodies anywhere near. Ships' processes and sentience cores deferred to the failsafes because they were infallible, and an equivalent of instinct; but not this time. This time an attack had come disguised perfectly, as a legitimate command, and they were going to obey it.

And when they did, and the MT Drive was activated, She would kill Her forcefield and let the universe and its gravity and radiation come flooding back in, and the *Charles Manson* would go wherever the other five went. *A good weapon to start the engagement,* thought Smithson sourly, as he fought for control. *Like my Breathtaker, imaginative and singular. But better, because it fucking works.*

To the MT Drive, which had no motive other than to function legitimately, everything was at first routine and normal. It awakened in the stern, found itself the recipient of what could only be a legitimate order to activate, and checked and rechecked each of its failsafes to ensure there were no planetary or other large bodies within the stipulated radius; then checked them again. Once these preliminaries were completed, it sent a stream of neural impulses to the ship's other sentience cores (weapons, drives, life support, scanners, communications, damage control, flickerfields) giving them formal notice of its activation and requesting them to prepare appropriately; and then it paused, expecting the usual acknowledgements but receiving none. Smithson had blocked each impulse, negating and countermanding and, where necessary, burning out synapses altogether.

The Drive could never be argued into disbelieving its basic imperatives, and Smithson didn't try to, so at first it was aware of him only as a procedural obstacle; but when he moved from blocking to counterattack, striking through his network of emergency overrides at the core of the

Drive itself, it became aware of him as a set of motives. It considered him, and he it. They came together, touching intimately along their interface, and quietly agreed that they shared nothing except the need to obliterate each other. Then they moved apart and began again, but this time without rules. It was no longer a game of procedural chess, and the *Charles Manson* was no longer their chessboard, but their weapon.

While the alien tractor beam continued to play softly over the stern, feeling for the MT Drive like some molester's fingers fumbling with zips and buttons—and while some parts of the ship, ambiguously, stopped resisting and started opening themselves to it—the *Charles Manson* began to falter. It saw its own physical and mental processes in turmoil, and since those processes were its idea of itself, it became the turmoil. It listened to the Drive telling it to cut life support from the Bridge and destroy Smithson, and to Smithson telling it to isolate and burn out the Drive, and found itself speaking those orders with its own voice while it listened to them.

The interface between Smithson and the Drive was longer than the ship, as bloodvessels when unravelled are longer than a body, and the ship knew that the interface was the scene of a terminal conflict. What remained of its lower-level systems tried to sound damage control and life support alarms, but with no more force than the reflex not to die of something dying. Smithson and the MT Drive swept through it like two infections, destroying it only as a by-product of their attempts to destroy each other, and that was the last thing the ship realised before they swamped it and its consciousness ended; that, and the fact that if it ever existed again, it would only be as *one* of them and not as both.

The object She had sent became suddenly inert on all wavelengths. The tractor beam fell away. The convulsions faded. The MT Drive shut down. Horus 5 and the starfield returned to the Bridge screen. Smithson had succeeded, and Foord opened his mouth to breathe again, but

"Commander," Joser said. "She's coming for us. Position 08-07-08 and closing rapidly."

Time started moving again, rushing back into the ship like thoughts after a coma. Foord could actually *hear* the seconds rushing back: they blew through the corridors and burrows, at first slowly then faster. The next phase of the engagement was already growing out of the body of the last.

"I'm handing back what's left of your ship, Commander," Smithson said. Foord had never heard him sound tired before. "Most of the damage will be within the capacity of the self-repair systems, but not the MT Drive. That, you can forget. You'll never be able to use it again."

"Position 07-04-08, and closing rapidly."

"Smithson…"

"I know, I know. Time. I'd finished, anyway."

Time. Blowing cold through the corridors. Smithson had saved the ship, but it had also partly died. It had lost one of its sentience cores and one of its drives; it was now a ship for which time could run out, like it ran out for other, ordinary, ships.

"Commander! She's 06-03-06 and closing."

"Yes. How much time?"

"Ninety seconds, if…"

"Thahl, Cyr, feed the closeup weapons and ignore everything else—scanners, life support , drives, everything."

He turned to face the forward section of the Bridge screen. Nothing was visible, yet. But it wouldn't be. She was shrouded.

"Fifty seconds, Commander."

"No, Joser. No more countdowns. Hit the alarms when there's twenty seconds to go. That's all."

She continued to approach at high speed, but was still below the horizon of Horus 5. The screen continued to show Horus 5, but no simulation of Her approach; the scanners were operating at less than twenty percent capacity, and by the time they generated any simulations, She would be on top of them. The *Charles Manson* continued to bleed off what remained of its resources to feed its closeup weapons. It had done well. It had already grown them carefully back to near-optimum, like a crippled animal growing a perfect set of claws for its final defence.

The alarms started murmuring.

Foord heard himself thinking *No. This isn't what She wants. We must do what She wants.*

"Cyr, cancel my orders! Stand down all closeup weapons."

"Commander?"

"Thahl, stand down everything except the Bridge screen. Leave us inert. No drives, life support, scanners…" When Thahl looked up inquiringly,

Foord snapped "Binary Gate. Work it out yourself. Cyr, cancel closeup weapons, now! I mean it!"

A roaring swamped the Bridge and something rose over the horizon of Horus 5.

It was a patch of empty space. Just like the empty space around it, but something was wrong. This was like a patch of empty space from another day, or seen from another angle, and it came towards them

paused, and *glanced* at them

and rushed past. Foord swore as the forward screen erupted with light and a deep violet afterimage settled across his eyes like a piece of hot iron, and when his sight returned the screen was still shuffling filters and the *Charles Manson* was left bobbing in the wake of whatever had passed.

The inert missile had been allowed to lay close by the *Charles Manson* ever since Smithson disabled the MT Drive; there was neither the time nor the resources to destroy it. As She came over the horizon, it quietly disappeared, collapsing itself down to nothing.

She was gone, too. Past them, and into Horus system.

There were several distinct kinds of silence. Joser's was one of inadequacy, Kaang's of puzzlement, Thahl's of no comment, Cyr's of accusation (You said She'd go closeup, Commander. You *said*.) and Smithson's, of something unspoken but obscene. Put together, they made an ugly shape in the dark air of the Bridge.

Foord laughed, softly and knowingly. At least, that was what he intended. The sound he actually made was high-pitched and uneasy, which surprised him because he felt less uneasy now. He was beginning to understand Her, though only in minor things, and only in penny pieces.

"It's alright," he said; then, catching sight of the glances around the Bridge, he went on quickly "I mean it, it's alright. This part is over, that's all... Joser."

"Commander?"

"Would you please confirm something for me? She should have started to slow down by now."

"Slow down? But She's just got past us and into the system! She'll be heading for Sakhra!"

"Your scanners won't have enough power to put an exact value on it," Foord continued, as if Joser had said nothing, "but there should be a perceptible slowing."

More glances around the Bridge.

"We must go after Her," Smithson said. "I need to start damage repairs now."

"Commander," Joser said suddenly, "You were right. It doesn't make any apparent sense, but She is decelerating."

"And," Foord resumed, "She'll continue to decelerate. I expect Her to switch down from photon to ion drive within the next minute; though there's no need for a countdown, thank you, Joser."

He gazed around the Bridge. One by one, they fell silent.

"She isn't going to Sakhra, not yet. She knows we can't follow until we've made repairs. She knows this will be fought all the way back to Sakhra, so She'll wait for us. When we're ready we'll find Her there, in the Belt, waiting. Now.... Thahl, please cancel battle stations, and go back to secondary alert. Smithson, how long will a full damage repair operation take?"

"Four hours if we hurry, Commander."

"Take five, and don't hurry."

"You realise the MT Drive is permanently down until we make port again?" He hesitated on Until; Foord knew he had been about to say Unless.

"Yes, I realise that."

"And you're serious about not hurrying?"

"Yes. Five hours, six hours, She'll wait."

"Commander," Joser said, "She's just switched down from photon to ion drive. Still decelerating, and heading into the Belt."

"Good.... Smithson, we owe you." He left a short pause, so Smithson could play out his usual game.

"You should have seen it earlier, Commander, what She was doing. I can't always be the first to see things."

"I did see it, eventually."

"Eventually."

"Tell me, do you think that inside Her there was someone like me who asked someone like you to think up something like your Breathtaker? Something unusual, to mark the start of the engagement?"

"You'd better hope not, Commander. Because if there was, Her version worked."

"It didn't, because you saw it in time and disabled it. Perhaps it was like ours. Not made to succeed, just to make us wonder."

"You're wrong, Commander, and you're self-indulgent. Ours got snuffed out, and we don't even know how. Hers started working, and we only just stopped it. Don't have any illusions about what happened here. It was a near disaster."

The alarms stopped murmuring. Red telltales disappeared one by one from the consoles, impact harnesses retracted, and the Bridge lighting increased from near-darkness to its more customary twilight. Thahl, Smithson and the others began implementing damage repair operations. Muted conversations between the Bridge and other parts of the ship restarted, like conversations at a restaurant after an altercation.

"Commander," Smithson said, "how did you know She wouldn't attack ?"

This time, when Foord laughed, it came out precisely as he intended.

"Because we were defenceless."

"You gambled that She wouldn't attack if we *made* ourselves defenceless."

"Yes. She even glanced at us, to make sure. Did you see?"

"You gambled *the ship* that She wouldn't..."

"Undefended civilian targets, She doesn't attack. Undefended warships, who *make* themselves undefended? Yes, I gambled. Work out the odds for yourself. But only for the next five hours or so. Then we go after Her."

●

Four hours fifty-one minutes later, Thahl announced completion of damage repairs. Foord immediately insisted on a further series of external working parties to check the hull's integrity, even though the original repairs included external working parties, and even though the hull's sensors confirmed no breach of integrity. He also requested a further systems overhaul to ensure the MT Drive was irrevocably dead and could never, as Smithson said, be reactivated. These operations took a further eighty minutes before they were completed to Foord's satisfaction. Almost completely restored, he told himself; except, of course, that one of its nine sentience cores, the one controlling the MT Drive, was dead. Along with the Drive itself.

He spoke to the ship's Codex, the agregation of its sentience cores, to verify that it understood. It told him it did, that nine were now eight, that one was amputated, and the eight would go on without it.

Status reports were taken, battle stations resumed, and the *Charles Manson* moved off for the Belt at an unhurried thirty percent ion speed. It arrived without incident and found Her waiting—waiting almost politely, just as Foord had expected—and the second phase of the engagement began.

PART SIX

1

The weapons core instructed the computers which served it to configure themselves to Attack, SemiManual. A warning harmonic warbled politely through the Bridge. Headup displays and target simulations were superimposed on the Bridge screen.

Cyr sighed; she had been grooming her nails. She rested her right hand palm down on a panel, and pressed. The *Charles Manson*'s particle beams lanced out. Target Destroyed, said the headup display redly; it was referring to AN-4044, a minor asteroid near the outer rim of the Belt, scarcely larger than a small city and only just large enough to merit a classification number. Faith had been using it as cover for the last five minutes, which was all the weapons core had instructions to allow. Now it was vaporised, neatly and hygienically, by the beams; reduced to almost nothing. She was running again, and the Bridge screen simulation depicted Her movements. She was too distant for a visual, and in any case was still shrouded. It did not matter. Shrouding could not hide Her drive emissions, despite Her occasional half-hearted attempts to disguise them.

Kaang now joined in. Her instructions, like Cyr's, had been pared down by repetition to an unfailing routine. The manoeuvre jets fountained and the ion drive played up and down the register as she made the *Charles Manson* parallel exactly Faith's ducking and weaving. The *Charles Manson*'s particle beams had superior range, and Kaang kept Her always at an exact distance.

For six hours they had bombarded Her monotonously through the Belt. It seemed like six days. She had not succeeded in hitting back, though the constant use of Her flickerfields would be draining Her more than the constant beam-firings were draining the *Charles Manson*. Her counterattacks had been irregular, and were dwindling.

Cyr fired the beams again. Target Reached, said the screen headup. The weapons core predicted where She would go for cover, ignoring the evasive manoeuvres, and aimed the beams accordingly. As usual, the prediction was correct, and as usual Her flickerfields held; just. She made cover again, a small unclassified asteroid this time, and the weapons core started counting off another five minutes. The headup display dimmed. Kaang brought the ship to rest, still exactly at maximum beam range, and Cyr resumed grooming her nails. It was not a theatrical gesture; there was little else to do. Their tactics had been successful, but grindingly repetitive.

Most asteroid belts were sparse and meagre, but this one was huge, and it teemed. Horus 4 had created it by destroying two, maybe three, giant planets, leaving the Belt crowded with surrealist shapes and quivering with gravity. Its outer rim areas, where they were stalking Her, consisted mainly of smaller and more irregular asteroids, hanging in space at contradictory angles, like rock formations growing out of nothing. Parallax made some of them look so close they were about to collide. Gravity in the Belt was a latticework of forces, near and distant, small and large. The asteroids exerted it on each other, and had it exerted on them by Horus 4 and Horus 5 and the sun Horus. They moved in whole or partial orbits, balancing and counterbalancing each other like one of Foord's brass clockwork mechanisms.

Smaller asteroids crowded the rim areas of the Belt. Larger asteroids, the largest as big as small planets, crowded the middle. There were so many asteroids that only those about the size of a city, or larger, had classification numbers. Even then, there were hundreds of thousands; and ten times as many unclassified.

Five minutes later the weapons core instructed the computers which

served it to configure themselves to Attack, SemiManual. A warning harmonic warbled politely through the Bridge. Headup displays and target
simulations were superimposed on the Bridge screen. Cyr fired once (Target Destroyed) and twice more (Target Reached) as She started running
and Kaang parallelled Her movements. Cyr was about to resume grooming her nails, but this time there was a slight break in the usual pattern.
The warning harmonic sounded again, louder.

"Counterattack coming," Joser said. "She's charging down our throats,
like She did with the *Cromwell*."

"That's the second time in two hours," Cyr said, with a trace of irritation.

But it was now only a matter of standard procedure. It was dealt with
routinely, as on the previous occasion; Foord's preparations included an
array of counters to the Cromwell Manoeuvre. By the time Cyr finished
complaining, it was over. The *Charles Manson*'s weapons had refocussed on
Her without difficulty as She rushed towards them; Kaang had matched
Her course and speed, but in reverse, to maintain beam range; She had
slowed, realising the manoeuvre was compromised, and Cyr had beaten
Her off with a succession of beam-firings. Her flickerfields held and She
retreated deeper into the Belt, to find fresh cover. Kaang moved them
slowly forward, maintaining range. The weapons core started counting
another five minutes.

"I wonder," Kaang said, to nobody in particular, "why Her fields aren't
energy absorbent, like those on that missile?"

"The missile was unmanned," Joser said. "Maybe energy-absorbent
fields are harmful to living things."

"Are you assuming," Cyr asked, "that there are living things on that
ship?"

"Are *you* assuming," Smithson asked, "that it's a ship?"

"I hardly think," Foord murmured, "we have time for metaphysics."

"Yes we do, Commander," Cyr said. "If it goes on like this, we do. I'll
start on my toenails next."

Almost unnoticed, one of the ship's other sentience cores updated the
navigation files by deleting various numbered asteroids from the Belt. It
was a thoughtful and necessary exercise; the *Charles Manson* had already
rewritten the map of a substantial part of the Belt's outer rim, and would
probably continue to do so. Proper and accurate records had to be kept.

Five minutes later the weapons core instructed the computers which served it to configure themselves to Attack, SemiManual. A warning harmonic warbled politely through the Bridge. Headup displays and target simulations were superimposed on the Bridge screen. Her cover was AL-4091, a mid-sized asteroid whose destruction took two beam-firings. She broke and ran, again deeper into the Belt, and Cyr reached Her with four shots before She found cover. Kaang took the *Charles Manson* forward sufficiently to maintain beam range.

The second phase of the engagement had now lasted six and a half hours. Foord called a short break for status reports; they were duly made and he duly listened, though they revealed nothing more than the quietly satisfactory situation of which he was already well aware.

"Thank you," he murmured. "No further orders."

He nodded to Cyr, and the weapons core started counting another five minutes. Allowing for the taking of status reports, it was eight minutes elapsed time when the core instructed the computers which served it to configure themselves to Attack, SemiManual. The break in the rhythm was noticeable, like a delayed heartbeat, but the iterative cycle easily reimposed its pattern. The warning harmonic warbled politely, and the headup displays and target simulations reappeared on the Bridge screen. Her cover was AK-5004, another mid-sized asteroid whose destruction took two firings. She broke and ran, still going deeper, and Cyr reached Her with five shots before She found fresh cover. Kaang parallelled Her movements, maintained beam range, and brought them to rest again. Another five-minute count began.

"Cyr."

"Commander?"

"If we were Her, how much more of this could we take before the use of our flickerfields started to drain us?"

"Fifty hours before actual danger, but noticeable impairment after thirty."

"Smithson, can we assume..."

"If She's a ship like us, and not something else, Her flickerfields are likely to drain Her at a similar rate. Say impairment after thirty hours. But we'll bore Her to death in ten."

And that, thought Foord comfortably, would be just as acceptable. He had entered the second phase strangely unaffected by the near-disaster of the first, yet he entered it with the most ordinary and commonplace of strategies: careful, dogged, monotonous, unvarying attrition. After nearly seven hours the advantage it yielded was still only slight; but it was measurable, like a pile of shopkeeper's pennies. And it was growing, in penny pieces. There had been no *sudden* realisation that they were the first opponents ever to gain any advantage over Her; like the advantage itself, the realisation came gradually and without drama.

Ironically, the institutional processes to which Foord had been subjected, the learning of conventional methods before being allowed unconventional ones, had often been useful to him. At Horus 5, he had wanted to open with a flourish of the unexpected. In the Belt, he had decided to open with conventional, mind-numbing routine. A free-form battle in the Belt would have played to Her advantages, whereas this monotonous attrition played to one of his—the superior range of their particle beams. And it was working. Even if Her flickerfields didn't drain Her, She still couldn't break out of the stalking pattern they had locked on Her; and if they did drain Her, and the pattern could be held for long enough, She would be impaired, perhaps fatally.

"Communication, Commander," Thahl said.

"I thought I told you we're accepting no…"

"I think you should accept this one, Commander."

Thahl pointed at the antiquated microphone which stood incongruously on Foord's console. Its red Incoming light was glowing. Such microphones were the Department's standard means of communication. They were voice only—the Department did not do visuals—and carried a dedicated MT channel from Earth; they were not as antiquated as they looked.

"Department of Administrative Affairs to Foord, *Charles Manson*. Acknowledge, please."

Foord saw Joser stiffen; then irritated himself by wondering, Did I see it because I was looking for it?

"This is Foord. Identify yourself, please."

"Clerical Officer Lok, Office of Miscellaneous Vehicles, Department of Administrative Affairs. The Department is sorry to trouble you, Commander; this is a routine procedural matter only. If it's not convenient…"

"Hold for validations, please."

Foord glanced at Thahl and Joser, who began checking—Thahl for the source of the signal, Joser for its distinctive embedded signature and its voice pattern. These were three of the validations: the fourth was vocabulary and forms of address.

So far, the fourth appeared to check. In the unlanguage in which the Commonwealth clothed its private parts, the Department dealt with many Affairs, none of them Administrative; it never felt sorrow, or anything else, for those it troubled; the Office of Miscellaneous Vehicles was the Department's Outsider section; Clerical Officers had more power than generals; and routine procedural matters, were not.

"Commander," Lok said, "I have a message from the Department. Will you hurry the validations, please?"

"Joser? Thahl?"

"I'm rechecking the voice analysis, Commander," Joser said.

"*Re*checking?"

"It doesn't completely match Lok's pattern."

"Commander, it's a fake!" Thahl said. "It's from Her."

"Cyr, fire before She breaks cover!"

Cyr, swearing loudly, was already doing so. She overrode the five-minute count. A warning harmonic warbled politely through the Bridge. Headup displays and target simulations were superimposed on the Bridge screen, but...

"Too late, Commander, She's gone. Out of range. Heading into the Belt on ion drive, high acceleration."

Foord swore, more softly and less obscenely than Cyr, then subsided. It had only taken Her a second to divert them, but now She might as well have been hours gone.

"Commander," Kaang said, "I can get Her back in range if we move now."

"No, not this time. There's no need."

"I'm sorry, Commander....*No Need?*"

Foord glanced at her, surprised. Kaang never questioned tactics; part of their understanding was that she was *only* a pilot.

"She isn't running, Kaang, so we don't need to catch Her. She'll wait."

"Commander," Cyr said, "with respect, I think you should reconsider."

"What's Her speed and course, Joser?"

"It's on the screen, Commander. She's going into the Belt at sixty percent, but the speed's dropping."

"Take us forward on Her course, please, Kaang. *Thirty* percent." He turned to Cyr. "You're right, we can't just sit here. But we won't have to chase Her. Now She's out of range, She'll wait."

Like Foord, the Bridge swore softly to itself and subsided.

Kaang quietly engaged ion drive and took them deeper into the Belt. Foord turned an icy gaze on the microphone, whose Incoming light still glowed.

"You can go now" he told it.

There was no reply. The light stayed on.

"I said, You can go now. You aren't real."

"Neither are you. Neither is the Department. Neither is the Commonwealth."

2

Both ships possessed a similar array of drives, and a similar performance in each of them. When they entered the Belt, Kaang had cleverly feinted and doublebluffed Her into range of their beams, but that wasn't going to happen again. In fact, quite the opposite: the second part of their engagement in the Belt was a reversal of the first.

For ninety minutes, She danced in front of them exactly beyond the reach of their beams, countering even the attempts of Kaang to get Her back in range. She did sideslices and curlicues, rolls and tumbles and even the occasional somersault; She hopped behind asteroids which were just outside beam range, breaking out and running for cover just before they came within range. They still couldn't see Her—She hadn't yet decided it was time to unshroud—but they tracked Her path, including the dancing manoeuvres, easily enough through Her drive emissions, as of course She wanted them to. It was deadpan and sly, like a Sakhran might mock a human.

"Bring us to rest, please, Kaang," Foord said, ninety minutes later. He gazed around the Bridge. "If *Kaang* can't get Her back in range, we need something else."

Kaang carefully refrained from comment, as did Thahl, but the silence of the others was more pointed. He repeated wearily *She'll wait, She's not running, we don't have to chase Her.* He knew that for certain; one by one, he was adding pieces to the huge clockwork he had designed to engage Her. But he was still shivering from what She had done, how She'd faked a Department call but hadn't even bothered, apparently, to fake it properly. What if She decided next time to fake it properly?

He needed time, to see if they were affected as badly as he was. To draw out their reactions. But his first attempt was ill-judged.

"She *spoke* to us in that call," he said. "She's never spoken before."

"She didn't speak," Joser said. "It wasn't Her voice. It was a fake, and not even a very good one."

"It was good enough," Smithson said sourly.

Foord tried again.

"She spoke," he insisted. "She said we aren't real."

"Why didn't She fake it better?" Joser was almost plaintive.

"It was good enough," Smithson repeated. "It got Her out of range."

"She should have faked it better."

"Perhaps," Cyr said to Joser, spitefully, "it really *was* the Department."

"But the voice patterns and signature…"

"They could have been testing you. They're at least as clever as She is."

"It said we aren't real."

"Then it must have been the Department. Call them back."

Good, thought Foord. Smithson and Cyr seem unimpaired. Kaang doesn't count, not in this. Joser is suspect, but always was. So that leaves

"Thahl," he said. "This was the first time anyone's got an advantage over Her, and it disappeared because She distracted us…"

"Yes, Commander."

"…but maybe She *let* us get an advantage, so She could show us how easily She could make it disappear."

Thahl looked up sharply at him. "Do you really believe that, Commander?"

"Of course not!" he said, a little too loudly.

There was a silence. Feeling a need to fill it, Foord rushed on.

"Thahl, how did She know the vocabulary and forms of address? Is She able to monitor the Department's MT channel to us? Because if She is..."

"No, Commander, it's more likely She monitored the Department's calls to Director Swann. Sakhra's a communications beacon at the moment. We could probably monitor it ourselves."

"Yes, that must be it."

"I said More Likely, Commander. We can't be certain."

Foord didn't reply. *Is he*, thought Thahl, *waiting for me to make a suggestion, or is he faking? He can be irritating, sometimes.*

"Commander, you already decided to kill normal communications. I suggest you kill the Department's MT channel. It's as useless as the MT Drive, and for the same reason: *She* got into it."

"If we kill that channel, we're alone. And another part of us goes down."

"You wanted to be alone when we faced Her. You insisted on it. And as for another part going down..."

As for another part going down, Foord completed what Thahl did not need to say, this is an Outsider. Each of its parts, and each of *us*, has no perception of needing each other. A Sakhran would know that better than anyone. We can go through each phase of this engagement having limbs lopped off one by one, and still the mouth will bite.

"Yes, you're right," Foord said eventually. "Kill the Department's channel."

Thahl and Foord briefly made eye contact across the Bridge. Foord was thinking *I'm not only unsure how much he's faking, I'm unsure how much I'm faking.* Thahl was thinking the same thing.

"Joser, what's Her situation?"

"Still heading into the Belt, Commander. Forty percent ion speed and dropping. Position 12-16-14."

Foord was silent for a minute. Then he smiled.

"Take us *back* out of the Belt, please, Kaang."

"Commander?"

"Back the way we came. Ion drive, five percent." He looked round the Bridge. "Yes, I know. But I want to see what She does about it."

He looked across at Thahl and mouthed, *Nothing is simple.*

Foord and Thahl were perhaps the only two people on the *Charles Manson* who shared anything like trust, but just then they were both unsure.

Thahl looked back across the Bridge at Foord and mouthed, *Nothing is real.*

The manoeuvre drives fountained. Kaang turned the ship in its own length and commenced a slow, elegant departure towards the rim of the Belt, back in the direction of Horus 5.

A few minutes passed.

"She's still moving into the Belt, Commander," Joser said. "Position 14-17-15. But She's slowing. Like you said," he added, hopefully.

"Not quite like I said. I'd have expected Her to stop by now. I wonder if we should increase speed? No, let's not over-embellish..."

Another few minutes passed. The asteroids grew perceptibly smaller and sparser, but the *Charles Manson* still picked its way through them with the same unhurried delicacy. At only five percent, it would be a long time before they left the Belt; not that they expected to.

"She's cut Her drives at last, Commander," Joser said eventually. "But She's at rest, not following."

"Joser, watch Her position," Foord said. "I think She's going to..."

Foord studied the white dot on the screen showing Her current position. Still just out of range, of course. It wasn't that She'd stopped—She didn't need to stop in order to launch weapons—but he had a feeling this would be something unusual.

"Commander, She's launched something. It's not shrouded. I'll have a visual soon."

●

It was a cone-shaped object, tumbling towards them end over end; about thirty feet long by twenty feet wide at its base, said the Bridge screen. It offered no resistance to probes, and the probes showed it to be quite empty. It was not travelling under power (though outlets at its base indicated pulse motors) and there were no guidance or homing signals, so the screen concluded it must be on a preset course. As if to confirm this, it fired its motors briefly on-off to avoid a cloud of asteroid debris, then resumed its course towards them.

And, although the screen did not add any comment about this feature, its colour was pink; bright, nursery pink.

Comical and conical, Foord thought; *still pisstaking*.

"Stay at rest for now, please," he said. "Joser, the screen says there are no guidance signals."

"That's right, Commander: no guidance or homing signals. And ETA is ninety-nine seconds."

"So no guidance, and apparently—if we believe the probes—nothing inside it. So what's it there for? What's it mean?"

A section of the Bridge screen became locally magnified. The usual series of schematics was generated, unasked, by the screen: ventral, dorsal, side, front and rear. They added nothing not already visible.

"Cyr: lasers, please. I want to see inside it."

A single laser stabbed out, one of the ship's shortrange crystal lasers. It hit, and a section of the cone sheared off. Inside was as pink as outside; it really *did* seem empty. It still came on, tumbling end over end, but now more erratically.

"ETA fifty-nine seconds, Commander."

"Again, please, Cyr."

Two more shots, two more bits sliced off the cone, two more views of an apparently empty and featureless interior.

Still plenty of time, Foord thought, *to destroy it*. So what's it going to do to confound us at the last moment? He told Kaang to move them to port a few hundred feet and bring them to rest, which she did. The cone fired its motors, on-off, as it had done to avoid the cloud of debris, changing course so it still came at them, still tumbling end over end.

"ETA forty-five seconds, Commander."

"Cyr, finish it, please. Lasers."

If anything's going to happen it will be now, thought Foord. But it didn't. The cone exploded, not very spectacularly, and was reduced to pink dust which drifted away to add itself to the map of the Belt which Foord had been so assiduously rewriting.

Foord took a sip of inhibitor fluid—the tumbler had remained undisturbed on his chairarm during the recent flurry of activity—and settled back in his chair. He let out a long breath.

"Joser, what's Her position, please?"

"Unchanged and stationary, Commander."

"Good... So what did She mean with that missile?"

"Mean?"

"Yes. It was slow, empty, had no shrouding and no flickerfields, was coloured pink, and looked silly. Right?"

"Yes, Commander."

"And apart from the two occasions it fired its motors it wasn't travelling under active power. Right?"

"Yes, Commander."

"Yet it changed course when we did. Which means, doesn't it, that it either had an active homing system or was receiving guidance signals from Her."

"There were no homing or guidance signals, Commander!"

"You mean you failed to detect them." Foord did not say it unkindly, or accusingly. "Come on, this is the area She has most advantage over us. I just need to know how *much* advantage. I need to see how we failed to detect them."

"Detecting no homing or guidance signals is not the same as failing to detect them, Commander. I didn't fail to detect them. There were no signals."

"That's a clever answer," Foord replied, "but not a helpful one."

"Commander," Thahl said quietly, "you asked what She *meant* by that missile."

"Well?"

"It seems to have been empty. So, suppose it really *didn't* have an on-board homing system, and suppose it really *wasn't* able to receive guidance signals."

"Well?"

"Then its movements must have been preset by Her when She launched it. Including the move to follow our last-minute turn to port. She preset that move when She launched it. Before you gave the order to turn."

3

The *Charles Manson* was partly alive, but not alive enough to know that it could die. Its partial life made it serene and invincible; it knew that as long as the parts which made up its whole continued not to need each other, the whole could not be destroyed. It understood that when Foord, of all people, broke down it would probably not be noisy or sudden; with Foord it was more likely to be a careful, phased collapse. So it waited for the expected confirmation. It would then simply continue, minus the discarded part.

The ship had noted his increasingly unusual behaviour, the speech patterns and vocal nuances and repeated unanswered questions. It had prepared for his replacement by Thahl, or (if there were further contingencies) by Cyr or Smithson; Joser and Kaang were not on its list. It had noted that Thahl would normally be next, but had detected minor aberrations in him, too. It made no judgements—it wasn't able to—but only calculated contingencies. The contingencies were programmed into the computers which served its sentience cores which, when they came together, were its Codex.

But Foord did not break down. His reaction, when it came, was perhaps worse.

"What is She, Thahl?" he kept asking; the one question he always said he wouldn't ask. "What is She? How can She reach into our MT Drive and our communications and our thoughts before we think them? *How is it She already knows us?*" Eventually he stopped asking and fell silent, and then his reaction became clear: not breakdown, but withdrawal. He turned inwards, back to the time when the darkness came.

●

"Welcome to Morning Assembly, and a particular welcome to those joining us for the first time." Aaron Foord was one of these, and he looked round in bewilderment. Dust motes circled in the sunbeams which slanted down into the Assembly Hall. The Principal's voice echoed. "We know this must be a confusing time for you. We'll do all we can to end your confusion. To put right the events which brought you here to us. You'll find us a close community, but you'll find we particularly value new friends. We value the challenge you will give us. We look forward to making you part of something bigger than yourselves. You'll find a community here which will seem like it's been waiting just for you. You'll have experiences here which will last all your lives."

Twenty-five years ago, when Aaron Foord was twelve, his mother was diagnosed. She died within six months, and his father, after nursing her and becoming infected, within a further six weeks. He had no other relatives still living, so he went to a State Orphanage. He went because he was literally an orphan, though the term Orphanage was also figurative: it was a place for those Orphaned from the State, which considered itself their true parent. In other words, a centre for the treatment of young criminal and political offenders. The handful of genuine orphans who also went there did not usually survive unaffected.

It was not a stereotypical institution, at least in appearance: there was no forbidding architecture, only a collection of bland functional buildings with curtains and walls and furniture in beige and orange and brown. It was reasonably clean, and not immediately threatening. Aaron Foord noticed, with a sense of novelty, that things like teapots and saucepans and cooking vessels were all industrial size. All the things he had been used to doing alone, or as one of a family of three—eating, sleeping, going to the bathroom, reading and working and playing—he now did among dozens, or hundreds.

His parents had stayed together through his childhood. He couldn't define or recognise love, either then or later, but he noted carefully the details of their companionship, their ease with each other. He remembered summers on beaches, the murmur of voices. He always liked voices murmured and nuanced, and would try later to recreate them on his ship. His mother and father had given him a solitary childhood, but not an unhappy one. They were quiet and orderly people, and he grew up liking quietness and order.

He knew the Morning Assembly welcome was ambiguous. He knew there were unspoken words behind the spoken ones, and soon found out what they were: corporatist psychobabble. No room for optouts. No room for outsiders. You're Us or the Enemy. Community, Greater Good, One Of Us, There Is No I In Team. Most heavy gravity planets supplied Special Forces and mercenaries to other parts of the Commonwealth, and their societies were corporatist and authoritarian. Aaron Foord's planet was no exception.

The orphanage was run by State officials, some of whom were civilians and some, to his surprise, priests. The priests had a particular way about them. They had open regular faces and smiled a lot. They didn't walk but strolled. They didn't shout but spoke quietly, something he found likeable until he started listening to them. They punctuated their speech with swingings of their rulers, those instruments of love and certainty;

three feet long and made of dark heavy hardwood and even marked with calibrations, though he never once saw them used as instruments of measurement. Some of the priests, he learned, liked beating girls, some of them boys, and some of them both. Some did it out of simple cruelty, some out of complex cruelty. Others, the worst, did it out of genuine love.

The girls wore uniforms with box-pleated skirts. He had raped one of them, the last one he should ever have forced, the one who had shown him how to make places where the priests couldn't reach. She was a year younger than him, and came a year later. Her name was Katy Bevan.

"Welcome to Morning Assembly, and a particular welcome to those joining us for the first time." Aaron Foord noticed her among the newcomers. The others were bewildered or afraid or defiant, but not her; she was different. Dust motes circled in the sunbeams which slanted down into the Assembly Hall. The Principal's voice echoed. "We know this must be a confusing time for you. We'll do all we can to end your confusion. To put right the events which brought you here to us. You'll find us a close community, but you'll find we particularly value new friends. We value the challenge you will give us. We look forward to making you part of something bigger than yourselves. You'll find a community here which will seem like it's been waiting just for you. You'll have experiences here which will last all your lives."

Afterwards, he went up to her.

"Where is it?"

"Where is what?" She was unusually small and slight; blonde, with sharp features. She had a way of looking askance, as if smiling privately.

"The place you go to escape them when they're talking."

"Oh, *that*. It's in my head." She glanced at him. "You're the first one who's seen. I'll show you how to do it."

She called it Subvocal Subversion. *Where did she get that from*, he thought, *at twelve? Politically deviant parents?* She never told him why she'd been sent there and he never asked. "You create a space where they can't reach you, and the way you do it is by simple subvocal denial of everything they say. Even if the denials are contradictory. Actually it's better if the denials *are* contradictory, because it means that what they say is too. And follow their grammar, so the denials are grammatical. But think it, don't say it, and don't ever ever write it. Then it stays where they can't reach. It won't make their institutions collapse, but it'll give you a place they can't reach. Everybody needs that."

They did it together in Assembly, stealing glances at each other.

"Welcome to Morning Assembly, and a particular welcome to those joining us for the first time. We know *(No you don't)* this must be a confusing time for you. We'll do all we can *(No you won't)* to end your confusion. To put right the events which brought you here to us. You'll find us a close community *(No we won't)*, but you'll find we particularly value new friends...."

It was a small private act of rebellion, invented by a small private person. She did it when they were beating her, and *telling* her why they were beating her; and he adopted it when they were beating him. It worked, because it existed only as thought. But it was small and silent and private, and what the priests taught was large and loud and public, and supremely confident of its ability to prevail. They heard its confidence echoing in the Principal's voice at every Assembly. Even the dust motes were scared.

"This community we share has a mighty strength. It will not be denied. It embraces all of us and each of us, and it will not be denied. It demands to make us greater than we are, and it will not be denied. Compared to it, we are almost nothing. Like pebbles before a mountain. Like the *atoms* in pebbles before a mountain. Almost nothing. My reading this morning is from Job, chapter 9.

He is wise in heart, and mighty in strength.

He removeth the mountains, and they know not: He overturneth them in His anger.

He shaketh the earth out of her place, and the pillars thereof tremble.

He commandeth the sun, and it riseth not: and sealeth up the stars..."

But the Subvocal Subversion still worked for Katy Bevan and, increasingly, for Aaron Foord. It was small and private, like Katy, and perhaps that was why. Reach outwards, the priests said, become part of something bigger than you. No, she said, turn inwards. Build a private space where they can't reach you. Then another and another. Add them together and make a universe. It'll last you the rest of your life.

And it did. The more they thrashed him, the vaster the private spaces he created. He always carried his private universe, then and for the rest of his life. Apart from Katy Bevan, he made few friendships. To the others around him he was always an outsider, indifferent to their shifting cliques. They learnt to leave him alone, because of his physical prowess and his strangeness.

But don't *always* turn away, she said, on another occasion. I didn't, from you. I had to reach *out* to you to make you turn *inwards*. She laughed and said, That's ironic. He laughed too, then quietly consulted a dictionary. He didn't completely understand the word then, but would later.

Two years passed. Puberty came late to him, because of his circumstances. But when it came, it mated with his obsessiveness and created a monster. He started looking at the box-pleated skirts. He liked their swing and sway, and the shape and regularity and tidiness of the pleats: inviolate, and symmetrical. He longed for them with the same fastidiousness and thoroughness which he carried into adulthood. He longed to lift them and see what was underneath. To lift them slowly and carefully, without resistance. When Katy Bevan resisted him, it all became untidy and his hands became more urgent and afterwards he couldn't meet her gaze and he went away from her.

She refused to tell the Principal who raped her. That was a more serious crime than the rape itself, because she was deliberately putting herself beyond the community, denying the community its *absolute right* to help one of its own, and they thrashed her. When Aaron Foord burst into the Principal's study there were five of them, each one about three times her size, five massive adults thrashing a small private person who'd made a small private act of rebellion. She was bent over a desk (the second time he'd seen what was underneath her skirt) while two held her down and the other three thrashed her with their rulers, even taking turns and deferring to each other, You next, No you next. What, he screamed, do you believe in which makes *this* right? This is what we believe in, they said, that we love her so much we'd even do *this* for her, and he knew they meant it. He was one fifteen-year-old against five adults but he discovered instincts he would keep for the rest of his life (the Principal was right about that) and he killed two of them with his hands, wishing he could find a Sakhran who might teach him how to kill more of them, more efficiently.

Days later, the Department heard of it and called for his psychological and physical and academic records, which they studied. Then they recruited him.

Years later, Katy Bevan became Director of State Orphanages, kicked out the priests, and gradually made things better; not perfect, but better. The priests were still embedded in other State institutions, but she stopped them sniffing around the classrooms and playgrounds of the orphanages. By then Foord had at last met a Sakhran and knew more about the meaning of Irony, so he was able to ask himself, Which of us has made the most of our years? Which of us has been the most use? He never asked questions to which he didn't know the answer.

Also years later, he had learnt enough to know that the Commonwealth was not an Evil Empire. Most of it was not corporatist or authoritarian; in twenty-nine solar systems, planets like his were a small minority. The Commonwealth was not the same as the Department, either; it sometimes needed the Department to do certain questionable but necessary things, that was all. He added all that to his private universe, under Nothing Is Simple.

Foord only returned once to his planet and was not made welcome. He wanted to see Katy Bevan again, but didn't; he had already intruded on her once, and knew that he'd hurt her as viciously as the priests. More viciously, because his love for her wasn't as genuine as theirs.

●

Half an hour passed. Still neither ship moved.

Foord had fallen silent and seemed, for a couple of minutes, almost to have died. The others studied him, noting details with the quiet precision they'd learnt from Foord himself, and putting a value to each of them: voice inflexions, broken sentence constructions, repetition of unanswered questions. They assessed him in the same way as his own ship assessed him, ascribing values. Perhaps they should have considered discarding him; the ship had that on its list of options, but the ship was only partly alive. And when he fell silent, none of them felt equal to filling the empty space; except, unexpectedly, one.

"...And," Joser concluded, "Her position is 17-14-16 and holding. She's still shrouded, of course, but we have a reliable fix on Her position, which is probably what She intended." (A provocative assumption, which like others before it provoked no response from Foord.) "She's outside our beam range, of course, and no doubt She'll use Her superior low-speed acceleration to stay outside."

Joser's mouth had wandered into Commander's territory, but still Foord stayed silent.

"We do," Cyr snapped, "have weapons other than particle beams."

"Yes," Joser said, "but we can't use them if we can't catch Her."

Why, Cyr thought, *is he saying this? He's supposed to be just a Department stooge. So why this? Is he cleverer than I thought?*

"We can catch Her!" Cyr insisted. "Our top speed on ion drive is higher."

"Maybe. But She'll have calculated that." Joser paused, but still Foord stayed silent. "She can choose *where* we catch Her, and what She does about it."

"Not," Foord said suddenly, "if we catch Her sooner than She expects."

"Commander?"

"If we catch Her. Sooner, Joser. Than She expects. Don't you follow?"

Looks were exchanged around the Bridge. At that stage they didn't, except for Smithson. Insofar as his structure allowed it, Smithson went rigid at the thought of what Foord *might* mean.

"You're right, Commander," Joser said confidently (he had discovered that he liked defining a static subject, even if it was their own possible destruction). "But you see, Her superior low-speed acceleration…"

"If we *start* after Her on ion drive," Foord mused, "and then switch up suddenly to photon drive, just long enough to get Her back in range…"

"Commander!" Smithson bellowed. "This is a fucking *asteroid* belt! Ships *don't* engage photon drive in asteroid belts, not even *this* ship! Ships have to go *slow* in asteroid belts, Commander, because if they go *fast*, the asteroids bang into them. I have a better idea. Why not just invite Her to surrender?"

"…and it needn't be for long, or at full photon speed. Just ten percent on photon would be way above her top speed on ion drive. About…..I'd say, about eleven or twelve seconds at ten percent photon would catch Her."

It was not possible that Foord could have done the necessary mental arithmetic amid the uproar which engulfed the Bridge, unless he had simply not noticed it.

"Commander, we wouldn't last three seconds," Joser stammered. He had not done that calculation but he did know, quite accurately, the effect on everything he had just defined—thoroughly *defined*—of a new variable, even if it was a variable which tended towards their survival rather than destruction. "It's not an acceptable risk. It can't...it won't..."

"*You* tell him, Kaang," Smithson invited. "He expects you to take us through part of an asteroid belt on photon drive. Let's hear from *you*."

"For once," Cyr added.

"I'm only the pilot," Kaang mumbled, miserably. "That was the agreement."

"Tell us," Cyr said, "please. As a pilot. Can you do it?"

"Perhaps," Kaang said, "but I'm not certain."

"It gets better," confided Smithson to the air above him. "The Commonwealth's greatest pilot and weakest human being, executing the orders of a Commander who died half an hour ago. I want all this entered on the record." He looked at Foord and lowered his voice, for tragic effect; lapsing again into self-pity. "I don't know why, particularly. But I do. Someone may read it sometime."

"I don't intend to sit around while She knocks pieces off us one by one," Foord said mildly.

"Isn't that what you've been doing for the last thirty minutes?"

"We might die from this engagement," Foord answered, still mildly.

"You've died from it already," Smithson muttered.

"Commander," Cyr asked, "you said She might know our thoughts before we think them. So we use photon drive, and so does She. Then what?"

"Then we both survive or both die. If we both survive, we lose and gain nothing. If we both die we get a draw."

"I liked you better when you were alive," Smithson said.

For the first time, Foord looked directly at Smithson. "This ship can't collectively survive or die. Only its parts survive or die. Alone. When the MT Drive activated, we left *you* to fight it. Alone. The crew of an ordinary ship would have fought it together, and you know what would have happened."

A person of any sensitivity would have recognised that as the conclusion. Smithson, however, was not sensitive and only approximately a person.

"You oversimplified just now. If we both use photon drive, we don't necessarily both survive or die. She could survive and we could die."

"Of course. But only if She has a pilot better than Kaang. Do you think

Her pilot is likely to be better than Kaang?"

And that, even Smithson recognised, *was* the conclusion. "No, Commander."

Kaang sat quietly by in the half-light, following the conversation from one face to another. She often found herself like this: listening to them talking about her as if she wasn't there.

Smithson caused a muscle to ripple in his upper torso: not a shrug, but some other gesture Foord had never seen before. Perhaps, as he'd never seen it before, it was an apology. "Of course, that's if She *is* a ship, with a crew and Commander and pilot, and not something else. But we've been through that before... Commander, we haven't even seen Her yet, and She's made us say these things. We've never said such things before."

Thought them, maybe, Cyr told herself, *but never said them. What's happening to us?*

And that was the mood in which they passed on to the details of what they were about to do. To escape it, they went over the details again and again. A ten percent photon burst to bring Her back in range, executed by Kaang who, while it lasted, would become the focus of the ship as Smithson was when he fought the MT Drive. Then, if they survived, the re-establishment of the particle beam bombardment. And first, a series of slow moves towards Her on ion drive; on the basis of Her responses, Foord would decide when to engage photon.

The repetition of the details was like the restoration of a heartbeat after trauma. It brought the Bridge back to something like its normal quietness.

"Photon drive is ready whenever you want to use it, Commander," Smithson said, a few moments later.

"Thank you. Cyr?"

"If we survive the photon burst, I can re-establish the particle beams."

"Thank you. Kaang?"

"We now have figures for the duration and course of the photon burst, Commander. Duration is fourteen seconds."

"Fourteen? I underestimated."

"The course includes eleven major evasive manoeuvres, Commander," Kaang said evenly, "around intervening asteroids."

Eleven manoeuvres, in fourteen seconds, at ten percent photon speed.

She might have been describing a routine parking orbit. Foord tried to match her lack of expression, and failed. He could *feel* expressions moving over his face, as if they were external forces. Eleven, fourteen, ten. What Kaang was about to do, on his orders, had now been given figures, and they were monstrous.

"I understand. Then," as the alarms politely cleared their throats, "please take us forward on ion drive, Kaang. One percent."

"Done, Commander."

The manoeuvre drives fountained. The alarms increased a semitone, but stayed well within the bounds of politeness. The ion drive cut in, almost silently. The asteroids on the encircling Bridge screen whirled and resettled as the ship established direction and attitude; otherwise there was no sensation of movement.

"She's moving away, Commander," Joser said. "Ion drive, low register."

"Increase to three percent, please, Kaang."

"Done, Commander."

"She's matched us," Joser said.

"Maintain at three percent, please, Kaang."

"Done, Commander."

Foord settled back. He glanced at Kaang. She was checking—unnecessarily, since she had already checked several times—that the navigation and drives cores had instructed their computers to make minor adjustments to the course and duration of the photon burst to allow for the last few movements. Foord knew he could do Thahl's and Joser's jobs about as well as they could; Cyr's, almost as well; and Smithson's, adequately. But Kaang's, never.

"Joser?"

"Still matching us, Commander."

"Good." It was settling into a pattern, muted and orderly, with the leisure to observe one's draughtsmanship and doublecheck the details. "Kaang, we'll stay at three percent, please. Give you time to ready the overrides for execution. And I'd like to observe Her responses a little longer."

"Done, commander."

"No, Commander, your order's refused. I'm engaging photon drive now."

The first answer was what Foord expected and practically believed he'd heard. The second, delivered with exactly the same inflexion, was what he actually heard. It silenced the Bridge.

"I'm engaging photon drive now, Commander."

"But the overrides—"

Kaang pressed a palm panel and gazed calmly round the Bridge. One by one, the other five consoles went dark.

"Done, Commander. As of now, I'm the only other living thing this ship recognises."

Insanely, Foord caught himself noting her use of the word Other. The alarms were rising, beyond their normal politeness; they were beginning to sound loud, like alarms on ordinary ships. And the *Charles Manson*, since it did indeed recognise only Kaang, was now proceeding with complete logic and reasonableness to move against all the others. To immobilise its own crew.

"Kaang!"

"If *you* didn't see this coming, Commander," she replied, as the ship closed its burrows and corridors and bulkheads to isolate its inhabited sections, "then maybe She won't either."

Foord knew she was right. He wanted to say so, but there was no time. The last thing he was able to say, knowing that anything more would be cut short by the alarms' rising noise and/or the ship's destruction and/or the shutdown of internal communications, whichever was the sooner, was *Cyr, if we survive this, come out firing.*

In its haste to obey Kaang's priority overrides, the ship almost attacked itself. It slammed shut the final bulkheads; slammed down and locked the seat harnesses of its crew; burst open Kaang's harness as the last one (Foord's) locked; and made Kaang the focus of all its systems, sending neural implant wires to burrow into her face and head like maggots, pulsing with information. From the rest of its crew it turned away, leaving them isolated from itself and Kaang as though they were infected.

It killed internal communications. It killed its own Damage Control systems, since Damage could not begin to describe what would happen if Kaang failed. It killed the Bridge screen and all other onboard screens except Kaang's, because although it had nothing to say about whether a photon burst through asteroids was sanity or insanity, it knew that only Kaang was far enough from either to be allowed to see it happening.

It almost killed its own crew, reducing them to sixty-two near-corpses, buried in their own harnesses and in darkness. Then, when they were no longer necessary, it killed the alarms.

The photon drive cut straight in at ten percent. What might be the last fourteen seconds of the ship's life had already begun; nine seconds were left.

Two sets of events were taking place, one inside and one outside the ship. They should have been galaxies apart, not separated only by the thickness of the hull. Outside, the *Charles Manson* was plunging through the Belt, wrenching itself past, under, above, below and between those asteroids it had not already vaporised, ten times as quick and vicious in *missing* them as it had been in destroying them. Inside, everything was filtered and compensated out to almost nothing, the Bridge and corridors and burrows as dark as the vacated interior passages of a corpse; the ship might already have been dead and buried, or embedded in crystal like the Book of Srahr.

Nine seconds to go. They dropped like water from a tap.

Plop.

Eight seconds to go.

While his mother was dying his father had found a letter she had written, while she could still write, setting out her will; her last secret. And now Foord was seeing the last secret of his ship; how it had ordered its final affairs so that only Kaang, in the sense the ship would have recognised it, was still alive.

Plop. Seven seconds to go.

He did not actually hear the sound, just as he did not actually see the seconds poke out, one by one, into the stillness of the Bridge and fall to the floor, *Plop*

Six seconds to go.

but he realised they reminded him not only of water dropping from a tap (that was too obvious) but of human faeces dropping from.... *No.* He recoiled from that. That was something his own senses, deprived of input, were providing

Plop. Five to go.

from somewhere in his memory, perhaps Her use of faeces in the famous Isis engagement. But in one way it was accurate. Inside the *Charles*

Manson time really was passing that slowly, and the last few seconds of the photon burst really were falling that softly; solemn, dark brown, and blunt.

Plop. Four to go.

The *Charles Manson* was not alive enough to know that it could die. But it knew all about subdivision downwards into isolated parts, and Kaang was its last moving part.

Plop. Three.

Except that she wasn't Kaang any more. At Kaang's place on the Bridge, watching on the last working screen what would have been unwatchable to the others, there was now only an *object*. It looked like an exploded diagram, its seat harness burst open around its waist, its face and head fountaining with neural implants. Only its eyes and hands moved. They seemed speeded up by a factor of at least ten, but still—as always—unhurried.

Kaang was going to succeed. Foord was so certain of that that he even stopped listening for the last seconds to fall. He would never have heard them anyway. They were obliterated by the noise of a gigantic explosion. It wasn't the ship's destruction—that would have been beyond their hearing—but the ion drive, cutting in at full reverse thrust as the photon drive died, to kill their momentum and bring them out of the photon burst at rest.

The ship turned away from Kaang, like it had previously turned away from the rest of its crew, and forgot her. It left her lying in the tatters of her seat harness, her face bleeding where it had pulled out its neural implants; it routed her pilot's functions through to Thahl, and her console died as the others came back to life. It reopened its main systems along their usual channels; withdrew the bulkheads; unlocked the seat harnesses; reactivated the screens and lights and alarms; and awaited further instructions.

They had reached their moment, but it was already dying on them. It was the one moment when She might be vulnerable; when they had done something that might genuinely surprise Her. But the moment was dying on them even as it began, and the only way to give it meaning was to forget Kaang. Like the ship, they turned away from her, not even pausing to see if she was alive. Without speaking to each other they resumed the engagement, now with Thahl as replacement pilot; and Cyr, before any of them, resumed firing the particle beams.

4

The smaller asteroids in the Belt were mostly irregular, as lumpy and stolid as potatoes emptied from a sack; and two perfect killing machines stalked each other through them, like tarantulas.

At least, one was a perfect killing machine—the one which was visible and which had just executed a photon burst through asteroids, a near-impossible manoeuvre from which it had emerged with weapons firing. The other one stayed shrouded, a dark spot in darkness; it appeared to be surprised by the unheard-of manoeuvre, and appeared to be running.

But the battle between them was complicated and enigmatic. They fought in different languages, and with different weapons, and at times hardly seemed to be fighting each other at all. Their definitions of Battle and Fight and Weapon seemed to correspond only obliquely. And the space between them, by a kind of relativity, was changing as the battle changed. Things were happening to it. In some ways it was no longer space at all.

Space joined the two ships, and separated them. It was empty, but full of the weapons they fired across it at each other. It was shapeless, but given shape by the *Charles Manson*'s particle beams, whose range exceeded Hers. After emerging from the photon burst, the *Charles Manson* had reverted to the same monotonous attrition which had worked so well before, draining Her and systematically destroying asteroids as She sought cover behind them, keeping Her always at a range from which She could not return fire, at least not with Her own beams.

The space between them read like a book, its pages visibly crammed with the *Charles Manson*'s language: it was shot through with the dull blue of the particle beams, always one way, stabbing incessantly at Her. But it also contained something else, travelling back from Her to the *Charles Manson*; something unreadable. Something like the white areas of pages, wrapping round the *Charles Manson*'s beams like white spaces round printed words.

The *Charles Manson*'s language was one of physical attacks on physical targets. And Faith, while occasionally replying in the same language, seemed also to be conducting another kind of battle, on different targets. On people. On a person in particular. They were all known to Her, but She fixed on one.

5

Two hours had passed since the photon burst. They had won back their advantage, putting Faith within their beam range and themselves out of Hers, and they were driving Her before them through the Belt; but they still remembered Kaang. Not as a colleague (they liked to think there were no such things on Foord's ship) or as an individual (she had never been interesting enough) or even as their pilot (Thahl substituted adequately). It was much more specific than that. They remembered her because the whole Bridge stank of her shit.

Only pack hunters tended their injured: solitary predators, like cats and Sakhrans and the *Charles Manson*'s crew, preferred to ignore them. For that unspoken reason, and for other reasons, they had left Kaang where she fell after the photon burst. It was nearly an hour before Foord summoned attention, and as the doctors carried her out she had defecated, massively. It had gone everywhere.

For the twenty-fourth time in the two hours since the photon burst, the weapons core instructed the computers which served it to configure themselves to Attack, SemiManual. A warning harmonic warbled politely through the Bridge. Headup displays and target simulations were superimposed on the Bridge screen. Her cover this time was AD-2049, a small asteroid whose destruction took only one beam-firing. She broke cover and ran. Cyr reached Her with eight shots, all of which She held with Her flickerfields, before She reached fresh cover. Thahl parallelled Her movements, maintained beam range, and brought them to rest again. The computers serving the weapons core started counting off another five minutes. Somehow the time didn't seem to pass as slowly as when Kaang had been pilot. Thahl's competence was monotonous, but Kaang's near-perfection was even more so.

They had counted out the last two hours in careful five-minute pieces like this one; but the first five minutes, following their emergence from the photon burst, *really* counted, because they had done something remarkable. They had become the first of Her opponents ever to surprise Her. When She had seen the only other ship in Horus system which might be able to threaten Her, emerging from the insanity of a photon burst through asteroids and coming at Her firing, She had—not exactly panicked, but *hurried.* And in the first few minutes, the engagement had been reshaped.

She fled from them so hurriedly that by the time She found fresh cover (Cyr reached Her with seven shots that time, all of which Her flickerfields held), She was two-thirds of the way through the Belt. Now, two hours later, She was three-quarters through and still running. Occasionally She tried other tactics—missiles on parabolic courses, decoys, even a shrouded mineswarm—but each time Joser spotted them and Cyr destroyed them.

The five minutes were eventually counted. For the twenty-fifth time, the weapons core instructed the computers which served it to configure themselves to Attack, SemiManual. A warning harmonic; headup displays; target simulations. Her cover this time was AD-2025, a miserably small asteroid (they all were, now that the Belt was starting to peter out) whose destruction took only one beam-firing. She broke cover and ran, trying to double back on them—She tried this every third or fourth time—but was easily headed off by the particle beams. Cyr reached Her with eleven shots, all of which She held with Her flickerfields, before She reached fresh cover. Thahl parallelled Her movements, maintained beam range, and brought them to rest again. The computers serving the weapons core started counting off another five minutes.

"You're getting better at this," Cyr remarked to Joser.

Joser gave her a slight nod of acknowledgement. "It's the repetition. I like the repetition," he said, and meant it.

The Bridge was pleasantly quiet, and Foord, quietly pleased. The Belt was dwindling, the asteroids She was using for cover were getting smaller, the spaces between them larger, and each time She broke and ran She had to take more of Cyr's unwaveringly accurate beam-firings. She was being drained; not only, it seemed, of energy through Her flickerfields, but of will. Even Her occasional counterattacks carried no real conviction. And most important, they had locked Her back in beam range and She seemed unable to break out of it.

Foord's wristcom buzzed.

"Commander, may I talk to you?" Kaang sounded as bad as she had looked the last time Foord saw her.

"Kaang. It's good to hear your voice again." (It wasn't.) "How are you?" ("How is she?" Foord had asked, an hour ago, of one of the doctors he had finally called to the Bridge. "She was half-dead, Commander, when the ship discarded her. She's still half-dead.")

Kaang didn't reply. He tried again.

"How are you, Kaang?"

"I'm in Medical, Commander."

"Ah," Foord said. He had never been able to sustain a conversation with Kaang about anything, except her duties as pilot. He tried again; this time, the last resort of any visitor to any sickbed. "Is there anything you need?"

"That's what I want to talk about, Commander. The doctors say there's no permanent damage."

"That's good...Kaang, I don't know how to tell you what we owe you." This was literally true: he genuinely didn't know how to say such things. He had blurted the words out, as though admitting to some personal disease.

"Commander, I think I should return to duty."

"No." Foord was relieved; this at least was familiar territory. "When you're fit, yes, but not before. Until then we have adequate cover."

"Who's acting as pilot, Commander?"

"Thahl. Both he and I hold current Pilot's Certificates."

"Commander, excuse me." The one area where she would show resistance. "What did you and Thahl score on your last annual tests? Seventy-five percent?"

"Thahl scored seventy-five. I scored seventy-four."

"The best military pilots score about eighty. I've never scored below ninety-five. She won't let you stalk Her forever, Commander. You need me back on the Bridge."

"And you need rest, according to my medical advice." ("She's gone unattended for an hour longer than necessary, Commander," the doctor had snapped, his forearms covered in shit and blood, "and she needs rest. More particularly, a rest from *you*.") "I most need you back, Kaang, when we've finally driven Her out of the Belt and this engagement really begins. If it is one. Until then we have adequate cover."

He snapped his wristcom shut, too abruptly.

Joser sniffed the air. "It's like she's never been away," he murmured to Cyr.

"Her absence," Cyr agreed, "has been deeply smelt."

Foord glanced at them curiously. The rapport between them had started to grow after the photon burst, and coincided with Joser becoming more effective. It was not something he would have expected.

He gazed round the Bridge. "I believe I asked for status reports." He hadn't. "Do I have to ask for them again?"

While the reports were being given—they were short, satisfactory and required only half his attention—he was thinking about Kaang.

"Thahl."

"Commander?"

"Block off communications from Kaang, please. I don't want any more calls like that."

In the first few minutes after the photon burst, when they erupted upon Her, they'd had no choice but to leave Kaang where she fell. But later, when the engagement resettled into the dual monotony of asteroid-hopping and beam-firing, they continued to ignore her. Their agreement to do so, like much on Foord's ship, was unspoken. Each of them found tasks to attend to, rather than attend to her—tasks which often required them to speak to each other over, and around, and through, where she was slumped at her console. It was only much later, and almost too late, when Foord summoned help. Outsiders always went self-contained during missions; it was their nature to turn inwards.

"That's all seen to, Commander. She won't...."

"Disturb us again?"

"Yes, Commander."

Everybody else on this ship, thought Foord—himself, even Joser, even the three doctors he summoned—had at some time either given or received violence. But never Kaang. She was the purest specialist, the least violent and least interesting of all the *Charles Manson*'s inhabitants. When the violence of the engagement touched her, it touched the ship's most private part. By not dying, she made it impossible for them to deny it.

And the result was monumentally disgusting: the smell, the stains on the lower areas of her light grey uniform, the facepack of dried blood and yellow moustache of mucus. Her breath had smelt, too. Foord did not even stop to think that at least she was still breathing, only that her breath *smelt*.

●

For the twenty-sixth time, the weapons core instructed the computers which served it to configure themselves to Attack, SemiManual. A warning harmonic; headup displays; target simulations. Her cover this time was AC-1954, another small asteroid whose destruction took only one beam-firing. Cyr reached Her with nine shots, all of which She held with Her flickerfields, before realising that Her target simulation, the white blip on the screen indicating Her position, had not moved.

At AC-1954, She had stopped running.

Cyr was surprised enough to glance up at Foord, but not enough to stop firing. Fourteen shots, fifteen. *What*, she wondered as she continued to fire, is She about to do that's worth this drain on Her?

The same thought had occurred to Foord. "Joser, I expect this is another missile. Check it, please, will you?"

"Already done, Commander. It is a missile. Closing at twenty percent. Details and a visual will be on the screen shortly."

"And the other missiles?"

"Other missiles, Commander?"

"Other missiles, Joser. Remember? She tries this every third or fourth time. The first one is a diversion for the others, coming in on parabolic courses while the first is on a straight course."

That speech had taken Cyr up to twenty-three shots.

"I remember, Commander. I'll find them."

"Yes, I think you will. She used to run you ragged, but not any more. Perhaps when we have more time"—Foord was dangerously unaware, then, how little they had—"you'll tell me how you did it."

Thirty shots. She remained still, Her flickerfields holding the beams.

"Here are the details, Commander. Visual will follow."

The Bridge screen displayed headups confirming the missile was under remote guidance from Faith, and showed its position and speed: 26-14-19 and closing, at ninety percent.

"*Ninety* percent!"

"It was twenty—"

"It's now ninety, Joser. Impact in seventy-nine seconds, it says. Cyr, *get it*, please."

(Smithson scowled at the headup display. "Something wrong about that missile," he hissed at Joser. "It doesn't *need* remote guidance. Too fast to manoeuvre, and on a straight course. So why guidance?" Joser shrugged, oddly and mechanically, as though remotely operated. Smithson turned to repeat the question to Foord, then decided not to. Oddly, he never knew why. It was one of his very few bad decisions.)

The long-range gas and semiconductor lasers lanced out at the missile, almost but not quite parallel to the particle beams which Cyr was still stabbing at Faith. The particle beams were malignant dull blue, the lasers brilliant white. The particle beams reached their target, the lasers didn't. The approaching missile simply avoided them. It flicked to one side, let them pass by, and returned to its course. All at ninety percent.

Smithson swore. "*That's* why remote guidance," he muttered.

Joser's expression was unreadable, almost shrouded. "Impact in sixty-four seconds."

The missile was now visible on the Bridge screen—though Joser had omitted to supply local magnification—and the screen generated the usual side, ventral and dorsal images, and, unasked, added magnification: a grey ovoid, about twenty feet long, with no markings or external features. Considering what it had just done, it should not have looked so ordinary.

"Cyr," Foord inquired, carefully—but his voice fooled nobody— "how can it do that?"

"Do you want it explained, Commander, or destroyed?"

Again the lasers lanced out. Again they missed.

"How can it do that?"

"Impact in forty-four seconds."

"Oh, *fuck* you," Cyr whispered, probably to herself. The missile's performance was extraordinary, and whoever on Faith was guiding it was reacting so quickly that Cyr was actually firing lasers and missing—almost unheard-of, and she took it very personally.

The lasers lanced out again and again, and missed both times.

"Something *wrong*," repeated Smithson. Joser did not reply; as the missile got closer, he seemed to get further away.

"Impact in thirty-seven seconds."

"*Behind it!*" Smithson bellowed. "*Look behind it.*"

"Thahl," Foord began, "can we—"

"Yes, Commander, we can outrun it. But if we run, we put Her out of beam range."

"No!" Joser shouted, but only at Thahl's grammar. "It's not *it*, it's *them*." He paused, oddly, as though afraid of being overheard. "*There's a second one*, Commander. Directly behind the first. Duplicating its movements. Hidden in its drive shadow. And when the first one's destroyed, the second one will…"

Explosions flickered on-off in front of them, knotting space like a muscle cramp.

"*Got you*, you bastard," hissed Cyr, who after her setbacks had switched to shortrange crystal lasers and had simply kept firing.

"…the second one will come straight for us. Impact in nineteen seconds. I'm sorry, Commander."

And as the second grey ovoid hurtled towards them through the wreckage of the first, something else flickered on-off: a glance between Smithson and Foord, concerning Joser. They left it unspoken. Other things mattered more, like the need to get out of Cyr's way so she could defend them against a rapidly approaching, largely unexpected and wholly ridiculous death.

But now, perversely, Cyr was enjoying herself. The weapons array was her language, and she used it fluently. She composed in it. She hunted the second missile with every closeup weapon in her vocabulary. To the crystal lasers she added motive beams, harmonic guns, tanglers, disruptors and others; she put them together like words in a haiku, each one amplifying each other's meaning until her composition grew dense and ferocious. She continued also to tap out an unwavering barrage of beam-firings directly at Faith, but that was only punctuation to the main composition. Cyr's attack on the second missile was an almost perfect statement of her abilities. It lasted exactly nineteen seconds, and then the missile hit the *Charles*

Manson; but it hit as a hundred pieces of wreckage.

And in its wake something else, equally alien, engulfed them. From his console in one of the weapons bays, Cyr's deputy, Nemec, started cheering. Others on other parts of the ship heard and joined him. The sound was distant and tinny, at first difficult to recognise because even the comm channels which carried it to the Bridge were designed only for muted individual voices; but then, when Thahl formally confirmed only minimal impact damage, the congratulations redoubled and even spread, at first tentatively, to the Bridge.

It was Cyr's moment and she basked in it, though not to the extent of forgetting her beam-firing. Seventy-two shots, said the screen headup display. Seventy-three.

Foord's gaze flicked from the screen to Cyr; then to Joser, where it rested for a moment; then back to the screen. He stayed silent.

"…very fast and manoeuvrable," Cyr was explaining to the Bridge in an it-was-nothing-really drawl, punctuated with glances at Foord, "but they had no flickerfields. They weren't a new type of missile, just one of Her known types, but stripped down for speed—probably nothing but drives, warheads and guidance. They had no defences."

"Like that kid you shot at Blentport."

Seventy-eight, said the headup display. Cyr's beam-firings did not waver, even after Foord's remark. Seventy-nine.

Even Smithson gasped at what Foord had said. The Bridge fell silent, then the silence died down into uproar. Foord stopped it with a glance.

"Thahl, this is an emergency. Get us out of here, now!"

The manoeuvre drives fountained. The *Charles Manson* began to turn away—from Faith, who had seemed at its mercy, and from the nuzzling wreckage of Her missiles—and ran.

"Why?" Cyr demanded. "You ordered Her missiles destroyed and I destroyed them!"

"Two of them." Foord laid the words down in front of her, like small corpses. "Ask Joser about the third."

"*Third?*" Cyr screamed at Joser, then "Oh no." She had seen Joser's face.

"There's no third missile," Joser said with quiet precision.

"No," Cyr kept saying, not to Joser but to herself. "No."

"If there's a third missile," Joser said with quiet precision "the scanners will detect it."

Thahl took the ion drive to ninety percent, almost as smoothly as Kaang. An hour seemed to pass.

"The scanners won't detect it," Joser said with quiet precision. He had just bitten completely through his lower lip. "Not this. This is the one She intended for us."

Foord glanced at the headup display—now, at last, Cyr had stopped firing the particle beams; the count was eighty—and turned back to Joser.

"See," he said. "What's been done to us."

He might have been talking to Joser about Faith, or to the rest of the Bridge about Joser. Both, suddenly, made sense.

They ran. At ninety percent ion drive Thahl took the *Charles Manson* back into the Belt, surrendering in seconds the ground they had won in penny pieces over hours, rolling and swerving at random because they might still evade whatever pursued them; they might have entire minutes left.

Foord looked at Joser. "I want you to relinquish scanners. Please hand them to Smithson."

"The one She intended for us."

Joser's console went dark. He hadn't relinquished —probably hadn't heard —but Thahl did it for him, routing the scanners through to Smithson. Later, thought Foord, I'll get him removed. But not now. Definitely not now.

"While Thahl is pilot," Foord asked Smithson, "can you do scanners as well as drives?"

"Running out of people."

"Can you do scanners as well as drives?"

"Of course I can, Commander. I can also take in your laundry, if you wish."

"Two out of three will be enough."

"Then forget the scanners and I'll take in your laundry."

"The one She intended for us."

"Thahl," began Foord, "could you…"

"Use photon drive? If you order it, Commander. But…"

"But you're not Kaang." At least, thought Foord, we still finish each other's sentences.

Faith remained at rest, while they digested what She had done to them and tried to run from it. But what She had done was already inside them, ahead of Her missile. It concerned Joser.

●

They ran for ninety seconds, and were still alive. The Bridge screen showed the Belt corkscrewing around them. Thahl showed no obvious signs of stress, but he never did.

"Nothing yet," Smithson said.

"The one She intended for us." Joser was repeating the phrase as regularly as Cyr had repeated her beam-firings; and with the same accuracy. As far as they could, they ignored him.

Had She, thought Foord, somehow possessed Joser's mind? That was the obvious explanation, but Foord knew it was wrong. The truth was more subtle, and much worse: not possessed it, *predicted* it. But so precisely that mere possession was unnecessary.

"Something out there," Smithson said. "An echo. No, it's gone. But the signature was unusual. It's big."

"The one She intended for us."

"Stop saying that," Cyr said.

"Leave him, he can't hear you," Smithson said.

"And anyway," Foord added, "it's all he'll ever say."

This was the first real event of the engagement; all the others had been fakes, fought in different languages. In their language Her attacks had been real, and had only just been beaten off by the abilities of Smithson, then Kaang, then Cyr. In Her language there had only ever been one attack, as gradual and patient as erosion, and She had directed it—all of it—at Joser.

"There, another echo!" Smithson shouted.

"The one..."

"Gone again. But it's *big*."

"...She intended for us."

"I'd like him to stop saying that," Cyr said.

The ship shuddered as it ploughed through some asteroid debris. Thahl quickly righted it.

Foord glanced at the screen. The speed was impossible. The Belt whipped past them, boiling, and flung bits of itself at them like antibodies. He knew Thahl couldn't sustain this, but said nothing yet.

Merely being run ragged by an opponent's superiority would not have done this to Joser. What She had used on him over all those hours was more than just technical superiority. His failure was not the cause of his collapse, only a symptom. He was finished long before then.

"More echoes," Smithson said. "I think I can pinpoint it, though…"

She might have killed Joser there and then just by telling him what She was, but that wasn't how She worked. Not by telepathy, and not by possession. The truth was more subtle, and much worse. She arranged the events he experienced; and then, because She knew him and knew all of them, She predicted, to the second, how he would react. She used events to make him believe, gradually, that he wasn't as bad as the others believed him to be, or as he feared himself to be; She did it piece by piece, letting him see things on his inadequate scanners which She could easily have concealed. Then, when he'd started despite himself to believe, even to the point where he could exchange banter with Cyr, She dashed him by making him miss things he should easily have spotted, even on his inadequate scanners; and She predicted, down to the last second, when this would prove insupportable to him.

By the time Her third missile was launched, he was already finished.

"I need the missile's position," Foord said, a minute later. They were still alive.

"You can't have it," Smithson said.

"What?"

"It's shrouded, so I'm only getting random echoes. You'll get the position when I can trust our scanners."

"Recall Kaang, Commander," Cyr whispered.

"Don't be ridiculous. Kaang's not fit. There isn't time."

"There *already* isn't time. Look at the screen. How long can Thahl keep doing this?"

"Smithson, we need that position."

"Later. There are too many echoes."

"The one…" Joser began.

"I'd really like him to stop saying that," Cyr said, and this time he did stop, because they hit another swarm of asteroid debris, more heavily this time, and went reeling.

"The one…"

For entire seconds they were out of control, and then the manoeuvre drives fountained and Thahl started to right them, but Foord didn't notice any of this. He had heard someone speak, just before the Impact alarms murmured.

"Kill the alarms, I can't hear!" Foord yelled.

"…She intended for us."

"What? What was that?"

"I said, The one She intended for us."

Foord froze, horrified: it was Smithson, not Joser, who had spoken.

"Why," he said carefully "did you say that?"

"Position of Her third missile," Smithson said, "is 05-03-06 and closing. And," he added, killing the alarms and what was left of Foord's composure, "this time She means it. It's sixty feet long."

The Bridge screen was shot through with light. The shroud fell away, and the third missile appeared, another featureless ovoid but bigger. They watched it *push* through its shroud into sudden existence, as if something invisible had just given it birth.

"It's just a ship's length away," Smithson breathed. "Impact imminent."

It filled half the rear screen: grey, featureless and huge. Foord stared at it, for too long.

"Impact *imminent*!" Smithson bellowed at him.

"No," he whispered. "Check its speed."

It was keeping an exact distance. It was plunging *with* them through the Belt, more a companion than a pursuer, its grey elliptical dot behind their slender silver delta making a deformed exclamation mark; and because it could hit them at any time, it wouldn't yet.

Smithson swore. "It's cut speed to match ours! It's…"

"Playing with us," Foord agreed.

"I have ten percent ion speed left, Commander," Thahl said.

"Use it, please."

He did, and so did the missile. On the screen, since it maintained distance exactly, nothing happened.

"That's enough. Cut back to ninety percent, please. We have to leave ourselves something."

"For what?" Thahl kept his voice carefully neutral, but he cut back, and so did the missile. On the screen its position and distance were unchanged. Thanks to Thahl's evasive manoeuvres, which it parallelled exactly even in their growing raggedness, it was the only other object in the Belt which wasn't trying to fling itself at them or away from them.

Cyr was already attacking it with closeup weapons. It carried flicker-fields, and even used them for a few seconds, but then ceased: perhaps there was no need. Either She would make it hit, or Thahl would get exhausted, or both, long before Cyr could damage it.

There was a huge explosion, but not the missile; not yet. They had clipped the rim of an asteroid fragment, and went reeling again until Thahl righted them. The missile reeled and righted itself with them, and maintained exact distance.

Another asteroid loomed ahead, and Thahl wrenched them over its horizon, with the missile following, and plunged into a swarm of asteroid debris. Somehow he got through it, and somehow so did the missile. They ran before it through the Belt, sidewinding and somersaulting. They ran like a dog through dustbins, hitting some and missing others; a dog trying to escape its own tail, and turning rabid because it couldn't.

"The one…"

"Please keep him quiet, Commander."

They entered another swarm of debris. The minor impacts mounted, and Thahl ignored them. Cyr kept firing at the missile, and it ignored her. Joser was trying to speak to Foord, and Foord ignored him.

The next major asteroid marked the change. It wasn't a sudden looming obstacle to be avoided: Thahl was actually making for it. It was large, potato-shaped and lumpy. Its face grew until it filled the forward section of the Bridge screen—and continued to grow, until Forward became Down and they were diving into it. Diving, Foord thought, into a giant face of W. C. Fields…there was where the hat should be, and there the cigar. It even had the complexion, veined and pocked and wrinkled, the details hurtling into and inside focus as it rushed up at them.

To their credit, none of them shouted at Thahl to pull out of the dive until they were sure he'd left it too late; and then he ignored them. He held the dive until they were inside final landing height, then turned the ship in its own length, heading up and back into the Belt. The ion drive, where he turned, hit the asteroid's face like a broken bottle.

And the missile followed them. It did not, as Thahl hoped, dash itself to pieces on the asteroid. It turned as quickly as they did, and was where it had always been: on the rear Bridge screen, a ship's-length away. It was as though Kaang was piloting it.

Smithson began a long vomit of foul language, which seemed to splatter over the walls of the Bridge and hang dripping like Kaang's faeces; though it made no difference to the missile. Nothing did. Joser couldn't detect it, Thahl couldn't lose it, Cyr couldn't destroy it, and Foord—

Foord couldn't take his eyes off it. Whatever it did to them finally, right now She was using it to speak to them, mocking them for surrendering in seconds of retreat what they'd gained after hours of pursuit. Foord even thought he recognised the tone of voice She used to mock them: understated and ironic, like voices used to be on the *Charles Manson*.

Joser was trying to speak to Foord, but the wrong words kept coming out. He kept saying "This is the one She intended for us," and Foord heard but ignored him.

They reached a rare pocket of open space in the Belt. Thahl paused, then wrenched them to port, heading for the next asteroid, and Smithson snorted in derision. So, almost, did Foord, and for the same reason: they were running ragged, a frothing dog diving for the dark of the nearest alley.

But literally an alley this time.

The asteroid for which Thahl was running was BZ-1014. It was huge, the size of a small planet. He flung them into orbit around it—after nodding briefly to himself, as if he actually knew what he was doing—and it spread out below them, like a giant unmade bed. It was humped and folded from horizon to horizon, a landscape of craters and mountains. Pulled this way and that by the Belt's shifting gravity, it breathed in slow geological violence. One of its breaths was ten of their lifetimes.

Thahl tightened orbit; the effect, of dropping closer to the surface while maintaining speed, was like a surge of acceleration. As BZ-1014's landscape rushed below, vomited out by one horizon and swallowed by the other, he turned and looked directly at Foord.

"Particle beams," he managed to say; and "Alley."

And then Foord understood, and had to fight an impulse to laugh out loud—in relief that Thahl had found something they could still do, and in disbelief at what it was.

"You heard him, Cyr. Fire particle beams."

"And destroy the asteroid? When we're on top of it?"

"No," Foord said, "when we're *inside* it."

Cyr was too amazed, and frightened, to reply. She glanced up at Foord; then at Smithson, who also understood; then at Thahl, who was going to do it anyway; and nodded.

They ran for their alley.

At ninety percent ion speed, Thahl tightened and lowered orbit; then dived

vertically

for the largest of the craters.

The particle beams—even stronger than Hers, the one weapon She couldn't match—stabbed ahead, perfect and recoilless, and *ate.*

The asteroid spasmed. Now they could see it breathe. Its metabolism sped, accelerating to match theirs, until its internal processes were running—and would run out—as quickly as theirs. Its surface contours turned liquid, concentrating a thousand years' movements into seconds, and its voice, now as audible as its movements were visible, roared up at them through the throat of the crater as they dived, and entered Thahl's Alley.

Because particle beams were recoilless, the *Charles Manson* broke through the asteroid's surface without impact. There was only a soft concussion, as of a finger poking into an eyeball; and then, abruptly, a shuffle and flicker of universes. The forward screen simply shifted from one frame, where they broke orbit and dived vertically, to another, where space turned to rock and outside to inside. Cause and effect tripped over each other. The screen showed impossible events by the light of impossible colours.

Thahl's Alley was a moving wormhole. They were the forward tip of a burrowing internal wound which opened ahead as it closed behind. Rock turned viscous, roared and fell away boiling before them where the beams ate it, but Thahl's Alley only existed ahead. Behind them it collapsed and coagulated, its collapse chasing but never quite catching them. Ahead and Behind worked in counterpoint, like a pair of thighs, to draw them deeper inside.

"Missile still there?"

"Yes, Commander," said Smithson, and swore. "Even through *this*."

And again, the engagement turned on itself. Their orders were to engage and destroy Faith in single combat, and now those orders—even the shapes of the words—melted. Thahl had injected them into an asteroid, and they were burrowing for its core where their beams would annihilate it and (perhaps) burst them free of its explosion in a manoeuvre not even Kaang had attempted; and all of this to destroy, not Faith, but just Her third missile.

The beams ate, they moved forward, the wound closed behind them, the beams ate, they moved forward. By now Cyr was laughing aloud ("Kaang should see *this*! Thahl, it's brilliant. It might even work!") and firing continuously, and the colours were breathtaking. Ahead of them where the wound opened, the beams had made something which was almost a sun, a swirling whiteness of molten colours fracturing and recombining, but its colour never reached the Bridge screen. The dark bruise-blue of the beams filtered its glare down to polite pastels of peach and mauve and lilac: delicate, lying colours which imparted a wash of wonder to their creation of Thahl's Alley, but drained it of its enormity. And hid its ending.

"There's no more I can do for now, Commander," Thahl said. "Not until we reach the core."

Foord nodded. For the last few minutes—it felt like seconds, but the screen said minutes—he had watched Thahl as closely as the screen, because the idea that Thahl could have devised *this* was as bewitching as any of the roiling interior-decorator pastels ahead. He knew less of Thahl, after years, than he did of Faith, after days.

More minutes passed. The beams ate, they moved forward, the wound closed behind them, the beams ate, they moved forward. It was a simple internal-combustion cycle, driven by post-Einsteinian physics. Foord would have given a lot to see what Thahl's instruments (roll, pitch, yaw, speed, spatial coordinates) were making of it; they were still on ninety percent ion speed, but *inside* an asteroid. And the missile...

"Still there, Commander," Smithson said.

"And," Thahl added, "we're not on ninety percent speed. We're on ninety percent power, but speed is down because we're not moving through space."

Did I think aloud? Foord asked, or thought he asked, And did I ask aloud if I was thinking aloud, or only think it? And did I—

That was when it started to change. They were slowing down, like his thoughts. Their speed had dropped when they entered the asteroid, and was dropping further. Nearer the core, matter was denser and penetration harder, the pastel illusion of an alley ahead growing darker and closing tighter. The colours themselves were slowing down and deepening. Events were suddenly gradual, slowing too fast; even sounds came more slowly.

"The one. She intend. Dead. For us." Joser's voice crawled around his head, trying to get in.

"Can you tell us how long before we reach the core?" Foord heard himself asking Thahl.

"No, Commander, because I can't predict our rate of slowing. Maybe we won't."

"Won't?"

"If we reach the core the beams will explode the asteroid. If we don't we'll be embedded. Like…"

Like the Book of Srahr in its crystal, Foord thought. Or said.

The beams ate; they edged forward; the wound closed behind them.

The air was as thick as tree-resin, trapping events like insects. It smothered light and sound, made thoughts meander, and conversations mumble to nowhere. Time inverted itself. Minutes stretched into seconds, or longer.

Foord found himself repeating his last conversation with Thahl. He walked around the words. They stood like stones in a cemetery. This time there were *three* voices in the conversation, not two. The third voice was a roaring which obliterated some words at random like an idiot's finger daubing a page.

"Can you"

"Us how long before we reach the"

"Won't?"

"Like the Book of Srahr in its"

Then the third voice reversed itself, and became the words it obliterated. Tell. Core. Crystal. The words crumbled, and the voice was wordless again. It chased its own echoes, caught them and became continuous, and

Foord began to dread it, so he went away.

Back in the cemetery the words were still standing like stones, but something else was there too. Where the word Crystal should have stood was a darkness. It spread. First it put out thin tendrils, like hairline cracks in the air; then thicker tendrils, which chased and caught the thinner ones and wandered among the words, engulfing and denying them. Then it joined itself and became a black web, as large as a planet. It turned to face Foord, swivelling on him simultaneously from above and below and all around, and—suddenly intimate—it pulled aside part of itself and showed him its inner recesses. Foord dreaded it. He went away, back to his ship, but the darkness followed him there, where it became the third voice.

The third voice was the voice of the asteroid, roaring at them from above and below and all around, swelling towards explosion: the rending of rock through which a dark web of fault-lines radiated, first thin then thick, chasing each other. It was wordless but held hints of words, growing and dying inside it; and Foord, returning to his ship from wherever he had been, found himself returning to a madhouse.

"The one…" Joser began.

"*Got* you," Cyr whispered, firing, and "Now hurry up and die." The asteroid rushed to obey her.

"…She intended for us." Joser was talking to himself, and being ignored.

"Still there!" Smithson bellowed, jabbing at the rear screen. "And it won't *ever* go away!"

And Thahl, the most shocking of all, because Foord had never heard him shout before. *Too early, it's exploding too early, we haven't reached the core yet and I'm not ready—*

"Thahl?"

"Commander. I'm glad you're back. I thought you'd gone away."

"I thought so too."

"Look out there, Commander. Look at what we've done."

They were talking quietly together, as if nothing else existed; as if the ship wasn't trying to collapse around them, as if the asteroid wasn't trying to pull open the walls of Thahl's Alley and make itself burst.

"So the beams—"

"Were too strong for it, Commander."

Still, thought Foord, finishing each other's sentences. "I didn't think it would go quite so quickly, though."

"Didn't you? It was only an asteroid."

They both shrugged, a gesture equally fitting as an end to their conversation, or to their years together; then they turned back to the Bridge screen, and considered what they had done.

The air changed. Thickness and slowness drained out of it. It turned sharp and crystalline. Light and events, having almost stopped, began to move again; *but away from each other*, parallelling the movement of each atom in the asteroid. They were all moving away from each other, like Sakhrans after reading the Book of Srahr.

Time restarted. Light shook itself free of the brown rotting gloom, crawled back through familiar pastels and burst into solar white, breeding new events like life-forms.

Thahl's Alley opened out into light. Fault-lines radiated from it, reaching through the asteroid's body like the fingers of a hand, and when they reached the surface the asteroid exploded, blowing through the fingers like sand.

6

Grains of sand.

Time restarted, multiplied, became abundant. Even events couldn't breed fast enough to fill it, and as the asteroid exploded and the ship fought to outrun the explosion, Foord had time to reflect on those events: on their scale of magnitude. Scales of magnitude had occupied him a lot, ever since he saw a perfectly ordinary Class 037 cruiser pass endlessly overhead at Blentport.

When they approached the asteroid, it was breathing in long geological cycles, heaving its flanks in response to the Belt's gravity. On a scale of magnitude, they and their ship were microbes in a phial, approaching a mountain.

Sometimes you could trust scales of magnitude. They were simple and linear. For example, two scorpions fighting. They would clack their claws and wave their stings, faces moving like gearboxes, while lesser things around them scurried away aghast. Then an elephant would step on them as it wandered by.

But sometimes, scales of magnitude were ambiguous, hinting that small events were the tip of something larger. For example, two animals glancing at each other, but they were the last dinosaur and the first mammal. Or a small pallid corpse on a beach, but the corpse of the first creature to crawl from the sea.

And sometimes, scales of magnitude were treacherous. They could turn full circle, letting the smallest overpower the largest. The microbes in the phial approaching the mountain were not themselves a threat, but they had *made* the phial which carried them, and it had the power to explode the mountain; and did so.

She remained at the outer edges of the Belt, still shrouded, and watched them. She had seen them execute a photon burst through the Belt, then burrow through an asteroid to explode it from within, and then try to outrun the resulting explosion. She still held all the advantages; they might not escape the explosion, and Her missile had come out of the asteroid with them and was still dogging them, and She knew they couldn't shake it off. But still, they had done such things that She was beginning to take notice.

7

"This is the one," Joser was saying "She intended for us this is the one." He was trying to say something and didn't know what it was, but he knew it wasn't *that*. Every time he tried to speak to them it came out as those words, but it didn't matter because nobody heard him or, at that time, even remembered him.

They ran, just ahead of the asteroid's explosion. The Bridge was chaotic and unrecognisable. Part of the minor core which ran the Bridge's gravity compensators had been damaged, and now was not the time to repair it. Things which had no business but to be fixed pieces of furniture and equipment had taken to an aerial existence, ricochetting off walls and ceilings like shoals of fish frightened one way and another. They went everywhere. Foord and the others were shouting, not in fear but in outrage that mere external events could dishevel them so.

After what they'd done it would have been fitting to have burst clear and to have seen the asteroid explode from a safe distance. It would even have been fitting, though less satisfactory, to have perished instantly in the centre of the explosion. The fact that their situation was neither of these, but something less than either, was an outrage.

They had burst clear of the explosion, but it had not stopped. It was gathering a wavefront behind them which was now racing and radiating through the Belt, so huge it would be visible to instruments on Sakhra. And their own instruments told them that if they ran as they were now— desperately, at ninety-five percent ion drive, because Thahl wasn't Kaang and couldn't use photon drive—then the wavefront would catch them before it dwindled to nothing.

It would hit them in about five minutes. They'd probably survive, the screen added insolently, but whether the damage would be serious or minor couldn't be predicted.

So they ran, just ahead of the wavefront. How could one asteroid, however massive, go on and on exploding like that? It was throwing out more matter than it was made of. As though someone at the other end of the galaxy had found an MT wormhole where the asteroid exploded, and was throwing fresh debris down it. As though the people in the apartment next door had knocked a hole in the wall and were shovelling things through it: cans, and cornflake cartons, and cat litter, and condoms.

"And the third missile?"

"I already told you, Commander," Smithson snapped. "We didn't lose it. It's still there, a ship's-length away."

"And damage reports? I want damage reports."

"No *time*, Commander, it came out with us and it's still there and it's like none of this ever happened."

"I said, damage reports. Cyr, closeup weapons; Thahl, try to lose it."

"I'm already trying to lose it, Commander."

"Like none of this happened," Smithson muttered.

"And I'm already using closeup weapons," Cyr said. *Just like before, and they didn't work then either,* she thought, but didn't say.

"The one She…"

Foord turned again to Smithson. "I said, Damage reports."

"Oh, for fuck's sake. Look behind us."

Her missile was still there, so close it filled half the rear screen. But behind it, filling the entire rear screen, was the wavefront which, like Foord's elephant, threatened to squash them all without noticing. In about three minutes, added Smithson.

The wavefront rolled on and on. It seemed like it would reach back to Sakhra. They had already rewritten part of the map of the Belt, in the form of the asteroids they had vaporised; now, a bigger part was being rewritten right behind them, and seeking to include them.

That extraordinary missile, Foord mused, and that wavefront. Two ticking bombs.

"This is. The one She."

Three, with Joser. Three was too many, so again he forgot Joser.

"Intended for us."

"Thahl, use the last five percent ion drive, please."

He did, and so did the missile.

Still stationary, relative to them. Filling half the rear screen. Neither gaining nor falling back. Like before, it had started deploying its flickerfields against Cyr's attacks, and like before it stopped. No need. No time, either to drain it or destroy it. It had perhaps two or three percent ion drive left, and they had nothing. And two minutes from now the wavefront would catch them, and they had nothing for that either.

There was an impact, but not the missile; not yet. They had ploughed into some asteroid debris, and momentarily went reeling until Thahl righted them. The missile reeled and righted itself with them. More impacts. Thahl's control of the ship was collapsing; he was fighting the collapse carefully and intelligently, but losing.

The Belt closed in on them. Asteroids and asteroid fragments came at them from ahead and above and below, looming and roaring and whipping past and leaving afterimages through which new ones loomed and roared. The Bridge screen listed them coldly and without comment as they passed, some of them the remains of those destroyed earlier. AN-4044, AL-4091, AD-2025. A series of minor impacts, and then something more serious, a sickening impact to port as they hit and glanced off a fragment from a smallish asteroid, AC-1954. Foord remembered that one. The alarms sounded: *real* damage.

"Port manoeuvre drives impaired, at least twenty percent," Smithson said.

Foord shrugged. They didn't, at that time, have any pressing need for manoeuvre drives. "And the wavefront?"

"Fifty seconds, Commander. But it's dwindling."

Joser tried again. He had something to tell Foord but not the words he'd been repeating. His mouth *his mouth* wouldn't make any other words.

"This is the one She intended for us."

He screamed, and it came out as those words. Shouted, and it came out as those words. Then he drew a last breath, dredged up all his willpower, dragged himself back to sanity, and spoke in clear ringing tones; but it came out as those words.

"This is the one She in*tend*ed for us. This is the one She in*tend*ed for us. This is the one She in*tend*ed for us."

This the way the world ends, thought Foord, picking up the rhythm with a line of old poetry, This is the way the world ends, This is the way the world ends, not with a bang but a

BANG.

It was, amazingly, the report of a pistol. A big, blue-black, old-fashioned pistol which Joser was holding. He had just shot himself in the temple, and seemed to be staring down at the pistol through his nostrils, since the half of his face which still remained began from the nostrils downwards. He slumped, and the seat took him.

His blood and brains, like Kaang's faeces, went everywhere. As with Kaang, they turned away.

"She's actually killed one of us," Cyr said.

"She did that long ago," Foord said, as the wavefront caught and hit them.

"And," he added, "none of us is One Of Us."

●

The wavefront was already dying. The further it reached the more insubstantial it became, until finally when it caught them it passed over them like sand. Their desperate flight from it had been just enough. The ship still spasmed as it hit, but the flickerfields held; and then it was gone, roaring past them and dwindling, in the forward screen, to nothing.

But the missile was still there.

"Smithson: damage reports, please."

"Hull, rear dorsal section, and manoeuvre drives, port and rear dorsal. Nothing we couldn't repair, if we had time."

The Bridge was suddenly quieter. Foord watched the asteroids looming and whipping past. Despite what had happened, they seemed almost peaceful.

"Missile's gaining. She's decided it should hit now, I think."

"Commander…" began Thahl.

"It's OK. There's no need."

The grey ovoid swelled slowly in the rear screen, since its speed exceeded theirs by only one or two percent. Naturally they deployed their flicker-fields, but were past surprise when it somehow slipped inside them; this was a missile like none they had ever encountered. They watched it grow larger, then blur prior to impact as it passed inside the screen's final focus. But there was no explosion, just a soft *thump*; and something obscuring the rear screen.

"No. I don't believe it."

"What?" Foord said. "Who's that speaking?"

"Slesar, Commander. Officer Joser's deputy. I'm sorry, my call should have gone through to him."

"Never mind that, what's happened?"

"It's on the screen, Commander."

The rear Bridge screen refocussed, and became a stained-glass window of dark red and terracotta, of burnt umber and sienna streaked with ochre. Headup displays provided a spectrographic analysis, but it wasn't necessary. As soon as Smithson started laughing, they knew.

The third missile had been packed full of shit, probably the last of Her stock from Isis. It was as though Kaang had returned to them, on a grand scale.

8

Two hours later, Kaang did return to the Bridge. She found that it and its occupants had changed; perhaps for better or worse, but certainly for good.

"Welcome back, Kaang."

"Thank you, Commander."

She stood in the main doorway, swaying slightly, and blinking at what she saw.

"Yes, I know," Foord said, waving an arm around, "A mess." His voice was still quiet, but he spoke more quickly, and with more emphasis, than she was used to. "One small repair, to one small gravity compensator, and all this debris would disappear. But I wanted it left like this. I *ordered* it left like this. I had my reasons. You'll see."

Joser's body was gone—she knew about Joser—and the Bridge consoles were impeccably tidy as usual, but everything else seemed chaotic. Kaang was bewildered. She had never seen it like this.

"Thahl has rerouted the pilot's functions back to your console, Kaang."

She nodded and began to pick her way, slightly unsteadily, through the mess and wreckage. Foord took her arm—he had never touched her before—and walked alongside her. His movements were different, somehow more abrupt and jagged; she was used to him moving about his ship silently and carefully. He kicked pieces of debris out of the way, and led her (not directly, but following the walls) to her console.

The others nodded as she passed—she mouthed Thank You to Thahl—but said nothing. Their expressions were hard to read.

She looked diminished. Her hair was lank and greasy, the scars on her face and forehead from the neural implants had not yet healed, and her eyes were larger and duller.

"Smithson," Foord called over his shoulder, "damage reports?"

"Moderate structural damage to rear ventral hull. Manoeuvre drives severely impaired to port, moderately impaired to starboard. MT Drive shut down and inoperable. And we're covered in shit."

"How long?"

"Another five hours. But we can't completely restore the port manoeuvre drives; they'll still be ten percent impaired."

"And Faith?"

"No change, Commander. She's stationary at the inner edge of the Belt, and out of beam range. At asteroid CQ-504."

"What's She doing there?"

"It's strange, Commander, She's—"

"No, leave it. I remember, you told me before…" He turned to Kaang. "You see?"

She blinked up at him. "What, Commander?"

He pointed to the Bridge screen. "What She's done to us."

She saw, though it took her a moment to adjust. The screen was subdivided into a mosaic of smaller screens. Each one showed views of the ship from outside, transmitted to the Bridge from remotes floating under, over and around the hull. The hull itself was swarming with figures, human and nonhuman, living and mechanical and synthetic. Apart from the six (now five) on the Bridge, the *Charles Manson* had a crew of fifty-seven. About thirty, Kaang estimated, were on the hull, outnumbered by mechanicals and synthetics.

The slender delta shape at first looked, as ever, perfect and inviolate; until random stabs of the arc-lights from the working parties threw into sudden relief the jagged edges of damage, mostly around the rear and port sections. Kaang could see the gashes and striations which, suddenly lit then dark then lit again, seemed to pulse like infected areas. And as her eyes adjusted further she saw where the hull was streaked and daubed.

She resumed her seat at her console. She seemed to grow back a little, but only a little, into her normal shape and identity.

"Thahl's rerouted the pilot's functions back to you, Kaang."

"Yes, Commander. You told me."

"He *has* rerouted them back." Foord spoke as if he had to be certain of that before he could say anything else to her, about anything. "We have a lot to do. Now you're back, we'll begin. By saying goodbye to Joser."

●

They waited for Foord's signal. When he gave it, each of them—including the synthetics and mechanicals—stopped working on the hull and turned to face the nearest remote, so that back on the Bridge Foord could see them all looking into the screen. The sealed capsule containing Joser's body was ready for ejection through one of the ventral airlocks.

Like most of those on the *Charles Manson*, Joser had no family or relatives—or none with whom he kept contact—and had elected, In The Event Of My Death In Service, for burial in space. The nine Outsiders had standard words for such occasions. Foord spoke them over the comm.

"Before he was born, he already existed. As a set of possibilities. As something unknowable. While he lived, he was the visible tip of that same thing. Now let him return to it, and still exist. Perhaps."

Joser's capsule ejected from the rear ventral airlock, and drifted away.

Faith's first victim went out in the same direction as that taken by Her third missile, after it impacted the ship. The missile had collapsed its molecular structure, become an irregular inert object about three feet across, and drifted away. Nobody felt disposed to follow it. Joser did, now.

●

"You added a word to the standard service," Kaang heard Smithson say to Foord.

"Perhaps," Foord said.

"Yes," Smithson said. "Perhaps. It's not in the service."

"Perhaps it ought to be…. Is the comm still on?"

It was. Work had not resumed. All over the hull, they were still staring into the Bridge screen.

"This opponent," Foord said into the comm, "is like none we've ever encountered. Before we finish repairs and go after Her, I want us to consider Her. To consider what She is."

"Commander," Cyr began, "this isn't—it won't—"

"It *is* and it *will*. This is important. I have my reasons. You'll see."

The figures on the hull were motionless. All of them, including the mechanicals and synthetics, seemed to be listening intently.

"Kaang, you start. What is She?"

"Commander, what's happened while I've been away?"

"What do you mean?"

"Our orders said destroy Her and ignore what She is. *You* said that. What's happened to make you change?"

"I'm sorry, Kaang, it was unfair to start with you. I'll come back to you later, but listen and you'll see why I'm asking….Thahl, what about you? What do you think She is? Is She from the Commonwealth, maybe a rebel?"

"Perhaps, Commander. But a ship like that—"

"Like what? We've been fighting Her all this time, and we haven't *seen* her yet."

"We know what She looks like, and we know some of what She can do, from records of previous engagements...She's not a Commonwealth ship."

"Or maybe She is, but just not one that we know of."

Thahl paused. "Then maybe we *don't* know what She looks like. She can bend and confuse scanners. Maybe how she appeared in previous engagements isn't how She really is."

"Maybe. So what is She?"

Thahl thought for a moment, then glanced up at Foord.

"Maybe She's been secretly built and funded by some of the I2Js," (he meant those Invited To Join) "to strike back at the Commonwealth."

A ripple of something, perhaps amusement, went through the Bridge. It was impossible to tell, from the heavily-suited figures on the screen, whether whatever it was had been echoed outside.

"Better," said Foord. "But it's not what you really think...Smithson, what is She?"

"How about something made secretly by the Commonwealth to eliminate Outsiders? You know what they think of us, Commander."

"Much better," approved Foord. "I like that one, it's so self-obsessed and so paranoid. So: Kaang."

"Commander?"

"What is She?"

"I wish I could take part in this, Commander, but you know I can't. We agreed. I'm only a pilot."

"Come on, Kaang."

"I really don't know...perhaps your suggestion, that She's some kind of rebel."

"Too obvious, and She'd need a better pilot. She'd have tried to recruit you...Cyr, what is She?"

"Do we have to go on with this, Commander?"

"Yes. What is She?"

"Maybe She really is just an alien. Maybe this is the first real threat we've ever known. The first of many. Maybe this is the start of a war, against the first enemy we've ever met who can really match us."

"She came here three hundred years ago, Cyr. It wasn't the start of a war against Sakhra."

"It didn't need to be. Whatever She did was enough for Her to leave and let Sakhra decline." She glanced at Thahl, who remained expressionless. "The Commonwealth is bigger. Maybe a war is more appropriate."

When the silence on the Bridge had grown long enough to be uncomfortable, Cyr added "You did ask me. And it's what we all heard back on Sakhra."

"And is it what *you* think?"

"Yes, Commander, because it's the most likely. The best fit."

"Except that the Commonwealth has ordered *us* to engage and destroy Her alone. Just *us*."

"That doesn't make it untrue."

"It doesn't matter whether it's true or not, Cyr."

"Oh? Then what is all this about, Commander? You told us—"

"To *consider* what She is. Not discover. Not decide. *Consider!* Consider all the explanations, because all the explanations, whether they're true or not, tell us the same thing."

"Do *you* have an explanation for us, Commander?"

"Yes, I think She's an alien. But not like you described, Cyr. Something quite different. Perhaps…"

"I meant an explanation for your behaviour here, Commander."

"…Perhaps what we've been fighting all this time isn't even a ship. Perhaps it doesn't have a Commander, or crew, or pilot. Perhaps it's a single life-form, evolved to live in space like a fish in water. Or a marine mammal, which looks like a fish but preys on fish. Yes: it looks like a ship but preys on ships."

"And how," Cyr inquired politely, "does it prey on ships? Does it eat them?"

"Absorbs their energies," Smithson offered. "You know, feeds on their feelings of mortification, after it's defeated them in various elaborate and enigmatic ways."

"Yes! And," Cyr went on delightedly, "and its drives, its scanners, its beams, its missiles, all the things that make it look like a ship, they're evolutionary mimicry."

"You see? It's getting better. You're adding details. Building internal consistencies." Foord stood up and gazed round the Bridge. His gaze was almost feverish, but it had something almost like certainty. Kaang saw each of them, herself included, try but fail to hold it.

"All the explanations, even the wrong ones—even that last one of mine, which is the most wrong—tell us the same thing. Even the explanations we haven't thought of yet, when we think of them, will tell us the same thing."

Abruptly, he turned and walked back to where Kaang sat at her console. As before, he went around the walls rather than directly, kicking debris as he went, and when he reached Kaang he towered over her.

"Let's recap. A renegade who hates the Commonwealth, and strikes at *us* because we're its most dangerous instrument. A resistance force from the I2Js who hate the Commonwealth, and strike at *us* because we're its most dangerous instrument. Something made by the Commonwealth, because the Commonwealth hates *us* and strikes at *us* because we're its most dangerous instrument. Something from another civilisation, the first ever to threaten the Commonwealth; and it strikes at *us* because we're its most dangerous instrument. You see where this takes us?"

Kaang felt the base of her neck aching as she stared up at him, trying to read what was in his face.

"We're alone. Trust nothing. Trust nobody. We're all we've got."

He glanced at the screen. The comm was still working, and none of the figures on the hull had moved. And Kaang, who didn't yet understand his meaning but had started to sense it from his voice, felt her scalp tingling.

"This is why I don't care who or what She is. I never have and never will. We're an Outsider, one of only nine, and we're alone. The Commonwealth created Outsiders as its ultimate weapon. It kept them outside normal command structures. It named them after killers and loners. It crewed them with killers and loners, people unable to fit normal social structures, but too brilliant and too valuable to discard.

"And when they came into those nine ships they brought only their abilities, and nothing else. No shared culture and no friendship. They were alone together. The other eight are still like that, but we've encountered Her and it's made us different. And this is why we can destroy Her. Because we know what we are."

On the screen, in the distance, there was a brief and silent flare. The required standard period had elapsed and Joser's coffin ignited, returning him to the set of possibilities he had always been. Perhaps.

"We're going after Her. We'll repair the structural damage and drives; but the surface damage, stays as it is. The shit over the hull, stays as it is. The Bridge, stays as it is. We, stay as we are. We'll taste and smell each other. This is what we are.

"Joser won't be replaced on the Bridge; we'll share his duties. And when we next face Her, it won't be for Joser, or the Commonwealth, or friendship or professional pride, it'll be because of what *She* made us. She was right: everything outside this ship is an illusion, and it hates us. Or She was lying, and everything outside this ship is real; and it still hates us. We're all we have, and outside this tin can we can trust nothing and nobody. We're all there is. Nothing else exists. That, out there, is painted scenery.

"We're no longer an Instrument of the Commonwealth. We're an Instrument of Ourselves."

9

For once, thought Smithson, *Kaang was ahead of everyone*. She had sensed Foord's meaning before anyone else—even before he, Smithson, sensed it. He saw that shudder, that frisson, go through her *before* Foord said Instrument of Ourselves. Afterwards he saw it go through everyone on the Bridge, and everyone outside on the hull, and he'd felt it go through himself; his long grey body, with its almost random construction, visibly rippled. Nobody cheered—this was, after all, still the *Charles Manson*—but Foord's words had an impact. They had gone everywhere.

When Foord finished, most of them just nodded briefly—to themselves rather than to each other, because again this was still the *Charles Manson*—and resumed work. Smithson too. Oh *yes*, he'd said to himself, I can buy some of that. Fuck everyone except us. Fuck the universe. Painted scenery. And, he thought sourly as he looked out from the Bridge at the stars, not even very well painted. Those stars look alive but most of them, by the time their light reaches us, are dead or dying. They look alive but they're dead. Trust nothing.

The *Charles Manson* nosed its way carefully through the Belt, towards Faith. Her current position was unchanged, and had been for some time, even while Her third missile chased them. She was on the inner edge of the Belt, at the asteroid CQ-504. She could have moved off ahead of them, out of the Belt and deeper into Horus system, and they could not have stopped Her, as She was out of beam range. But She didn't move off. It was curious, thought Smithson. She seemed to be building some kind of structure there.

Cyr too was considering what Foord said. She took each word, held it up and examined it from every angle: port, starboard, ventral, dorsal, front, rear. She particularly liked Instrument of Ourselves. It resonated. He made it sound spontaneous, but she knew he was too careful, and too clever, to say it without calculation. But it had a resonance. Now, we know what we are.

Cyr didn't like the bit about being able to smell and taste each other. She understood the symbolism perfectly; but she liked to be immaculate. To be anything less than immaculate was a high price to pay—for her, almost the ultimate price—but she weighed it carefully and decided it would be worth it. And she could already smell and taste Foord.

The *Charles Manson* nosed its way carefully through the Belt, towards Faith and the asteroid CQ-504. It was curious, Cyr thought to herself. She was apparently building some kind of structure there.

Kaang kept remembering The Shudder. Having felt instinctively what Foord said, she tried again and again to analyse it literally, the way Cyr and Smithson and Thahl would do; and failed. It didn't matter. She knew that what Foord said would change them all. It meant a shift in some previously immovable balance. And more specifically, it meant that she would be needed. She didn't understand where her extraordinary skills came from, but they would be needed and she was back in time to provide them, so that was alright. She missed Joser, though.

The *Charles Manson* nosed its way carefully through the Belt, towards Faith. It was curious, Kaang thought. She was apparently building some kind of structure on CQ-504. She had shrouded it against their probes, but they intended to know more about it by the time they reached Her.

Since Foord spoke, Thahl had been thinking about the Book of Srahr, and how one day—if they survived this—Foord would return to Sakhra and would be permitted to read it. And then a pattern would be completed, a long slow pattern three centuries old.

Thahl made himself turn to specifics. The *Charles Manson* was the most formidable ship in the Commonwealth; and what Foord said made it more so. Even She, when they next engaged Her, wouldn't know that. She would expect them to act like an Instrument of the Commonwealth, which they no longer were. Foord was right. Now we can beat Her, because now we know what we are. An Instrument "—of Ourselves," Foord repeated, as the *Charles Manson* nosed its way carefully through the Belt. "And we have to make it irreversible. So…" He picked up the incongruous microphone on his console, the one with a channel to the Department, dashed it on the floor of the Bridge and ground it with his heel. He drew a breath. "Thahl, please close down ALL external comm channels."

Thahl glanced up, but did not hesitate. Foord watched his hands, slender talons with two opposed thumbs, moving over his illuminated console, leaving darkness wherever they landed.

"Done, Commander. We're alone."

The microphone was only symbolic. Thahl knew the Department would have put several other probes on the ship; he knew about most of them, but not all. Later, Foord would order him to disable them, which he would do, but he wouldn't get them all. So, the microphone was only symbolic, but the symbolism was powerful.

The Department would want to retaliate. If they destroyed Her, they would put themselves beyond the Department's retaliation, and if they didn't destroy Her then She'd destroy them; and they'd be beyond the Department's retaliation. Either way, Foord had now locked them outside. They were genuinely outside the Department's reach.

The symbolism was very powerful, but Thahl knew Foord had also calculated it carefully, as he always did. And it wasn't only, or at least wasn't entirely, a mere cynical calculation—Thahl, too, had felt The Shudder. They all had. Exactly as Foord had calculated.

●

There was a silence on the Bridge. Even when they started speaking the silence remained in their speech, jumping from the end of one sentence to the beginning of another.

"They'll want to know why," Kaang said.

"When this is over," Cyr said, "and when we rejoin, we can tell them."

"Perhaps we won't rejoin," Smithson said.

"Of course we will," Cyr said. "Instrument Of Ourselves is right for what we need now, but we'll have to rejoin. When She's gone, there will be..."

"Nowhere else to go," finished Kaang. "That's right, isn't it?"

"Yes," Smithson said, "but for now I prefer it like this. It feels right."

The silence was quite unlike the *Charles Manson*'s usual repertoire of silences: reflective, rather than pregnant. Some of them gazed out across the plane of the Belt, in the direction of the inner edge where She waited. The stars twinkled. Some of them were dead.

"Some of us will die," Smithson said.

"Yes," Foord said. "But now we really can defeat Her. And She doesn't know it, yet."

"She'll know," Kaang said, unexpectedly, "when we engage Her. Ships have a body language."

"What will She..." Cyr began, then stopped for a moment and glanced curiously at Kaang. "What will She do when She finds out?"

"It isn't important," Thahl said suddenly. "We all know, She isn't concerned either way."

The others looked at him.

"Anything sent up to stop Her is irrelevant. She may destroy it, play with it, or let it go. She isn't concerned either way."

"For once..." Foord began, then stopped for a moment and glanced curiously at Thahl. "For once, I think you're wrong. Where we're concerned, She *is* concerned. She won't run ahead of us to Sakhra, and She won't stay put in the Belt. She wants to fight us all the way through the system. All the way back to Sakhra. I *know* it."

And then something else occurred to Foord. These pieces of knowledge about Her which he'd been gathering so carefully, based on his observation and research and on what he thought was his growing instinct about Her, perhaps they weren't real. Perhaps they were planted by Her, as She had done with Joser. Not by telepathy, but events. *She does things, and predicts their effect on us, which means that somehow She already knows us.*

He was so struck with this idea that he scarcely noticed when Cyr excused herself from the Bridge. Something I need to check in the weapons bays, she had said. I'll be back in thirty minutes. He nodded abstractedly.

●

Unnecessary, Cyr told herself, as she picked her way through the cramped corridor leading to the weapons bays, Unnecessary. *Like the kid you shot at Blentport.* It was a vicious thing to say, more like something *I'd* say, and it made him sound ugly. I should have spoken to him. She imagined the conversation, in his study. —You wanted to see me? —Yes, what you said. How could you say that, after I'd just destroyed Her missiles? —Yes, I know. I'm sorry. Was there anything else? Foord had a habit of receiving an attack, draining it, and tossing it back to the attacker like a dead empty thing; it was a habit Cyr knew he could apply to his personal dealings as well as his military ones.

The main corridor branched into several narrower corridors, with naked lights and unfinished plaster, and she took the one leading to the bay she wanted. On the way she had to squeeze past one of her junior officers, a young woman called Hollith, so tightly that at least one of them enjoyed it, and then she was in the particular bay she had come to visit, staring up at Foord's two missiles.

She had come here to try and figure them out: not what they did, but how he'd *use* them. Everyone knew he delivered every time, against every opponent, but how would he deliver *this* time? And against *this* opponent? Even Smithson, arguably the cleverest of them, had not been able to see how Foord would use these things. Smithson, in fact, had been quite disparaging about them, perhaps irritated by their simple design and by Foord's cryptic answers to his questions.

Smithson, arguably the cleverest of us? She did a double-take on that, just as Foord might have done. First, as he would have said, there is no Us. And second, she knew Foord operated on the principle that they were all at least his intellectual equals. Still, if even Smithson can't figure them out and I can…Then she looked up at them again, at their ugly flanks with overlapping blue-black metal plates, their strange nosecones and obscenely swelling drive bulges. They seemed to stare back at her insolently, giving her nothing. How could Foord devise weapons whose use even Smithson couldn't figure out, though Foord had got Smithson to *build* them? Two reasons, she told herself. One, because he'd put the answer in plain sight where it would be most hidden, and Two, because he was clever; at least as clever as Smithson, which meant very clever indeed.

Cyr was from a wealthy Old Earth family which provided the Commonwealth with a monotonous stream of diplomats and bankers and senior civil servants. She had opted instead for a military career, and her family had disowned her, not because of her career choice but because of another choice she made.

Her family was as large as it was wealthy. Her childhood and adolescence was full of brothers and sisters, aunts and uncles, grandparents and cousins; full of mahogany and velvet, lawns and landscaped gardens, parties and functions and friends; and full of the particular ease which came from wealth worn lightly. Even by their standards she was unusually clever and attractive and they adored her and surrounded her, sensing she would distinguish herself but not, then, knowing how.

For her, the darkness came later than it did for Foord, and came differently. Her fifteenth birthday was marked with a party in the grounds of her home. It lasted through most of the day and she slipped indoors to go to the bathroom. A friend of her father's, also a diplomat, followed her inside. He had always been attentive and kind, a regular guest at the house. This is our secret, he said as he started touching her, A special birthday present. Her instincts took over; she fought back with her hands and then, when he still wouldn't go away, with her father's cutthroat razor. The stroke which actually stopped him was a lucky one, but he collapsed abruptly and bled copiously. It went everywhere.

It was a revelation; the birth of her private universe. It made her want to lock the door and masturbate. If he'd still been conscious she'd have let him have her. She *owed* him. He had written down for her, all over the walls and floor, exactly what she was.

Later the stories about him came out, how he used to cruise at night for partners, usually younger or poorer or less intelligent than himself. He had hidden it from his family and had kept it apart from his public career, as would she; but she would do it better. His attempts to hide it were really quite mediocre. She hated mediocrity.

Her early sexual experiences were unsatisfactory, and now she knew why. Sex didn't have to be shared with others. It could be *done* to others, and could be heightened by hurting them. She cruised for strangers. She never chose family, or people she knew at school or university, or military colleagues: always, it was strangers. She cruised cities for them like a smaller-scale Faith, random and motiveless, beautiful and brilliant. And perhaps also like Faith, she did it out of a compulsion which she wouldn't acknowledge, preferring to call it choice.

Occasionally she thought *What have I become*, but that voice was distant, and the voice that said *This Is What I AM* was louder and more insistent. It would not be denied. Her earliest episodes were technically rapes, but even that distinction grew blurred: some of the later ones, though disturbingly violent, were almost consensual. Nothing, even then, was simple. And occasional episodes of pain and violation in dark teeming rooms weren't enough. She wanted more than bits of opportunism. In the future it should be larger-scale, not the exception but the rule. It should be what it *really was,* a regular part of her life.

That was when she made her other choice, and became something quite unusual, a female serial rapist. She preferred Multiple or Random; Serial implied a process of growth and increase, whereas she saw it as a large but stable part of her life: something important, but something which had found its allotted place and wouldn't grow to engulf her. Later, the distinction would be lost on the media who covered her trial. Predictably, they labelled her The CYRial Rapist.

At first, her military career flourished. She was high-achieving, high-profile and glamorous. She won Commonwealth and Olympic small arms medals, but that was only her hobby. Her career was large scale weaponry, ships' weaponry, and she excelled at it. Her ability was natural, but not like Kaang's; she had to work hard at it. Her military colleagues, sensing this, surrounded her and adored her, unaware of the moral toxin she carried.

She had chosen this career in the hope that she would find a legitimate outlet for what was in her, but this was one of her few mistakes. The conventional military of course dealt in violence, but only as a means and not an end; and not, usually, random or gratuitous violence. It was the suspicion of fellow crew-members which finally brought her to trial.

No, she told the court, it's absolutely *not* a compulsion, it's a conscious choice. I can choose not to. Mere serial rapists have to follow a pattern. I don't. It's *not* a compulsion. The prosecuting counsel nodded in agreement, then told the court *It's a compulsion. She's described it very precisely. Her descriptions are always very precise.*

She was sentenced to indefinite confinement in a secure mental institution, and then the Department came for her. Part of the arrangement—the unwritten part—was that, in return for using her proven talents on an Outsider, she could continue cruising; she could even continue enjoying the pain and violation, but—they told her—she had to be able to prove it was consensual and negotiated. Get them to sign a contract, they told her. Here's a draft we've prepared.

And she remained very wealthy; the Department supplied her with lawyers to fight her family's attempts to disinherit her. Her family could afford the very best lawyers, but the Department's were better.

Most of the others on Foord's ship had done things by compulsion. She absolutely *knew* this wasn't the case with her. For her it was always by choice: free, rational, conscious choice. And because she realised she wasn't the same as the others, she treated them warily, even though many had abilities she respected. She regarded Smithson as foul and pompous but very clever, with an intuition which was irritatingly accurate; Kaang as uninteresting except for her almost supernatural ability as a pilot; Thahl as competent but enigmatic; and Joser, before he had the good taste to die, as someone whose scheming far exceeded his talent.

Foord had some of all these features, but not enough of any to unbalance or skew his performance; the best and worst of them, but mostly the best. Cyr could not deny that she had feelings for him, but they were bleak and grudging. They could hardly be anything else, given what each of them were. She often teased herself with the irony; they might almost be viable partners, if it wasn't for everything they were.

She gave herself a project: to find out what he had done to make the Department come for him, as it had come for her.

She had the wealth and resources to uncover his story. She embarked on the project as carefully and obsessively as Foord himself might have done, and eventually she found it; all of it. His parents and the orphanage and the rape and the priests he'd killed. Even the bit where he had later told the Department that he wished he'd known a Sakhran who could teach him how to kill more priests, more efficiently. She smiled. I wish you'd known *me* back then, I'd have taught you; and I'd have taught you how to enjoy it.

—You realise what this is? Mr. Gattuso, the proprietor of her favourite couture house, asked her when she described what she wanted. —Yes, she said, I know exactly what it is. Please make it for me. —I don't, Mr. Gattuso said, want to annoy one of my best customers, but I have to ask, Are you sure? If you wear this, it may produce An Effect. —I'm aware of that, she said. Now please make it for me. You know how I want it tailored. It must hang *just so*....

And it did produce an effect, one which amazed her. She had no idea that a mere garment could have such an extraordinary effect on grown men, but she quickly adjusted and learnt how to use it. She found it very satisfactory; she could glide among them acting as if she was unaware of it.

Prior to meeting Mr. Gattuso, she had completed her research and knew exactly what she wanted. She found the designs for the orphanage uniforms, and described them to him with her usual precision: box pleats on the front and back of the skirt and bodice, a fabric belt and belt-loops, buttons on the shoulders, and so on. Going into such details, so obsessively, was like entering Foord's private universe. She found herself following the paths of his obsessions as tortuously as she followed the cramped burrows of his ship.

Cyr suddenly let out a laugh of delight. It startled her deputy, Nemec, who'd been lurking in a corner of the weapons bay, quietly ogling her.

She understood it. Suddenly, and instantly, and all of it. Not even Smithson had seen *this*. Cyr only saw it because she had an instinct for weapons and how they were used, but now she knew it all, exactly how Foord would use them. *You clever bastard,* she thought. She'd seen what Foord had specified: what was inside the nose cones, what kinds of charges were packed in the distended bodies, what kinds of drives they had and the range over which they'd operate, and—most important—how fucking *simple* they were. *You clever, brilliant bastard, she thought. If only*

●

So the *Charles Manson* nosed its way carefully through the Belt, towards Faith. Its MT Drive was shut down. Its port manoeuvre drives were impaired. Its hull was plastered with shit, and carried a series of jagged open wounds round its rear ventral and dorsal areas where the wavefront had caught it. It resembled Cyr after a night's cruising: normally immaculate, but now with her makeup smeared and her perfectly-tailored clothes locally disarranged.

The *Charles Manson* retained at least ninety percent of its former perfection. The damage to the hull looked superficial; but it went deeper, and it was not damage. Like those inhabiting it, it had changed; perhaps for better or worse, but certainly for good.

They had executed a photon burst through the Belt; had burrowed into and out of a planet-sized asteroid; had turned away from the Commonwealth and Sakhra; and were still there, more formidable than before. Instrument Of Ourselves and Trust Nothing were powerful phrases. Eventually they found their way back to the Department, where they were noted.

●

They began their final approach to CQ-504. Faith was no longer there. Having made sure they were approaching the asteroid, She had moved away, still in the Belt but beyond the reach of their beams. They slowed, and stopped. Foord ordered local magnification of CQ-504, and for the first time they saw the structure She had built.

A silver pyramid.

CQ-504 was a smallish asteroid at the inner edge of the Belt. It was grey, lumpy and asymmetrical. The silver pyramid nestled in the folds of its lower hemisphere, pointing out and down. It might have been the first sign of an outbreak of some regular, geometrical infection.

They probed it. Apart from the surface, which read as an unremarkable mix of metallic alloys and ceramics, they got nothing.

"Commander," Thahl said, "I don't know what this means, but the length of each side of its base is one thousand, six hundred and twelve feet. The exact length of our hull."

"What does that mean?"

"I don't know."

They probed it again. Nothing. They probed the asteroid underneath it, and again got nothing: no excavations, tunnels or buried devices.

A short silence followed.

"What is it?" asked Foord.

"It's the thing," Smithson said, "She's put there to make you ask, What is it."

Another short silence. Foord ordered further probes on the pyramid (nothing), the asteroid (nothing) and Faith (still shrouded, position unchanged, out of range). An inconclusive start to their new incarnation as an Instrument Of Themselves.

"Cyr, has She done anything like this before?"

"No, Commander."

"Nothing like this, in any records of Her previous engagements?"

"No, Commander. Nothing remotely like this."

"Are you ready to fire on the pyramid?"

"Yes, Commander."

"And do you have any idea what will happen if you do?"

"No, Commander."

"Neither do I. But we know it will be something enigmatic; something cryptic and unreadable; don't we?"

"Yes, Commander."

"So we know what to do next, don't we?"

They went around it.

Maintaining exact range, now that Kaang was back, the *Charles Manson* turned in its own length at forty-five degrees and headed out of the Belt. In doing so it described a perfect semicircular path around, and to the left of, CQ-504, the pyramid, and—beyond them—the still-shrouded Faith. All three, when the semicircle was completed, were at the same distance from the *Charles Manson* as before; but this time, astern.

They headed out of the Belt and into Horus system, in the direction of Horus 4 and, ultimately, Sakhra. Whatever the pyramid would have done, had they fired on it, remained a mystery; one which they chose to ignore.

Foord glanced at the rear section of the Bridge screen, and smiled faintly. Let Her chase us now, he thought. She beat us at Horus 5, we got a draw here, and now comes Horus 4. And there, I know how to defeat Her.

PART SEVEN

1

Horus 4 had none of the roiling colours or tectonics of Horus 5. It was dull grey, with a giant flat face; massive and impassive, like a crouching sumo wrestler. They approached it slowly, and with infinite care.

Gravity had long ago struck it dumb and flat and featureless. Gravity even distorted the edges of its light, so that on the Bridge screen it appeared blurred and out of focus. On and under its surface were untold heavy-element riches, but they were unreachable. Horus 4 was the most massive planetary body in the known galaxy, and nothing living or mechanical would ever be able to stand on its surface. It was like the true landscape of Hell: not the flaming flamboyance of Horus 5, but flat unending monotony.

When the Sakhrans moved aside for the Commonwealth (which they did without resisting, and almost without noticing) the Commonwealth took stock of its new member. Sakhra had plenty of living space and minerals and raw materials, and that alone made it invaluable, but there was more. Although the inner planets were negligible, there was an abundance of heavy elements in the Belt and Horus 5.

And there was yet more: Horus 4 had more natural riches than the rest of the system put together. The Commonwealth set out to explore it. And then came the realisation.

The Commonwealth knew about the extraordinary mass and density of Horus 4, how it had torn to pieces three or more giant planets the size of Horus 5 and left their remains as the Belt. Calculations were made about how Horus 4's gravity would operate as a function of its mass and density, but the calculations were misguided. Horus 4 was so massive it had some of the properties of a neutron star. Gravity, the strangest form of violence, was not just the product of mass and density, but something which in extremes could spill over into light and even time, and no planet had gravity as extreme as Horus 4. The first Commonwealth ships to attempt an approach were captured by it, long before they expected to be within its reach, and so were the unmanned probes which followed. Horus 4, the Commonwealth concluded, gave nothing back. Its riches were unreachable. It was even more violent and threatening than Horus 5. It was best left alone.

Only some of this was true. It was certainly best left alone, but it was not violent, or even—in the conventional sense—threatening. It was a mass of absences: absence of noise, of colour, of movement, of tectonics, of surface features. Its gravity flattened and silenced everything, made everything absent. It simply existed, and within a certain distance around it all other existence was impossible.

The *Charles Manson* was still far outside that distance. Its approach to Horus 4, cautious and ever-slowing, had so far taken five hours, with at least another three to go. As the planet's image grew on the Bridge screen, they had quite early grown tired of looking at it, because it gave them nothing to see. They knew all about it, but they knew also that in their lifetimes—even if their lifetimes ran a normal span—nothing of theirs would ever get near its surface. It was strangely uninteresting—literally, massively uninteresting—considering all the things they intended it to do for them.

2

These days, Sulhu often found himself walking listlessly through the corridors of Hrissihr. Every day it got a little colder and, with families leaving for the highland and mountain hillcastles, a little emptier. *She* was coming again, and there were stories of disturbing events in the Bowl, and even here, in the Irsirrha foothills. The other day they had brought him someone called Blent, a rather bellicose and stupid young man. He was a descendant, apparently, of Rikkard Blent (great-great-great-grandson? Sulhu could never quite fathom human lineage) and had been caught trying to do what his ancestor tried, to enter the vault and read the Book of Srahr. Sulhu had him sent back to the lowlands, still alive, but without doing to him what was done to his ancestor two hundred years ago, which would have been pointless; not undeserved, but pointless.

Later the same day, Sulhu stood in front of Hrissihr, wrapping his cloak against the wind and looking up at the huge frontage of the hillcastle just as Foord had done when he first arrived. The srahr, symbol of zero and infinity and symbol of Faith, was still there where someone had daubed it. The black paint was beginning to peel and shred.

She was coming again, and events were taking place on Sakhra. They were not mass events, because both the Sakhrans and the humans who had settled on Sakhra (the Sakhran humans, Sulhu called them privately) were too enigmatic, too apolitical and fragmented, for mass movements. It was ironic that they had those features in common. Sulhu sometimes amused himself with the thought that one day, Sakhran humans might become human Sakhrans. The simple reversal of adjective and noun would mean a world of difference.

So they were not mass events, just individual episodes. Still, they were troubling. Like the strange gathering on Grid 9 at Blentport, and the manner of the *Charles Manson*'s departure. With his son on board. Sulhu wondered whether he would see his son return to Sakhra, but on other days he also wondered if he'd see *Her* return to Sakhra. There was something about Foord and his ship that made him fear for any opponent they engaged; even this one.

●

Swann felt tired. Not so much physically—he had been on sleep inhibitors for the last few days—but spiritually. There were too many things to deal with, all of them troubling. And the burns on his hands and face, although they'd been treated and would heal, were throbbing persistently.

Blentport was now relatively quiet. All the Grids were empty, all the Horus Fleet ships were refitted and had joined the defensive cordon, and most of the port's military personnel were evacuated to the highlands. Swann had personally directed this from his Command Centre in the basement of one of the Blentport buildings. When it was complete he had stayed there to observe the long-range scans of the events in the outer regions of Horus system, where the *Charles Manson* was engaging Faith, and to direct responses to the mostly isolated, but disturbing, incidents in the lowlands. He had been there, almost continuously, for days.

"The *Charles Manson*. Still dead?" He meant its communications.

"Yes, Director."

"Alright. Keep hailing it."

Like Foord, he was large and black-bearded and came from a heavy-gravity planet; but his bulk was not conditioned muscle, as was Foord's, and he lacked Foord's tidiness and grooming—a lack which had been apparent during the events preceding Foord's liftoff, and again during the incident with Copeland's ship. Nothing had happened since to improve either his appearance or his demeanour. The outbreaks of violence were mostly in the lowlands, and were neither large-scale nor orchestrated. But, like all lowlands politics, they were difficult to read; and troubling. Swann and Sulhu unknowingly shared the same private expression— Sakhran humans—to describe the Commonwealth settlers who colonised the lowlands.

Grid 9 was now empty. Swann had walked through it a couple of times, as listlessly as Sulhu walked the empty wings of Hrissihr. A few days ago, those who had gathered there (civilian and military) milled around for some time after the *Charles Manson*'s departure. Some of them slaughtered the six chimaera. Later, when they heard Boussaid had died, they set fire to the landchariot and threw the Sakhran driver's body into it. In the side window, unseen, the web curled and died.

Swann had tried personally to drag the Sakhran's body clear of the burning landchariot, sustaining burns to his hands and face. That was the first of only three times that he had left the Command Centre in the last few days. The second was to receive Rikkard Blent's descendant (was it great-great-great-grandson? Swann couldn't remember and didn't care) from the Sakhrans who returned him, unharmed but still bellicose, from Hrissihr. His name was actually Blent-Gundarssen: the Blent family name had sunk and resurfaced, through generations of bedsheets.

Swann asked them to convey to Sulhu his thanks, his promise that the man would be prosecuted, and his regret at the death of the Sakhran driver. All this had been acknowledged with polite inclinations of Sakhran heads, while above them the last few ships of Horus Fleet rose to join the cordon. Swann had to shout to be heard.

The third time he left the Command Centre was to tell Boussaid's family, personally, what had happened. There could have been a fourth time, when Copeland was shuttled down to Blentport to face arrest and trial, but Swann had sent others.

"*Charles Manson* still dead?"

"Yes, Director…Director, we'll tell you if anything comes in."

"I know you will. But you don't think anything will come, do you?"

"No, Director. Foord cut communications deliberately."

Swann looked at the cordon on one of the many screens in the Command Centre. It was a classic formation. Battleships and cruisers formed the outer ring. Destroyers and interceptors inside, ready to engage Her closeup if She got through the larger ships. Everything was deployed logically and sensibly, facing out towards the Belt and the Gulf and outer planets from where She would come if Foord didn't stop Her. All of them, of course, had been ordered to stay in formation, no matter what happened with Foord.

It was the largest fleet in any of the Commonwealth's twenty-nine systems, except for the Earth fleet. Swann wondered if it would be enough. If it wasn't, and if She ignored the evacuation and launched a catastrophic attack on Sakhra's now almost undefended Bowl areas then a handful of people on Sakhra, Swann among them, would be personally responsible. He accepted that. He was fiercely, but intelligently, loyal to the Commonwealth.

Swann's planet, like Foord's, had been authoritarian and corporatist, but unlike Foord he had come to the Commonwealth in the ordinary way, through the regular armed forces and not the Department. Like Foord, however, he had found that planets like his were only a minority. Most of the Commonwealth was a lot better. On balance, he told himself with his usual clumsiness, far more about it was right than was wrong. Even when it did something wrong, such as the law about removal of poison glands from Sakhrans in the lowlands, plenty of its citizens—himself included—were ready to stand up and campaign.

There were other banks of screens in the Command Centre, to which Swann had been increasingly drawn over the last few days. They depicted events at Horus 5, the Belt, and—now—Horus 4. They were not actual views but simulations, because of the distances involved and the cessation of transmissions from Foord. Some would be accurate, others based on the best guesses of Swann's mission analysts.

At Horus 5 She had outthought Foord, as Swann expected; but something had happened in the Belt, coinciding with Foord's cutting of communications. There had been a burst on photon drive through asteroids, an apparent collision with one large asteroid, an apparent hit by one of Her missiles, but the *Charles Manson* was still there. Then, it had left the Belt and headed for Horus 4, and after a pause She had followed. But was She chasing Foord, or making for Sakhra?

Foord was obviously planning some sort of action involving Horus 4. Everyone knew about Horus 4; if you got too close, it killed you. So did She, but She was more dangerous because She killed by choice and motive. Or maybe not. Maybe She was like Horus 4, and had no choice or motive. Maybe She was just made like that. There was a thought.

Swann looked again at the careful pattern of the cordon; *it's everything we have,* he thought, and again wondered if it would be enough. He had found the *Charles Manson* and Foord and his crew to be quite alien, outside everything he understood and valued. But *She* was different by magnitudes. She made the *Charles Manson* seem like something it could never, ever be: One Of Us. One Of Ours.

3

They continued their approach to Horus 4, cautious and ever-slowing.

Gradually, their perception of Her had changed. In the Belt they had become the first of Her opponents ever to gain any advantage over Her, and that removed some of Her mystery. So too did Foord's remark about Instrument Of Ourselves. They knew he had calculated it—he calculated everything—but it was compelling, and it changed how they saw Her.

And what completed the change was when Foord told them how he intended to use his two missiles. When he finished, there was a long silence.

"That's very clever," Smithson said, at first grudgingly; then, as he walked around it and looked at it from all angles, he added what was, for him, the ultimate accolade. "I wish I'd thought of that."

Cyr murmured "So do I" and Foord glanced at her sharply, maybe suspecting she'd already figured it out; or maybe she read too much into his glance. Foord's ability, like the garment Cyr wore, produced a remarkable effect on those around him; he could glide among them, like she did, as if unaware of it. The difference was that with Cyr it was just a garment, something she'd paid to find out about, and paid again to have made for her. With him, it was more: everything he was.

So they realised now that She could actually be defeated. And as they moved closer to the planet whose unique properties would make it one of their weapons, so the planet—because of its unique properties—became less interesting.

Even Foord grew tired of looking at Horus 4, though he was careful not to appear so. They had seen the wonders of Horus 5 and the Belt. They had crossed the Gulf between the inner and outer planets on their way to engage Her, and might—depending on what happened here—have to cross it again. But Horus 4 was different. Looking at it was as dull as looking at a door—duller, because at least someone might go in or out. It was like looking at a photograph of a door.

And yet Horus 4 was one of the weapons which would destroy Her. The other one was Foord's pair of missiles. Foord wished he had made Blentport build him more than just two, but that would have been difficult given the circumstances there. And if they worked, two would be plenty; one would be enough. Not for the first time, Foord found himself wondering how and when he had thought of them. Smithson had been watching him.

"When I asked you before, Commander, you said you didn't know. You said it was like you always had it."

"What?"

"The idea about those missiles."

"Well, I still don't know. I can't remember the exact moment."

"That's also what you said before, Commander... Ever thought that perhaps *She* planted the idea?"

Foord looked up sharply. He had been about to give Smithson a Smithsonian reply, then noticed the angularity of posture which, for Smithson, denoted humour.

It was infectious.

"Why ever," Cyr wondered, "would She do that?"

Smithson shrugged, approximately. "Because She's Enigmatic?"

"Perhaps," Foord ventured, "Cryptic is a better word."

Kaang had been following the conversation from face to face with some puzzlement. "What's the difference, Commander?"

"Do you mean, what's the difference because we're going to destroy Her anyway, or what's the difference between Cryptic and Enigmatic?"

"Yes, Commander. I mean, yes, I meant what's the difference between Cryptic and Enigmatic."

"There isn't any difference," Cyr said.

"Yes there is," Thahl said, "but it's hidden."

Lazily, the irony fed on itself, chewing backwards and forwards while they worked on Her destruction. The approach to Horus 4 continued, slower and slower.

Slower and slower. Cautious, and more cautious. There was a point on their approach to Horus 4 when they would be captured by its gravity. Long before then, they would stop and make their final arrangements: the arrangements whose idea, like the design of his two missiles, seemed to be something Foord had always known. "And Faith?" he asked Thahl.

"She's left the Belt, Commander, and is heading for Horus 4. Her position is approximately 15-10-16."

"Approximately?"

"She's still shrouded, and Her drive emissions are faint. She's on low ion speed, about nine percent, and the gravity distorts our scanners."

"Oh, of course," Foord said. He added "Still Enigmatic, then."

"Don't you mean Cryptic, Commander?"

"I thought you said the difference between them was hidden."

"It's only hidden if you try to find it, Commander."

Foord inclined his head slightly in acknowledgement, and the conversation chewed and savoured itself a little more.

"Commander," Thahl said, a few minutes later, "I still recommend caution. She might simply be heading for Sakhra, not pursuing us. She could just pass us by. Like…"

"Like we did to Her at the Belt. I know. But…"

But Foord knew. He had his growing instincts about Her, and his mounting pile of penny pieces of knowledge. Unless She really had planted it all, She would come for them before making for Sakhra. He *knew*.

"What's Her ETA, Thahl? Approximately?"

"At least three hours at Her current speed, Commander."

"Good. Then we have plenty of time. Let's get it done."

●

The orbit around Horus 4 was the simpler part. The missiles would be a bit more complicated.

They had calculated the orbit they would need. It would be a pronounced elliptical orbit. At the two opposing high points they would be able, with momentum plus bursts of ion drive, to break free of Horus 4's gravity. But for the rest of the orbit they would be genuinely trapped, unable to do anything except move along its elliptical path. That was essential, if She wasn't to pass them by. They had to be genuinely trapped. And Faith, approaching them, had to know it.

But that was the easier part; they had calculated all of it. All they had to do was continue their ever-slowing approach to Horus 4 and wait until they reached the critical point of commitment. Then, when they knew She was coming for them and not heading past them for Sakhra, they would inject themselves into the orbit. They would do it suddenly, making it look like an overreaction to Her approach. They had planned it carefully, and practised it repeatedly; but when they really did it, they would be committing themselves to the gravity of Horus 4. Nothing was worth that, except the chance to defeat Her.

"Commander," Cyr murmured, "I know what the difference is."

"Difference?"

"Between Cryptic and Enigmatic."

"Well?"

"I'll leave it unspoken."

The more complicated part was the preparation and launch of the two missiles. It was more complicated only because the missiles were what shaped everything else. If they didn't work, She would pass by unhindered to visit Sakhra, and the *Charles Manson* would go down to visit Horus 4.

But they would work. Nothing Enigmatic about *them*. They were simple, relatively small, and—most important of all—inert. They would be released quietly before the *Charles Manson* entered its orbit, at a point (calculated) which would put them in orbits parallel to the *Charles Manson*'s but further from Horus 4, where they would not be trapped.

They were almost nothing but drives and warheads. Their warheads, cramming every inch of their limited size, were charges of E91, the most concentrated conventional explosive ever made. It did exactly what it said on the packet, and, over a small area, did it with nuclear intensity; but unlike a nuclear device, it was inert and undetectable until the moment of its explosion. Their drives were high-intensity particle motors, giving huge initial acceleration but only over a short range. Each missile had in its nosecone a lense and low-power microcomputer, programmed to recognise only Faith, from whatever angle they saw Her. They would project nothing and transmit nothing; and receive nothing, except Her image.

The missiles would float like fragments of Horus 4, dark and dead, and too inert—Foord hoped—to be noticed by Her as She approached. She would realise that apart from the two high points of the elliptical orbit, the *Charles Manson* was genuinely trapped; it could still fight, but could not move out of its orbital path. It would be fatally hampered. She would choose somewhere midway between the two high points for Her attack. She wouldn't have to destroy the *Charles Manson*, just damage it enough to make it unable to break free at the high points. Then, She could pass on to Sakhra while Horus 4's gravity did the rest; or She could stay and watch, and then pass on to Sakhra. Either way it would be decisive, and at decisive points in any engagement She always unshrouded. That was where Foord's two missiles came in.

"Cyr, if you know what the difference is, you can't say that you'll leave it unspoken. You can't use speech to announce that you're leaving something unspoken."

"If I didn't say I was leaving it unspoken, Commander, nobody would know about it."

"Exactly."

This word-construct was getting more and more self-indulgent, thought Foord, but its whimsicality somehow worked: considering what they intended to do, it seemed oddly right. They could each murmur their additions to it while they worked towards creating Her destruction.

The lenses in the nosecones of the missiles would be shortsighted, almost squinting. And they would not be sending, only receiving. They were no more than automatic cameras: operating on low power, absolutely conventional, and programmed to recognise Faith's image from any angle the moment She came in their sight. She would obviously approach slowly and cautiously, drawn by the *Charles Manson*, this strange opponent who'd got more out of Her than any other; drawn by the *Charles Manson*'s predicament, but never becoming anything less than cautious.

The missiles would not be in any way controlled by, or in communication with, the *Charles Manson*. There would be nothing, no signal or emission, for Her to detect. Almost every part of them would be inert. When the cameras recognised Her, which they would only do over short range, the missiles would activate. They would—Foord hoped—be almost point-blank and would reach Her too quickly even for Her flickerfields.

This was the idea which Foord had always seemed to have in him. It depended on a lot of Ifs: if She didn't pass them by, if She didn't detect the missiles, if the missiles worked, if She came close enough, if She unshrouded. And, of course, if they'd calculated Horus 4's gravity correctly. It was simple, and might be decisive; high-risk, but dependent on low-tech devices. It was the kind of thing nobody had ever offered Her before: a threat. If it succeeded, then Faith, if not destroyed, would be damaged; too damaged—Foord hoped—to prevent the *Charles Manson* from reaching the high point of its orbit, breaking free, and finishing Her. That was likely to be, as Smithson had said, the point where Some Of Us Will Die. But nobody before them had gained any advantage over Her, and here they were, realistically working towards defeating Her. And even, along the way, snatching some self-indulgent wordplay while they worked.

"Smithson."

"Commander?"

"Let's suppose She *did* plant the idea. But not to win the engagement. Only to plant the idea that She'd planted the idea."

"You think so?"

"I only said Perhaps."

"You didn't say Perhaps, Commander."

"Yes I did, at Joser's funeral. Remember? But I intended it for now."

Self-indulgent, Foord thought again; but the tone, dry and lazy and circling, made it a counterpoint. What they were about to do needed a counterpoint.

They had plenty of time to complete the final preparation of the missiles, and had done most of it already; but they still triple-checked them. Since the missiles would be launched inert, there was very little pre-launch priming to be done. Nevertheless they did it, then did it again, and again; especially the lenses and nosecones.

The preparations continued, lazily but thoroughly, and so did the word-construct they were building together. They each added a part, as the impulse moved them. They liked it for its intricacy. It was quiet and nuanced and understated. It felt like it *belonged* on the *Charles Manson*, just as Foord himself belonged there. It was almost like building a replica of Foord, something subtle and complex which they admired but didn't fully understand.

"Cryptic or Enigmatic," Cyr mused. She turned to Smithson, and smiled engagingly. "What do you think?"

"Perhaps both, perhaps neither. How about Unreadable?"

"Like the Book of Srahr?" Foord immediately wished he hadn't said that, but Thahl didn't respond.

Their mood started to change. The word-construct had grown over-intricate. Like Her pyramid in the Belt, they left it behind them. Its time had passed, and something else was beginning.

4

"She's disappeared, Commander," Thahl said.

"Are you sure?"

"Yes."

"Where?" Kaang said. "Where's She gone?"

"He didn't say Gone, he said Disappeared." And don't, thought Foord, ask if there's a difference.

"Is there a…"

"She's cut Her drives, Commander," Thahl said. "She's shrouded, so we can only track Her by drive emissions. And She's cut them. All of them."

"Is there a…" Kaang began again, then "Oh. I see."

"I think it might be working, Commander," Thahl said. "She's slowing. I think it means She's coming for *us* before heading for Sakhra."

"It's really beginning," Foord said softly. "We've passed the first If. You know what to do next."

The next part had been calculated, but it could not be allowed to look that way. Making it not look that way was part of the calculation.

●

Like water dripping in an empty building, something moved inside Her.

She was approaching the *Charles Manson*, slowly and apparently with caution. She was still shrouded.

Whatever She was, She existed physically. There was an inside and an outside. Inside was a crew, or something else not yet imaginable, which studied them. It moved, and reached for a conclusion.

●

Faith's last known position was 15-10-16 approximately. She was approaching Horus 4 from the direction of the Belt and Horus 5; the *Charles Manson* was on Horus 4's opposite side, beyond which lay the Gulf, Sakhra, the inner planets, and the sun Horus. She was still coasting and slowing, all drives cut, otherwise they'd have reacquired Her position from drive emissions, and a series of alarms and screen headups, now dead, would come to life all over the Bridge; but they could estimate where She was from Her probable rate of slowing.

The Bridge screen, unasked, superimposed a schematic showing Her last known and present estimated position. Relative to the *Charles Manson*, She was somewhere below the horizon of Horus 4. When She came for them, either visible or shrouded, She would at some point rise above the horizon like another sun, but in opposition to the sun Horus; perhaps where a moon should be, except that Horus 4 had no moons. It had destroyed them all.

Foord became aware of a faint background noise on the Bridge: a rustling, like a woman moving inside a ballgown. Thahl and Cyr had also noticed it.

"Gravity on the hull," Smithson said. "Horus 4. It'll increase."

It did. And She continued to come closer.

She studied them.

They were well aware of Her superiority over Commonwealth ships, even Outsiders, in the areas of scanners and communications. She had a large repertoire of techniques and devices which were normally undetectable, although on the Bridge they could sometimes sense when She was using them; it was a difference in the quality of Her silence. Cyr was usually quickest to sense it.

"Yes" she told Foord. "I feel it too. She's looking at us."

The noise from outside changed, from rustling to rasping.

She studied them. Given that She'd changed course, cut drives and was heading towards them, this was hardly surprising; but they needed the confirmation, to get them past the next series of Ifs. They'd planned it meticulously, but it still depended on the Ifs. Not only the obvious ones they'd all recited, but the more subtle and troubling ones.

If She believed they were planning a move of some kind.

If She believed they intended to use Horus 4 somehow as a part of their move.

(And if that was how Her thought-processes worked, in linear paths like theirs.)

If She believed that they'd hurriedly brought their plan forward when

She cut drives and they could no longer track Her.

And most of all, if She acted then as *they* would have acted, and came closeup to finish them. If She did that, it would not only help them, it would diminish Her. They'd know there was at least one part of Her that was like them, among all the other parts that weren't.

●

The *Charles Manson*'s ion drive flared twice and took them in a wide elliptical orbit round Horus 4, but the orbit had been entered too hurriedly. There was something wrong about it, and something inside Her noticed.

The *Charles Manson* shuddered as the ion drive took it and whirled it towards Horus 4. The bits of debris on the Bridge, untouched by the compensator Foord had deliberately left unrepaired, moved in response, gearing down the ship's larger movements to small rodent scurryings across the floor.

Nobody spoke, so they never knew that they were all thinking the same thing at the same time: they had left the Bridge, and themselves, untidied since the Belt as Foord asked, and were beginning to notice the mess and smell. It was in their nature, perhaps learnt from Foord, to notice things like that at times like this.

Foord looked around the Bridge, and nodded. The weapons core gave instructions to one of the sub-computers serving it, which checked for time and place, and started a countdown. At the calculated point the two missiles were released; not fired or launched, but dropped. It was done without ceremony or comment and done while the *Charles Manson* was still moving, like an animal defecating while walking. The *Charles Manson* continued on its way. Behind it the missiles just floated, like two turds.

A little later, Foord again looked around the Bridge and nodded. Again a sub-computer, this time one instructed by the navigation core, checked for time and place and started a countdown. Again the *Charles Manson* shuddered as another ion burst whirled it closer to Horus 4. Both bursts had been calculated, repeatedly. This one was not significantly different to the earlier one, and produced a similar flurry of rollings and slidings from the bits of debris strewn over the floor; but this was the one which finally trapped them in orbit around Horus 4. *Kill them all*, Foord had said. *All your reactions.*

The torsion-sound from outside became almost continuous. The gravitational stress on the hull during orbit had of course been part of their calculations, but the sound hadn't. They were used to the ship filtering and compensating everything before it intruded upon them, but this time it couldn't. The sound increased as the planet reached into them.

The two missiles were in orbits parallel to that of the *Charles Manson*, but further out from Horus 4 and not yet trapped by its gravity. Their orbits were the product of the *Charles Manson*'s motion when they were dropped, and would decay soon as they were not travelling under power. Apart from the low-powered and shortsighted lenses peering through the transparent nosecones, they were inert. They would remain inert until She appeared. And if She didn't, or if She did and they didn't work, they'd overtake the *Charles Manson* on its way down to Horus 4.

And *down* was where Horus 4 now was. The realignment was complete, although they were still a massive distance away and saw it as a complete sphere; a giant autistic face, empty of expression. Unlike other planets, it wasn't cloud-cover that made it look out of focus, but something its gravity did to light and space. And perhaps also to time.

Foord looked through the Bridge screen at the same segment of Horus 4's horizon as that which the missiles were scanning. He wanted to watch Her rise over that horizon, unshrouded, so he could see Her destroyed before *anyone* knew what She was or where She came from. Thahl looked out at the same horizon; he too wanted Her destroyed, for reasons which at that time would have been incomprehensible, even to Foord. Cyr hoped the missiles would damage but not destroy Her, so she could finish Her while She was wounded. And Smithson, watching Foord trying to tempt Her closer, was reminded of his ancestors on the plains of Emberra: how they would tempt and trick those hunting them to come closer so they could tear them to pieces, and how the outcome of those combats was that one species of herbivores evolved to dominance while several species of carnivores and omnivores didn't.

None of them spoke, so another moment passed in which, unknowingly, they all shared similar thoughts. Except Kaang, who was busy deliberately making them a prisoner of Horus 4.

They had built something which wasn't real, but had all the internal consistencies and inconsistencies of something which was. They'd built a detailed narrative of how they'd acted hurriedly; not in panic, just hurriedly. As a further detail they flared their manoeuvre drives and reversed their ion drive, deliberately a few nanoseconds after it would do no good. Then—because the initial hurriedness would have been understandable, but panic would have been inconsistent with their reputation, and therefore unconvincing—they cut all drives and went with the orbit, conserving energy until the orbit's high point where they could escape Horus 4's gravity; and they powered up their closeup weapons and checked their flickerfields, consistent with a calm and rational reaction.

It looked convincing, even to them.

The hull continued to make torsion sounds. They were genuinely trapped, and genuinely frightened.

●

The two missiles were beginning to diverge from each other and from the *Charles Manson*, but only to a degree which had been calculated. The lenses in their nosecones swept the same area of Horus 4's horizon as did Foord and the others back on the *Charles Manson*, but without any accompanying thoughts. They were simultaneously focussed and short-sighted. Apart from the lenses, the missiles were inert. Their drives and warheads were dead, and they had no communication with the *Charles Manson* and no knowledge or memory of its existence. They were beyond its contact or control; instruments of themselves.

They had no life, and would have none until She appeared. Then, their life would flare and die. It would begin and end almost simultaneously, with the performance of a very specific task.

They seemed ill-equipped for it. They were small and quite primitive. Against Her many and mysterious abilities, they were like a pair of clawhammers. And where they floated, they were at the focus of another If: *If* they managed to stay unnoticed by Her. Because if, at any time, She did notice them…

●

"Nine hours to the high point," Kaang reported.

A long, dead time. The engagement had congealed around Horus 4, producing a minor planetary system. Horus 4 now had a new, silver, artificial moon orbiting it, one which it might later destroy like the others, and that moon itself had two smaller moons, dark and inert; and there was another moon, even more unreadable than Horus 4, which would soon rise above the planet's horizon. Until it did, the new planetary system was almost stable; quiet and balanced and Newtonian.

Foord was beginning to wonder, idly, if he'd rather see the missiles damage Her than destroy Her—it would open Her up, you could learn things about Her—when, like a polite tap on his shoulder, every alarm on the Bridge started murmuring discreetly, and Thahl said "Object approaching, Commander. Look at the screen, please."

Foord wondered then whether She too had a sense of irony. For what rose over the horizon of Horus 4 was not Her, but a small silvery object. A pyramid.

On the Bridge screen, local magnification showed it tumbling end over end, but in a slower and somewhat more stately way than the pink cone She had sent them in the Belt. It was much smaller than the pyramid at CQ-504, in fact only about the size of a small lifeboat. It was featureless, and appeared to have no drive emissions, but it was headed in their direction.

"The dimensions along its base and sides have exactly the same proportions as the one in the Belt," Thahl said.

Foord nodded, unsurprised. "Anything else?"

"Our probes get only surface readings, like the one in the Belt. If we trace back along its trajectory we get to 11-15-13, where we think it was launched. That's also where we estimate She would be, at Her present rate of slowing."

They paused, and studied it. Thahl's expression was unreadable. Smithson snorted and muttered something about Cylinders, Ovoids, Pink Cones, and Now Fucking Pyramids. Cyr laughed unpleasantly, a laugh that Foord knew and didn't like; it made her ugly.

"Ignore it again?" Smithson ventured.

"Yes," Foord said, "ignore it. And we know what it's going to do next, don't we?"

It passed them by, exactly as they had done to its larger relative back in the Belt, and with exactly the same precision. It described a careful semicircle around them, so careful that at any given point it was the same distance from them. Then it plunged down into the face of Horus 4. It flared briefly, not from atmospheric friction—Horus 4 had no atmosphere; that too had been destroyed by gravity—but from the friction of being compressed down to nothing, to not even a smear. That was the last they saw and heard from Her of pyramids.

"So what was that about, Thahl?"

"Perhaps She was telling you something, Commander."

"Kaang, how long to the high point of the orbit?"

"Seven hours, Commander."

"Thank you…Telling me something, Thahl?"

"About how we ignored the pyramid at the Belt."

"And what do you think She was telling *you,* Thahl?"

"Commander?"

"You're the only one on board"—he'd been about to say The only one of Us, but caught himself just in time—"who might know what She is."

The Bridge was already silent, otherwise it would have fallen silent then. Thahl paused a long time before replying.

"I know what Srahr said She is, Commander."

"And what Srahr said She is, would it…"

"Affect this mission? No. And if it—"

"If it did, you'd tell me?"

"Of course I'd tell you, Commander. Why are you asking all this now?"

"You're a Sakhran, but you're also First Officer. Deputy Commander of my ship. Which comes first?"

"The ship does, Commander."

"Which ship?"

"This one, Commander. You know I meant this one." Thahl was not angry, but reproachful.

What made me suddenly ask him all that? thought Foord. Then the alarms started murmuring, differently this time. Different alarms for different events. Monitor displays, dark since She cut Her drives, lit up again. Foord whirled round to look at the Bridge screen

"She's here, Commander," Kaang said softly

and saw Her.

●

Slowly, and apparently with caution, She rose over the horizon of Horus 4

Her position, said the Bridge screen, was 8-7-12; close to where they expected, far enough from Horus 4 to avoid its gravity, and not yet close enough to be seen by the missiles. The Bridge screen, unasked, shuffled filters and switched to local magnification. She was a slender silver delta like the *Charles Manson*, but the proportions differed; Her length was about eight percent less than theirs, and Her maximum width, at the stern, about eleven percent less. Her surface had interlocking hull-plates, like theirs but smaller; the size of scales on Sakhran skin. The contours of Her hull were covered in small ports and slitted windows and apertures, but there was no light or movement behind any of them.

They had seen images of Her before, on recordings. They knew Her dimensions, knew what She would look like from every angle, and knew Her shape would be like theirs. But all that was before they had actually *seen* Her. None of it mattered, now.

They watched Her in a silence which grew around and between them, neither joining nor separating them. This time, they knew they shared the same thought. She's brought more than just Herself to face us here, She's brought a universe.

Foord went away somewhere on his own. They all did. And a few miles and a universe away, She noticed; and waited for them.

●

The *Charles Manson*, Thahl told himself, had simple lines which were visibly curved or straight; Hers were neither. The *Charles Manson* had a simple, recognisable geometry with an inside and outside, ending at the outside; Her geometry was different. She *began* at the outside.

Thahl tracked the line from the needlepoint tip of the nose to the broad stern end of the delta. He imagined that line extending forward millions of miles, perhaps to Sakhra, and knew it would deviate by less than a millimetre; but he could *see* it, a fifteen-hundred-foot straightness which was part of a cosmic curvature. He imagined each line of Her shape extended in a cat's-cradle millions of miles in all directions, beyond Horus system and out into the galaxy, until they all began to curve. Faith was just the visible part, hanging at their centre. That was what She had brought with Her.

Is this, he thought, *what Srahr saw three hundred years ago?* I'm the first of us (no, the second) to see Her since him. And what happened to us will happen to the Commonwealth, unless we destroy Her. My father believes Foord might be able to do that. So do I, now.

Smithson recalled Copeland, seeing Her at Anubis and whispering Face of God; the recordings captured it, the last thing he ever said. And Ansah at her trial (Smithson had read the transcripts) describing the moment when She unshrouded: a shape not unlike an Outsider, but on Her it's different, as if She's only the visible part of something larger. She moves like a living thing and looks like a part of empty space, a small part made solid and visible. And the rest looming around Her, unseen. He understood now what Ansah meant by The Rest: everything else She had brought with Her out of the shroud.

I'm not ready for this, he thought. *You don't see it on the recordings.* It'll affect *us* more than ordinary crews, because we're more imaginative, and more self-indulgent. More dangerous, and more vulnerable. How had Ansah stayed functional when she saw *this*? Because, he thought sourly, she was trying to lose those ridiculous Isis ships, and she had no time for what *we're* indulging in now (he had looked round the Bridge and seen it on their faces, as surely as they would see it on his).

Smithson had read all the transcripts and knew Ansah's trial was an injustice; but none of that mattered, now.

"She cruised the cities, random and motiveless, beautiful and brilliant." Cyr recalled the the phrase from her trial; unlike Isis, trials on Old Earth were adversarial, not inquisitorial, and tended to produce such rhetoric. The prosecuting counsel was a small stout man whose sonorous diction was oddly out of keeping with his appearance; a man given to flights of verbosity, but also incisive and clever.

His phrase had always troubled her, and now she knew why. Cyr remembered the faces of her family as he said it; the trial had turned them into people who no longer recognised her, but now Cyr recognised herself. If you took The Cities out of that phrase, his description of *me* is a description of *Her.*

Maybe Foord really meant it when he said Instrument of Ourselves. Maybe She's what we would be, if we didn't have the Department looming behind us.

Kaang thought, *What's Her pilot like, has She got a pilot like me?* I don't think so, I'd have felt it when She unshrouded, ships have a body language. That's a shame, I'd like to find someone like me one day.

Then, unaware of the thoughts of the others on the Bridge, she shrugged and turned back to her instruments.

It's like seeing a new primary colour, Foord told himself, *or finding a new prime number.* Her shape didn't belong here, it belonged outside ordinary perception and geometry. Outside, inside; straightness, curvature. Orders of magnitude. She looks like us, but She's a universe of things we aren't.

He watched Her on the screen and thought, Do you know why you're doing this? Or are you like Cyr, are you following a compulsion which you tell yourself is free choice? Are you doing this because it's how you were made? If you are, who made you?

Later, when they returned from wherever they had separately gone, She was waiting. She knew the effect Her unshrouding had on opponents. Normally She would not have waited for them to recover, but this opponent was different.

5

Foord was breathing heavily. There was a ringing in his ears. He had an erection, and tasted brine in his mouth and along the sides of his tongue. He gestured at the screen.

"Her position..." Thahl began. He paused, partly because he needed to and partly to help Foord compose himself. "Her position is 8-7-12, Commander. She's matching our speed and maintaining an exact distance."

"Within range?" Cyr asked, before Foord could speak.

"No. She's outside closeup range."

"She'll come closer." Cyr moistened her lips. "We're going to hurt Her."

The two ships were directly facing. They watched each other. There was a particular quality to their watching, like the first meeting of two people who would share the rest of their lives together.

"Has She seen the missiles?" Smithson asked, minutes or hours later.

"I don't think so," Thahl said, "and I know they haven't seen Her."

"Of course they haven't!" Smithson snapped. "She's not close enough."

"She has to come closer," Foord said.

"She will," Cyr said.

"She might," Thahl said. "If it doesn't look like we want Her to."

There were a couple of curious glances at Thahl, but only a couple. Most of them couldn't take their eyes off the Bridge screen.

Foord's erection wouldn't go. He studied the others' faces, trying to see if they were similarly affected. Normally you could tell; there was a certain fixedness of expression which characterised people nursing an unwanted arousal. But two of them were nonhuman, and one of those was asexual, and the light on the Bridge was too subdued to be certain of the others, so he gave up. He preferred looking at Her anyway.

She hung there, like light turned solid. *I had no idea*, Foord thought, *that She'd be like this. I'll remember this for the rest of my life. How long is the rest of my life?*

"How long since we saw Her, Thahl?"

"Nearly three hours, Commander."

"*What?* Are you sure?"

Thahl ignored that.

What was happening to time? It had seemed to slow down at other points in the engagement, but now it was doing something stranger: *sharing* itself. It drained out of Faith, and out of the *Charles Manson*, and into the space between them. Almost as if it was doing an act of courtesy to them, so they could hold this moment together, the moment of their first meeting. Time filled the space between them, setting itself out for them like a gaming table on to which, later, they would lay their cards.

"How long," Foord asked, "till we reach…"

"The first high point? Three hours, Commander," Thahl said.

"So we're about midway, where She'll probably attack."

"If," Smithson said, "She believes we're really trapped here, and if She hasn't seen the missiles."

Foord said "She does believe. And She hasn't seen them."

"And She's coming," Thahl hissed, suddenly, as alarms murmured. "She's coming closer. Look at the screen."

●

The two missiles waited to perform their task. When the time came they would sacrifice themselves to perform it, but they would not make the sacrifice knowingly or freely. They would do it because that was how they'd been made.

They floated in unpowered orbits, behind the *Charles Manson* and further out from Horus 4, on trajectories which still bore some of the *Charles Manson*'s imparted motion. The shortsighted lenses in their nosecones tracked back and forth in search of the only shape they'd recognise; but She was still too far away.

They could see the *Charles Manson* in front of them, but they didn't see it. They were not programmed to recognise it and not equipped to communicate with it. They didn't know it had made them and launched them. They didn't know about any of its sixty-two (previously sixty-three) living inhabitants. They didn't know it existed.

They could see the grey flat face of Horus 4, but they didn't see it. They were not programmed to recognise it and not equipped to feel its gravity. They didn't know it existed.

They didn't even know there were two of them. Each was the centre of its own universe, in which only one other thing existed, the shape they hadn't seen yet. If they didn't see Her soon, their orbits would decay and they would go down into the grey flat face they didn't see, and would die before they attained their very limited life. And if they did see Her and did attain life, it would begin and end almost simultaneously.

Instruments of Themselves.

The crude shortrange lenses in their nosecones tracked endlessly back and forth, and still didn't see Her. Their universe was empty. She had to come closer.

●

The Bridge screen displays showed that Her ion drive, which She had been using in reverse to maintain distance, was gradually reducing. She was closing the distance between them, slowly and apparently with caution. And She was still studying them, with the probes they couldn't block, or detect, or trace back to Her. They could feel it.

"Everything," Smithson was saying to Thahl, "comes down to those missiles." As usual, he was irritating but right. "How are you sure She hasn't seen them?"

"If She'd seen them," Thahl said, "She'd know this is all a simulation and She'd destroy them. They're inert and defenceless."

Smithson grunted, but said nothing for the moment. Thahl reflected on Smithson's wording: not Are You Sure but *How* Are You Sure, as if he wanted to avoid giving offence. Unusual for him.

"What if," Smithson said suddenly, "She's already launched missiles of Her own, similar to ours, and *they're* waiting for *us* to come in range?"

"I'd considered that," Thahl responded.

"And?"

"And I probed the areas around Her. Nothing."

"They might have evaded you."

"Then She'll win."

Smithson sighed theatrically. Foord said to him *"Listen. We're trapped in this orbit, and She's coming closer, both of which we planned. If She's seen our missiles, what do we do differently from what we're doing now?"*

"Particle beams?"

"No. We've been through that. We both fire our beams, we both use flickerfields, and we both keep our distance. That isn't what we want. She has to come closer."

"Is that what She wants?"

"Yes. She wants to finish us closeup, and She will if we're trapped and vulnerable, and we've *made* ourselves trapped and vulnerable. She has to come closer."

There were gasps from Cyr and Kaang, but when Foord turned quickly from Smithson to look at the screen, She was still there, unchanged.

"What happened?"

"Didn't you see it, Commander?" Kaang asked.

"No, I wasn't watching. Replay it, please."

On the screen She *flicked*, like a visible hand on the end of an invisible arm, whipping sideways and instantly back to its previous position. It was over almost as soon as it began, and everything else was unchanged. The space between them was still closing, but slowly. The Bridge screen returned to real time.

"Has She ever done that before?"

"No, Commander. Not on any of the recordings."

It was a strange unreadable movement, thought Foord; *not done for us but for some purpose of Her own.* The way it ended immediately it had begun reminded him of the lifecycles of their two missiles. She has to come closer.

●

Minutes passed. Foord still had his erection; and the bitter taste in his mouth and along the sides of his tongue had returned, gradually stronger as She came gradually closer.

His head throbbed like his penis. His thoughts were slowing down, like an ancient clockwork. Every time one of his thoughts tried to move it tripped a counterweight and generated an equal and opposite thought. No it didn't. He'd never felt like this before. Yes he had, on the occasions he'd caught himself looking at Cyr, and remembering the orphanage: first an arousal, then something darker, a need to open and penetrate and see underneath. He hadn't done it with Cyr, but had to with Her. He was afraid not to.

The Bridge screen reduced its local magnification to keep the same image as She came closer. Her ion drive was still reducing. The ports and windows and apertures remained dark. Probes showed no evidence of Her weapons powering up, and no trace of any missiles like theirs, floating inert nearby; although, as Foord knew, their probes were not effective against Her.

"I want Her, Thahl. What do I do to bring Her closer?"

"She's already closing, Commander."

"Not fast enough. What do I do to bring Her closer?"

"Commander, don't gamble. Not now. If She thinks we *want* Her closer..."

"I do want Her, Thahl...So something *opposite*. I don't want Her."

The taste along the sides of his tongue. His penis, pumping. Time to lay a card.

"We've changed our minds about fighting Her closeup. Haven't we."

Phrasing the question as a statement gave his voice a downward cadence at the end of the sentence. So did the deadpan recital of their motives, in the way he intended *She* would interpret them.

"We've seen Her and it's affected us. Hasn't it. Now all we want is to keep Her away. Don't we. So we fire our beams."

"That's what I told you!" Smithson crowed. "It seems hours ago."

"Commander," Thahl whispered, "*don't gamble.* You don't need Her to come in faster."

"Yes, I do." Before I have time to think what it means to destroy Her. "Fire particle beams, please, Cyr."

The beams lanced out, twice, across the piece of space that had set itself out between them. It was like they'd violated that space and the unwritten sharing of time. Foord didn't care. Time was up for the sharing of time.

They watched the beams reach Her and watched Her flickerfields hold them easily. Then She reacted.

"She's increased Her reverse ion drive," Thahl said. "She's moved back. I don't think it's worked."

But it had. There was a brief pause while She hung at a fixed distance from them—as though She had drawn back to examine Her conclusion, one last time—and then the Bridge was full of murmuring alarms and headup displays recalibrating to accommodate what She did next. The Bridge screen needed no more shufflings of filters or local magnifications, because She filled it. She had switched Her ion drive to forward, fifty percent, and was coming straight at them.

The screen showed violet flickerings around Her hull as She powered up Her closeup weapons. That was almost reassuring; it was how they must look to Her, as they powered up theirs. Time to lay another card. Foord glanced at Cyr.

"Fire particle beams again, please."

The beams lanced out. Again, She held them easily. As She did so, She came within visual range of the two missiles. They saw Her, and began and ended their lives.

From the two points where they floated, they erupted towards Her.

Amazingly, as though She had the reflexes of a single living thing, She *whirled* in Her own length to face them, a move the *Charles Manson* could never have made; but they were nearly point-blank, and they both slammed into Her, the silent explosions of their impacts following as, nanoseconds too late, Her flickerfields came on.

Both missiles hit Her port side, the first amidships and the second, while She was still rolling from the first, near Her main drives at the stern. She continued to roll, bringing Her port side fully into their view, and they saw it, as if lit by a naked bulb swinging in a cellar: the enormity of what they had done to Her.

Two great craters had been hammered into Her hull, glowing in a colour they couldn't name. Inside the craters they glimpsed for the first time what lay underneath Her surface, spidery substructures like their own. Bits of Her fountained out of the craters, turning end over end. They came in all shapes and sizes, and some were almost recognisable, like ordinary bits of wreckage from an ordinary ship; but

(Thahl got the Bridge screen to focus on them, and gestured wordlessly at Foord to look)

each piece of wreckage, whether it was a girder or a nut or a bolt—yes, She was made of things like that, as well as other unimaginable things—as soon as it left Her, reproduced in miniature the main damage to Her hull. Each piece, as it was thrown out, developed two craters in its side, and burnt away to nothing in the same unnameable colour as the craters they had hammered into Her.

Each piece, as it burnt away, was replaced by others which did the same, and others after that. The Bridge screen only focussed on the larger ones, but they were all burning away; and they were continuing to pour out of the craters, long after the missiles' explosions died. Later the Bridge screen would analyse and calibrate every piece of wreckage, individually and exhaustively. It would report its findings upwards to its sentience core, which would report them upwards to the ship's Codex, which after adding its own comments would report them further upwards to Foord and the others; and they would be no wiser then than they were now, watching it happen.

Thahl switched the Bridge screen back to the main view, where She was still rolling from the two impacts. The edges of the two craters in Her hull were *still* peeling back, pulsing like cell walls, as She completed the roll and Her port side passed out of their view.

She turned and ran. What was left of Her main drives flared, and She swung away, heading into Horus system and towards Sakhra. There was an oddness about how She moved, an asymmetric rolling produced by the way Her drives flared over the jagged wreckage at Her stern; asymmetric but repeated, the limping of something injured. They wouldn't be able to follow Her until they reached the high point where they could break free of their orbit, but that hardly mattered. She was hurt, intimately and massively; and She was going into the Gulf between Horus system's inner and outer planets, where She would have no cover.

Her screen image slowly receded, but She had left them something on the Bridge: a silence. It settled among them like another crew member.

It was one of the *Charles Manson*'s old silences, teeming with things unsaid. The reason for it, they all tried to persuade themselves, was Foord's injunction: Kill your reactions. Kill them all. It fitted well, and each of them—including Foord himself—tried to take refuge in it, in the enormity of what they'd done. But it wasn't real. There was no enormity. That was, literally, too large a word. What they had done felt smaller and dirtier.

It felt like it should never have happened. As if they were a gang of rapists, standing around after their victim had crawled away.

Later, the silence She left with them began to die.

"What have we done?" Kaang said.

"What we intended," Cyr said.

"It felt wrong. Like it shouldn't have happened."

"Because nobody's done it before."

"And it's trapped us," Thahl said. "After this, we have to go on and destroy Her."

"Or kill Her," Smithson said. "It's like She really is a living thing."

"No," Cyr said. "A ship, like us."

"You saw those bits of wreckage."

"Like us."

"But what they *did*—"

"No!" Cyr snapped. "A ship. Like us."

"Whatever She is," Foord said, "I don't want to know. I never have. I'm afraid of what we'd find."

"Is that why the Department said don't communicate with Her? Do they know what She is?"

"I don't know, Cyr." Foord glanced at Thahl, who for once would not meet his gaze. "But I'm afraid *not* to destroy Her."

There was a pause. A piece of the silence broke off, like one of the pieces of Her wreckage, and began to die in the same way as the main silence.

PART EIGHT

1

They reached the high point of their orbit around Horus 4, broke free without difficulty, and entered the Gulf. Later they got the first images of Her on the Bridge screen, crawling brokenly ahead of them. The two great craters on Her port side, midsection and stern, were still pulsing in the same unnameable colour, like chemical fires in a derelict building. Radiating out from them, and spreading over Her hull, were dark lines in swirling watered-silk patterns.

The Bridge screen patched in closeups. Her hull plates, the size of thumbnails, were diamond-shaped and bounded by submicroscopic hairlines which both joined and separated them. The dark swirling lines cut across these boundaries, and (from earlier time-lapse closeups) were spreading like a skin infection. Further from the craters they grew paler, their colour finally merging into the silver of Her hull.

Apart from the craters and the spreading dark lines, She showed nothing. No light or movement behind the windows and ports and apertures which punctuated Her hull, and no emissions other than the damaged main drive.

"A ship, like us," Cyr said.

"Not like us," Smithson said.

"Substructures," Cyr said. "Windows. Ports. Drives. Even hull plates."

"Not like us," Smithson repeated.

"Something was in there once," Kaang said. "I don't think it's there any more."

Foord looked at her curiously.

"Body language, Commander. You can usually tell."

"Cyr: particle beams, please."

"I thought you wanted it closeup, Commander."

"That's all finished. Just destroy Her."

The beams stabbed out. Her flickerfields deployed, and held them.

"It seems…" Cyr began.

"Again," said Foord. And "Again."

Again the flickerfields held. Other than that, She did not respond.

"You were right," he told Cyr. "It does seem."

"So we go closeup?"

"Yes…Kaang, slow approach, please. On Her port side."

The *Charles Manson*'s manoeuvre drives fountained, and they shifted to port; theirs, and Hers. They were still at long range, behind and above Her. They had chosen Her port side because of the craters.

Her starboard manoeuvre drives fountained, and She shifted to port—Hers, and theirs. Like a clock-face where She was at the centre and they were at the periphery, She had only to move a fraction of the distance they did to keep Her port side turned away. Other than that, She did not respond. She was dark and inert on all wavebands, and continued to crawl brokenly ahead of them.

Cyr said "It seems that She doesn't want us there."

"Again, Kaang," Foord said.

Again Her manoeuvre drives fountained to match them.

"Again," Foord said.

And again.

"Fine. Kaang, make it starboard."

Their port manoeuvre drives fountained, and they commenced a slow approach to Her starboard side. She did not respond.

●

The Bridge screen stopped shuffling and magnifying Her image; as they drew closer it enlarged naturally. Something did seem to have gone out of Her, and left only an empty container. No longer light made solid, or the junction of lines stretching to infinity.

They had cut their speed to a couple of percentage points above Hers. Their approach was so gradual that Foord was almost taken by surprise when Thahl stopped reading out spherical co-ordinates, and was replaced by Kaang reading actual closing distances.

"Fifteen thousand feet. No response."

There was a dorsal ridge running the length of Her slender delta hull, from the needlepoint tip of the nose to the flat, wide main drive outlets at the stern—both of these extremities, like much in between, resembled corresponding features on the *Charles Manson*—and it divided Her damaged and undamaged sides. The damaged port side faced away from them and was hidden, but even the undamaged starboard side had been somehow lessened. It was no longer even half of perfection or half of infinity, if that was mathematically possible. It was half of a lessened whole.

"Twelve thousand feet. No response."

The dark lines were apparently spreading over both sides of Her hull, uninterrupted by the dorsal ridge. None of them gave any readings when probed. They wrote patterns on, and over, and around, all Her other features: windows, portals, manoevre drive outlets, weapons apertures. All were dark and silent, like the outside of a deserted building. Something really had gone from Her.

"Eight thousand feet. No response."

Once Foord had found an injured turtle, dragging itself across a beach. Its face was expressionless. Great birds wheeled above it waiting to pluck out its entrails and eyes, but the turtle wanted only to make one step follow another; to cross the beach to the sea, dragging its injuries with it. The way She crawled across the Gulf towards Sakhra made Her both lesser and greater than before. Lesser, because She was crippled and had lost whatever animated Her. Greater, because She was crippled and had lost whatever animated Her, and still crawled.

Foord caught himself thinking that they'd seen Her just once when She was perfect, when She unshrouded. No one would ever see Her like that again.

"Six thousand feet. No response. Commander, it's like we don't exist for Her."

They were at the distance where, on more routine occasions, they would be commencing docking procedures. She filled the Bridge screen now, both horizontally (with the entire length of Her undamaged starboard side) and vertically (with Her wounded up/down rolling motion). The surface features of Her hull, some similar to theirs but others unguess-able, were sharply detailed—no clearer than when the Bridge screen had patched in local magnifications, but now they were closer to Her than they'd ever been, and genuine closeness somehow let you see better.

"Four thousand feet, Commander," Kaang said. "Still no response."

Foord glanced at Cyr.

"For what you want to do, Commander, it needs to be closer."

"Kaang, take us to one thousand, six hundred and twelve feet."

"Commander?"

"The length of our hull and the measurement of Her pyramid…Is that close enough, Cyr?"

"It's exactly close enough, Commander. Do you think She'll notice?"

"The distance? Yes, but I don't care either way. The gesture is for us, not Her."

"One thousand, six hundred and twelve feet," Kaang said, "and hold-ing. She's made no response."

"Thank you, Kaang." He turned to Cyr. "Well?"

"Tractor beams first, Commander, as we discussed. Then, everything else."

Tractor beams were what you used on a beaten opponent, merely to hold him in place while you tore him to pieces with other closeup weap-ons. They were the birds' claws, before the beaks went in.

"Agreed. Deploy tractor beams, please."

Then She made Her response, and it erupted in their faces.

2

She had found a conclusion. She woke and fought for Her life, desper-ately and passionately.

Tractor beams were invisible on normal wavelengths, so the Bridge screen displayed them in glowing red: fat red lines, moving slowly, heavy with torsion. When Foord gave the order, Cyr did not send just one or two. She launched them in a swarm, from points along the entire length of their hull, aimed at points along the entire length of Hers. They extended slowly out from the *Charles Manson* across the sixteen hundred feet in a classic Hands formation of groups of five, each group with two leading and three trailing: fat red sausage fingers, feeling for Her in fives.

They never reached Her. She put out a swarm of Her own, one of Hers for each of theirs, in the same Hands formation—they also showed red until the Bridge screen adjusted, and displayed them as pale blue—but they never reached the *Charles Manson*, because She never meant them to.

They watched unbelievingly as the Bridge screen showed each of Her beams hitting each of theirs headon, halfway across the sixteen hundred feet. The two colours bled into each other. It was like an injured fighter suddenly recovering to throw punches, not at his opponent but at his opponent's punches. And each one was accurate.

Foord swore. When he'd started to think She had no more mysteries left, he'd found at least two: desperation and passion. There was also the unfailing accuracy, but he already knew about that.

It continued. Seen unaided, there was nothing but sixteen hundred feet of empty space between them. Seen on the Bridge screen there was a moving diagram of two sets of beams: a tangle of two sets of motives, one to destroy, one to survive. The two formations of fat fingers met and interlocked in a multiple handshake, red and blue and purple. Where two opposing beams met, they subdivided into branches—always one of Hers for one of theirs, and Hers always accurate—and where branches met they subdivided into tendrils, tendrils into threads, threads into veins, vanishing into complexity; like their motives.

The initial exchanges—their beams attacking, Hers defending—were replayed in denser concentrations, inside the tangle of the thing which grew between the two ships. As the tangle got denser, the red/blue/purple colours bled deeper into each other and were shot through with further subdivisions: violet and mauve, lilac and pink, burgundy and cobalt.

The original formation of their beams had been deliberately conventional. Cyr swept a hand over her console and randomised it. The red fingers extending from the *Charles Manson* swirled like seaweed in a sudden current, then ceased to be groups of five and attacked in an undefined swarm. Faith randomised the pattern of Her own beams to mirror theirs, again one for one and again unfailingly accurate.

Foord thought, *Could we have done that? And where's She getting Her power?*

He watched Cyr, who had stayed cool and resourceful throughout, as she launched another swarm, this time of inceptor beams. Inceptors were high-power tractor beams, ten times fatter and stronger. Cyr had had enough of complexity and tangling. She had decided simply to punch the inceptors through the thing between them and get a direct hold on Her.

They never reached Her. She launched inceptor beams of Her own which met theirs one for one and tangled them like She had tangled their tractor beams, so the result was the same.

Stalemate.

On the Bridge screen, the thing which had grown up between the two ships now filled the sixteen hundred feet. It was bigger than either of them, and almost as complex. Red fingers from their hull, and blue fingers from Hers, poured into it and fed it. It was a living thing which they'd created together and were feeding together. It swelled and pulsed. Colours chased each other across its surfaces.

Cyr swore. So did Foord, and gestured at the thing on the screen. "Kill it, Cyr. Cut the beams."

"But *Her* beams—"

"Were intended to stop ours, not to reach us. When ours go, Hers will go."

"Are you sure?"

"Yes. But if you're not, cut them one at a time. Cut one."

Cyr cut one tractor beam. On the Bridge screen one red finger disappeared, together with its branches and subdivisions, leaving empty tunnels in the body of the thing between them.

Faith immediately cut one of Her beams; a blue finger disappeared, leaving a mirror-image network of empty tunnels.

"You see? Now cut the rest, one by one."

Cyr did so, and so did Faith, one of Hers for one of theirs. It was like taking veins and arteries out of a body, one at a time. They'd created and fed it together; now they pulled it apart, together.

It proceeded slowly but methodically. *We work well together*, thought Foord sourly, watching it on the Bridge screen. We almost *belong* like this, working with each other. Building up something that doesn't exist unless you see it on a screen, and then dismembering it.

Eventually it was done, and the space between them on the Bridge screen was as empty as it had been in real space. The two ships were still separated by sixteen hundred feet. They still travelled together through the Gulf, side by side, at a matched thirty percent. They regarded each other. Whether She watched them as they watched Her, through eyes and screens, they didn't know. But they could feel their gaze returned.

"I need your next orders, Commander."

"Everything, Cyr. Hit Her with everything." He looked at Thahl, who looked away.

●

A new set of apertures opened along the port side of the *Charles Manson*'s hull: short-range crystal lasers. They stabbed at Her like horizontal rain. The range was too close for Her flickerfields—or theirs, if She responded—and every one of them hit Her, but spattered off like raindrops. Cyr shrugged, then boosted their strength to maximum. A few of them brought small puffs of surface debris from Her hull, but did not penetrate. Cyr boosted them again, beyond maximum.

For the first time, She attacked. She fired a broadside of low-intensity light beams. Their colour was pale gold.

"Harmonic guns," Foord muttered. Cyr nodded, apparently unconcerned.

Faith's harmonic guns were like those of the *Charles Manson*—multiband harmonic noise generators, running up and down the audible and inaudible scales to disrupt the molecular structure of a ship's hull. In previous engagements they had torn apart the hulls of at least three Commonwealth cruisers, but the *Charles Manson* was different: stronger by several magnitudes.

The harmonics were encoded in the light beams, and the light beams, when they hit, released them. They sounded like an organ toccata and fugue overlaid with too much bass, and a choir singing in counterpoint overlaid with too much treble, both sequences of notes deconstructed and put back together at random.

They played—literally—over the *Charles Manson*'s hull. They set up resonances which rolled through the Bridge and the cramped corridors and living-spaces. They brought noises like those from Horus 4, noises of torsion as the ship's inner skins were twisted in opposite directions to each other, and to the outer skin. They brought concentric ripples to the surfaces of the drinks in the chairarm dispensers, and stirrings from the rubbish on the floor of the Bridge. They induced nausea and muscle cramps, but nothing more; they were designed to tear ships apart, not their occupants. And they failed, because they weren't strong enough. They rolled the length of the *Charles Manson* and back again, then subsided.

Cyr boosted the crystal lasers to danger level, and held them there; they brought more puffs of surface debris from Her hull. Cyr glanced at Foord, smiled briefly, and fired the *Charles Manson*'s harmonic guns. Their golden beams reached across the sixteen hundred feet and released their encoded notes over Her hull, which was still being hit by the crystal lasers. They couldn't hear the music of their harmonic guns, but they knew it would resonate inside Her at least as powerfully as Hers had, inside them.

For ten seconds, the time it took to run the sequence of notes up and down Her hull, She didn't respond. That was enough to suggest She was being damaged; and the crystal lasers were adding to it, persistently and in penny pieces. Cyr powered up the harmonic guns for another broadside.

Her hull blurred and shone, like Her soul was leaking out of it, and at the same time the *Charles Manson* was hit with a series of small impacts. While they were still trying to understand what had happened, the Bridge screen patched in local magnifications and showed them. At each place where the crystal lasers had been hitting Her, the thumbnail-sized scales of Her hull had silvered over and reshaped themselves into collimating mirrors, raised at angles to reflect back the *Charles Manson*'s lasers; not just to hit it, but to hit it on the corresponding points of its hull. Again, desperation; again, unfailing accuracy; and again, Foord swore.

Cyr recovered quickly. The reflected lasers were causing only limited surface damage, like they had done to Her, and it was easily remedied; Cyr turned them off. She glanced at Foord and fired a second broadside of harmonic guns. Again they reached Her and played their notes up and down Her hull, and again She didn't respond. Cyr fired a third broadside.

They knew Her internal damage must be mounting. They knew She'd have to fire Her starboard manoeuvre drives to get out of range of their harmonic guns, and She did so; but what came out of them was not drive emissions. It was heavier and slower, dark and bulbous and glistening, like dozens of separate streams of entrails. About five hundred feet out from Her the streams joined, and became a single cloud of corrosive plasma, the colour of insects' wing-cases: dark but crawling with iridescence. She flourished it like a cloak, and sent it billowing towards them.

Foord immediately ordered retreat. The *Charles Manson*'s port manoeuvre drives fountained, and the gap between them increased to three thousand feet. Then the manoeuvre drive apertures widened, and fired a neutraliser cloud.

Foord was right, She'd wanted to widen the gap, but She'd made *them* do it. And faced with a plasma cloud, they'd had no choice. They couldn't let it near them. It would corrode their electronics, infect their bionics, eat their outer hull layers, and—worst of all—would carry on doing those things even after an engagement had been won and the enemy who launched it was destroyed. But a plasma cloud could be countered; by retreating, and by launching a neutraliser.

Across three thousand feet, they watched their cloud billowing out to meet Hers. Theirs was light in colour and Hers was dark, but that didn't imply any symbolism. The lightness of their cloud was the colour of dirty bandages, and the darkness of Hers carried the iridescence of jewels. They met, and this time there was no stalemate. Their cloud crawled over and under and inside Hers, putting out the jewelled colours one by one as if it had grown fingers and was poking out eyes. Her cloud collapsed under the pale crawling shadow of theirs, folding back into itself until it ceased to exist. In the space between the two ships their cloud was left suddenly alone, like something floating in a toilet. Cyr touched a panel and it folded back into nothing, like Hers.

Iridescence, thought Cyr. *I'd almost forgotten.* "Commander, please have Kaang take us to sixteen hundred feet. I have an idea."

●

In the *Charles Manson*'s underbelly, something moved. A door in the rear ventral section of the hull started to slide open; then jammed. Cyr switched to backup systems and it started moving again. At one point it actually creaked (an incongruous, gothic noise which they could hear even on the Bridge) as it resisted, but the backup systems forced it to continue. It slid back, opening a dark gash in the *Charles Manson*'s underside.

The weapon which would emerge from the gash had never been used operationally. It had only been tested once, seven years ago when Foord took command of his ship on its first proving flight. The test had been successful but Foord and Cyr had both thought the weapon was too elaborate and specialised.

Seven years later, he glanced at her.

"Fire Opals," he said. "I'd almost forgotten."

"So had I," said Cyr. "We were both wrong."

The starboard manoeuvre drives fountained. Kaang brought them back to exactly one thousand, six hundred and twelve feet. Faith did not respond, but was watching them closely. They could feel it.

Out of the gash poured a stream of iridescent globes, each one the size and colour of an opal. The Fire Opals were designed (in Foord's opinion, over-designed) to attack an already damaged opponent in a particularly roundabout way. Each globe was individually programmed to enter a ship's hull through openings caused by battle damage, to seek out electronic and bionic circuits, get close to them, and burn itself to destruction. The circuits they attacked would not be destroyed outright, but—perhaps worse—would function too erratically to be trusted. Any ship they entered would be lobotomised, deprived of senses and sentience.

Seven years ago, Foord had said that if you'd knocked a hole in your opponent you wouldn't need such an oblique way of finishing him. Now, he told himself, if such a hole existed the Fire Opals could be decisive; and Faith, on Her unseen port side, had two.

They dropped endlessly out of the gash in the *Charles Manson*'s belly like eggs out of a fish. After the darkly beautiful iridescence of Her plasma cloud, their greens and pinks and blues were as fresh as rain in sunlight. There were a hundred and ninety thousand of them.

The Fire Opals extended underneath the *Charles Manson* in a long rippling filament. The door in the ship's underbelly slid back, buckling slightly as the backup mechanisms forced it past the point where it had jammed on opening.

Cyr touched a panel and the Fire Opals whipped out from underneath, then up, and hung quivering in the space between the two ships. She smiled to herself, then touched a few more panels. The Fire Opals formed themselves into a slender openwork sculpture: a delta shape with Her proportions, woven in opalescent ice. Cyr indulged herself further, and touched more panels. The sculpture started to hump up and down in imitation of Her crippled gait, and two holes appeared in its port side, one amidships and one at the stern.

Faith made no response.

"That's enough," Foord snapped. "Just get it done."

Cyr's sculpture melted. She reached into it through her panels and pulled out the forces holding it together, and it collapsed back into what it had always been, a large swarm of small opalescent globes. The Fire Opals were still under Cyr's control and would remain so until she locked in their path and launched them; then they would become individually self-directing, like Foord's missiles.

She pressed Launch, and said goodbye to them.

The path she had locked in for them existed for microseconds and was gone, as they flowed into and out of it. It was a straight line to Faith, converging at a point only fifty feet from Her starboard, then branching in a giant Y, arching *over* Her and down towards the two craters on Her unseen port side. The path existed only when they travelled it, closing in their wake until all that remained of it were the two prongs of the Y above Her, pointing down at the craters like mantis claws. Then that was gone too. They had entered Her.

Cyr locked off her panels. "They're self-directing now, Commander."

Foord nodded, and stared into the Bridge screen.

Sixty seconds' propulsion, as they entered Her through the craters and found paths through the wreckage, seeking circuitry. Then thirty seconds' burning. Most of them would find nothing and would fall and die alone in an unimaginable interior, in a darkness they would illuminate briefly but uselessly; but some would succeed. Maybe another two minutes, and the effect would be visible.

It would act like a nerve poison. First convulsions, violent rolling and pitching motions; then erratic flaring of Her manoeuvre drives and what remained of Her main drives; then desperate attempts to use Her scanners and probes; then shutdown, as She realised that Her senses were crippled.

Foord watched, across the cramped space they now shared with Her after having fought Her through half a solar system. Again he thought of a cellar with a naked bulb swinging from the ceiling. That was the kind of place where you did things like this.

After three minutes She started to shudder. It was not a convulsion, just a gentle pitching motion which overlaid the rolling caused by the damage they had already done to Her, but it was visible. Foord leapt to his feet and stared greedily into the Bridge screen, trying to pull more movement out of Her image, but after another minute it subsided. Only the original rolling remained.

"What..."

Cyr waved him to silence, and continued watching the Bridge screen closely. After thirty seconds she straightened.

"They've failed, Commander."

"You said they'd destroy Her."

"They didn't."

"But you said..." He could hear an almost indignant note in his voice. *Listen to yourself,* something tried to tell him, but he ignored it. She'd wronged him: Cyr, or Faith, or both.

"...you said they'd destroy Her."

"They *didn't.* She's still there." After a moment, Cyr added "Look. You can see Her, if you study the screen. Instead of yourself."

"All of them? All of them went inside Her and all of them died?"

Cyr threw up her hands, making her clothes move interestingly.

"Yes, Commander. And we still have to destroy Her. If that's what you want."

"Of course it's what I want! I even..."

"You even had the words ready. I saw your face. Playing at regret. 'We'll never know who or why; Her undeclared war; Her strangeness and beauty; Was there no other way?' You had the words ready. I saw your face."

"But you said..."

"Listen to yourself, Commander," Thahl hissed.

There was something like contempt in Thahl's voice, and Foord suddenly shared it.

"Cyr, I..."

"Leave it, Commander."

"It was because…"

"Because we have to destroy Her and you're afraid not to. Leave it."

He should have left it, but he'd wanted too much to apologise and explain. And now, to counter that, he went into denial and started reassuring himself: at least he and Thahl still understood each other, finishing each other's sentences. But it wasn't real. It was whistling in the dark, the same unguessable dark where the Fire Opals had burned and died.

On the Bridge screen, against the emptiness of the Gulf which was both huge and cramped, She did nothing but roll stolidly alongside them with the same crippled gait. On the Bridge, he saw Cyr and Thahl and Smithson—Kaang hadn't noticed—staring at him across another gulf. As if he was on a path which would take him away from them.

"Is She working on me, like She did with Joser?"

"If She is, Commander," Thahl said "it won't be like Joser, not after what we've done to Her. We're going to find out new things about Her."

"And She isn't," Smithson added," Working On You. That's self-indulgent, I've seen it before on Outsiders, too much imagination. If She's working on one of us it won't be you. Off this ship you can be vulnerable, but on it you're stronger than any of us."

Foord looked sharply at Smithson, who added, for good measure, "Yes, you heard me correctly, Commander. If She's working on one of us, maybe it's me. Why else would you expect *me* to tell you how strong you are?"

Foord looked at their faces. He couldn't read them. He didn't know if She was playing him like Joser. Or playing one of them, or all of them.

We're going to find out new things about Her. About ourselves. It will get strange.

"Thahl, if I'm right, you may have to…"

"Take command. I know. But you're not right, Commander…"

"Cyr, what do we do next?"

She exchanged glances with Thahl. "I'm already doing it, Commander. Look at the screen."

3

Cyr's combat instincts were more Sakhran than human. She was un-moved by failure. It produced in her neither despair nor defiance, neither desperation nor determination; only an expressionless glance, and then she continued past it. So when the Fire Opals died, she simply switched to what had worked before: the harmonic guns. While Foord indulged himself elsewhere, she powered them up, and now a broadside of golden beams played up and down Faith's starboard flank.

As before, they took about ten seconds to travel the length of Her hull and back, but this time it was different. Something was happening inside Her.

The windows and ports which lined Her hull had been dark since they first saw Her. One of them, close to Her stern, lit up. The Bridge screen immediately focussed on it, but nothing was visible inside: the light was as depthless as the dark had been. It was the same unnameable colour which burned in the two craters on Her port side, so far removed from any colour they had ever seen that they had difficulty recognising it as light.

The window darkened. The one next to it lit and fell dark, then the one next to that. It was like a lantern floating, or being carried, inside the length of Her hull, stern to nose; then back, nose to stern, the windows lighting and darkening sequentially. When it had passed back through Her hull, it disappeared. The line of windows was dark again.

The dark, like the light, was depthless. It seemed to be only a coating on the inner surface of each window, or to go on for an infinity behind it; either way, it showed nothing of what was inside Her. The process had taken twenty seconds.

Cyr again fired the harmonic guns, directly into the windows. They lit and darkened again, but this time from outside, as the golden light passed over them and released its harmonics. Then, simultaneously, they exploded. Molten silver—a lighter colour than Her hull, the colour of the pyramids– gushed out of them and cascaded down Her flanks. Shards of dark glass, or crystal, or diamond, from the exploded windows fountained and swirled around Her like a swarm of dead Fire Opals, visible only against the cascading silver of Her hull, disappearing against the dark backdrop of the Gulf as they flew further away from Her. A few of them reached as far as the *Charles Manson*, and bounced off harmlessly.

For the third time, Cyr fired the harmonic guns. More liquid silver poured out of the sockets of Her windows. She was bleeding ten times as copiously as before. There didn't seem room inside Her for what was pouring out. It was no longer cascading down Her flank, but moving horizontally across it. In ten seconds it covered Her entire starboard side from nose to stern, and built contours which didn't follow the contours of Her hull underneath it, or the contours of anything they would have recognised as a ship. She altered, and their perspective altered with Her.

Waves of molten silver were moving over Her hull. They moved against or around each other to create peaks and troughs, in long sinuous ripple patterns like wet sand after a retreating sea; then, as the peaks rose and the troughs deepened, they started to look like something else. What was building itself over Her starboard flank made no sense if you saw it as shapes extruding horizontally from a vertical surface, or as shapes covering a ship which was alongside them. You had to be looking *down* on it, and then it made sense.

Her starboard flank had become a silvered landscape, a relief map of hills and valleys and plains. The sockets of Her windows were lakes of liquid silver. The landscape filled the Bridge screen. A headup display said they were travelling through the Gulf alongside an object whose shape and size were similar to theirs, but it was a lie. They floated miles above it.

As perspective altered, so did magnitude. The lakes became oceans, the hills became mountains, the valleys grew as deep as the Sakhran Great Bowl. Now they were floating above the face of a planet. The Bridge screen couldn't contain it; the silver landscape filled all 360 degrees of it, and rushed out past sight beyond its top and bottom edges. They'd seen the roaring fiery face of Horus 5 and the blank blurred face of Horus 4, and this was bigger: and all done in silver, height and depth picked out in gradations of silver-white through silver-grey to silver-black. They floated miles above it, and it swam years below them.

As perspective and magnitude altered, so did colour. Shadows welled up inside the liquid silver, never quite reaching its surface, but tinting it like internal bruises: silver green in the valleys, silver blue in the oceans, silver white on the mountain- peaks. Thahl made the Bridge screen magnify one of the oceans. Once it had been a window, then a lake. Now it had bays and inlets, and on its silver-yellow beaches things were crawling out, some to die and some to evolve.

Then the last alteration: time. Alternate bands of light and darkness chased each other across the face of the silver, first slowly, like the turning of pages, then faster. The things which had crawled out of the ocean moved away into the land, from which others returned, altered. They made geometric shapes and grid patterns which grew and reached out lines, some straight and some curved, to cover the landscape and join each other. The pages turned faster and the patterns grew; then stopped growing and stayed the same, page after page; then dwindled and lost their connecting lines; then stayed, diminished, page after page. Was it the face of Her home planet? Or of other planets, after She had visited them? It was too enormous and small, too fast and slow, to have any meaning. Or, like the layers of darkness and light on the inner surfaces of Her windows, when they had been windows, its meaning might go on forever.

"It's a lie," Foord said. "Get us out of here."

●

The *Charles Manson* turned in its own length, engaged ion drive at fifty percent, and headed away: not only to escape what She was doing or becoming, but to escape the sixteen hundred feet of confinement they shared with Her in the vastness of the Gulf. Already the oppressive weight of the last few hours, to which none of them would have admitted, began to lift.

The image on the Bridge screen was now a rear view, but it still filled the screen because more of it poured back into the screen from its upper and lower edges as they moved away. At thirty thousand feet, which they reached almost instantly, it still hadn't diminished. They knew it was a lie. They knew She'd done something to the screen or to the sensors feeding it, or to the fabric of the space between them, but it wouldn't go. Thahl killed the headup displays which recorded its distance and mass and composition, and wished he could also kill the image. One was a lie, and both were meaningless.

"No," Foord answered Cyr before she asked, "we're not running away...

Kaang, what's our distance?"

"Eighty thousand feet, Commander."

"Take us to a hundred and fifty thousand, please. Cyr, be ready with particle beams."

"Commander," Cyr said, "that silver is the same composition as Her pyramid."

"And it's a lie. Whatever She's done to our instruments or our senses, it's a lie."

"We never fired beams at the pyramid! If we fire them at *that*, we don't know how it'll react."

"Whatever it does, will also be a lie."

"Commander, you seem…"

"*No.* This is me talking, Cyr. Not Her."

"That could be Her talking."

"No. She doesn't do possession, She does events and predicts our reactions." Because, he was beginning to suspect, but didn't dare say, *She knows us and has always known us.*

●

At one hundred and fifty thousand feet, the image stopped filling the screen. For the first time they could see the whole of it receding, just as if it was a real object, but that only made it stranger.

They had expected that when they could see its boundaries, when they could see the whole of it floating against the backdrop of the Gulf, the lie of its magnitude would give way to what it really was: just a ship, like them. But the silver extrusion blurred its edges and made it look like an oil-smear on a wet pavement. It turned the distance between them into an imagined alleyway, smelling of rain and urine.

Kaang turned the *Charles Manson* in its own length and brought it to rest, facing Her.

"Thank you, Kaang. Cyr, particle beams, please."

They stabbed out. Foord imagined them as a wind blowing through the wet alleyway, making rubbish stir on the ground, and posters flap against walls like bats nailed there by one wing. All of this was a lie: particle beams were near-instantaneous, and while Foord's imaginings were still forming, the beams had already impacted Her starboard side. She did not use Her flickerfields.

The silver extrusion turned the bruise-colour of the beams, then flared white. It swirled away from Her hull, cleanly and easily, as if it had never been more than a cloak someone had thrown over Her which She was now throwing back. As it swirled away from Her, it used the beams' energy to re-order itself, and became something else. A replica of Her, done in gradations of grey.

"Full-size," Foord said to Cyr. "Yours was less than quarter-size." She shot him a venomous glance.

The replica moved slowly towards them, leaving the original behind it. Like the original, it was sideways-on to them, presenting its starboard side. It stopped. Foord motioned Cyr to hold fire.

In front of it, between them, light grey and dark grey shadows of tractor beams—Hers, and theirs—fought each other to stalemate, form-ing a tangled mass from which, one by one, they removed themselves and were gone. Pallid grey washes of harmonic-gun light played up and down the length of its hull. Grey shadow-lines of lasers peppered it, and were turned back as some of its hull-scales became pewter-grey mirrors. Pale Fire Opals branched in a giant Y above it, swarmed down to enter the two great craters on its unseen port side, and were gone.

More harmonic-gun fire. Light moved inside the replica, an unname-able shade of grey. A line of its windows exploded. From the replica burst a replica of the silver extrusion from which the replica was made. It became a landscape, then a planet's face. It was a lie, telling a replica of a lie. Pages of light and darkness chased each other across its surface, networks of lines grew over it and diminished, and *then* it rushed to-wards them, filling the screen. The shadows of its surface details grew larger. The moment before it hit them one of the grey seas, which had been a lake and before that an exploded window, opened to swallow them.

The replica passed over, under and around them, raking their hull. The Bridge screen switched to a rear view showing it swirling away, dissipating back to what it had always been: almost nothing. Thahl reinstated the Bridge screen headups, and they said it was insubstantial and incapable of analysis. Smithson relayed damage reports one by one: superficial stria-tions on the hull, to add to those they already carried. She should have continued to infinity, Foord thought: one replica makes another, which makes another.

Ahead of them, She remained at a hundred and fifty thousand feet. Nothing of the silver extrusion was left on Her. The Bridge screen, before anyone instructed it, focussed on the line of exploded windows. Their edges were jagged where the explosions had torn out a few surrounding hull-plates, but in each one, set deeper inside than the dark glass had been, was an opaque surface the same dark shade as the patterns spreading over Her. It looked as if they'd been boarded up from inside.

"Particle beams, please, Cyr."

This time there was no illusion of a dripping alleyway. The beams reached Her immediately, and immediately She deployed Her flicker-fields. They held, and continued to hold, with no detectable weakening, as the beams fired again and again. She even returned fire with Her own beams, just once. It was no more than a gesture, and the *Charles Manson*'s flickerfields held it easily; but the gesture stayed, hanging between them. *Maybe*, thought Foord sourly, *it was only a replica of a gesture.*

Again Foord had the beginnings of an erection and the taste of vomit along the sides of his tongue. He still carried the compulsion to destroy Her, and the ambivalence that went with it. He wondered if the compulsion came from him and the ambivalence from Her, but he knew the truth was worse: the ambivalence was his too.

All of this made it a bad time for Cyr to say what she said next.

"'Insubstantial and incapable of analysis.' It wasn't real. We're still here."

His glance at her was as venomous as the one she had given him.

"Why is *She* still here?"

"Because you haven't done what I suggested, Commander. We should go for Her port side." She returned his glance; they shared, not body fluids, but venom.

"Kaang."

"Commander?"

"Take us closeup again. Same distance as before, but this time on Her *port* side. And Kaang."

"Yes, Commander?"

"This will be difficult. She doesn't want us there."

Faith crawled through the Gulf at thirty percent ion speed. The crippled gait, a mixture of roll and pitch produced by Her impaired drives flowing over the wreckage of the stern crater, was asymmetric and repetitive. Her hull was covered in the swirling watered-silk patterns, dark against the silver of the hull plates. It was like the darkness of the Gulf was bleeding into Her.

A hundred and fifty thousand feet away, Cyr watched Her on the Bridge screen and considered the dark swirling patterns, and how they lessened Her; Foord's two missiles had changed everything. Made Her fight for Her life. *But we haven't seen a hundredth of what She'll do to live. It'll get strange.*

Kaang also looked at the patterns. *Like an airless version of oxidation,* she thought, and forgot them.

The Bridge screen panned back, and back. Faith became invisible against the immensity of the Gulf. Ahead of Her were the inner planets, Sakhra and Horus 1 and 2. They were so far away they showed only as specks, scarcely more visible than Faith, and indistinguishable from the backdrop of stars. Only Horus itself was bigger than the other stars, and not by much.

A sound like doors slamming in a corridor ran up and down the ship. It was the locking of seat harnesses, for everyone except Kaang; hers would come later. She glanced across at Thahl and noticed that he had extended the claws of one hand and was tapping them absently on the rim of his console, tap-tap-*tap*, tap-*tap*, tap-*tap*-tap-tap. The sequence was irregular but, when Thahl repeated it, became part of a larger regularity; the same rhythm as the sequence of Her rolling motions, which Thahl was echoing as he watched Her on the screen. Repetition: the watered-silk patterns spreading over Her had of course been analysed for repetition, but none was found. Perhaps if there was another one of Her, or another million, the end of the sequence would be seen and it would start to repeat. That was as near, and as far, as they could get to the meaning of what was happening to Her.

Kaang watched the screen for a few moments more. Her face was expressionless.

She locked her seat harness, and wrenched the *Charles Manson* to port.

The starboard manoeuvre drives erupted as she pushed them directly from zero to overload, and she augmented them by vectoring the main drives. The *Charles Manson* whipped sideways and diagonally, and flung them down a straight line which would end sixteen hundred feet on Her port side. The move was too quick for the gravity compensators, and everything loose on the Bridge exploded into midair. The ship strained and shrieked as loudly as it had at Horus 4, but there it was only fighting one force; Kaang was throwing forces at it from all directions. By the time the debris on the Bridge had landed, but before it bounced, they had almost reached the point on Her port side for which Kaang had aimed; but She rolled with the move, and still presented Her starboard side to them. Kaang did not decelerate but flew past Her, turned at fifty thousand feet and executed the same move, with the same result. She executed it again, turning the *Charles Manson* at twenty thousand feet this time, standing it almost vertically on its nose and plunging it *under* Her, to come up again on Her starboard side because Faith, again, had rolled with Kaang's move. Kaang turned immediately and headed back, apparently on a ramming course; at nine hundred feet she wrenched the *Charles Manson* above Her, but again Faith rolled and presented Her starboard side. Kaang had expected this and fired the ventral manoeuvre drives, then vectored the main drives to augment them. It looked like the *Charles Manson* had hit an invisible wall. It stood for an instant on its stern, then pitched backwards over Her, aiming again for a point sixteen hundred feet on Her port side. This time it was closer, but still Faith rolled with the move and kept Her starboard facing them. When Kaang saw it had failed she did not decelerate or turn but continued until they were eighty thousand feet from Her, and still facing Her starboard side. Kaang brought them to rest, and glanced around the Bridge.

One by one, minor damage alarms sounded. She ignored them. She glimpsed the expressions of Foord and the others, and ignored them too. She knew it was always going to be unequal; whatever move she made, however complex and spectacular, Faith had only to wait for it and roll with it. Kaang shrugged, and started over again.

She fired the starboard manoeuvre drives, more gently this time. They fountained, and the *Charles Manson* moved—very slowly—to port. Kaang made some minor balancing adjustments to the ion drive, so the *Charles*

Manson maintained distance at exactly eighty thousand feet, and began circling Her. On the Bridge screen they saw Her starboard manoeuvre drives fountain briefly, then cut; fountain again, then cut; and repeat the sequence, so that She turned minutely as the *Charles Manson* circled Her massively, always presenting Her starboard side. It linked them together, as if they were at opposite ends of the minute-hand of a giant clock face, they at the outer rim and She at the centre: a fixed relationship, defined by clockwork. They both knew it was a lie, and when she was ready, Kaang ended it.

She went straight to a hundred and ten percent ion drive and shot the *Charles Manson* down the invisible line of the minute hand. At sixteen hundred feet, when everyone expected Kaang to decelerate, she didn't; she held the impossible speed but poured it into a series of rolls and slides and feints and somersaults which plunged them back seven years, to when she had first piloted the ship. She vectored the main drives to augment the manoeuvre drives, pushed the manoeuvre drives to thirty percent above danger level—two of the outlets burst after ten minutes, a third after fifteen minutes, and she ignored the alarms—and executed all her previous moves over and under and around Faith, but this time within the compass of only sixteen hundred feet, so She had less time to roll with the moves. But She did roll; although Her main drives were impaired Her manoeuvre drives were still operational, and they fountained in changing combinations up and down Her flank as She played them, just as Kaang did. The two ships tempted and toyed with each other as if they were knifeblades in the hands of two invisible but closely-matched opponents. *Her pilot,* thought Kaang after twenty minutes, *is good but he isn't a freak like me. Why can't I find another freak like me?*

After twenty-three minutes alarms were sounding throughout the *Charles Manson*, the minor-damage alarms now joined by the deeper notes of hull-integrity warnings, and Kaang ignored them. *This will be difficult,* Foord had said, *She doesn't want us there.* Kaang neither knew nor cared why. She had no idea what they'd see when she finally got them there, or what they'd do about it; that wasn't her territory. She blocked out everything except the imperative to pile move upon move until they emerged on Her unseen port side, and as time went on—it was now over thirty minutes—each move was getting them closer, and each of Her rolls was getting a little later. A little closer to too late.

Kaang poured more and more moves into the compass of sixteen hundred feet. If she'd left a visible trail, it would have looked like the tangle of tractor beams. She knew the balance was shifting but her face remained expressionless. Her hands blurred over the panels of her console, bringing convulsions to the *Charles Manson* with every touch, but she still seemed unhurried. The alarms and hull-integrity notes and warning headups on the screen were multiplying, and Kaang continued to ignore them. With each move she built her advantage and edged closer to a final outflanking, but with each move something burst or broke or failed. She knew exactly what she was doing to the ship, without needing alarms or headups, and she knew she was getting close to its real limits. She knew, even better than Foord, that the *Charles Manson* was almost alive and she was almost killing it.

Kaang sensed what would happen next, just before it happened. Faith stopped firing Her manoevre drives; She had given up.

Kaang cut the move she had just started and let momentum take them, slowly, in an arc over Faith's dorsal surfaces, and down, facing Her port side. On the Bridge, and up and down the length of the *Charles Manson*, seat harnesses burst open with hisses of compressed air. It was like the ship was letting out a breath.

Kaang finally brought them to rest, at a distance of exactly one thousand, six hundred and twelve feet, and they saw.

4

The two great craters on Her port side, one amidships and one near the stern, were still there. She hadn't miraculously repaired them. Around their edges, and in their interior where twisted latticeworks of substructures could still be glimpsed, the craters pulsed with the same unnameable colour. It shifted between all the colours they knew, without becoming any of them.

The craters went at least fifty feet into Her flank. Nothing poured out of them any more. They were filled with wreckage near Her surface, but the deeper they went the stranger they became. There was a darkness at the back of them which seemed either depthless or infinite: a curtain of something neither gas nor liquid nor solid, with a pattern of whorls like watered silk. It reminded Foord of the patterns on the endpapers of his father's books.

The craters pulsed into and out of focus, their apparent depth growing and diminishing as the light inside them shifted. Sometimes they seemed only as deep as they really were. Sometimes they seemed deeper than Her hull was wide, making corridors into somewhere else which was also filled with wreckage, like cameras taking pictures of cameras taking pictures into infinity. Then the light would shift again, and the craters would return to what they really were: something that nobody had ever done to Her before.

The damage was not only in the craters. Around their edges the fabric of Her outer hull had been torn back so violently that it produced an effect of inversion, as though the two missiles had burst out of Her, not in. The dark swirling patterns covered Her port side more densely than Her starboard, and around the edges of the craters they were darkest and densest of all.

The damage was massive. But it looked like it had gone beyond damage, and become something else.

Something about the craters had started to worry Foord. Thahl too, because before Foord could ask him he superimposed on the Bridge screen an earlier image of the craters, when the missiles first hit Her. The ship picked up on Thahl's request, and added text headups before Thahl asked for them.

The two craters had grown in area, by about two percent according to the headups; but they remained exactly the same shape as before, down to the smallest indentation, as though the present image was merely a slight magnification of the earlier one. They still looked like pulsing wounds, but wounds didn't spread so uniformly. They had the appearance of stability; of balance. Of the achievement of steady state.

Steady State, thought Foord, and froze as he started to understand.

"Commander," Cyr said loudly, "we need your orders."

Cold, organised shock hit Foord. It should almost have killed him, but it didn't; instead it spread through him steadily and uniformly, a replica of what was happening in the craters. He'd just learned, as Thahl promised, something new about Her. Something truly new; and intimate, and obscene.

She's eating Herself.

"Commander!" Cyr was shouting now. "We need your orders!" She turned to Thahl, and whispered "What's eating him?"

"No orders," Foord said quietly. "No questions. Please, listen to me."

This, he told them, was how She could go on crawling through the Gulf to Sakhra when the damage they'd done should have destroyed Her. She'd reached a conclusion. For the first time someone had made Her fight for Her life, and She'd fought desperately and passionately; and this was how. This was where Her conclusion led.

She'd turned the craters into a controlled process of self-digestion, mass to energy.

He waved away their questions. Maybe where She comes from, he said, this is what every living thing does when it's wounded: puts its muzzle into the wound and eats, to give the rest of itself, the unwounded part, strength to go crawling on. Maybe whoever built Her put replicas of that reflex into Her, as we put crude analogues of ours into our ships. And No, he said, I don't have evidence. How could I, when nobody's ever been able to probe Her? But you've seen what's happened to Her since Horus 4, and I know I'm right.

Their questions died out.

Foord remembered a character in one of his father's books, a minor Dickens character, who kept saying "If I'm wrong I'll...I'll *eat my head.*" The sheer impossibility of it had entranced him; he had pondered it for days. He thought, *If She ever reaches Sakhra at this crawling pace, She'll have eaten Herself entirely and She won't exist. Yes She will. What's eaten will still exist, but it will be something quite different...*

This wasn't a frenzy of self-mutilation. It was steady and careful and measured. She was digesting the damaged parts of Herself at exactly the rate She needed to provide the energy to go on fighting, to go on crawling through the Gulf. Her motives were desperate but Her conclusion was cold and considered, and Her execution unfailingly accurate. Like everything She did.

Both his parents, in the later stages of the illness which finally took them, had fought a losing battle to keep their appearance. He'd pretended not to notice the incontinence-stains on their clothing, or their subter-fuges to conceal them. This was similar: something private about Her which he shouldn't have seen.

"What She's doing to stay alive, Cyr, is in the craters. Go for the craters."

●

For ten seconds, the golden light of the *Charles Manson*'s harmonic guns swept along Her flank, pumping their resonances into Her. She seemed to shudder, but it could have been the effect of the shifting colour from the craters. Lit by that colour, nothing seemed real or measurable.

Cyr fired the harmonic guns again, once, along and back. This time she also fired the Friendship guns (used only when close) at Her flank; they shot Jewel Boxes, self-guiding shells which on impact released jagged slivers of synthetic diamond able to shred almost any known surface. They didn't shred Faith, but each one succeeded in digging a small shallow gash in Her flank, dislodging three or four of Her thumbnail hull plates, and that was enough for Cyr's immediate purpose. There were nineteen such gashes in an irregular line along Her flank, between the midsection and stern craters.

Why doesn't She respond? thought Foord. Cyr was thinking the same thing, and added *Perhaps She already has.*

Cyr launched a swarm of grapples across the sixteen hundred feet. She called them Hands of Friendship, diamond-tipped claws on the end of black monofilament lines which tumbled out like spider-secretions from ventral orifices on the *Charles Manson*. The claws were shaped like Sakhran hands, and were self-programmed to find any irregular surface, grip it, and never let go. One, and occasionally two, of them landed on each of the nineteen shallow gashes, and held. Now, Cyr thought, we're directly touching Her.

Cyr's long jewelled fingers played another combination of panels, open-ing another pattern of apertures on the *Charles Manson*, this time along the starboard midsection. The objects which emerged were globular and milky and quivering. They made their way towards Her like a slow-motion ejaculation, each one targeted at one of Her port manoeuvre drive outlets. Cyr called them Diamond Clasps, because they were plasmas of altered carbon which turned on impact into plugs of liquid, then solid, synthetic diamond. They landed on Her and dressed Her, covering each outlet with a brilliant sparkling scab. Two missed, but the other fifty-three landed accurately.

She responded. She must have known what was coming next—that Cyr would hold Her in position and attack the craters—yet it was strangely half-hearted. She fired just three of Her port manoeuvre drives, presumably to test whether She could dislodge the diamond scabs. She couldn't; thin streams of drive emissions squirted from underneath them, but most of their force was contained. Then, using Her starboard manoeuvre drives only, She tried to roll away, but the claws and monofilament lines of the grapples held Her. She didn't try again.

"Now the craters," Foord whispered.

"This is too easy. Something's wrong."

"The craters!"

"Commander, it's too easy. She wants us to go for the craters."

"She wants you to think that, so you won't go for them. You wanted my orders. Carry out my orders."

Cyr hesitated. Something, perhaps Faith, was still telling her not to attack the craters directly. As her hand hovered over a panel she hadn't pressed before, she thought *This may be wrong, it may keep Her alive.* She pressed the panel.

A long ventral aperture slid open, releasing an object like an ancient battering-ram, ninety feet long: a Diamond Cluster, a missile whose bulging warhead was a cluster of five hundred Jewel Boxes, which would explode their fractal diamond slivers simultaneously. It could shred any known Commonwealth ship. If it hit Her where She was already damaged, it should break Her in half.

It dropped out of the *Charles Manson*'s underside, made one calculated burst of its motors and went dark, crossing the sixteen hundred feet to Her. On the Bridge screen they watched it entering the midsection crater. It went deep inside until, like everything else in there, it passed beyond focus. The latticeworks of wreckage and shifting colour swirled and swallowed it, like it was entering a forest of seaweed.

It exploded, but not in a way which made any sense. First, the explosion blew *out* of the crater, not in. And second, it was hundreds of times slower than it should have been, so slow that it was drained of force. And third—

The pattern of force and fragments, of blast and flying diamond-slivers, which should have erupted *into* Her and should have been unstoppable, came blossoming *out* of the crater in a slow and syrupy and ever-widening funnel, almost a gesture, reaching out to the *Charles Manson*; then reversed itself. The huge burst-open body of the Diamond Cluster and its multiple warhead came back together, unexploded itself, and sank back into the midsection crater like treacle down a throat. They never saw it again. But the dark watered-silk patterns around the crater's edges turned darker.

She's digesting it, thought Cyr, aghast. Converting its mass to Her energy. She never cared about it exploding, She just wanted it inside Her. And we gave it to Her. Part of *us* is now part of *Her.* What have we started?

The dark swirls continued to darken, for about fifty feet around the midsection crater. There was a shuddering at Her stern as She started to repower Her crippled main drives, and alarms were sounding on the Bridge. Cyr tried to think it out for a few seconds more. If there's a mass-to-energy process in the crater, the dark patterns must diffuse it through Her. And if you diffused that process, if you subdivided it hundreds or thousands of times as She had done, you could change it and change the laws it obeyed. You could *write* the laws it obeyed.

And we gave it to Her. "Commander…"

Alarms sounded again on the Bridge. She had fired Her main drives and was starting to move away, and Kaang immediately matched Her course and speed: like before, She moved through the Gulf at thirty percent, in the direction of Sakhra. The two ships were travelling alongside each other, still linked by Cyr's diamond grapples and monofilament lines; and still separated by one thousand, six hundred and twelve feet.

Cyr felt a mounting horror. "Commander…" she repeated.

Foord shook his head, and pointed at the screen. Something was coming out of the midsection crater.

●

The Bridge screen had spotted it at the same time as Foord, and patched in local magnification. It came into focus as it came out of the shifting colour. It became definite only when it left the crater, and started crawling over the surface of Her hull.

It was about the size of a man, and shaped like a spider. Its body was triangular, with three jointed and clawed legs extending up and out from each corner. It was the same metallic-ceramic silver as Her hull, and its body was featureless, with no recognisable sensory devices, so there was no focus of its identity; no face.

Another one emerged behind it, and another, and another.

"Thahl?"

"No, Commander. These are new."

Even so, they weren't surprising. The *Charles Manson* carried its own self-programming EV synthetics, used for hull repairs and occasionally for close combat. They were not unlike these, both in shape and size.

"Hold our position," Foord said. "No matter what happens."

More came out of the crater, one by one. The Bridge screen counted them: nineteen. They darted across Her flank towards the shallow gashes where Cyr's grapples were anchored, the diamond Hands of Friendship which were designed never to let go. The spiders dug them out of Her hull, busily and precisely, then fired onboard motors and rode them, and their monofilament lines, back across the sixteen hundred feet to the *Charles Manson*. The lines had come out of the *Charles Manson*'s underside, and now they curved back on themselves as the spiders flew them back towards the *Charles Manson*'s dorsal surfaces. It was like they were folding a giant bedsheet.

Hundreds more of them poured out of the midsection crater, not in the same tidy order as the first nineteen. They were climbing over each other to get out, as if they were running from something in the crater rather than running to attack the *Charles Manson*; but that impression lasted only a moment. Each one, as it emerged, fired its onboard motor and jumped the sixteen hundred feet, following the original nineteen. Some were blown to pieces by Cyr's Friendship guns as they jumped, and others were vaporised by the motors of those immediately in front of them; but nearly two hundred landed on the dorsal surface of the *Charles Manson*'s hull, where, like prospectors in a gold rush, they ignored each other and started digging where they landed.

Nobody ever made you fight like this *before*, thought Cyr, talking both to herself and to Her, as she activated the *Charles Manson*'s own synthetics to meet them.

On the Bridge, the usual murmuring of alarms was again supplemented by the deeper notes of hull-integrity warnings. Faith's synthetics dug busily; the claws which dealt so easily with Cyr's Hands of Friendship were shredding the hull's topsurface. Some had already penetrated to the first inner layer. They worked quickly and precisely, with an air of self-absorption, as though competing. Rising vertically above each of them, like smoke from factory chimneys, were floating columns of shredded hull-fragments.

Groups of hull-plates on the *Charles Manson*'s rear dorsal areas rose up into blisters and burst open, disgorging the *Charles Manson*'s own synthetics. They too were like spiders, but spiders from the planet where they were designed and built, with globular bodies and eight multiclawed legs. They were the dark bluish grey of gunmetal. They were slightly bigger than their opponents, and there were more of them, five hundred against two hundred. They swarmed over the top of the *Charles Manson*'s hull as though they were a shadow cast by a third ship. Faith's spiders ignored them and continued digging into the hull until the last possible moment, then turned one by one as the swarm reached them.

One of the *Charles Manson*'s many external viewers picked up the moment of first contact, and patched in to the Bridge screen. One of Faith's spiders was digging deep into the hull when three of the *Charles Manson*'s reached it. It stopped its work and turned to face them, though it had no face and neither did they. The three closed on it from different angles. It impaled the first, extending a leg to strike down through the dark globular body and into the hull, then rose and pivoted on that leg to grasp the second, holding it aloft while it snipped off its eight legs one by one, and rolled its body away. It completed its pivot and landed, then *flicked* the leg by which it held its first opponent impaled; in a torrent of cogs and gears and catarrh-coloured machine oil, the first opponent was cut in half and the two halves left painlessly but uselessly twitching. Faith's spider seemed to consider for a moment; then carefully nudged the two sets of dismembered remains to send them floating up to join the column of hull-fragments rising above its excavation, to which it returned. The third of its opponents, which it had either forgotten or decided to ignore, leapt after it and struck downward, severing a corner of its triangular body complete with three jointed legs. Faith's spider died, or became nonfunctional, so strangely that on the Bridge they could only stare at what happened; but the Bridge screen magnified it, and recorded it in detail.

The two pieces of Her spider did not bleed oil or spurt mechanical innards. The surfaces where they had been severed were smooth and solid, like a stone sheared in two, with no inner cavities or workings. The two pieces grew still; then broke in half, again with a solid shear, and broke in half again and again, beyond vision, until they became nothing. Except that nothing which continually halves itself ever becomes nothing.

The Bridge screen patched in two more viewers. They showed similar individual battles, dark against silver.

A silver spider cut two opponents to pieces, and turned back to continue its excavation. But one of the two, its dark globular body split almost in half, and dragging the empty half of its body and the strings of its insides behind it, crawled after the silver spider on its three remaining legs. It looked like bravery, but was not; the dark spider, like Foord's two missiles, recognised nothing in the universe except its programming. It struck down at the third joint of one of the silver spider's legs, and severed it. The silver spider fell into halves, and subdivided down to nothing; almost as if it wanted to.

Five dark spiders encircled a silver spider. It let them close in; then whirled balletically, pivoting on first one and then another corner of its triangular body, striking with its claws at different parts of the circle around it. Every time it struck, an opponent was mutilated. They fell back. Finally one of the five caught a claw and severed it at the joint. They stayed back and waited for it to start subdividing—which it did almost eagerly, as if that was even more important than digging into the hull—and then they moved off to the next battle.

The Bridge screen patched in more viewers, shuffled them one after another, then subdivided them into a mosaic. Then it started to pan out. Only one side fought collectively; the other fought in intervals between attacking the hull, and then only as isolated individuals against two or three or more opponents. They never went to help—or even seemed aware of—each other.

The Bridge screen panned out further. Along the top of the *Charles Manson*'s hull were nearly two hundred excavations, some of them now dangerously deep. Each was the scene of a battle, and each was marked by a floating vertical column of pieces of hull, to which were being added the dark dismembered bodies of the *Charles Manson*'s spiders. They were smokestacks in a diseased industrial landscape; and, like giant lice running over it, things with no faces or voices or identities fought with unrelenting vacancy.

The *Charles Manson* had never before had to repel a boarding by an opponent's synthetics, and Faith had never before had to reveal or use Her own. Both were somehow violated, but together they had made *this*. *We work* very *well together*, Foord thought sourly, watching it. Thahl sheathed and unsheathed his claws, Cyr unconsciously licked her lips. Smithson was expressionless. Kaang, until Foord told her to stop, had actually put her hands over her face.

The Bridge screen again subdivided into a mosaic of individual battles. It had seen a pattern, which it judged worthy of attention. The *Charles Manson*'s spiders were no match individually for their opponents. In direct combat, even three or more against one, they were being annihilated. But their self-programming told them something else. They only had to sever one body-part, even the last joint of one leg, and the silver spiders would cease to operate and start subdividing down to nothing, almost as if they wanted to.

What made you? thought Foord, staring across the sixteen hundred feet. *What are you?* She looked and behaved like a ship, sustained damage, showed internal substructures—they were still visible now in the craters, lit by the unnameable colour, as the two ships flew alongside each other through the dark of the Gulf. And the wreckage that had poured out of those craters, each fragment repeating the main damage and burning away to nothing. And the silver landscape. And the self-digestion, mass to energy, diffused through Her damaged body by dark swirling watered-silk traceries.

And now the silver spiders, easily able to shred the *Charles Manson*'s hull and dismember its spiders but subdividing down to nothing when any part of them was severed, so they could only be whole or be nothing. And when not whole, they seemed to *want* to be nothing, and that was what the Bridge screen had seen. That was what had started to turn the battles.

The Bridge screen displayed the numbers. Five hundred against two hundred became four hundred against a hundred and fifty, and then the change set in: three hundred and fifty against eighty, three hundred against twenty. The Bridge screen patched in the end of the last silver spider. It had shredded six opponents and, moments before it was overrun, snipped off one of its own legs and subdivided down to nothing.

The top of the *Charles Manson*'s hull was a leprous landscape: excavations like open sores, sprouting vertical columns of debris, and everywhere dismembered spiders. Nearly three hundred of the *Charles Manson*'s dark spiders remained, though few of them had all their body-parts. Without ceremony, they set about repairing the excavations. They used plugs of synthetic diamond like those Cyr had launched at Faith, carrying them to and fro across the hull in their original form, like quivering opalescent eggs. They picked their way through the debris with the slow injured gait of soldiers after a battle, except that the bodies they stepped over were only those of their own kind. Their opponents had gone, subdivided to nothing.

The Bridge was silent except for a few exhaled breaths. Faith continued to fly alongside them. The craters continued to pulsate. The Gulf just continued, before and behind them; and so did whatever had just taken place over the topsurface of the *Charles Manson*. There was no sense that something had just ended successfully.

When Smithson said "What next?" he was the first to speak. Nobody answered, because he wasn't asking what they would do next, but what She would do next. And She had already begun.

The columns of debris floating vertically over the abandoned excavations grew taller and thinner. They waved backwards and forwards in unison as they grew. Their waving was repetitive and hypnotic, like hair on a drowned corpse. Each backwards-and-forwards cycle left them a little more off the vertical, inclining a little more in the direction of Faith; and a little taller and thinner, as if they were not just accretions of debris but something ductile, being teased out longer and thinner by their own waving motion. As they extended and thinned they looked even more like strands of hair: diseased hair, piebald with the colours of the *Charles Manson*, the silver of its shredded hull-plates and the dark gunmetal of its dismembered spiders. And always getting thinner, easing gradually further in Her direction.

Cyr shook off the near-hypnosis of their waving motion long enough to ask herself why she wasn't firing on them, or why none of the others had asked her; then became aware that something else was happening, back on the topsurface of the *Charles Manson*.

At first it seemed like a minor optical fault on the Bridge screen, a faint double image of the landscape of the hull's surface. There was a barely visible mirror-image of the surface of the hull, floating inches above the real surface; as though part of the hull had shed a molecule-thick layer of its skin which, as it floated upwards, retained the shape of the original. The *Charles Manson's* surviving spiders, moving slowly to and fro repairing the damage done by the excavations—*their* movements were also repetitive and hypnotic, as if they were shadows cast by the waving columns above them—passed through the apparent double image without noticing it. Those on the Bridge saw why when the Bridge screen spotted it and attempted to magnify it locally: up close, it was almost nothing. You had to be at a distance even to glimpse it, and then you weren't sure. But it existed. The Bridge screen didn't deal in optical faults, even minor ones.

It rose higher, and grew more distinct as it rose. Now it was six feet above the surface, still mirroring the shape of the hull beneath it, and had thickened and turned silver grey. And now, when the Bridge screen again magnified it locally, it had acquired substance and texture: it was granular, made up internally of swirling and eddying particles. Cyr cried out, and Foord again tasted bile along the sides of his tongue, as they both realised what they were watching.

It was the collective ghost of the silver spiders.

Nothing which keeps halving itself ever becomes nothing. They had divided down beyond visibility into atoms and their subatomic components, and were now recombining into something else.

Cyr fired on it with the Friendship guns and shortrange lasers. They passed through it, leaving useless rents which closed as the particles inside it swirled back. It rose into a conical shape, as though it was a bedsheet and a figure underneath it had stood up. The conical point rose higher, pulling the rest after it until it too became a column, thicker and taller than the others. It waved backwards and forwards in time with the other columns of silver and gunmetal. Together, they took their leave of the *Charles Manson*.

A soft concussion rolled up and down the hull as they moved off it in unison and started to cross the sixteen hundred feet back to Her, a slow slanting elongated armada. Cyr fired on all of them with no more effect than before.

They converged, coiling and twining round each other, two hundred strands into a single rope which carried Her colours and theirs, and Her substance and theirs. Cyr fired tanglers and disruptors after it, and more lasers and Friendship guns, but they passed through it and spent themselves. Like a coil of matter spiralling from a captive sun into its black hole companion, the giant rope of their substance and Hers reached out towards the midsection crater on Her port side.

Foord stared. *We can't let Her take it inside Her. But we're too close for particle beams, there's no time for plasma clouds, and nothing else works.*

"Kaang."

"Commander?"

"Ram Her, please. Aim us at the crater."

The Bridge froze. Cyr glanced at Thahl.

"Commander," Thahl said carefully, "She'd assimilate us. All of us. And then She'd go on to Sakhra."

Foord nodded impatiently, gestured with a raised hand: You didn't think I was serious, did you? "Thahl, you said we'd find out new things about Her. Look at the screen. That wasn't a battle. She wasn't fighting us, She was *farming* us."

The great coiled rope, light silver and dark silver, grey and gunmetal, reached closer to the midsection crater. It floated between the two ships, away from one and towards the other, touching neither of them. It had never physically linked them, had never simultaneously touched both of them, but it held them together by what it was, their substance and Hers.

Perhaps this was all the silver spiders had wanted: to subdivide into molecular ghosts and offer themselves back inside Her for assimilation, together with the shredded pieces of the *Charles Manson*'s hull and spiders which they'd collected for Her and coiled together into this giant rope which would feed Her so She could go on to Sakhra. Perhaps She wanted the *Charles Manson* by Her side all the way back through the Gulf, to feed off it as required. Partly companion, partly farm animal.

On the Bridge screen they watched as the midsection crater seemed to open itself to the reaching rope. It entered, and continued and continued to enter, until all its length was enfolded and swallowed into the nameless colour. As She took it into Herself a shockwave radiated out from the crater across Her flank. It was a darkening of the watered-silk lines, diffusing through Her the energy She created from the mass She had received, dividing and subdividing it down thousands of branching paths. She moved forward relative to the *Charles Manson*. Her ion speed increased to forty-five percent. Kaang matched it, and they stayed alongside Her; for now, they had nowhere else to go. Where do farm animals escape to?

By one more increment, one more order of magnitude, they had become part of Her. As they flew together through the Gulf to Sakhra, there might be further increments. She would take and use what She wanted of them, and they couldn't stop Her. That, now, was their relationship.

●

"Relationship? *Relationship?* Commander, this is a military engagement!"

"Call it what you like, Cyr."

"Relationships don't stand still, Commander. They grow. They die. And they can be *changed.*"

It seemed like hours ago when Foord said that. In fact it was only minutes, and they still flew alongside Her through the featureless dark of the Gulf. She still moved with the same crippled gait—Her image lurched vertically up and down on the Bridge screen—but now She was travelling at forty-five percent, and so were they. The swirling patterns over Her hull were darker. Once they'd stalked each other through the Belt like a pair of tarantulas. Now it was different.

"Permission to speak freely, Commander," Cyr said.

"Of course."

"You said we can't stop what She's doing. That's unforgivable. In fact I wonder if it was you speaking at all."

Foord gazed at her steadily. "Don't go there."

She held his gaze. "If you're saying we can't stop it, it's my duty to go there."

Foord had never heard her use the word Duty before.

"I mean it, Commander."

"I *want* to stop it, but we need a weapon that works. We've tried most of yours."

Other conversations on the Bridge had stopped. There were several paths Foord and Cyr could have taken from this point, none of them good; but they were all closed off, unexpectedly, by Smithson.

"You're both," he said, "missing the point! Weapons aren't always called weapons. Anything which produces Cause and Effect can be a weapon."

"That's very true," Foord said drily. "Like Relationships Don't Stand Still. But do you have anything more specific?"

"Yes, I do. Something very specific, *and* it makes things stand still. The Prayer Wheels."

The Prayer Wheels. The stasis generators used to isolate the MT Drive. The *Charles Manson*'s MT Drive needed three of them for safe containment. The *Charles Manson* always carried nine. And the MT Drive had been shut down since Horus 5, when *She* had tried to activate it.

"Go on," Foord said.

"You know it already," Smithson said impatiently. "Cannibalise two Prayer Wheels, launch them into those two craters. Gamble. Maybe they'll freeze those mass-to-energy processes…"

"Why should they?"

"…isolate them, freeze them like an MT Drive, and then the craters will go back to being just holes in Her side, holes which *we* made, and we can fire whatever we want into them. Get inside Her. Break Her up."

"Slow down. Why should they freeze the processes like an MT Drive?"

"Look at those craters, Commander."

Foord looked. They looked back at him across sixteen hundred feet, unblinking and calm. Despite the nameless colour, despite the tricks they played with focus and perspective, they were above all calm. Stable, steady-state.

"Commander, those are not simple mass-to-energy processes. They've been slowed down and subdivided, millions of times, until they sidestep the equations. To produce that steady-state energy, to diffuse it through Herself in usable amounts, probably takes only a millionth of what those craters have swallowed. But it also takes a new kind of physics."

"MT physics."

"Yes, Commander. *We* couldn't do it, we don't know enough about MT.

But we know how to freeze it in stasis fields."

"So will She. She'll be able to stop the Prayer Wheels."

"Of course She will, Commander! But immediately?"

"I don't know, and neither do you."

"Then would you rather go on like this? In the time it takes Her to stop the Prayer Wheels, She'll be vulnerable and those craters will be open to us. Maybe. And Maybe is better than *this*. Now: my people can get two of them from the stern, weld some guidance systems and motors on them, and have them ready in one of the ventral launch bays in less than an hour. Is that specific enough?"

5

Later, Foord would realise that Smithson had probably saved the ship, simply by having an idea and getting them working on it. It almost didn't matter whether the idea would work, though it was an extremely clever one; at that moment, if they'd had no goal, they might either have been infected by Foord's mood, or relieved him of command. Both courses would have been fatal. So Smithson got them working, and Foord stayed in command, though his mood—and its source—remained unreadable and worrying.

Smithson was often impatient with superiors and equals, but less often with subordinates. On this occasion his behaviour was faultless, and a source of some amazement; he was as thoughtful, meticulous and quietly authoritative as Foord himself would normally have been. The two Prayer Wheels were taken from the six reserves not connected to the MT Drive. The work of confirming they were operational, testing and welding in place the guidance and propulsion units, and manhandling them down to a conveyor tube which shot them through to one of the ventral launch bays, took Smithson's people forty-seven minutes. Once in the launch bay, final testing and routing of the controls through to Cyr took another seven. During that time, Cyr—at Smithson's suggestion—briefed Foord on what she would be firing into the craters, and in what order. Foord was more responsive than previously, but not much. He sat quietly with Cyr amid the rubbish and debris on the Bridge—which he still insisted should not be cleared—listening to her briefing, and watching Faith.

Faith made no more moves towards them. She increased Her speed to forty-eight percent, and they matched it to stay alongside Her. She did not appear to notice.

Foord was concerned about his behaviour. He tried to determine why he was concerned, but the reason kept sliding past him, as though his concern belonged with the rules of the normal universe, and his behaviour now held an MT-like ability to sidestep it. He was feeling better now, closer to what he remembered as normal, thanks (not for the first time) to Smithson's cleverness. But he'd come close to accepting what *She* had done to them. Cyr was right, he should never have behaved like that. He never had before. He resolved never to again, and immediately set about reciting rules for ensuring he never would; and again it sidestepped him, and left him trying to remember why he needed to recite rules. But he felt better now, closer (he told himself) to what he remembered as normal.

After Cyr briefed him, and after he reacted with apparent enthusiasm, she stayed with him (another suggestion of Smithson) and let him talk. Her dark pleated skirt had ridden up behind her as she whirled lithely to sit next to him, so she was not actually sitting on its fabric. The pleats were rucked up around her bottom, but he knew they would fall back gracefully into place when she stood up; they always did.

"A millionth, Cyr."

"Commander?"

"Smithson said She needs only a millionth of what She swallowed in that crater, to convert into a steady stream of usable energy. I thought She'd turn us into a farm animal and carve off bits of us to eat when She needs to, but She doesn't need to."

"Apparently not."

"But She'll probably do it anyway, just for the symbolism…Cyr, you see those dark patterns over Her hull?"

"Yes, Commander. They've spread."

"They haven't moved."

Originally, Cyr had just wanted to let him talk. Now she looked at him sharply.

"How could they be spreading over Her and not have moved?"

Because, he told her, they were always there; they'd just grown darker.

And they weren't just on Her surface. If they really did diffuse the processes through Her body then they'd have to go all the way through Her
in three dimensions, like a tangle of veins and capillaries. So what we see
is just the surface of something bigger; the story of this whole mission, he
added wryly.

"When they weren't needed," he finished, "they were invisible; the same
colour as Her hull. But when She needed them, when She was damaged
and had to use them, they grew darker as they…"

"Diffused energy through Her," Cyr said. "So if Smithson's idea
works…"

"The process will be temporarily frozen, and the patterns will disappear."

She looked at him again. He smiled and said "It's like with a new partner. When you start living together you find out new things. Intimate
things, like how her varicose veins work."

Cyr almost smiled back. She stood up. The pleats fell gracefully back
into place.

"It's nearly time, Commander. Will you be ready?"

He undersood why she had to ask him that. His behaviour had been
disturbing; less than was required of him. It would be tempting, and quite
reasonable, to think that Faith had been working on him like She'd done
with Joser. But now he felt that the truth was worse—that his behaviour
came from *him*. Or maybe that was also Faith working on him, but more
obliquely.

"If I'm not ready," he called after her—the pleats fanned out as she
turned to face him—"you know that you must ask Thahl to consider…"

"Yes, I know that. I've already come close to it."

●

"They're ready," Smithson said, after fifty-four minutes had elapsed.

"Thanks," Foord said. "I owe you."

"For moving your furniture?"

He smiled briefly, then nodded at Cyr. "Launch them."

The two Prayer Wheels dropped silently out of the ventral bay and floated underneath the *Charles Manson*. They were rings of dark metal nine
feet in diameter, with a hub and four radiating spokes. Smithson's people
had actually rolled them, like oversized cartwheels, from the cramped

MT Drive pit near the stern to one of the cargo tubes, where they were shot through to the ventral bay. The motors and guidance systems were simply metal boxes welded to their circumference at irregular intervals; they looked like bits of mud caked on the rims of real cartwheels.

Cyr pressed a panel. The motors round the rims fired once and went dark. The Prayer Wheels glided slowly, and on diverging paths, towards the midsection and stern craters. Faith seemed not to have noticed them. They passed three hundred feet, then six hundred and nine hundred. Twelve hundred. The light in the craters glowed. As the Prayer Wheels got closer, the light formed a backdrop against which they became diminishing silhouettes.

At fourteen hundred feet Cyr fired the final course adjustment; the motors flared and died. She glanced at Foord, on an impulse mouthed Varicose Veins, and pressed another panel. The Prayer Wheels started to turn. The dark metal of their rims became transluscent and glowed pearl-white as they began generating stasis fields. The motors and guidance systems exploded silently off the rims. The Prayer Wheels entered the craters and were swallowed.

That was not what they'd expected. They'd expected Her to realise what they were doing, and to try flight, evasion, counterattack, anything, to prevent it. If She didn't it meant either that they'd genuinely surprised Her (for the third time—first the photon burst, then the two missiles) or that it wouldn't work. But it *is* working, thought Foord exultantly, as he saw things on the Bridge screen he'd never expected to see.

The dark swirling patterns on Her flank grew faint, then darkened and grew faint again. The nameless colour which both lit and obscured the two craters died, then flared and died again. She started to do the things She should have done before. She fired Her manoeuvre drives in sequence and tried to roll so the *Charles Manson* wouldn't be facing the craters, but Kaang rolled with Her, maintaining relative position and distance—still exactly one thousand, six hundred and twelve feet—and the light in the craters flared and died again. She pushed Her speed to fifty percent and Kaang matched Her. She stopped dead and resumed at forty-five percent, and Kaang stopped dead and resumed with Her. She fired Her manoeuvre drives at random—two of them exploded, bursting their diamond caps—trying to roll or pitch or yaw in any direction which would take the *Charles Manson* away from the craters, but Kaang mirrored everything She did; sometimes, it seemed, before She did it, as if Kaang was taking the lead and making Her follow. The two craters flared one more time, and went dark. The patterns over Her flank darkened one more time and went pale. Another of Her manoeuvre drives exploded, this one near the stern crater, and pieces of wreckage fountained out from Her. The Bridge screen tracked them. Each piece grew two replica craters of its own, but this time they flared once and went dark, like eyes closing.

She seemed to give up, as She had done once before against Kaang, and let them fly alongside Her. Cyr pressed a series of panels, and two of the *Charles Manson*'s main ventral launch bays opened. Objects dropped out of them, fired once and made their way towards Her.

In the few seconds before Cyr's attack hit Her, they had time to look into the craters. Both of them were lit, not by the unnameable colour but by the weak pearlescent flicker of the Prayer Wheels deep inside them (*another naked bulb in a cellar*, thought Foord) and they saw, despite all the ways in which She was utterly unlike them, a piece of their own likeness. She too was packed solid, almost to dwarf-star density. The stern crater was packed with the cathedral slabs of Her main drive housings, the mid-section crater with a melted chaos of cables and conduits, like a bucket of dead eels; and both craters with broken latticeworks of structural girders, even with the same H cross-section as their counterparts on the *Charles Manson*. Angles were random and contradictory. Everything had flowed into everything else and frozen at the instant of melting. Escher and Dalí.

The furthest recesses of each crater were still out of focus, obscured and sealed by the darkness whose surface swirled with watered-silk patterns. If She had a crew, some of them would have moved through these areas; but nothing had kept enough shape to be corridors or doors or anything else recognisable. Or to be their bodies. *We* did that, thought Foord, and then he froze as another thought came, a very unwelcome one.

Maybe we only damaged Her outside, not Her inside. Maybe this is how Her inside *really* is. Maybe She always carries this chaos inside Her.

●

Cyr watched the two ninety-foot Diamond Clusters she had just launched, the last two the *Charles Manson* carried. Like the Prayer Wheels they had fired once and were now gliding on diverging paths towards the two craters. Like the Prayer Wheels, She must have seen them coming and should have responded but did not. Cyr had told Foord they were the best weapon to follow the Prayer Wheels into the craters. Foord still wanted beams, but Cyr persuaded him. She *knew* that energy weapons in the craters would be wrong.

Cyr watched the two of them, and watched her instruments; she calculated that if Faith continued to do nothing, no final course correction would be needed. As with the Prayer Wheels, there was a moment when She could have tried rolling away, and everything would then have depended on Cyr's preparations and Kaang's reactions; but the moment passed. The two ninety-foot missiles reached Her and slowly entered the craters and continued and continued to enter until their entire lengths were swallowed. *And this time,* Cyr thought as she watched them explode, *You can swallow but you can't digest.*

They were simple explosions, massive but conventional, not linked to MT physics in any way and not affected by the stasis fields. They flashed On-Off in a nanosecond, On to light the two craters with fire—almost a mundane colour after the colour which had previously lit them—and Off to leave them lit again only by the flicker of the Prayer Wheels, which generated their own space-time and were untouched by non-MT events around them.

This time the explosions went *into* Her, the way they should have done before, and She had no means of reversing them or slowing them, but the explosions themselves would not have damaged Her. It was what they released into Her, a million fractal diamond razors the size of Sakhran claws, flying through Her at a million times the speed She had slowed them to last time. They were a simple physical weapon, carried to massive extremes. Their eruption and flight inside Her had already happened. It would have lasted only another nanosecond after the two explosions, On-Off in their afterimage. If She had been a Commonwealth ship, even a battleship—or even an Outsider—She would have broken in half. Because She was not, Cyr had the next attack already prepared for the craters; and, if necessary, the one after that and the one after that.

She came to a halt, and the *Charles Manson* halted with Her. Alarms murmured on the Bridge. Whatever had happened inside Her, found no other expression outside.

Alarms murmured again. She started to move forward slowly, at twenty percent. The *Charles Manson* paralleled Her. She showed nothing they could read, either as life or death. Maybe the diamond razors had shredded Her interior and crew, and She was moving only on automatic, or maybe they had failed. As usual, She gave them nothing. Her interior, like Schrödinger's cat, was neither dead nor alive, but something else which might become either.

Cyr and Foord exchanged glances.

"Commander, do we still…"

"Yes. What else is there?"

Cyr pressed some more panels, and the next attack began. Blisters rose and opened along the topsurface of the *Charles Manson*'s hull. Their three hundred remaining spiders swarmed out, fired their onboard motors, and made for the midsection crater. It was something Cyr and Foord had both wanted: to do to Her what She had done to them, to assault Her internally and intimately. Always attack the wound, Cyr said.

"Cyr," said Foord, "if this doesn't work…"

"I know. I have the next attacks ready."

The dark gunmetal spiders fanned out as they crossed the sixteen hundred feet. They were silhouetted against the silver of Her hull as they floated slowly towards Her. Many of them were missing limbs. As they neared the midsection crater they fired their motors and funnelled into a narrower formation—almost a coiled rope, like the one She had taken into Herself. Their silhouettes became less distinct as they came within the compass of the crater's backdrop, where only the flicker of the Prayer Wheels illuminated them. The mouth of the crater was almost the same colour they were.

The slowness and uncertainty of what they were doing made Foord suddenly tired. He looked across the sixteen hundred feet and almost prayed to Her, Respond.

The alarms had earlier murmured on the Bridge, like polite punctuations to the other conversations, but now they shouted. Both craters, stern and midsection, were black. At last, She had neutralised the stasis fields, and the weak illumination from the Prayer Wheels had died.

Cyr glanced at Foord. He shook his head, No.

"Hold them back, Cyr. Don't let them enter the crater. Not until…"

He had expected to see both craters re-ignite with the unnameable co-lour, and to see the dark swirling patterns reappear over Her hull, indicat-ing the resumption of Her mass-to-energy processes. So had the Bridge screen, which patched in local magnifications of both craters and of Her hull around them, but nothing showed. At least, nothing they expected.

The midsection crater filled with shivering white light. It was so bright it hit them like a wind, crossing the space between them with almost physical force so they expected the *Charles Manson* to rock. It was like a billion arc lights. It silhouetted the floating bodies of the spiders, reaching itself and their shadows back at the *Charles Manson* like alternate dark and light fingers, projecting their silhouettes onto the *Charles Manson*'s flank in a broken rewriting of the earlier dark patterns on Hers.

And it was only the midsection crater, not the stern. That remained dark. Foord had glanced back at the stern crater to check, and so missed what happened next at the midsection, and found himself wondering what the alarms and shouting were about until he looked back to the midsection crater and saw the figure which walked out of it—*walked,* not crawled—and which was now standing in the crater's mouth, looking at them across the sixteen hundred feet.

It was human-sized, and human-shaped.

It was human, and they recognised it.

6

"It's a good analysis," said the voice, "of the events at Horus 5 and the Belt and Horus 4. The last bit, in the Gulf, is harder to read. Our analysts see it differently to yours."

"*Our* analysts," Swann said, "had to work from limited information. From long-range monitoring of drive emissions, from radio and optical telescopes on Sakhra, and a few remote probes that happened to be in the system. We had no ships in the area, because *you*"—he tried to keep his voice even—"because you told us to recall them and deploy them around Sakhra. If you have a different view of what's happening in the Gulf, it's because you know more about it than we do. For once, just say yes or no."

Swann's Command Centre at Blent was full of screens, most of them showing live feeds of events around Sakhra which he didn't want to see, but Swann was speaking not into a screen but into a—superficially, at least—old-fashioned microphone. The Department of Administrative Affairs didn't do faces on screens. It only did voices on mikes.

"Yes, of course we do. We'd hardly build things like the Outsiders and not build in ways of monitoring them. Just because Foord has killed all communications—by the way, with us as well as you—"

"We have only your word for that," Swann said, then wished he hadn't. His voice wasn't shrill, but the remark was.

"Just because Foord has killed all communications," the voice went on evenly, "doesn't mean we can't track him. He knows that, of course. He's neutralised some of our devices, but not all of them. And Joser wasn't the only observer we had on the *Charles Manson*. Foord knows that, too."

"So you have information which we don't about what those two ships are doing in the Gulf. I insist you share it."

"Insist?"

The days Swann had spent in the Command Centre, since Boussaid's death and since the *Charles Manson* had left to engage Her alone, seemed longer than the rest of his life. They stretched back behind him, worrying and unfathomable, noisy and fetid. He hadn't washed or changed his clothes. Neither, by his orders, had any of his staff—the military and security people he'd charged with monitoring events on Sakhra, the communications people he'd charged with tracking the *Charles Manson*'s engagement of Faith, and the mission analysts he'd charged with interpreting it. Their cups and meal trays and half-used toiletries were strewn over the floor, left where they fell. The atmosphere was as thick and furry as the inside of his mouth.

Without any possibility of realising it, Swann had done to the Command Centre what Foord had done to the Bridge of the *Charles Manson*.

"We have an apparently invincible opponent," Swann said. "She's entered the outer reaches of Horus system, almost certainly to attack Sakhra. The only ship with any chance of defeating Her has, on your orders, engaged Her alone. According to our analyses She's made the *Charles Manson* shut down its MT Drive, execute a photon burst through the Belt, and burrow through a large asteroid. Then, apparently, Foord succeeded in damaging

Her at Horus 4." Swann became aware that he'd been counting the points on his fingers, the nails of which were stained and bitten; Foord's hands, he remembered, were always immaculate. "And now there's a series of strange closeup exchanges between them in the Gulf, and those two ships are travelling alongside each other. Through the Gulf. Towards *us*. And Foord won't communicate. Maybe it's not just one invincible opponent coming for us, but two. *Yes*, I said Insist!"

The voice did not immediately reply.

One of the screens in the Command Centre showed a live address from the President of Sakhra, appealing for calm. The irony was not lost on Swann. Apart from the disturbing but still largely isolated incidents shown on various other screens, calm was what Sakhra still had. Things were falling apart, but calmly. Since the *Charles Manson*'s departure from Sakhra—if *She* ever came here, would *She* cause as much chaos?—the disturbances had increased, but they were still apparently unconnected, and hard to read. The humans on Sakhra seemed to share the Sakhrans' sense of separation, of having turned away from each other. Election turnouts were small. When Swann gave interviews, which he had done frequently in the last few days, he got ten times the President's coverage.

Or maybe these events were the tip of a larger pattern, as were the events in the Gulf with Foord and Her. Maybe—Swann immediately regretted this thought, because its afterecho wouldn't go away—maybe they weren't just hard to read, but too big to read.

"No, not two opponents," said the voice, eventually.

"What do you mean?"

"Not two opponents, Director. Foord is still attacking Her."

"Attacking?"

"She's been damaged: nobody has ever done that before. She's fighting back, so the *Charles Manson* is still attacking Her. We don't fully understand what She's doing, but She's fighting back."

"You don't know, do you?"

"I told you, Foord has killed communications with us."

"But you have your devices. Do you or don't you know what's happening in the Gulf?"

"We don't know. He seems almost like *Her*."

"I met him here, remember. And dealt with him over Copeland. He was always like Her."

"But we know he's damaged Her, Director, and we know he's trying to finish Her. We can't read Her responses. But we don't interpret it as any joining of forces."

"You've contradicted yourself at least three times, but let that pass. We can agree that he's damaged Her, and that nobody else has done that." Despite what he felt for Foord, he remembered the genuine sense of wonder he'd had on hearing that. "So why isn't anyone helping him? Does *all* of Horus Fleet have to remain around Sakhra?"

"Director Swann, believe me. If Foord fails, you'll need the entire Fleet."

"Not even the *Charles Manson* could take on the entire Fleet. Are you saying *She* can?"

"If Foord fails, She'll come for Sakhra. It may be over-provision, but it's better that Sakhra's defended with the whole Fleet."

One advantage of the microphone was the amount of sceptical expressions Swann could safely direct at it. Not even the voice seemed to believe that last answer.

Swann let the silence grow long enough to become uncomfortable. "If," he said, "they're so closely matched that one Outsider can damage Her, how many would it take to be sure of defeating Her?"

"What do you mean by that, Director Swann? Specifically?"

"One Outsider's damaged Her. Two or three more could finish Her. Send us two or three more. Is that specific enough?"

"No. Outsiders don't fight in teams, they fight alone. And if She defeats Foord and comes to Sakhra, the Commonwealth will need all of them for what happens next."

7

Foord stood in the mouth of the midsection crater and looked across the gap, blinking, at his ship.

He felt cold. He held his hand in front of his face and flexed his fingers. There were veins and tendons and nails—immaculate nails—but the flesh tones were gradations of grey and silver. He felt cold, then it occurred to him that he was standing open to space and didn't have a suit. He was standing—gravity worked here—and breathing; he took in what felt like air through his open mouth, and his chest rose and fell. I'm a construct, he told himself, a construct of liquid silver made by whatever lives in this ship, but I'm also *me*, with all my memories and motives. I've just woken to life, but I remember all my life leading up to this. Why didn't they just make something that *looked* like me? Why did they make me like this, full of everything I am? It seems like overengineering.

He looked down from his raised hand, along his arm, to the rest of his body. Large, heavily muscled; toned and tidy; everything I've woken up to, every day, over there on the *Charles Manson*. How did they know it all? And why have they put me here? He felt cold.

Outside the mouth of the crater, between him and his ship, floated nearly three hundred dark gunmetal spiders. They'd been about to pour into this crater, this open wound we made in Her side. They'd been about to enter Her and attack Her, like She had sent Hers to attack us, but when this cold light filled the crater I told Cyr to hold them back. (Did he remember that, or just assume it? He didn't know.) And behind him, in the crater's deepest recesses—behind the swirling darkness which hid those recesses from the *Charles Manson*—were the giant coils and festoons of The Rope, the thing She'd made by joining pieces of them and Her, and had then taken into Herself.

He felt cold. Not because he was standing open to space—that was a cold he'd never have had time to feel, he'd have died from it instantly, if he'd been alive. The cold was inside him. He knew he couldn't possibly be alive, but he avoided the temptation of trying to define Alive. I have motives and memories and sensory inputs and outputs and a sense of myself, just like me in my ship over there. Maybe more so. I'm almost more than me. I must be looking across from the Bridge and seeing me here, but I can't look back and see myself over there because I'm hidden in the Bridge and I don't have a screen that gives me magnifications of things moments before I ask for them. The grammar doesn't work, it's too clumsy. Words don't work. I'm here in the crater and I'm over there sixteen hundred feet away in my ship. I can't call the Foord over there Him, it's Me.

Self-referential, like a book reading a book. Same software, different hardware. The software is all my memories and motives, everything I am, but I'm made of liquid silver which remains solid while it keeps my shape.

I'm not organic—no, don't go there either, don't try defining that. I've been *made*.

I grew out of a pool of silver on a floor somewhere behind me on this ship. I've been made by the people who live in this ship. (Yes, People. Who Live.) I know them as Them and People, not Her or It, because there's more than one and they interact socially, but I don't know what they look like or why they made me or why their ship has done these things. I know less about them than a hammer knows about the owner of the hand holding it—less than an atom in the handle of the hammer—but they made me like this, and put me here, for a reason.

And that's what it is, he thought, looking out at the spiders floating between him and his ship. They were motionless, dark against the silver of the *Charles Manson*. They floated in a narrow compressed formation so that he only saw the front five or six bodies but saw hundreds of limbs, some broken, sprouting from those behind, like figures of Kali. He knew he would try to stop them when they entered the crater. He neither wanted to nor was aware of being compelled to; it was just how he was made. It was inevitable, like breathing, though he stood open to space and wasn't alive.

Something made him turn round and look back into the recesses of the crater. He wasn't surprised at what he saw coming out of it to join him and stand by him, in the crater's open mouth, facing the spiders.

●

On the Bridge they were dumbstruck as they looked at the single figure which stood, looking back at them, in the mouth of the midsection crater. The others saw what the figure looked like, but Foord saw what it *was*. He took in every detail of its body-language and posture and demeanour. He knew what was behind its eyes.

The Bridge screen patched in a closeup of its face.

"That isn't just..." Foord began, then his throat closed up. He took a deep breath through his open mouth, his chest rising and falling.

"That isn't just a replica. It isn't just a construct. It's *me*, everything I am, soul and self-awareness and everything."

"How can you know that?" Smithson asked.

"The same way you'd know, if that was you standing there. It knows it's everything I am, but it knows it was made, and it's trying to understand why. Not It, *Me*. I know I was made, and I'm trying to understand why... There aren't words for this, words don't work."

Foord looked through the Bridge screen into his own icy silver soul. He felt cold.

On the screen, the figure turned round to look back into the recesses of the crater. Other figures were walking out to join it, one by one, and to stand at its side.

●

Foord turned to see them walking out of the crater to join him.

Cyr was first. She too was silver and grey, the grey ranging from almost-white to almost-black. She raised a hand in greeting. Her fingernails, immaculately manicured like his and dark blue back on the *Charles Manson*, were here almost black, at the tips of long silver fingers. Her tunic and shoes, dark blue on the *Charles Manson*, were here dark grey. Her skirt swung gracefully as she walked, just as it always did, and Foord could feel himself getting the first stirrings of an erection, just as he always did.

They even let me have erections, he thought. He wanted to take it out and look at it, but thought it probably wasn't the time. He expected it would be silver and grey.

She smiled at him. "Commander."

"Hello, Cyr."

And they've let me hear spoken words, open to space. You can't hear noises in space. But you can't stand in it or breathe in it either, and Cyr was breathing like him; her chest rose and fell under her tunic. And her voice sounded just like it did on the *Charles Manson*, just like he remembered.

He looked her up and down. "I know you wear that to arouse me," he said, "and it does. It looks good on you. You're beautiful."

Before she could reply they were joined by Thahl, Kaang and Smithson. Thahl, slender and graceful like Cyr but slighter. Kaang, pleasant but unremarkable, a little plump, and looking terrified. And Smithson—

Smithson was the strangest of all, because back on the *Charles Manson* he was naturally grey. Only his eyes really differed; normally they were warm and golden, here they were mid-grey. When he extended a limb in greeting, Foord heard the wet plop.

They all had self-awareness. As Foord on the *Charles Manson* had re-alised when he first saw himself, something about them made it obvious. They had everything, physically and spiritually, which they'd ever woken up to every morning of their lives; yet they knew they were made, and knew they would defend the crater. They knew also that they should go back into the ship and find the people who made them, but they knew they never would.

They came and stood at Foord's side in the mouth of the crater, imagin-ing (they could also imagine; they'd been given that too) what their other selves on the *Charles Manson*—no, their *selves*: words didn't work properly for this—would be thinking.

●

"You see?" Foord said to the others on the Bridge. "They're *us*. They're everything we are. Tell me they're not."

"What are we going to do, Commander?" Kaang said. She was looking at herself and the other four figures in the crater, and sobbing.

"What are *they* going to do?" Cyr asked. She too was unable to take her eyes off the crater.

"You already know," Foord said. "She made them and She put them there. Put *us* there. To defend the crater against our spiders."

"But She could have made ordinary devices," Kaang said. "Ordinary synthetics. Even if they *looked* like us, they didn't have to *be* us."

"Yes they did," Smithson said bleakly. "That's the whole point. Make us fight them and kill them."

The silence returned. The way they each thought about family and loved ones, if they had any, varied with their biology and culture and circum-stances, but the way they thought about *themselves* did not vary. Some of them could even imagine killing loved ones or family, but this was worse. Worse than suicide. Deliberately killing something with sentience, when that sentience was your own, and when you knew—unlike suicide—that you'd still be alive and aware of what you'd done....

"We have to attack the crater," Foord said.

"I know, Commander," Cyr said. "And if they defend it we have to kill them. Kill *us*. I wish the words would work better."

"She never did anything like this," Thahl said, "when She last came to Sakhra."

"You said we'd find out new things about Her."

"Yes, Commander, I did. But this…"

"This is because we hurt Her. Made her fight for Her life. Nobody's seen this, because nobody's done that before." He took a long breath, and felt it rasp through his throat. "We have to watch ourselves die." He nodded to Cyr, who sent out the signal to the spiders.

●

They stood together in the open mouth of the midsection crater, and watched as the spiders started moving towards them.

"Why have they brought me here, too?" Kaang asked. "I'm nothing to do with this, I'm only a pilot. We'll die here."

Foord laughed. "Are we alive enough to die?"

"Commander, we're only five against…how many?"

"Nearly three hundred," Cyr said.

"And we're unarmed," Smithson said. "Not even sidearms."

"Five against three hundred or three thousand. It hardly matters," Foord said. "They didn't make us like this and put us here just to be wiped out."

"Didn't they?" Smithson said. "Maybe that's the whole point. Make us, over there, kill ourselves over here."

The spiders were moving slowly towards the mouth of the crater; so slowly they were almost drifting.

"I think," Thahl said, "that when they made us, they must have given us some special abilities."

"I think," Foord said drily, "that you have them already."

"No, Commander. Extra abilities. Otherwise why would they…?"

"I'm not aware," Cyr said, "of anything over here that I don't have over there."

"We ought to go back through this crater and find them," Smithson said. "But we know we can't. *That's* something we don't have over there."

"Then," Foord said, "over here we'll die. Fighting our own weapons."

The spiders drifted closer. Without thinking, they all stepped back from the mouth of the crater, to allow room for the first ones to enter.

"When they snip our arms and legs off," Smithson muttered, "will we subdivide down to nothing?"

"Nothing," Thahl said, deadpan, "is ever completely nothing."

"Thahl, were we..." Foord began.

"...like this over there?" Thahl finished. "I don't remember, Commander. Maybe we left more things unsaid."

●

Foord looked around the Bridge, and focussed angrily on Cyr.

"Watch the screen! Don't turn away. They're *us*. We'd want that dignity. We wouldn't want us to turn away."

"You're right, Commander. I'm sorry."

Cyr had been the only one on the Bridge to turn away. Normally she would have been first to watch what her weapons were about to do. She enjoyed the use of weapons, but not against these opponents. She turned back to the screen, where her replica and the others stood blinking back at her through the cold light in the crater, and reached a conclusion. There was something she could do.

She pressed a series of panels.

●

The spiders floated closer, and the first one entered the mouth of the crater. It was missing one of its middle limbs and had gouges all over its body. It crawled forward. It did not make for Foord, but for Cyr. She moved away from the others, to isolate herself. She guessed what she had done, back on the *Charles Manson*.

"Cyr?"

"I have to be first, Commander, not you."

"Why?"

"Because back on our ship, I'm controlling them."

"I don't understand."

"You will."

The spider approached her clumsily; almost, it seemed, by accident. The missing limb gave it an awkward rolling gait. Cyr saw it silhouetted against the silver hull of her ship, sixteen hundred feet away. On the *Charles Manson*, those on the Bridge saw it silhouetted against the silver figure of Cyr, slender and graceful.

Cyr took another step sideways. As she expected, no other spiders had yet entered the crater. She looked into its nonexistent face. It was *her* weapon. She was controlling it on the *Charles Manson*. It stepped towards her, its feet clacking on the floor of the crater; it extended a couple of forelimbs as if in greeting, and reconfigured the claws to manipulator mode. Cyr was making calculations about how long she could engage it, how long she could hold it off before those who made her were triggered into revealing whatever abilities they had given her to counter it. While she was making her calculations, it rose on its hindlimbs and pronged out her eyes. She screamed. Foord thought it was more in horror than pain, but couldn't be certain because he'd never heard her scream before. More spiders floated into the crater and settled, and more waited behind them. Cyr continued screaming. Her screams didn't incorporate obvious phrases like My Eyes or Help Me, but were entirely wordless. Foord motioned to the others to fan out. This can't be, he thought. If they made us, why would they let us be massacred like this? They must have given us something. But what?

●

On the Bridge, Cyr watched the local magnification on the screen. Her palms were bleeding where her fingernails dug into them; her manicured nails, painted darker than the blood they drew. In the crater, her nails and her blood were the same shade of almost-black. She could see it clearly on the Bridge screen, because in the crater Cyr had sunk to her knees and held her hands over her eyes and was screaming, and Foord had motioned to the others to fan out and face the spiders which had entered the crater and were now climbing over each other, pushing each other aside, to get at them.

"You told that first one to go for you, not for me."

"Yes, Commander."

"And you told it exactly what it should do to you."

"Yes, Commander." Cyr held Foord's gaze. Her eyes were dark and unreadable. "It was one thing I could do for them, I mean us, in the crater. They'd know I'd order the spiders to attack them. So I did it to myself first, in the most vicious way I could."

Foord went to say How can you think of something *that* vicious, but he already knew; it was how she was made.

In the crater they had turned away from each other; they were fighting separate battles, and they were going down. Cyr was still alive while the spider which had taken her eyes continued to work on her face, making it as featureless as its own. Only then did it finish her, slashing her throat. Her blood—dark grey, almost black—should have floated around her in globules, but gravity worked in the crater.

Foord went down easily, more easily than he expected. A spider simply stabbed him in the stomach—his entrails glistened silver and grey—then slit his throat. He didn't call to the others for help but just fell forward, shaking his head *No, this can't be,* and the spider stepped delicately over him and over Kaang, impaled on the claw of another spider and already dead, towards Smithson and Thahl. They knew Smithson and Thahl would be more difficult, because their programming said so.

On the *Charles Manson,* Smithson watched on the Bridge screen as five of them surrounded him and took it in turn to slice him, vertically. He felt grief but concealed it beneath outrage. He swore at them, as he was swearing at them in the crater while they sliced steaks off his body; his flesh in the crater had the same moist consistency as it did on the *Charles Manson.* They had severed one of his two main forelimbs, but he extruded a secondary limb, picked up one spider and used it to dash two others to pieces, then collapsed as the spiders halved and rehalved him.

Then there was only Thahl. They surrounded him, nine against one, with more and more entering the crater. He concentrated on disabling them by breaking their limbs with blows from his hands and feet. He had already disabled five, moving among them like a Sakhran customarily moves in combat—not only using his own speed and grace, but seeming to radiate something which made his opponents slow and clumsy. Just like a real living Sakhran, he thought wryly, but he knew he couldn't disable them faster than they were entering the crater. He knew that those who made him, and made the others, had put them in the crater to face the spiders, but he was puzzled.

There must be something they've given us to fight the spiders with.

The others hadn't revealed it, and neither had he, but it must be there. He wondered again what it was, and when and how it would show. He kicked away a couple of disabled spiders to make room to face the new-comers who were surrounding him. Then he realised what it was, and smiled.

●

On the Bridge, Thahl carefully studied himself as he fought in the crater.

The others on the Bridge had done what Foord demanded. They had watched themselves die, even when their emotions were insupportable. Thahl did not allow himself to show any emotion, even when he saw what they did to Cyr, though there was an irony about it because that was what Cyr *over here*—words didn't work properly—had told them to do to her-self. He continued to show no emotion when Foord went down so easily, and still showed none now, when he watched himself fighting—though he studied the screen closely, looking for but not finding any modification of his abilities.

He knew there had to be more.

She *made* us and She put us in the crater to defend it. She must have given us the ability to defend it, something extra beyond ourselves, and he wondered how and when it would show. He watched himself moving among the spiders—just like a real living Sakhran, he thought wryly—and then it occurred to him that just as he made the spiders look slow and clumsy, so had *Her* spiders, each one a match for at least six of theirs until they…

Then he knew, and smiled to himself. On the Bridge screen, which had focussed on him in closeup as he was the last of them left, he smiled back at himself from the crater.

●

In the crater the spiders Thahl had disabled were strewn around him, most of them limbless or broken-limbed but still rocking backwards and forwards to get at him. Now others had entered the crater and surrounded him: nine, ten, eleven. They made cautious feints to draw him out, but did not yet attack directly. More were joining them.

That was when he had smiled to himself.

I'd like to have lived longer, he thought, which is reasonable considering how they made me. They gave me self-awareness, and all my memories and motives. He might have added, And my soul, but Sakhrans—perhaps because of how they reproduced, or how they organised themselves so-cially—were not particularly religious. So not Soul, he thought, but my sense of what I am. And because they made me like this, I can do what comes next more easily. It won't be as complete as dying, because I also live over there.

He became still. He folded his arms across his chest, and collapsed into himself.

The process began at the top of his head and worked down through his body to his feet, like an ice-sculpture melting. He turned, from his head downwards, into liquid silver. Because it started at his head, his consciousness dissolved away while the rest of him was still collapsing. His last thought was They didn't make us telepathic. I wish I could tell them over there that our opponent is not just a Her or an It, there are *people* living here. Perhaps they'll find out. Even see them.

The liquid silver which had been his head cascaded down his body, which in turn cascaded down his legs to pool at his feet, which in turn be-came part of the pool. When Thahl was gone, the same thing happened to the bodies of the others. Cyr, Foord, Kaang and Smithson collapsed into themselves, leaving silver pools; five pools, including the one which had been Thahl. Suggestions of rainbow colours swirled across their surfaces, but otherwise the pools were inert. The spiders peered and poked at them, indifferently, because they did not signify opposition.

Simultaneously the five pools burst into thousands of separate silver beads, each the size of a fingernail. For a moment they stood apart from each other, quivering; then flicked across the floor of the crater, between and around the clacking feet of the spiders, combining and recombining until they became a single thing: a floorcovering of rippling silver, only molecules deep. Its shape was like a map, defined by the spiders around which it flowed and formed. It moved back into the depths of the crater, through the out-of-focus dark curtain, to where the silver-grey coils of the Rope festooned the walls. It rose and touched the Rope's coils, welcoming it down from the walls and into itself; the coils entered it, and continued and continued to enter. Then it flowed back towards the mouth of the crater.

Its volume had increased. Now it covered the entire floor, to a depth of inches.

●

On the Bridge, Foord cried out as he watched Thahl die in the crater. He had stayed outwardly impassive when the others went down, even himself, but now he could not look across the Bridge at Thahl; they were both embarrassed.

He watched the pools become beads, and the beads combine and recombine.

"Get us out of here, Kaang."

"Commander, our spiders—"

"Forget them, Cyr, they're already finished. Get us out of here, Kaang. Now."

The *Charles Manson*'s manoeuvre jets fountained, a gesture of parting. It turned away, engaged its ion drive at seventy percent, and ran. *We keep moving backwards and forwards*, thought Foord, *like masturbation.*

●

The carpet of liquid silver stretched continuously from the mouth of the crater to its recesses, where the darkness hung. Points on its surface rose into small conical shapes or sank into small conical depressions, within a vertical range of no more than plus or minus an inch; they formed and disappeared randomly, as though caused by the first isolated drops of a rainstorm. Colours—cobalt, violet, burgundy, dark bluish grey—swirled across its surface like cloud shadows.

About thirty spiders were in the crater; the others still floated outside. They walked through the silver liquid—it no longer flowed around them— picking their steps with human delicacy, swivelling to find recognisable shapes of opposition but seeing none. They saw the *Charles Manson* turn away from them and run, but it meant nothing to them; its location was not in their mission parameters, not until they had done what they came to do and were ready to leave Her.

Near the mouth of the crater a small conical point rose to about an inch above the surface, but did not subside. It continued to rise, drawing more liquid up after it. It was still silver but grew duller as it solidified and cohered and became the shape Foord had expected: man-sized, a triangular body with three jointed limbs pushing up and out from each corner, and no face.

If there was a moment when it could be said to have started its existence, it was when it stepped clear of the silver liquid, leaving a hole behind it which closed *Plop,* and pivoted to survey the *Charles Manson*'s spiders around it. They looked back impassively. Rising on first one corner of its body and then another, moving in spasms of right-angles and diagonals like a new chessboard figure, it plunged amongst the dark spiders and shredded three of them before they could react. A fourth, remembering the earlier encounters on the *Charles Manson*, snipped a joint off one of its legs, but this time the silver spider did not subdivide down to nothing. It stopped and looked, facelessly, into the recesses of the crater, where others like itself were forming.

Initially there were three more. The silver closed *Plop* behind them, *Plop Plop*, as they stepped clear of it and started their existence without ceremony. They joined the first and arranged themselves into a diamond, moving with stop-go oddness. They shifted from one direction to another, and from stillness to speed and back to stillness, with an abruptness which made the *Charles Manson*'s spiders look human.

●

The Bridge screen, without being told to, had maintained its local magnification on the crater as they ran. At a hundred and fifty thousand feet Kaang stopped the *Charles Manson* and turned it in its own length to face Her.

The screen showed more silver spiders forming. As they rose up out of the liquid carpet, the remains of their opponents—dismembered swiftly and without mess or passion by the original four—were dissolving down into the silver. It welcomed them.

The crater was now full of silver spiders. It seethed with the oddness of their movements as they stepped clear of the silver liquid; the *Plops* of the liquid closing behind them, if the Bridge screen had transmitted sounds, would have been like a choir of sphincters. Sideways, forwards, diagonally, they flicked themselves into diamond formations, four to a diamond, and made their way to the mouth of the crater, where they fired their onboard motors in sequence and launched themselves outwards.

The Bridge screen panned back. A vomit of silver spiders burst out of Her midsection crater and hit the rest of the *Charles Manson*'s spiders, still floating alongside the crater mouth, and the second and larger part of the massacre began.

96, said the screen's headup display impassively, against 261.

It was like Sakhrans fighting humans—more so, because Sakhrans fought as individuals and the silver spiders fought with perfect co-ordination. On the *Charles Manson*, they'd chosen to collapse and subdivide when damaged, and even then, any one was a match for at least six opponents. Now, they were outnumbered only three to one.

95, said the headup display, facing 187. 95, facing 163.

Two to one, Foord corrected himself, his horror rising as the odds fell; less than two to one. He had foreseen this, so his horror contained no panic; it was as coldly mathematical as the Bridge screen's accounting. What was happening was devoid of drama or uncertainty, but still horrifying.

94, said the headup display, facing 123.

The silver spiders were not fighting their opponents, they were merely shredding them and parcelling them into manageable pieces which were handed back down the line into the mouth of the crater where the silver liquid welcomed them into itself.

94, said the headup display, facing 87.

It was an industrial operation. They were loading cargo, not fighting a battle, and seemed genuinely unaware that the cargo was trying to resist them while they loaded it. And now that the operation was into its final stages, it accelerated.

93, said the Bridge screen, facing 45. 93, facing 9.

"Particle beams?" Cyr asked. Her voice betrayed nothing.

"No, not on the crater," Foord said. Neither did his.

93, facing 0.

"I meant on them, Commander, if they come for us."

"They won't. She's taken enough of *us*. Now She wants Sakhra."

●

Nobody spoke on the Bridge. They were thinking the same thing but wouldn't say it aloud. They all go into the dark, Foord recited to himself, they all go into the dark and become part of *Her*.

He wasn't thinking of the ninety-three that had just entered Her. Neither was he thinking of their own spiders, dismembered and parcelled into the crater, or of the spiders and hull-plates taken before from the *Charles Manson* and swallowed by the crater; that was just hardware and substances.

He was thinking of the original five silver figures; ourselves, blinking at us from out of that hole in Her side, the hole we made. Ourselves. Those five figures carried our souls, and our souls have become part of Her.

Not Have Become: *Always Were.*

"I've been thinking," he said, "impossible things. So have you. We can't leave them unspoken."

"I thought that's exactly what we do on your ship," Smithson said.

Foord ignored that. "Those five figures, we knew when we first saw them that they were *us*. We saw it behind their eyes. All our memories and motives. Even souls, if we have them. Everything that animates us, animated them.

"And *She already knew it*. When She made those five, She already knew what we are. She put it into them when She put them in the mouth of the crater. She took it back into Herself when She took *them* back. I think She's always known what we are. Since before we existed."

"Commander," Thahl said, almost gently, "we've turned away from the Commonwealth. *We* don't know what we are. Where do we belong now?"

"Perhaps more with Her than the Commonwealth. There's more of us in Her than we ever gave to the Commonwealth." What did I just say?

"Commander," Smithson said, "do you know what you're saying?"

"Are you saying you haven't thought the same thing?"

"Are *you* saying this, Commander?" Cyr asked.

"She means…" Thahl began.

"I know what she means. Is it me speaking, or Her?"

Again, nobody spoke on the Bridge.

"This is me speaking." Even as he said it, he wasn't sure. "I won't submit to passive submission to a higher power—Her, or the Commonwealth. Nothing outside of me has the right to know my soul. I never really knew what I meant when I said Instrument of Ourselves, but I do now. It means *that.*"

Foord looked at the Bridge screen where She still floated, apparently immobile. She was further away now, a hundred and fifty thousand feet instead of sixteen hundred, and travelling faster through the Gulf than before, but the screen maintained magnification and their course and speed matched Hers, and the Gulf was empty of reference points. It was as if they were both stationary, and She was only sixteen hundred feet away. She seemed always to be only sixteen hundred feet away.

"The Commonwealth has taken a lot from us, but not as much as She has. The Commonwealth is just a machine, not a god. We must fight the god. We must go on and destroy Her, no matter what things we learn about Her. There can be no time or space except the time and space we take to destroy Her." He knew he was close to incoherence, but he went on. "No space in front or behind. No time before, after, or during."

He only understood half of what he said, and had no idea what any of them would say next, himself included. And he would never know, because there was an interruption from somewhere outside.

"Commander," Thahl said, "we have incoming."

"I thought I told you not to—"

"The signal isn't from Sakhra, Commander. Or from Earth. It's from Her."

8

She had sent Her signal openly, with no attempt to disguise its origin. She even followed the standard Commonwealth ship-to-ship protocols, prefacing it with a code on the usual hailing frequency; in effect, a formal request for their acceptance of a communication, which with equal formality they refused. She ignored their refusal, and tried to bypass their defences and put Her signal directly onto the Bridge screen.

"Block it, please, Thahl."

"Commander, it might be...."

Foord looked up at him sharply. "Block it."

Her image on the Bridge screen became blurred and overlaid with static, a normal and temporary side-effect of the blocking of an incoming signal. When the block was accomplished, the static would clear from the screen; which ought to have been now.

"Thahl?"

"The signal's growing more powerful, Commander. I'll try to…"

"Thahl, *the screen.*"

The Bridge screen had never before gone dark while the ship was operational. The sudden absence of its light was like the sudden absence of air, a visual suffocation. Thahl switched to backup and it relit, showing Her image again, overlaid with static; and again it fell dark. The screen had many backups and failsafes, and Thahl used them all. It stayed dark.

"Smithson," Foord began, carefully controlling his voice, "do we…"

"Yes, Commander, we still have Her on scanners, and She hasn't changed course." His voice tailed away.

The screen relit. It glowed with a soft opalescence, but it was absolutely blank. Worse than dark. And it was changing, in a way it had no business to: changing its texture and surface contours.

The screen covered the curved wall of the Bridge, as thinly and closely as a coat of paint; but now its surface rippled like silk, and something was trying to form on it, *behind* it, which was impossible. On the segment of the screen facing Foord, two shapes were trying to push through it, a rectangle and an oval. Their meaning was clear to Foord, because the oval sat above the rectangle and suggested a head and shoulders, pushing through a silk shroud.

"Her face," Thahl said. He seemed to be talking to himself.

"No!" Foord shouted. "Not on my screen, not on my Bridge, it belongs out there. Thahl, we don't want to see this. Please, block it."

"It might be Her face, Commander."

"I said block it!"

Thahl pressed some panels. Nothing happened. He pressed some more. The silken texture, and the shapes forming behind it, slowly drained from the Bridge screen. The screen sank back to its normal contours, went dark and relit, this time with Her image, magnified as before so She seemed only sixteen hundred feet away. Her drives were flickering through the wreckage at the stern in a way they had not done before, and the screen's headups said that Her course was unchanged but Her speed had dropped to thirty-five percent; Kaang matched it. The midsection crater remained dark.

Foord slowly let out his breath. Something had told him that they should not, absolutely not, see whatever had tried to form on the screen.

He knew that no signal from another ship, however powerful, could force itself on the *Charles Manson* if they decided to block it; finally they had, but he was still uneasy. He knew Her abilities with communications. Or rather, he didn't know them, not all of them.

"Blocked, Commander." Thahl's voice was carefully neutral.

Foord nodded briefly, and looked again at Her image on the screen. Something about Her wasn't right. She had slowed to thirty percent, said the headups, and Her stern drives were flickering fitfully. He thought again of naked bulbs in cellars. We're fighting Her through a solar system, and She compresses it down to cellars and dripping alleys.

The alarms murmured.

"What—"

"Another signal, Commander," Thahl said.

Nothing reached the screen. Her image was still there. She was now down to twenty-five percent, and Her stern drives were cutting out, refiring, and cutting out again.

"Where? Where is Her signal?"

Thahl's hands flew over his console. His claws started to unsheath and retract, almost but not quite in time with the on-off stuttering of Her stern drives. For a moment he seemed close to panic, something Foord had never seen in him before; then he subsided, and resumed his normal demeanour. He looked round at Foord.

"This signal isn't aimed at the screen, Commander. It's aimed directly in here, into the Bridge...."

"*What?*"

"....and so far, we can't block it."

A white light filled the Bridge, like the light they had seen in the midsection crater. They blinked in it. It made them feel cold. It had no source and cast no shadows. It went everywhere; even the air glowed with it. It washed over them, turning their faces to pocked landscapes and their figures to dishevelled statuary.

Foord held his hand in front of his face and studied it, as he had seen himself do in the mouth of the crater. The ripe sweat under his clothes turned fish-cold and clammy. His breath actually frosted in front of his face, stinging his lips and nostrils; and through its vapour he saw, strewn over the floor, the rubbish and debris which he'd refused to move.

Now it started to move itself.

It swirled across the floor in miniature vortexes which sprang up and died at random, like the life-forms on Horus 5. A figure forming in the middle of the Bridge was making it swirl. The figure was solidifying out of the light. It was still indistinct and shifting, a hollow latticework of vapour, like the vapour of Foord's breath; but it had a head and shoulders, arms and legs, in approximately human proportions.

Foord drew his sidearm. Cyr had already drawn hers and was aiming, and Thahl had started towards it.

"Don't!" Smithson bellowed. "Don't touch it! Don't go near it."

The headups on the Bridge screen kept assessing and reassessing it: it was a hologram, it was a solid object, it was neither, it was both, it was unreadable. It was also unexpectedly beautiful, a roiling hollow vapour-shape lit from within. It flicked *on-off* as it tried to form. On the Bridge screen, Her stern drives flicked *off-on* in the same rhythm.

Her speed dropped to nineteen percent and She started to pitch and yaw. The energy required to project something into the Bridge against all their inbuilt defences was unthinkable, just as the act itself was unthinkable; not even another Outsider could have done it.

"Commander," Smithson said , "She's draining Herself. Just to communicate with us, She's draining Herself!"

"And your point is?"

"My point *is*, She might be vulnerable to our particle beams, so why haven't you thought of using our particle beams? And," to Cyr, "why haven't *you*?"

"You're right," Foord muttered. You're always right, you smug slug. "Fire them, Cyr. Not into the craters, but everywhere else."

The beams lanced out. Her flickerfields met them and held them, but— said the Bridge screen headups—only just. Her stern drives went dark, stuttered and refired, and the still-unformed figure standing in the middle of the Bridge actually doubled over, as if in pain.

"You see? You *see*?" Smithson shouted, adding unnecessarily "*That's* what you should have done!"

"Again, Cyr. Keep firing them."

Cyr did so, again and again, imagining her finger was not pressing a firing-button but digging into one of Smithson's eyes. Always, always, he was right, and always, always, she could never forgive him for it.

Her flickerfields still held the beams, but each time Cyr fired, the figure on the Bridge weakened in definition. It threw its arms up around its head. If they had been able to see its face properly, it might have been screaming. The vapour which made up its outline started to disperse, as if blown by a wind. It was fading, and finally faded to nothing, but the white light which had brought it, and out of which it had formed, still filled the Bridge. The debris still swirled fitfully across the floor. Their breath still frosted in front of their faces. They still felt cold.

Her stern drives fell dark and did not refire, and She came to a halt. The *Charles Manson* halted with Her, and Cyr continued stabbing out the particle beams. Her flickerfields—coloured a distinctive neon purple, unlike those of any other ship—were getting paler and thinner. When they deployed you could still see through them to the silver of Her hull underneath, and the screen headups showed that their power was dropping, and that She was deploying them nanoseconds later. With every firing, the beams were getting closer to penetrating the fields; to actually hitting Her.

"She's weakening," Cyr said.

"No She isn't," Smithson snapped. "Her *fields* are weakening, because She's diverting their power." He looked across the Bridge. "Into *that*."

The figure had returned to the Bridge, but it was fainter than before. It faded almost to nothing, reappeared, then faded again.

"Soon She'll be defenceless," Cyr hissed, "and the beams will reach Her."

All through the engagement their particle beams had been the only weapon which consistently outmatched Her. They pushed and probed through Her fields, a little closer to Her with each firing.

She had put everything into what She was trying to project, but it was not enough. Although the white light still filled the Bridge, the figure failed to re-form out of it, and the beams were still reaching for Her. Eventually She gave up, and routed power back to Her drives and flickerfields. Her stern drives stuttered and refired and She began moving through the Gulf at thirty percent—Kaang matched Her speed and course—and Her fields redeployed. Cyr continued firing, but Her fields held firm now. The white light drained from the Bridge. So did the figure which had tried to form.

Stalemate again.

The Bridge returned to its normal subdued lighting. The screen displayed the latest analyses of what She had attempted, but they added nothing new. What had entered the Bridge—Entered The Bridge, Foord read aloud, in outrage—was an electromagnetic signal which acquired physical substance. It was unreadable. Almost certainly, announced Smithson sonorously and unnecessarily, another example of Her superior use of MT physics.

"And that's it?"

"Of course not," Smithson snapped. "Commander, whatever She wanted to say to us, She still wants to say it. She *endangered* Herself to say it. She won't give up."

"And how will She not give up?"

"She didn't have enough power to put that thing on the Bridge *and* fight our beams. So…"

"So She'll find more power. And you know where She'll find it, don't you?"

Unusually, Smithson said nothing.

"You're always right," Foord told him, almost as an aside while motioning Thahl to divert power back to their signal-blocking, "but you're not always right at the right time. Thahl! That figure will be back again, and this time it will…"

The crater in Her midsection started to glow, not with the cold white light but with the unnameable colour, the colour which hid inside the normal spectrum. In whatever universe it came from it might be familiar and everyday, perhaps the colour of sky or grass. In this one it was many words, all beginning with Un.

There was an explosion in the midsection crater. She rolled with it, presenting Her undamaged underside and starboard and dorsal surfaces, and then, as She completed the roll, Her port side again with the midsection crater facing them. Headups crowded the Bridge screen, telling them what they expected and could already see. The midsection crater was two percent larger but exactly the same shape, lit with the colour which burnt steadily and patiently inside it.

Perhaps it was only another millionth of what She had taken into Herself—including their five simulations, and their spiders and hull-plates, as well as pieces of Her—but She was consuming it, and turning it into power which partly fed Her flickerfields, partly Her drives, but mostly this projection of white light into the Bridge which, this time, trampled down their defences and solidified into the figure standing in front of them. Not a simulation in silver and grey but a real figure, with real flesh tones, blinking in the light of the Bridge as it looked round at each of them, its breath frosting in front of its face like theirs.

●

Aaron Foord stood in the middle of the Bridge, blinking. He was about thirteen, dark-eyed and quiet. He wore the orphanage uniform, a white shirt and dark blue trousers. He felt cold.

He looked at Foord.

"Are you what I became?"

"Are you what I grew out of?"

Aaron Foord again gazed round at the others, and stopped at Cyr. "You're a bit old to be wearing *that*," he said, "but it looks good on you. You're really beautiful."

He turned back to Foord, and asked "Who are these people with you?"

"Weren't you told, before you were sent here?"

"No."

"They're like me," Foord said.

"The ones who sent me, the ones in that ship over there…"

"We call it Faith. Or Her."

"…seem to know you."

"What do they look like?"

"They wouldn't let me remember…. You don't know anything about them, do you?"

"No."

"Later you will."

"I must admit," Foord said, "you're even more convincing than the figures in the crater. But you're still made by Her."

"What do you mean, figures in the crater? I don't know what you mean."

"You're not me. You're not even yourself. *She* made you, you're a simulation of me when I was younger."

"What did you mean, figures in the crater?"

"How do you think you got here from the orphanage? Why do you think you're here?"

"I don't know. They wouldn't let me remember."

"You're not me. You're not even yourself. *She* made you, and when you've spoken to me, and said whatever She told you to, She'll unmake you. Your life exists only between being made and unmade, and it's short and pointless."

"And *you're* not *me*. How much do you remember about me?"

"I remember nothing about *you* because you've only just been made and soon you'll be unmade. About *me*, I remember."

"No you don't. Maybe that's why I'm here, to tell you what you've forgotten."

("Ghost of Christmas Past," Cyr whispered.)

"Ah," Foord said. "This is it. We've been circling around it, but you're right, this is why you're here. To tell me how I went into the orphanage and turned away from people and made my life tight and tidy and made myself unreachable and became Commander of a ship full of loners and outsiders like me, and I'm the loneliest and furthest outside of all of them. Because all the other circles of Hell get hotter and hotter, but the final circle is cold and quiet and sterile, like me. Is that what She sent you here to tell me?"

"Yes."

"Then you're done. She'll take you away from here and unmake you. Your life has been short and pointless."

"Cold and quiet and sterile…"

"What?"

"Cold. Quiet. Sterile. If you're what I became, it has been short and pointless."

Foord did not reply.

The next time Aaron Foord spoke, it was to someone else.

"I want you to take me away from here, please. I want you to unmake me."

Foord began "I shouldn't…"

Aaron Foord's figure stood there, but Aaron Foord was gone from inside it. Something moved across its surface: a swirl of silver, from its head down to its feet, washing away his features and colours and shape.

"I shouldn't…" Foord tried again. "I shouldn't have said that to him. But he…"

"He's gone, Commander," Thahl said. "Let it go." He reached out to put a hand on Foord's shoulder. They both drew back; he had not retracted his claws.

"I'm sorry," they both said, each for several different reasons.

The figure remained in the middle of the Bridge, blank and unmoving. It changed its shape and posture, growing slimmer, and standing at an awkward angle. Features pushed out from inside it, reached its surface, and stabilised. Colours and flesh tones followed. It had a new inhabitant.

●

Susanna Cyr stood in the middle of the Bridge. She did not blink, and as for feeling cold, she always felt cold. She was over ninety. She looked round at them one by one, until she found Cyr.

"Are you what I grew out of?"

"Are you what I became?" Cyr answered.

"Yes, exactly right, this is what you became. Look at it."

She was gaunt, where she had once been slim, and her voice bubbled through mucus. She still wore dark lipstick, but now its colour matched that of the burst veins beneath the stretched skin of her face. Her clothes—an expensive dark linen jacket and skirt—somehow did not hang properly on her.

"Why are you standing at that angle?"

"Arthritis. And incontinence pants."

"You're as convincing as the other one," Cyr said. "Flesh tones, details, everything."

"What other one?"

"You know that She made you and sent you here, don't you?"

"Of course I do. What did you mean, Other One?"

A quiet movement to one side made them both look round. Thahl had discreetly re-routed Cyr's Weapons functions to his own console, just in case.

They turned back, and locked eyes again.

"At least," Cyr said, "the other one was a copy of someone who did exist, in the past. You're sixty years in the future. You're a copy of someone who hasn't existed yet."

"This is supposed to be news to me? I already told you that."

"You didn't," Cyr said, "but I figured it out…Were you sent here to talk to me?"

"Oh, I see. Like the Other One. What am I, number two? Three more to go, then. Or four, if She does Joser too."

"And what would She have told you to say? Something like, There Are Many Possible Futures?"

"I'm sorry, I don't understand."

"Oh, you know, that the future isn't fixed, that it can be altered, that I might not turn into you and get a face like a sanitary towel, but first I have to Change. Everything the Commonwealth pays me to do, everything I do best, everything involving weapons and killing, I have to stop *liking* it. Liking it makes me a loner and an outsider, even on this ship. I have to Change. I might seem beautiful now but inside I'm full of poison, and unless I Change, the inside will push through to the surface. Like it has with you. But I can still Change: I can still turn my life round and find another future…Is *that* what She told you to say?"

"Every word of that," said Susanna Cyr, "is wrong, including And and The. Your future *is* fixed. You *can't* change. You *can't* turn your life around. You *will* become me. And you're a loner and an outsider because…"

"Because I like it too much?"

"Because nobody will want you. The future is fixed. Nobody will want you: not as a lover, partner, companion, or even friend. You have only colleagues. Most of them, you frighten. The ones you don't frighten—like these here—you sicken."

Cyr wanted to look around her, but could not.

"Occasionally," Susanna Cyr went on, "you think that Foord might want you, as much as you want him, and occasionally he does. He thinks you're the most beautiful woman he's ever seen, but also the most sickening he's ever known. You can make him ejaculate and vomit with equal ease, and in almost equal amounts….Yes, ejaculate. Sometimes in his cabin he thinks of you and masturbates."

Susanna Cyr paused, and laughed; the same kind of laugh Cyr occasionally did, which made her ugly.

"Always the same Foord. He can never share it, even with you. He'd rather take it with him and go off somewhere on his own. And you know, sometimes he *can't* ejaculate; that's when he thinks of what's between your ears, rather than what's between your legs."

Thahl was already moving towards Cyr, but maybe he hesitated; or maybe, for once, even he was not fast enough. She emptied her sidearm into Susanna Cyr's body. Bits of torn parchment flesh and broken struts of bone and bloodsoaked dark linen erupted from Susanna Cyr's midriff and chest and shoulders and thighs: real substances, not silver. She doubled over, then straightened. She did not fall, despite her arthritic hip, and the bits blown from her body floated around her in midair, stopped at the moment they left her. She looked like an exploded diagram. She smiled at Cyr.

"Why didn't you just aim for my face?"

Cyr could not reply, even to shake her head. Thahl's micromanipulator claws were around her neck, almost but not quite piercing her skin. She dropped the sidearm. Thahl's claws retracted, and his hands left her.

"Well, it doesn't matter," said Susanna Cyr. "I'm done here anyway. I'll see you in sixty years. The future is fixed. Your life will be long and pointless. I know, I've lived it."

Cyr sank to her knees. Thahl still stood behind her. He reached out to touch her shoulder, but she shrank away, even though his claws were sheathed.

Susanna Cyr's figure had emptied. As the exploded pieces returned to it, it washed itself clear of her features and identity and posture, and became blank.

"Ghost of Christmas Future," Cyr hissed. She locked eyes with Foord. Strangely, neither of them was embarrassed.

"Do you really do that? On your own?"

"Yes," said Foord.

"Why?"

"Habit."

Thahl looked from one to the other. He had only a partial understanding of human sexual dynamics, but a very good understanding of the nuances of human speech, and of things left unsaid.

"Kaang," Foord said, "get us away from here. Hard to port, eighty percent. Maybe that signal will weaken with distance."

She did so, though she didn't believe him. Neither did any of the others.

●

They fled through the Gulf. She made no attempt to follow them, but Her white light still filled the Bridge, and they still felt cold.

For the first time since Joser's death there were six and not five on the Bridge, but the sixth was blank and unmoving and empty. For those reasons Cyr—who knew it was essential to appear unaffected—hit on the rather spiteful device of calling the empty figure Joser. When she got unsteadily to her feet after Susanna Cyr left and Foord gave the order to run, she pointed to the figure. Forcing lightness into her voice, she asked Thahl

"Which of us will fill Joser next? You?"

When Thahl did not answer, she lowered her voice and said "Remember I was too quick for you. And please put the Weapons functions back to my console."

Thahl glanced at Foord, who nodded.

Cyr, without taking her eyes off Thahl, said "He didn't order you to reroute my Weapons functions. You don't need him to order you to put them back."

"The functions are back."

"Thank you."

"I would never have killed you, Cyr."

"I know. But you tried to stop me doing what I wanted."

And later, while they continued to run from Her in a silence broken only by operational remarks, Cyr turned to Foord and said "Is Joser still solid? Or does he seem to be turning back to vapour?"

The headups on the Bridge screen showed She was hundreds of miles away; soon it would be thousands. Her image had dwindled to almost nothing. In the absence of instructions, the screen had not seen fit to magnify it.

"I meant it, Commander. Look at him. Around his edges. Don't you see it?"

Foord tore himself away from her gaze and looked again at the empty figure. It took him a few seconds to see what Cyr had already seen: the figure was less distinct. It started to sway. The motion was most pronounced at its head while its feet stayed unmoving, and as it swayed it left flakes of itself, like scurf, floating alongside it until they dissolved in the light.

It was bleeding away into the light, in a reversal of the process by which it had first appeared.

"It *is* weakening with distance!" Foord shouted.

The screen headups showed She was now several thousand miles away. The figure on the Bridge was keeping its shape but losing its substance, turning back to an open basketweave of vapour. For the first time since Susanna Cyr had inhabited it it made a deliberate movement, putting what had once been its hands up to what had once been its throat. If it had been more distinct, it might have looked like it was trying to breathe.

She was now tens of thousands of miles behind them, less than a smear on the Bridge screen. The screen chose that moment to return to the original magnification, patching in Her image as if She was sixteen hundred feet away, and She chose that moment to consume another millionth of what was in the midsection crater. Again there was an explosion in its recesses and again the unnameable colour burned there; but this time, as She rolled with the force of the explosion, something was different. She rolled along Her entire length but also pivoted around Her midsection, backwards and forwards and side to side, turning the roll into a clumsy figure-of-eight movement which She fought to bring under control. Nothing She does is clumsy, thought Foord. She's in trouble.

They caught fragmented glimpses of Her underside and starboard and dorsal surfaces as She rolled. Her manoeuvre drives fountained to correct the movement and the roll ended before the port side came back into view; then began again in the opposite direction, dorsal to starboard to underside. Her manoeuvre drives fountained again to correct the movement, and again to correct the correction, and overcompensated. She rolled a third time, underside to starboard to dorsal to port, and came unsteadily to rest. They stared, across tens of thousands of miles and sixteen hundred feet, at Her port side. Maybe, they thought, these projections were damaging Her internally.

Cyr pounded her console in pleasure, then swore viciously as she thought how she'd look if she hit something important—not what damage she'd do, just how she'd look. Foord and Thahl were still watching the screen.

"Cyr..." Foord began.

"Yes, Commander, we're still in beam range."

Foord nodded, and looked at the midsection crater; it glowed exactly as before, steadily and patiently. It might have been another screen, patching in a picture from another universe. Alarms murmured.

The empty figure on the Bridge, Foord noticed, was no longer empty.

●

Elizabeth Kaang stood blinking in the cold light, her breath frosting in front of her face. She looked round the Bridge at them, one by one, and found Kaang. Their eyes locked.

"What's missing?" Kaang asked.

"Nothing, I think," said Elizabeth Kaang. "I'm just the same as you."

To the others on the Bridge, she was: blonde, plumpish, a pale complexion verging on pastiness, and pleasant but unremarkable features.

"I'm sorry," Kaang said, "but something's missing."

"Oh, *that*. Over there," Elizabeth Kaang pointed at the Bridge screen, where Faith hung in silent counterpoint to their mundane conversation, "they said you'd spot it immediately. To me it doesn't feel any different. It was never in me to begin with."

"Over there. Who are they?"

"I don't know. They wouldn't let me remember."

"What do they look like?"

"I don't know. They wouldn't let me remember. Look, I'm nothing, really. What they told me to say will only take a few moments, less time than the others, and then I'll go. …This ship has only two things which can outperform them. The first is its particle beams, which are stronger than theirs, but that's only tactical."

"And the second," Kaang said, "must be me."

"Yes. Over there they have nothing, living or otherwise, to match you. You know that yourself. You're nothing really—I can say that, you see, because I'm the same as you—except for what you do as pilot. Even genius doesn't describe it. Genius comes once in a lifetime, but what you have may never be repeated. You've always had it, and you've never had to work at it, and you don't know what it is. Neither does the Commonwealth."

Kaang glanced down at her console to check; Thahl had rerouted her Pilot's functions through to himself. "Nobody," she said, "has any idea what it is."

"*They* do, over there," said Elizabeth Kaang.

"No! I don't believe you!" Kaang's voice shook. "I don't believe you, you're lying."

"I'm sorry," said Elizabeth Kaang, "but they told me exactly what it is and how it works. Of course I didn't understand, and anyway they wouldn't let me remember."

"No! You're lying!"

"They made me without it, to show that if it ever leaves you, the rest of you will be unchanged."

"You can't prove any of that!"

"The first thing you said to me is 'What's Missing?'"

"You still can't prove it. You're lying!"

"Look, I said I won't take as long as the others, and I'm almost finished. You have a gift that you don't understand and didn't ask for. You're on an Outsider ship with a crew of outsiders, and it even sets you apart from *them*. They need you because of what you can do, but you're not anything like them, not in any way. You're a different kind of outsider. You've never done bad things. You wouldn't know how to *decide* to do bad things." She smiled, almost apologetically, and her features started to sink into the substance of the figure.

The last thing she said, sounding further and further away, was "I asked them over there, if they understood your gift, could they copy it and make others like you? They answered me, but they wouldn't."

"Let."

"Me remember."

"I'm alright, Commander," Kaang told Foord, for the second time. "There was nothing there I didn't already know…Thahl, can you route my Pilot's functions back to me? Thank you."

"Kaang, She didn't intend any of us to come through this unaffected. She took damage, just to put that thing into the Bridge. So please, go and rest."

"Because I'm nothing really? Because except for what I do as your pilot, I'm the weakest one here?"

Foord paused. "Yes."

"I'm glad you answered plainly, Commander. If you'd said anything except Yes, even Yes But, you'd have been lying."

Foord did not reply.

"But I can't rest, Commander. If She really does understand what I have, I need to be here. If She really can make others like me, She'll come after us."

"She doesn't, and She can't," said the figure on the Bridge. "She was lying."

●

The empty figure had become a seven-foot column, approximately humanoid. It was grey and glistening, and its eyes were startlingly large and intelligent; warm, and golden.

"She was lying," it repeated.

"And what business," Smithson said, "have you here?"

The rest of their conversation was conducted in Smithson's own language, a series of scratches and chirps made by the rubbing together of chitinous surfaces in the neck, amplified through the throat and modulated by the mouth: a language of almost electronic speed and intensity, evolved by Smithson's ancestors when they were herds of plains planteaters who needed to develop a more sophisticated social organisation than the packs of impressively-organised carnivores and omnivores who hunted them. That, and their physical strength, and their development of the most efficient digestive system in the galaxy for extracting energy from plant matter—it worked subatomically, and meant they didn't have to spend all their time grazing, but could develop intellectually—let them turn evolution upside down and become the dominant lifeform.

Foord could not understand, afterwards, why the conversation was conducted in Smithson's language. Initially he suspected it contained things She didn't want them to hear. But in fact, as they found out later when the Bridge screen played back the recordings with translations added, it covered matters of which they were already well aware.

The simulation began by reciting Smithson's original name, the one he'd had in his youth. This was a polysyllabic word the length of several paragraphs, enumerating his youthful achievements, both physical and intellectual. The word of his name was a mechanism which grew as he grew, some parts taken away and larger parts added, to show what he was and point to what he would become—how he might grow into his expanding future. And then, abruptly, it ended.

The simulation paused—it had only taken a few seconds, but the translation would last several minutes—and then recited Smithson's present name, the one which would never grow any further, because now he had no future. It followed the polysyllabic structure of his earlier name, and ended with two syllables which the Commonwealth had humanised to their nearest pronounceable equivalent: Smithson.

Smithson was where his present name ended. After it, no further additions would ever be made. It was an Ember slang expression, most closely translated as Septic Knob.

Children and accomplishments were of overriding importance to Smithson's people. They needed both, in massive amounts, for the strength and intelligence to beat off several predator species, any one of which would normally have become Emberra's dominant lifeform. Males and females alike piled up their accomplishments, used by the outstanding ones as bargaining-chips in their drive to create, at the expense of lower achievers, more descendants to strengthen an already rapidly-strengthening gene pool. This compulsion, to achieve to procreate to achieve, was fundamental to the social organisation the Embers had developed on the plains. It pervaded all their institutions. They were an impossibility: dynamic, aspirational herbivores.

And Smithson, even among the other high achievers, was pre-eminent. His position on Emberra was almost that of Srahr on Sakhra. But it had all ended when he was diagnosed as a carrier of the incurable disease known colloquially—Ember humour was always cruel—as Septic Knob. As a carrier he would not suffer its horrific degenerative effects, which spread out from the sexual organs to engulf the body and mind; but his children would. So he killed them, and then—because, he said bitterly, they would have become vegetables anyway, and he was a vegetarian—he ate their remains, hoping he would become infected; but carriers were immune. So he turned away from his people and his accomplishments—irrelevant now, because no more females would ever mate with him—and was recruited by the Department.

"And is *that*," Smithson said, reverting to Commonwealth, "all you came here to say? Everyone here knows it already."

The simulation laughed. "It bought some time. For Her to make more like Kaang."

"Only about one minute of *their* time," said Smithson. "And She can't make more like Kaang, that was a lie."

"Of course it was. That's why I'm here. To tell you a lie about it being a lie."

"Oh, go fuck yourself."

"You tried that, too. Remember? You still couldn't get infected."

●

Later, Foord remembered to check the figure on the Bridge. It was empty and unmoving. Smithson's dimensions and features had drained out of it; what remained was smaller, roughly humanoid, but blank.

"Getting ready for me, Commander," Thahl said.

"Why did She leave you to last?"

"We're in beam range, Commander," Kaang said.

"Thank you. Hold this position. Cyr, start firing, please."

Cyr had already started. Even before Kaang brought them to rest the beams were stabbing out, and even before they reached Her, Foord had seen something which made him shout in triumph. He had been watching the Bridge screen readouts, and it was clear She had made a mistake.

She had again diverted only minimal power to Her flickerfields, leaving them almost transparent and deploying them whole nanoseconds late. Cyr's dark blue beams punched into them and almost through them; but not quite. They dissipated less than fifty feet from Her flank. Foord felt his shoulders drop—that had been their best chance, maybe their only one—but Cyr swore, loudly and sickeningly, and fired again. This time She diverted more power to the fields. They were transluscent now and they deployed earlier, but they were still below strength and the beams again almost penetrated them; and again, dissipated less than fifty feet from Her. Cyr screamed at the image on the Bridge screen, smashed a fist into her console, and fired again, and again. She was firing manually; automatic fire would have preserved intervals for the beams to power up, and Cyr would not tolerate any intervals, even if she overloaded the beams. She said so, out loud, staring wildly round the Bridge where they stared back at her; she *explained* it to them, in terms, but it came out of her only as a scream. Foord had never heard her scream before, not on the ship.

Only Kaang and the beams can hurt Her, Cyr explained, and She might already know what's inside Kaang, so there might only be the beams, and the beams might only work *now*, when Her fields are underpowered, and Might Might Might the future *isn't* fixed and I won't, not Might but won't, limp around in incontinence pants at ninety. She *explained* it to them, in terms, but it came out of her only as a scream, broken by fits of coughing when she tried to draw breath, but couldn't.

Foord stared at her and thought, I've heard you be many things—spiteful, vicious, even merely unpleasant—but always in packets of words. You always choose words. I've never heard you like this. What's happened to you?

"Cyr! That's enough. Go back to automatic, you'll overload the beams."

She couldn't speak. She shook her head No, and tried to form words, then pointed at the Bridge screen.

Words came. "Fuck yourself!" she spat. Literally spat; it was dribbling down her chin. Her mouth was like one of Smithson's orifices.

"That's *enough*. Put the beams on automatic. Now."

She was still firing manually. The beams were still punching through the fields to within fifty feet of Her, but no further.

Cyr broke into more coughing. "Do you realise," she managed to say, "how close I was?"

"And put your emotions on automatic too."

Cyr glared at him, wiped the spit from her face and flung it in his direction—a gesture he chose to ignore, fortunately for both of them. Then she shrugged, and complied. The beams went back to automatic fire, and it settled into the usual pattern: their beams, and Her fields.

The beams continued on automatic, and She used their powering-up intervals to divert more power to the fields. As She did so, the cold white light on the Bridge started to diminish, and the unmoving blank figure diminished with it. It went from opaque to transluscent, as Her fields powered up from transluscent to opaque. The beams continued to fire, but got no closer. There was almost a co-operation in the way both ships settled into their usual stalemate.

This was part of what had incensed Cyr. She locked eyes with Foord.

"What's happened to you?" he asked.

"You wanted Her more than anything," she told him, "more than you wanted me, and I could have given Her to you, but you wanked it away."

Foord had no answer. She's like my own skin, he thought, even when she sickens me I can never cast her off. He turned to Smithson and asked "Are you all right?"

"Yes, Commander. All it did was recite my two names. It said nothing you don't already know." He performed a deprecatory movement of his upper torso. "The translations will be ready by now. Play them if you wish; we seem to have time." He gestured towards the Bridge screen, where the stalemate of beams and flickerfields continued.

Foord wasn't so sure about having time. The stalemate suited both ships, but only until one of them found how to do something extraordinary. Like, in Her case, duplicating Kaang's abilities.

"Kaang, what do you think? Was She lying?"

"I don't know, Commander," she said, unhappily. She never liked these conversations, and Foord usually let her avoid them. But not this time.

"Try. I need your opinion."

"You once told me that if the Commonwealth ever understood what I have, and if they could copy it and put it into others, they'd kill me to get it. Remember?"

"Maybe the Department rather than the Commonwealth, but I remember" said Foord, shifting his gaze between Kaang and the screen, where something had caught his attention.

"They tried everything to understand it, and they never could. Neither could I."

"Yes. And so?" While she spoke, Foord stole more glances at the screen. Something there was wrong.

"So I don't know if She was lying."

"Oh. I see." Foord would normally have been exasperated, but something else had distracted him. When he realised what it was he went to shout Cyr's name, but before he could do so, Kaang continued.

"We went through this when I joined you, Commander. I'm only your pilot. Please don't ask me about other things."

"Right, I won't...Cyr!"

More of the white light drained from the Bridge, and the empty figure in front of them started to fade. The reason was that She had diverted more power to Her flickerfields, and the reason for that was that Cyr had killed the automatic override on the beams and was again firing manually. On the Bridge screen they were stabbing at Her almost continuously. The fields too were almost continuous, a thick purple cloud roiling around Her; She looked like something bleeding underwater. Cyr's continuous fire was still punching almost through the fields, despite their extra power; the purple cloud was being pulled this way and that by the dark blue shafts Cyr was throwing into it, from different directions and angles.

Cyr had become quiet, as abruptly as she had become incoherent. Now she was playing her firing-panels coldly and without apparent haste, the way Kaang would pilot the ship; taking the beams almost but not quite to overload, the way Kaang would take the ship almost but not quite to destruction.

"Cyr!"

"No, Commander, I've almost got Her, I can give you what you want."

"Go back to automatic, Cyr. That's an order."

"Commander," Smithson said, "let her go on firing manually. I have an idea." He spoke briefly into his comm, and nodded. "Yes, we can do it. Commander, let her go on firing manually."

"Smithson, what—"

"No time." Smithson's gaze swept the Bridge. "Brace for an emergency. This will seem worse than it is."

But there was only a near-quietness, punctuated by the ship's murmurings to itself and the low rhythmic pulse of the particle beams. In the dwindling light the blank figure was barely visible. It stood among them like a dead tree in a copse of living ones, with evening falling.

There was a dull faraway explosion in the *Charles Manson*'s midsection, in the area of the particle beam generators. The alarms sounded, and the Bridge screen patched in a view of the starboard midsection, where some hull plates had been blown away. The ship lurched, but Kaang immediately righted it. Repair synthetics were already scuttling over the hull.

"It's nothing, Commander," Smithson said, over the shouts and alarms, "it's a fake. Best we could do at short notice, but She might buy it. Damage is minor."

"Damage?"

"Cyr," Smithson continued, "cut the beams' power by twelve point five percent."

"What?"

Foord said "Cyr, I see what he wants. Do it now. Don't disobey me again."

Cyr did it, and started to understand.

"Twelve point five percent," Smithson intoned smugly, "is consistent with a blowout of one beam generator. You overloaded the beams. Remember?"

"You mean," Cyr said, "that if She thinks a generator's blown, She might..."

"Might cut the power to Her fields and divert it back here, yes. So if that thing over there comes back to life and starts talking to us, you get your shot. You can fire your beams on full power."

Cyr laughed, softly. "You clever bastard."

The near-silence was still punctuated by the ship's murmurings to itself and the low rhythmic pulse of the particle beams; the beams were on automatic and firing on reduced power, and the thick purple flickerfields held them easily. The empty figure standing among them was almost nothing, a bruise on the surface of the air. A minute hung, quivering, and dropped. Foord felt something like vertigo, as if the floor had turned to glass and cracks were racing across it; he suddenly saw how much might hang on the next few moments.

Cyr caught his expression as it raced across his face.

"Are you scared She might not buy it, Commander?"

"Not scared. Unsure."

"Don't be. She'll buy it. *Then,* you can be unsure."

"What made you say that?"

"The future isn't fixed. Least of all for you, Commander."

Foord glanced at her curiously, started to reply, then forgot her. The temperature plummeted. Cold light was flooding back into the Bridge, Smithson was bellowing *I Told You So,* and the empty figure was starting to fill. The light went everywhere, and the figure drew substance out of it; then shape; then surface textures, and skin colour, and posture. And lastly, identity.

When it finally stood before them, slender and graceful and slight of build, it surprised none of them.

Thahl's replica did not blink in the light—Sakhrans rarely blinked—and it did not look round the Bridge to find the one it came for. Apart from a brief glance at Foord, it paid no attention to anyone except Thahl. It was not Thahl's exact double; perhaps slightly older, though signs of aging were difficult to gauge in Sakhrans.

"Well," Thahl said.

"Well," said the replica.

"Why did She leave me to last?"

"Because," said the replica, "the others were more interesting."

"Yes, of course. No secrets about me." Thahl's face and voice, like those of the replica, were expressionless; Sakhran humour was as quiet as Ember humour was cruel.

"Me neither," agreed the replica. "I have nothing to reveal."

On the Bridge screen, the stalemate of beams and flickerfields continued. Cyr had no intention of firing the beams on full power yet—it would be too early, and too obvious—but Foord still watched her closely.

"Or almost nothing," added the replica. "There's your mission."

"Well?"

"Well, it turned out satisfactorily. Three years ago—three years ago for me—the *Charles Manson* pursued Her through the Gulf to Sakhra, and finally destroyed Her one-to-one in front of Horus Fleet."

"Yes, that would be satisfactory," Thahl agreed. "And there's nothing else you have to tell us?"

"No, nothing," agreed the replica.

Foord still watched Cyr; she still fired the beams on reduced power, and made no move yet to go to full power.

"Or almost nothing. There's Foord."

"Foord?"

"Foord left me—sorry, left *you*—on Sakhra while he returned to Earth and enjoyed the glory. But on Sakhra we knew what Srahr had written. We knew what Faith was, and we knew She would always come again. There will always be more Faiths."

For some reason, the replica paused.

"Was there any more," Thahl prompted, "about Foord?"

The replica seemed embarrassed; unusual for a Sakhran, even a replica.

When it next spoke, its voice was different. Almost apologetic.

"Foord could never stop thinking about Her. Finally he returned to Sakhra, and read the Book. Then he wrote one of his own, which in deference to us he called the Second Book of Srahr, and he did to the Commonwealth what Srahr did to us. When they read what She was they turned away from each other, like we did. Something went from their lives, and they never got it back."

Cyr fired the beams on full power. The future consumed another millionth of itself, and exploded all the way back to Sakhra.

9

Something unexpected had happened in the Gulf, and Swann was about to feel its first ripples.

When the *Charles Manson* lifted off from Sakhra, and the strange civil disturbances began, Swann had retreated to his Command Centre at Blentport. Like a dying pharaoh, he had ordered that his staff be buried there with him. Through the days following, it had been full of their noise and movement and smell, and the mounting layers of their detritus. They had grown hot and dirty and tired together, struggling to read things which were unreadable: the disturbances on Sakhra, and the events in the Gulf.

The Command Centre had once been spacious, symmetrical and well-ordered; now it was crowded, not only with people but with chaotic piecemeal additions. The space between its orderly rows of consoles was filled with other consoles. It was walled and even ceilinged with screens, most of them—like the consoles—commandeered from other parts of Blentport. The screens were wide-angle and high-definition, paper-thin so they could be stuck like posters over any spare flat surface. Some of them showed the final stages of Horus Fleet's deployment round Sakhra, now almost complete, and all the others—except one—showed the civil disturbances.

Sakhra was not being engulfed by some mass uprising—neither Sakhrans nor Sakhran humans did their politics like that—but it was being prodded, here and there, by outbreaks of unease. Swann rubbed his forehead, feeling grit and sweat in his fingers. He was hot and dirty and tired from trying to read unreadable things. The disturbances were bad enough, but the events in the Gulf were worse.

There was one screen in the Command centre, the largest, which showed no images, only binary readouts and schematics and text headups, their windows crowding untidily over each other like a miniature of all the other screens on all the other walls. This was where Swann's analysts tried to piece together the engagement in the Gulf. All through the days of Swann's confinement it had been adding and subtracting information, as the analysts did sweep after sweep of their limited and partial data sources, updating them in sequence. The updates moved round the screen like an invisible clock hand, rippling the words and figures as it rearranged them. Each sweep took about a minute; then after thirty seconds the next one began, and the next, as unnoticed as the rise and fall of breathing.

The screen flickered as the latest sweep was completed; then attempted to turn itself inside out as it tried, and failed, to correlate what it had been fed. It went blank, then relit showing only gibberish. It started its next sweep. The invisible clock hand moved round it, casting shadows as it rearranged words and symbols and figures, but it was still meaningless.

To one side of the big screen was the old-fashioned floor-standing microphone—five feet tall with a weighted circular base—which Swann had swept to one side after his last troubling conversation with the Department. The weighted circular base had kept it from falling over.

It started to buzz, and its monitor light flashed Attention Now.

"Clerical Officer Oban, Office of Miscellaneous Vehicles, Department of Administrative Affairs. The Department is extremely sorry to trouble you, Director; this is a routine procedural matter only. If it's not convenient....."

"Yes, yes, I know you're real, cut the foreplay."

"There's been a development."

"I can see that. What does it mean?"

"Foord has had a success. A major success."

●

Whatever else they were, the inhabitants of Faith were sentient. They were not in immediate danger from the chaos Foord had brought them—they had never had, or needed, the capacity to feel personal danger—but neither could they ignore it. They reflected.

Nothing else in the universe was quite like them. They were invincible, but not immortal. They had always known what they were made for. For other sentient beings this might have been revealed by one unusual individual, who might have written a Book which would change their lives, but not for them: they had always known. It was part of the balance of the universe, part of its clockwork, that they were invincible. If they weren't, the universe was wrong.

●

"Foord has had a success. A major success."

"Good! How major?"

"He's damaged Her again, more seriously than the first time…We think the balance has started to shift. We think he's winning."

"There's something in your voice. What's wrong?"

The microphone stayed silent. As Swann watched it, it seemed—without moving—to acquire its own body language, reflecting the uncertainty he heard in its silence.

Behind the microphone, the big screen completed another update sweep. The invisible clockhand again moved over the words and figures and diagrams, and Swann's staff milled around it. They shouted things at him, but the silence from the microphone drowned them out.

When the voice next spoke, it seemed different, and Swann was bewildered when he realised why. The voice actually sounded embarrassed.

"You see, there's been a development."

"I *know*. You told me. Foord's winning."

"No; it's us. We're not unanimous any more."

"About what?" Make it be about something physical, or something operational, Swann prayed silently to the microphone. Not something unreadable.

"Some of us think we might not have fully appreciated something."

And Swann knew then that something was wrong. That something enormous was enormously wrong. If the voice had been merely frightened, he could have been frightened with it; that was normal when you encountered operational setbacks, and you could be frightened and still have a chance of putting them right. But the voice was *embarrassed.* You only sounded embarrassed when there was something you couldn't put right.

"And what is it," he asked carefully, "that you Might Not have Fully Appreciated?"

"Foord. We know what might happen if he loses. But if he wins, it might be worse."

"What?"

"If he loses, it might threaten the Commonwealth. But if he wins, it might threaten more than the Commonwealth."

"What can be more than the Commonwealth?"

"Everything."

●

It was part of the balance of the universe, part of its clockwork, that they were invincible. They did the work of gods, without being gods themselves. No single one of them was significantly more intelligent than Foord, or Smithson, or Thahl, or Cyr. But they were made differently. Nothing else in the universe had ever been made like them.

They would never encounter any opponent who wasn't already part of them. The motives and memories, hopes and fears, history and future of every opponent they had met or would ever meet, were contained in them at an unplumbable depth: in the curved and recurved space between the unique particles which made them, in interstices where no other physical laws reached. All of it was there to be drawn on when they met their next opponent and the next and the next, into eternity or for as long as the universe lasted. They didn't know why they did it, or who made them, but how they did it was a function of how they were made.

For an almost geological time they had faced opponents, singly and in multitudes. No opponent's abilities could ever be unknown to them. No opponent's ship could ever outfight or outperform theirs. And no opponent had ever done to them what this one had done.

●

"Everything."

"I don't—"

"Remember when you demanded we send the other Outsiders to the Gulf? We even thought of doing it, but now it's impossible. You're on your own. So are we. Everyone's going to be on his own."

"I don't—"

"You don't listen. *Listen*. Keep Horus Fleet in a defensive cordon, like we told you. Those two ships are still far away, but they're coming. They'll cross the Gulf and arrive at Sakhra, locked in combat, or in whatever else they're doing to each other. Pray that neither of them wins. Pray that they keep fighting for another year, or ten years, or a thousand."

●

No opponent had ever done to them what this one had done. They still had superiority, because of their unique ship and their own uniqueness, but now for the first time they felt a stir of unease. Not for themselves— they had never had, or needed, the capacity to feel personal danger—but for the balance, the clockwork, they served. If that was wrong, everything was wrong.

They still had superiority. Foord had done something unexpected, but they could still do other things, beyond even Foord's abilities. They reflected.

10

"Something went from their lives," said Thahl's replica, "and they never got it back."

Cyr fired the particle beams on full power. They tore through Faith's underpowered fields and hit Her, twice. She killed Her main drives, killed the signal She was putting into the Bridge, killed all the other things She had primed for later, and threw everything into Her fields, but by then Cyr—who was firing manually and continuously—had hit Her again, and again, and again: five times before Her fields, too late, reached full power.

Smithson's idea had worked; his ideas always worked. But this one would go on working, long past the point where it gave them what they wanted.

On the Bridge screen they saw Cyr's five shots raking along Her flank between the midsection and stern craters, vaporising Her hull plates and leaving five parallel clawmarks; then Her fields reached full power, turning opaque and almost solid when Cyr's beams touched them, and not even the Bridge screen could see through them. No further shots penetrated.

When She killed the signal She was putting into the Bridge, She killed Thahl's replica with it. It was swept to one side as if by a wind, dividing into particles which further divided into light, and then into nothing. The replica died abruptly and without ceremony, like a real Sakhran, and left nothing behind it.

The white light of Her signal disappeared, plunging the Bridge into the darkness of normal light. The cold went away, and their breath no longer frosted in front of their faces. Foord motioned Cyr to stop firing; Her fields cleared, and the Bridge screen showed what had happened beneath them.

There should have been at least one new crater, or even five new craters, gushing liquid silver and glowing with a nameless colour and throwing out pieces of wreckage which grew five miniature clawmarks and burnt away to nothing. Instead there were only five dark parallel lines, which the beams had scored along Her flank between the two craters; they looked like lines ruled on a very long sheet of writing paper. The Bridge screen did measurements and patched in a closeup: each line was nearly nine hundred feet long and less than a foot wide, the width of a few of Her thumbnail hull plates. The beams had scored out the plates as they raked along Her flank, uncovering the dark pewter of Her second hull layer, gleaming and undamaged.

"Surface only," Foord hissed at Smithson. "The beams were supposed to be the only thing, apart from *her*"—he gestured at Kaang, but continued to glare at Smithson—"which gave us an edge!"

"*She* said that, Commander," Kaang said. "Or rather, my replica did."

Foord ignored her, and turned to Cyr. "Craters. Where are the craters?"

"Commander," Thahl said, "our probes are detecting something inside Her."

"Our probes have never detected anything inside Her!"

"This is the first time."

●

It was a movement, slow and vast like something oceanic. The Bridge

screen patched in some data, but it was gibberish; it said the movement
had occurred nine thousand miles inside Her. The probes lost it and found
it again, nearer the surface. Now it was only three thousand miles inside.

"What is it, Thahl?"

"You can see the readouts, Commander. I don't know."

"What have we started?" Foord whispered to Smithson, and to Thahl
"Why isn't it showing?"

"I don't know."

The midsection and stern craters flared like before with the nameless
colour. But this time they flared only fitfully, and when the Bridge screen
went to patch in closeups of them, Foord for once overruled it—"Leave
it. That's nothing. Go *there*"—and ordered it back to the five clawmarks
on Her flank. Immediately the light from the craters died, as if She had
heard or anticipated him.

The Bridge screen tracked along the clawmarks.

"There."

At a spot three hundred feet from the edge of the midsection crater,
something was rippling Her flank; pushing up from underneath and moving Her hull plates, like Foord had sometimes seen the smaller muscles
in Thahl's forearms moving the diamond-shaped scales of his skin. The
screen patched in a closeup.

The movement covered an area no larger than the page of a book, fitting easily between two of the clawmarks; it made a slight bulge in the
hull plates. The microscopic distance between the edge of each plate
and its neighbours increased fractionally, showing a thin line of pewter
underneath—Her second hull layer, uncovered like the clawmarks had
uncovered it, but on a much smaller scale. Without being ordered, the
screen panned out.

There was another one, a hundred feet away; then a third, then dozens,
always *between* the parallel clawmarks, and only deep enough to uncover,
beneath the edges of the plates as they moved apart, the dark pewter of
the second hull layer. Now there were hundreds. Because they appeared
only between the parallel lines along Her flank, they started to look like
writing—an effect heightened by their regularity, because they always followed the outlines of the hull plates. The screen went to closeup again.

The lines made by the gentle parting of the hull plates, which from a distance had looked like lines of cursive writing, were almost granular when seen closeup; like ink under a magnifying glass, sinking into the weave of parchment. The screen went closer still, becoming almost a microscope. It concentrated on just two plates. Their edges, where they had gently eased apart to reveal the dark layer underneath, were like torn paper, with trailing filaments waving microscopic goodbyes to each other as they moved fractionally apart. The screen held the magnification for a few seconds, then panned out again.

Now there were thousands of them. The localised ripplings in Her flank were starting to join and become a concerted outward bulge along nine hundred feet. The fine cursive lines were visible again from a distance; that, and the fact that they all continued to stay within the lines of the clawmarks, made the suggestion of writing irresistible. They almost formed the shapes of recognisable letters: letters arranged in words, words in sentences, with an underlying grammar. Foord had to fight a temptation to try and read it.

Here and there, as the bulging increased, hull plates were gently popping off Her surface, uncovering a small solid blob of the dark pewter layer underneath. The screen patched in closeups of some of the plates: they didn't develop five miniature clawmarks of their own and burn away to nothing, they just lifted gently off and floated alongside Her. It was gradual, and did not seem threatening. The screen panned out again.

More hull plates were lifting off; dozens, then hundreds, leaving dark solid blobs behind them. Hundreds became thousands. The impression of unreadable writing along Her flank changed; now it looked more like a musical notation, and Foord fought the temptation to read a tune into it. Smithson even started trying to hum it.

Foord glared at him. "Stop that. Tell me what's wrong."

Smithson was unabashed. "What do you mean, Wrong?"

"What is She doing?"

"She isn't, Commander, it's being done *to* Her. She can't stop it because She's diverted Her power to the fields. To keep *us* off Her."

"Then we should be pleased, and you should be saying I Told You So. We're not, and you aren't. So what's wrong?"

Smithson did not reply.

"What have we started?"

Nine hundred feet of Her flank, between midsection and stern, blew open. There was no explosion. It blew open slowly, layer by layer, as if She was undressing for them.

●

Perhaps She really couldn't stop it, and could only slow it down; if so, She had slowed it thousands of times. It had the shape of an explosion, but not the speed. Every surface feature on the nine-hundred-foot section of Her flank detached itself and floated gently outwards: silver thumbnail hull plates in hundreds of thousands; lines of windows plugged with darkness; manoevre drive nozzles, scanner outlets, weapons apertures. Most of them floated away complete and undamaged, turning end over end, and when the Bridge screen showed closeups of them there were no miniature echoes of larger damage and no burning away to nothing. They lifted off and came to rest floating alongside Her.

There was no gushing of liquid silver and no nameless colour. Where the outer hull layer had lifted away, the second layer remained underneath: unbroken dark pewter, featureless except for echoes of the windows and apertures of the outer layer. Then it too blew slowly open.

The second layer was an unbroken whole, not miniature plates like the outer layer. All nine hundred feet of it blew out in five pieces, so large they retained fractions of the original curvature. The screen showed them in closeup as they lifted away. When they were clear of Her they broke into smaller pieces, always with clean sharp edges, and floated alongside Her where they bumped and nuzzled into the remains of Her outer layer.

Below the second layer was a cavity filled with a latticework of structural members and subassemblies which had linked it to the third layer, also dark pewter. After the second layer blew out, so did the latticework. They had glimpsed it once before when their missiles hit Her and opened the two craters, but now they saw it in detail as the screen went to closeup. Then, the explosions of their missiles had torn into it, breaking and twisting it; now it was exerting its own force, a thousand times slower but irresistible, to pull itself gently free from its fastenings to the third layer and float away from Her. Like before, some of it was recognisable and had counterparts in the *Charles Manson*: girders with an H cross-section, ducting, conduits, circular pipes squashed to ovals where they were sheared, platings with screw-fastenings and giant bolts (the screen even showed their threads in closeup, gleaming as they unscrewed themselves from their anchorage points). Other parts were unrecognisable, discs and triangles and polyhedrons made of something which hovered between gas and solid and liquid. It all lifted gently out of the nine-hundred-foot gash in Her flank, breaking into smaller and smaller pieces, and floated alongside Her.

For once, Foord thought, *Smithson's wrong. This isn't being done to Her, She's doing it to Herself.*

The third layer of Her hull, like the second, was dark pewter. All along the nine-hundred-foot gash, it was scarred and dented where the structural members had pulled free and floated outwards. The Bridge screen, anticipating that the third layer would also go, patched in closeups of sections along its length. When it blew out, the screen calculated, the gash would reach deeper into Her than the craters and they would see Her interior. But it didn't blow out. The gash in Her side became dark, either depthless or infinite, and nothing else came out of it. The screen's headups said the gash was a molecule deep, then nine thousand miles deep, then infinite, and then the headups cancelled themselves and said Unable. It belonged to another universe where physical laws unravelled and time went, not forwards or backwards, but sideways and inside out. Unable.

"Kaang," Foord managed to say, "you see that?"

"Yes, Commander."

"Fly us into it."

Around the Bridge, they turned on him in disbelief.

The alarms started murmuring.

"Commander," Kaang stammered, "do you really…"

"Alright, no. Cyr, fire the beams into it."

"We don't know what it is, Commander!"

"That's why."

Cyr went to press the firing-panel, then looked round at the others.

"I gave you an order."

The alarms were murmuring, louder because they were unanswered.

"Look at the screen headups, Commander!"

The alarms were murmuring because, for only the second time, their probes had detected something moving inside Her. The screen headups, like before, were unreadable. They said it was nine thousand miles inside Her, and ten times bigger than the previous movement; then three thousand miles inside, and a hundred times bigger.

"I've seen the readouts. Fire on it."

The beams stabbed out, but Her fields met them on full power, opaque and almost solid, and held them. Cyr stopped firing and the fields cleared. The movement had not yet reached the surface of Her hull. The screen said it was only a molecule's thickness inside Her and a million times larger than before, then cancelled. Unable.

Nothing further happened.

"She's waiting for us to go back to Her," Foord said, mostly to himself. New things about Her. "Kaang, take us to fifty thousand feet and hold us there."

Kaang did so.

●

When Kaang brought them to rest, She continued.

Something started to emerge from the darkness of the gash in Her flank. It was not a hundred times or ten times or a million times bigger than before, but it would become bigger than She was and it was impossible. Earlier, She had survived by eating Herself. Now, She defecated.

What came out of the gash looked like the fingers of a giant hand: five separate fingers, thicker than Sakhran trees, at intervals of about two hundred feet along the entire length of the gash. They were separate, but moving in a way which suggested that back inside Her, behind the darkness, they were linked together in a hand. They were dark blue, at first almost invisible against the darkness in the gash; then, as they emerged, they became visible against the silver of Her hull.

They were a particular shade of dark blue, the colour of bruises. They were the five strands of their particle beams which had hit Her, slowed down millions of times, so they looked like treacle. They even glistened like treacle. They crept glutinously out of the wound, and as they emerged— and continued and continued to emerge—they lifted and undulated away from Her horizontally, reaching like blind worms towards the cloud of wreckage floating alongside Her.

They kept coming out of Her, nanoseconds of energy slowed millions of times to mass, but mass greater than their energy when they had hit Her, as if She had reversed the mass-to-energy multiple; or imported another multiple from another universe. The screen analysed them. It said their composition was that of the particle beams, but their mass was impossibly big, then reverted to Unable.

They reached the cloud of wreckage and nuzzled into it, gently bumping aside some of the larger pieces. Inside the cloud each of the five fingers subdivided into thinner fingers, and thinner into thinner until the thickest were only threads. They moved inside the cloud of wreckage, binding its pieces and organising them and spinning them, with the instinctive delicacy of spiders, into an openwork sphere which was bigger than She was.

The five fingers kept coming out of the gash in Her flank, across the gap and into the openwork sphere. They turned pale blue, then transparent; and they were hollow. Objects were being carried along inside them in suspension, pumped out of Her and into the sphere: at first only dozens, but then hundreds. The five transparent tubes pulsed with them. Foord told the screen to show closeups, but it had already done so, and he already knew what they were: everything She had ever taken from them, and everything they had ever thrown into Her, and more, in mounting and impossible quantities.

There were things the size of a human head, black and sickle-shaped, each with a diamond tip and a trailing tangle of monofilament: pieces of the grapples Cyr called Hands of Friendship. Then hundreds of slivers of fractal diamond, which their Jewel Boxes had exploded inside Her. Then something larger, a turning tumbling curvature of dark metal: a broken rim from a Prayer Wheel. Then dark pieces of carapace from their dismembered spiders, trailing gears and claws and circuitry. They were coming in hundreds, through each of the five fingers, and the Bridge screen was labelling and classifying them in headups which flashed on-off in nanoseconds, as quickly as the beams had flashed when they were energy and before She had turned them to tubes of treacle. The screen tried to keep up, identifying and labelling each object in what Foord recognised, too easily, as monomania.

The objects were still coming in hundreds, out of Her and into the sphere. The five fingers were no longer just shaping and organising the sphere but feeding it, in quantities which could never have existed inside Her. Now the sphere was bigger than both ships put together.

Through the fingers the whole of their engagement, the whole of the last few days of their lives, poured out of Her. Silver hull plates which Her spiders had excavated so industriously and which She had taken back inside Her in giant entwined cables. The Fire Opals which had fallen and died somewhere inside Her. More jagged slivers of diamond, this time hundreds of thousands, from their giant Diamond Clusters. Even cylindrical bits of the the Diamond Clusters themselves, reduced to digestible pieces. More bits of Prayer Wheels showing fractions of curvature and attached spokes. And more hull plates, more diamond slivers, more bits of their spiders and more dead Fire Opals. Thousands and thousands of everything.

"There's too much," Smithson muttered. "Like the beams. There's more coming out than we put in."

"She's *making* them," Foord whispered. "Thousands of everything. What have we…"

"Started? Who knows." Thahl answered him.

The five fingers changed colour again. Different objects gushed through them into the sphere, objects which were not theirs but Hers, in silver and grey: Thahl's head, Smithson's torso, Cyr's eyeless face. Not one of each but hundreds. Foord saw his own simulation at least a hundred times. And then other things of Hers, but these were complete and not mutilated: the replicas of Aaron Foord, Susanna Cyr, Elizabeth Kaang, Smithson and Thahl, the ones which had stood on the Bridge, forming out of cold white light and dissolving back into it. Again there were hundreds of them. They bent and conformed to the contours of the five transparent fingers as they poured through them, like dead children on a slide, tumbling out empty-faced into the openwork sphere. The hundreds became thousands and the sphere was no longer openwork but dense and solid, a mixture of colours and textures and shapes from Her and from them.

The fingers came to an end. They never did turn into a hand. One by one they completed their emergence from the unplumbable darkness of the gash in Her flank, their trailing ends floating across to the sphere and entering it. The darkness, either a molecule deep or as deep as the distance between galaxies, remained.

Between the two ships the sphere, bigger than either of them, hung motionless.

A mixture of us and Her, thought Foord. "Fire on it," he told Cyr; but Cyr was not able to, because it became something else.

It started to compress, as if invisible hands were crumpling it prior to throwing it away. The compression was not uniform but abrupt and jagged. Its volume halved in a nanosecond, then halved again in five seconds, then stabilised; then halved again and again, to the size of a boulder and the size of an apple; then compressed, finally, to almost nothing. The two ships faced each other, speechless, across the space where it had been and still was.

The Bridge screen tracked it and would not let it go, chasing its collapse down from the size of an apple to a grain of sand to a molecule. The screen had become as obsessive as Foord; it would not say Unable again. It chased the sphere's collapse further down, past the size of a molecule. It ignored the lunacy of its own readings, refocussing down and down with the definition of a microscope, and showed the Bridge an empty point in space with Faith looming out of focus behind it, and told them *There,* at that point, was what Her sphere had become: either an atom or a universe.

It was not an atom.

●

It exploded, back to the size of a grain of sand. Then expanded, to the size of an apple. Then expanded further, but more slowly.

The screen had chased it down through its first collapse, and back through the explosion of its creation, the expansion of its infancy, and the stability of its steady state. All through the chase the screen had told them what it was or wasn't or might be, deleting and rewriting its readouts, combining contradictions into conclusions. Finally, like the object itself, the screen's conclusions collapsed to almost nothing, exploded outwards, expanded, and reached relative stability.

It was a universe, said the screen, the size of an apple. Inside it would be galaxies like molecules, solar systems like subatomic particles, lives and civilisations which would go from birth to extinction in nanoseconds. In maybe five minutes, said the screen, the explosion of its creation would reverse and it would collapse.

The screen magnified it beyond focus, and got only its surface. Its face filled the screen like Horus 4 had done, but was even less distinct. Its outer surface was impenetrable; more than solid. Its colour was the nameless colour from Her craters, but flat and unlit. And while it existed, it brought a noise they would always associate with it. Not its own noise but theirs, a dissonant mismatched chorus of all their instruments trying to probe or understand it, failing, and saying so.

If it was a universe, then what they saw wasn't its surface; that had no meaning. They saw its outer boundary, and that also had no meaning. What did the boundary of a universe look like from outside? Or from inside? If it was a universe it was infinite; inside was neverending so outside, where they were, was neverbeginning.

The dissonant chorus of instruments continued. Everything in the ship tried to probe it, but it was denser than Horus 4, or a neutron star, or billions of either. It couldn't exist in their universe, and the Bridge screen *said* it didn't; or couldn't, which was different. If it did exist its gravity would have annihilated both ships in the instant of its creation, but to one side of it was Faith and to the other side, further away, was the *Charles Manson*, and they registered no gravity. The thing between them, separating them by a few thousand feet and billions of light-years, behaved as if they didn't exist, just as it didn't exist for them; or couldn't, which was different.

Smithson was laughing. Not cruelly, as he usually did, but in wonderment.

"She's actually done it."

"The screen may be wrong."

"No, Commander. It may be wrong about details, how and when it collapses, but not about what it is." He laughed again, softly. "The only way She could hold us off is to put a universe between us. Can there be a bigger compliment? We thought we'd learn new things about Her."

"I don't…"

"Yes you do, Commander, you do understand. You were right, She made it deliberately. And it's made of *us* and *Her.* Together. Its life will be only seconds or minutes to us, but to them it's eternity."

"Them?"

Smithson looked away. He seemed to be blinking.

Thahl said "Commander, he means the living things that will grow and die inside it. They must have already evolved...we may all meet again in there, Commander, and not know it."

Foord looked away. He too seemed to be blinking.

"Commander," Cyr said, "do we still fire on it?"

"Not this time. Whatever She's done, it must play itself out."

"But..."

"First, it's not really there. Second, if it is it's beyond our weapons. And third...I've destroyed ships. I might destroy cities if I had to. But a universe?"

"Made by Her."

"The fourth reason. *We're* part of Her. We always were."

Again he found himself blinking back tears.

It hung before them on the screen. The ship's voice—its instruments, all unable to reach a conclusion—sang it through its life.

●

The alarms murmured. The two ships faced each other across Her universe, which could not exist as a discrete object between them because it was infinite.

In five seconds and a billion years following its creation, it formed its time and space and physical laws. It formed nebulae; nebulae congealed locally into stars; stars were organised and spun into galaxies, measuring molecules and light-years across their spiral arms. Around some stars it formed planets.

Fifteen seconds and three billion years into its existence, it was teeming with life and death. A minority of lifeforms developed civilisations, and a minority of civilisations flourished, lasting millionths of a second and thousands of years. A smaller minority of civilisations spanned more than one solar system. There was even an unidentified ship, prowling the dark spaces between galaxies. More than one, but they rarely met or communicated.

Her universe, like any other, was mostly empty. Its emptiness dwarfed suns, whose light guttered like cigarette-ends dropped in a derelict building. Only one time in millions would light produce life where it landed.

Civilisations began and ended their lives along its timeline, in packets of millionths of a second and thousands of years. The atoms and subatomic particles of Foord and Thahl and Cyr and Smithson and Kaang—of their replicas in the crater, or their replicas from the Bridge, or the thousands of reproductions of both which had tumbled out of Her—went into Her universe and reappeared in living things. Occasionally they existed in the same galaxy; less occasionally, in solar systems close to each other; almost never, in the same solar system; less than almost never, on the same planet; and less than that, in forms that would recognise each other.

Once, on a planet circling a dying red sun, an individual with some of Foord's particles came within a few feet of an individual with some of Thahl's. They glanced at each other and passed by. One was chitinous, part of a collective hive; the other was feathered, pecking at a fruit like an apple. Later they died. Five seconds and a billion years afterwards, their sun went nova. An unidentified ship watched it from a distance of atoms and light-years, and turned away towards the next solar system.

●

She began Her endgame. For the second time the Bridge screen went dark, and She brought them into Her universe. There was no compression: they stayed as they were, but reality around them changed, instantly, from outside to inside.

Every part of Her universe, because it was infinite, touched every part of theirs. It welcomed them with a noiseless rushing. Foord shouted to them, above the noiselessness, *We'll come out at Sakhra, then all this will be finished.* Finished abruptly. After everything which had gone before, Her endgame was simple and abrupt. Fast, and final. It was Her last throw of the dice.

Foord knew Her better now, and knew what She had done. She was a conventional ship with a conventional opponent, and the opponent was matching Her—perhaps, with Foord's careful penny pieces, more than matching Her. She was also something else, something which could make and encompass universes, and She had drawn on the second identity to meet the threat to the first. But that, Foord knew, would also threaten the second identity.

They passed through Her universe like ghosts, unseeing and unseen. They were almost nothing: a movement of air, an echo, a deepening of colour. As they passed, their traces altered with the magnitude of what they passed through—a planet, a continent, a room.

It contained random particles from them and Her, and multitudes from neither. It contained civilisations which grew and died in different galaxies at different times, without knowing each other. Some resembled the Commonwealth or the Sakhran Empire, and some were unimaginably different. Some were visited by an unidentified ship, and collapsed or declined after it left them. Some had an individual who wrote a book about what the ship was. Some sent an opponent to engage it singly.

They saw no more of Her universe than it did of them. For seconds, and billions of years, they ghosted through it. Orders of magnitude. If it was a universe, they passed only six of its planets, in six different solar systems in six different galaxies, on the route She had set to bring them out at Sakhra. It was a short journey, less than the span of one grain of sand on a beach; and in the mere seconds and billions of years it lasted, Foord finally understood.

I know what She is. I know what Srahr wrote.

●

On an uninhabited planet of dark slate, their passing was an extra quiver in a column of smoke. The smoke rose from a hut standing by itself on the slopes of a mountain. Someone had come there, to live and die alone.

On a grey-blue basalt planet their passing was a momentary darkening of one vein of mineral in a wall of cliffs. The cliffs were honeycombed with tunnels eaten into them by acid rain. They overlooked a beach.

A tsunami was coming, nine hundred feet high and nine hundred miles an hour. It dragged the shallow water across the beach towards it. It sent a nine-hundred-mile-an-hour wind ahead of it, which tore through the tunnels in the cliffs and made them scream.

In a room at the summit of a stone tower, their passing was a momentary deepening in the grain of a wooden floorboard. The room held the world's last two living things, a father and daughter, opponents of an unspeakable theocracy. The theocracy had impregnated them with a cellular stasis field, which halted their ageing and even their need for sustenance; then, having made them almost immortal, it sentenced them to life imprisonment. If Foord had been able to see them, he would have remembered his *own* father's old volume of *King Lear*: We'll wear out, in a wall'd prison, packs and sects of great ones that ebb and flow by the moon.

And they did. They lived to see, through barred windows, the extinction of their species. But they had become something else, and it no longer mattered to them.

On a planet once visited by an unidentified ship, their passing was a small vortex of wind in a pile of dead leaves. It had been the first planet of a civilisation that spanned half a galaxy, and would have dwarfed the Commonwealth. The spires of its cities were so tall they pierced the ionosphere, and so numerous they made the planet look like a pincushion. They were still unblemished, centuries after they were built, each one standing in parkland. After the unidentified ship left, people had turned away from each other; they no longer lived in cities or visited parks, and were no longer people. Small vortexes of wind played among the dead leaves in the parks, like the ghosts of terriers.

In a half-lit apartment, their passing was an unnoticed flicker in a lamp swinging from the ceiling. A couple had taken to meeting there, despite the sectarian and political forces ranged against them. Later they died, but their children founded a new society. It too died, but gradually and gracefully, and while it lived—hundredths of a second, and tens of thousands of years—it was glorious. Its systems of thought were so powerful that they lived on as ghosts, heard and seen in the dreams of the historians and chroniclers and archaeologists who sifted its ruins.

Their passing was a moment's dilation of an eye pupil in something which walked vast plains. It was a solitary carnivore with the same shape as the members of the herd it walked with. It had evolved the shape and smell and voice of herd members, so it could live among them. It would even help defend them against packs of other predators. It lived with them and outside them, and fed with them and on them.

●

I know what She is. I know what Srahr wrote. Her universe died. In four minutes, not five as the Bridge screen had said, but four, it went from singularity to universe to singularity. It collapsed, and they came out of it at Sakhra.

They cried out as the screen relit. It seemed months or years since they had last seen Sakhra. It pulsed before them as if lit by a naked swinging bulb, the main continent covering an entire hemisphere, the Great Bowl filling most of its interior. It looked like a giant eye.

She was waiting. For the first and last time, She spoke directly.

I almost love you, said Her words on the screen, in a cursive script like the one they thought they had seen spreading over Her earlier, but this time they could read it. I almost love you too, Foord thought, and almost love can almost never die.

She moved to exactly one thousand six hundred and twelve feet from them and they resumed fighting, if that was what it was.

●

The two ships passed by Sakhra, well outside its orbit. Horus Fleet, in its careful defensive cordon, watched them pass. Faith carried a huge gash which had opened up two-thirds of Her port side, and the *Charles Manson* was covered in shit and striations and an apparent infection of boils where its dorsal hull surfaces had been attacked. They were throwing closeup weapons at each other when they emerged at Sakhra, and continued as they passed by and left its orbit and headed for the two inner planets, and neither of them gave Horus Fleet more than a glance. Horus Fleet made no move towards them and no attempt to contact them. They were gone.

They approached the orbit of Horus 2, and it finished. There were nearly fifty impacts from missiles She had made, replicas of Foord's two, which had been floating inert all around them. They hit every part of the *Charles Manson*, even the Bridge. It wasn't Her private universe which had destroyed them, it was Her copy of Foord's idea. Now, thought Foord, looking for his closest friend, I really do understand Sakhran irony. And he's always been my closest friend.

The damage they did to Her was enough; she consumed herself. She was not able to turn back and attack Sakhra. She limped off, and passed out of Horus system, and would never come back.

Foord's ship died like Jeeves would have died: carefully, ordering its affairs, collapsing tidily and progressively, informing survivors of the disposition of lifeboats. It had always been in Foord's nature to wonder how Jeeves would have died.

The Bridge was wrecked. Kaang and Smithson were unhurt, but Thahl had died instantly and Cyr lay on the floor amid wreckage and rubbish. Foord went to her, and held her in his arms. He'd never touched her before, except once, more than seven years ago, to shake hands when she joined his ship. Now they kissed, tongues and everything.

Cyr looked up at him. "Almost," she said, and died.

PART NINE

FROM THE *SECOND BOOK OF SRAHR*, BY AARON FOORD

"Almost," she said. She could have meant the life we ought to have had together, or the engagement with Faith. The word works equally well for either.

If she meant the life we ought to have had, then I won't write about it here. It doesn't belong here. If she meant the engagement with Faith, I think she was right; we almost defeated Her.

●

We never did see what they look like, but with hindsight it doesn't matter. When you know what they do, what they look like becomes irrelevant. They do the work of gods, but they aren't gods themselves.

Maybe I should write about Her in the past tense. After all, the engagement is in the past: She went away from Sakhra because we damaged Her, and She won't come back. But Her effect on us, like Her effect on the Sakhrans when She first visited them three hundred years ago, belongs in the present and will belong in the future. It won't go away just because She went away. And there isn't just one of Her. There will always be more Faiths: the universe has several of them. Every universe does.

It was just before the end of the engagement, when everything ended for me, that I finally came to know what She is. And when I knew, I saw something else: a structure, made up of orders of magnitude. To describe what She is I must first describe the structure, because She's part of it.

Orders of magnitude. How many grains of sand on one beach? How many beaches on one planet? Planets in one galaxy? Galaxies in one universe? So, how many grains of sand in one universe? And how many universes? All those questions, except the last, have a finite answer. Only in the last question is the answer infinity. Or zero, which is the same thing turned inwards. In Sakhran mathematics they have the same symbol for infinity and zero: the srahr, so named when She first came here three hundred years ago.

When Srahr wrote his Book and told them what She is, they saw it was true and accepted it. They still carry it within them like the code of an ancient disease. It told them they were almost nothing, that they had nowhere to turn except away from each other and nowhere to go except into regression and decline. Sometimes I think they were right, sometimes not. What Srahr wrote, and what I will write, has more than just darkness about it; there's also a suggestion of infinity. The more you know, the more room there is for the unknown. Like something continually halving itself where the halves get *bigger*.

The first part of what I write can be easily proved, because the orders of magnitude demonstrate it. They're well known. Our galaxy's magnitude relative to the universe is quite negligible, perhaps no more than the magnitude of an atom, and we're only minor parts of the minor parts of that atom. We really are, in physical terms, almost nothing. And we can't see the whole universe because it's too big. Our encounter with Faith was only a momentary ripple in the lesser regions of one of its lesser galaxies.

The next part can't be objectively proved, but it's what I finally saw as the engagement ended, and it fits all the observed data. When it comes to observed data, nobody since Srahr has observed Her more than me.

●

We fought Her through a solar system, and piece by piece I got to know Her, one new thing after another, though I never put all the pieces together until the very end. *Her abilities* are the key. Her abilities explain not only how, but why; they're everything She is.

Her abilities meant that She knew all Her opponents, past and present and future. That She knew them before they existed, and after She defeated them. That they were always part of Her and always would be.

Her abilities meant that no system She attacked would ever defeat Her, and that every system She attacked would, after She left, sink into chaos or decline.

Her abilities meant that She knew everything we were, all our motives and memories. She could put it all into silver replicas of us that were better than the originals, and then make us kill them. We recovered from that, but only just.

Her abilities meant that She could send a second generation of replicas into the Bridge, *my* Bridge; replicas of what we were or might become, all misleading and all true. We never entirely recovered from that, though we did go on fighting Her somehow.

Her abilities meant that She could influence us by creating events to which She knew, exactly, how we'd react. She did it so accurately that mere telepathy, or possession, wasn't necessary. At times She seemed to know our thoughts before we did, but what She really knew was *us*.

Her abilities meant that She could confuse and block our scanners and probes, letting them detect only what She wanted them to detect, and leaving them otherwise useless.

Her abilities meant that She could change the building-blocks of matter, could create and re-create Her spiders and our replicas from silver liquid and white light; that She could take parts of Herself, and parts of us She'd collected, and convert them to energy to go on fighting even after the damage we'd done should have destroyed Her.

Her abilities meant that She could control the basic laws of conversion of matter to energy, slow them down thousands of times to a steady state, and diffuse them through Herself. Rewrite the laws in Her own language.

Her abilities meant that She could make a universe, apparently just for tactical reasons, and use its few minutes of life to move us and Herself through the Gulf to Sakhra.

Her abilities enabled Her to outfight, outmanoeuvre, outthink and outperform every opponent She ever met or would ever meet: the next opponent and the next and the next, into eternity or for as long as the universe lasts.

Her abilities were exactly what She would need if She was the universe's own, official, designated antibody. I notice I've lapsed into the past tense. She *is* the universe's own, official, designated antibody, and will be for eternity or for as long as the universe lasts.

●

I realized what She was just before the end of the engagement, when everything ended for me.... No, I shouldn't say that, it's what Smithson used to call self-indulgent. What ended was important to me personally, but it doesn't belong here. I'll start again.

I realised what She was just before the end of the engagement. The only way Srahr could explain his conclusion, and the only way I can explain mine after fighting Her across a solar system, is that the orders of magnitude were not made for inanimate objects; they were made for living cells in a living body, for galaxies in a universe.

The universe is a living thing, perhaps the final or even the only living thing. The only question is whether it's also sentient; a question to which I'll return presently.

I don't have the tone for this. The proper tone should be apocalyptic, or at least revelatory, but I'm incapable of either. I've learnt to see things differently now, and all I see are multiple levels of irony; the result of being around Sakhrans for too long. So our galaxy is only a cell in a living body too large to see, and the body organises and defends and preserves itself, either consciously or blindly, against disease. Disease is an imbalance in one part of a body, something spreading too fast. Civilisations which spread across solar systems become diseases; they threaten an imbalance, so *She* visits them and leaves them in regression or chaos. Our engagement with Her, into which we poured everything we had, was only a momentary spasm in some minor organ, not even noticed unless the body is sentient; a question to which I'll return presently.

●

So She's the universe's perfect, invincible instrument, yet we damaged Her so badly that She couldn't go on to Sakhra. Does that mean we proved Her inadequate? Does *that* mean there will be another generation of antibodies to replace Her, even more beautiful and brilliant than She is?

The universe made Her, but did it make Her consciously, or blindly? Could something like *Her* really be made blindly? Just reflexively secreted? Perhaps: antibodies and enzymes and secretions are made blindly, but if you see them as pieces of functional design, they're as beautiful and brilliant as She is.

And whatever made the universe which made Her, was *that* acting consciously, or blindly? How high up the orders of magnitude do you have to go before you get to the final sentience? Maybe you never do. Maybe it's neverending. Or maybe there isn't a final sentience. Maybe sentience is the inferior quality, and doesn't have a higher ultimate version but belongs lower down. Maybe the final nature of the final living thing is nonsentience.

We don't see evidence of sentience in the universe, or even nonsentience, or indeed anything at all, but we wouldn't. The universe is too big. We don't see it all, or even a meaningful part of it. Orders of magnitude: the fraction we see is incomparably vast and we're incomparably small. Almost nothing.

If it was sentient we could at least say it was a higher form of us, but I believe it isn't. I believe it's not alive enough to know it can ever die. I think its constructs, like Faith, aren't the work of conscious thought or intelligence, but of blind reflex. They're secretions. And we're the sentient and thinking lesser parts of a vast but nonsentient and nonthinking organism.

My ship was nine percent sentient. It died like I always imagined Jeeves would have died, tidily and thoughtfully. And one of the best insults to be found in literature comes from a Jeeves book, from Bertie Wooster's Aunt Agatha: "There are times, Bertie, when I think you are barely sentient."

But maybe not an insult. Nonsentience is where everything starts and where everything returns, full circle: the beginning and the end. Our sentience is only a staging-point, in the middle. The last living thing—the final, ultimate living thing—is as unthinking as the first. Irony doesn't come any bigger, or any more compelling.

●

All my life I've lived by nuances and inflexions, things unseen and unsaid. There's a kind of vertigo in trying to guess their magnitude, because it might be infinite.

It seems years, not days, since I last came to Sakhra. The engagement with Her still hasn't ended; its effects will come next. Its effects will be like a srahr, seen as a line from its edge or an oval from other angles, but never as a full disc. I never saw or did anything during the engagement with Her which wasn't the tip of something larger or the opening movement of something unseen.

What She gave us was like a srahr, either zero or infinity. It may make us turn away from each other and regress, or it may make us go into the universe and find out how it works, and if it really is living and really does make its own antibodies. Things like Faith were secreted to neutralise things like the Commonwealth. But this time, they may not.

I always professed indifference to the speculation about what She is. I'm the last person who should have found out, but now I know it as fully and deeply as Srahr himself. Irony, or what?

Maybe the Commonwealth will regress, like Sakhra. Maybe Cyr and I will meet again, the same sets of cells recombining after trillions of generations. The chances against it are infinite, but that means that the chances in its favour are infinite too. Or (another irony) we may just pass by without recognising each other. But that doesn't belong here. I'll start again.

Will the Commonwealth regress, like Sakhra? Will we turn away from each other, like Sakhrans? I don't know. For once, maybe they were wrong. The universe is vaster like this, with a dark majesty; more of a thing of wonder. The Sakhrans regressed when Srahr told them they'd become a disease and the universe had sent an invincible opponent to halt their spread. But Faith wasn't invincible: we almost defeated Her. She intended to return to Sakhra but couldn't, because of what *we* did to Her. No other opponent has ever damaged Her like that.

And what does Regress mean? When Srahr told them what She is it made them turn away from each other, though being Sakhrans they never regressed entirely. They didn't sink into total despair, because they always had their sense of irony as a long-stop. They have a highly developed sense of irony. So do I, now. Unlike Faith, I've been to Sakhra twice.

●

I know Sakhrans better than most. They reproduce asexually, but they're not mere copies; I could never have the kind of relationship with Sulhu that I had with his son. I always knew Thahl was my closest colleague, but it was only in the moments before he died that I realised he was my closest friend. I think he always knew that.

Orders of magnitude. I loved Thahl as much as I loved my mother and father, and almost as much (I realise this now) as I loved Cyr...but Thahl was only a fraction of Srahr. He knew what She was, because he'd read Srahr's Book. Srahr was the one who *wrote* it. What must he have been like? They all say he was the greatest of all Sakhrans, a combination of poet, philosopher, soldier and scientist. I'm just a warship commander; not even that, any more. But Srahr was also an author, and his people never recovered from his literary career. I may have at least that in common with him.

And even Srahr wasn't right all the time. He thought She was invincible, and I almost proved She wasn't. She could only defeat us by replicating our missiles, the ones which damaged Her almost fatally, and that's almost an admission of *Her* defeat. Or maybe I'm whistling in the dark, the same dark where our Fire Opals and Diamond Clusters and other weapons fell and died.

Almost is such a big word; almost infinite. We almost defeated Her, but in the end my ship was destroyed and half my crew were lost. This makes no sense, Smithson bellowed at me, after Cyr and Thahl died. He was outraged. I wouldn't have cared if *I* lived or died, but *she* should have lived and *he* should have lived. I ought to put his words in quotes, but they work equally well as they are. They're my words too.

When I'm finished here, I'll leave and go back into the Commonwealth on my own; and that leads me to one last piece of self-indulgence, one last shift from the general to the personal. When I leave here it will be without Cyr and without Thahl. I miss them, Thahl for what was and Cyr for what should have been.

I can never see anything in quite the same way as before: an apple, a dust-mote in sunlight, a grain of sand, my own hand in front of my face. I built empty spaces between myself and Cyr, and between myself and Thahl, when they were alive. Now they're dead, I still see the empty spaces. People die, but the empty spaces between them are immortal.

●

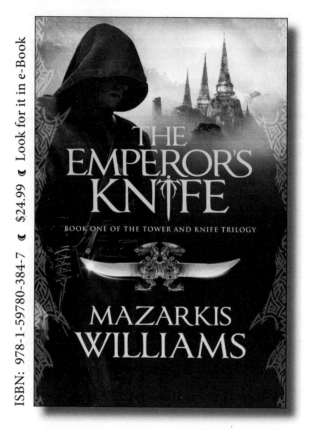

ISBN: 978-1-59780-384-7 ❦ $24.99 ❦ Look for it in e-Book

There is a cancer at the heart of the mighty Cerani Empire: a plague that attacks young and old, rich and poor alike. Geometric patterns spread across the skin, until you die in agony, or become a Carrier, doing the bidding of an evil intelligence, the Pattern Master. Anyone showing the tell-tale marks is put to death; that is Emperor Beyon's law...but now the pattern is running over the Emperor's own arms.

His body servants have been executed, he ignores his wives, but he is doomed, for soon the pattern will reach his face. While Beyon's agents scour the land for a cure, Sarmin, the Emperor's only surviving brother, awaits his bride, Mesema, a win-dreader from the northern plains. Unused to the Imperial Court's stifling protocols and deadly intrigues, Mesema has no one to turn to but an ageing imperial assassin, the Emperor's Knife.

As long-planned conspiracies boil over into open violence, the invincible Pattern Master appears from the deep desert. Now only three people stand in his way: a lost prince, a world-weary killer, and a young girl from the steppes who saw a path in a pattern once, among the waving grasses—a path that just might save them all.

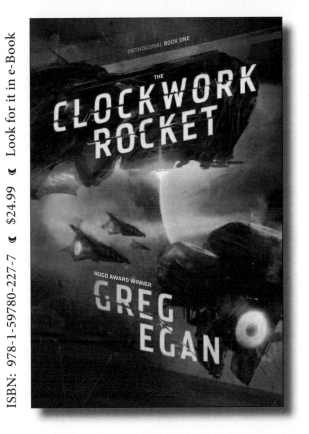
In Yalda's universe, light has no universal speed and its creation generates energy.

On Yalda's world, plants make food by emitting their own light into the dark night sky.

As a child Yalda witnesses one of a series of strange meteors, the Hurtlers, that are entering the planetary system at an immense, unprecedented speed. It becomes apparent that her world is in imminent danger—and that the task of dealing with the Hurtlers will require knowledge and technology far beyond anything her civilisation has yet achieved.

Only one solution seems tenable: if a spacecraft can be sent on a journey at sufficiently high speed, its trip will last many generations for those on board, but it will return after just a few years have passed at home. The travellers will have a chance to discover the science their planet urgently needs, and bring it back in time to avert disaster.

Orthogonal is the story of Yalda and her descendants, trying to survive the perils of their long mission and carve out meaningful lives for themselves, while the threat of annihilation hangs over the world they left behind. It will comprise three volumes:

Book One: *The Clockwork Rocket*
Book Two: *The Eternal Flame*
Book Three: *The Arrows of Time*

ABOUT THE AUTHOR

John Love spent most of his working life in the music industry. He was Managing Director of PPL, the world's largest record industry copyright organization. He also ran Ocean, a large music venue in Hackney, East London.

He lives just outside London in northwest Kent with his wife and cats (currently two, but they have had as many as six). They have two grown-up children.

Apart from his family, London, and cats, his favorite things include books and book collecting, cars and driving, football and Tottenham Hotspur, old movies and music. Science Fiction books were among the first he can remember reading, and he thinks they will probably be among the last.